FIC Freem
14 day   Spy/Intrigue.

D1068219

th

NO TIME FOR HEROES

NO TIME FOR HEROES

Brian Freemantle

ORION

First published in Great Britain in 1994 by
Orion
An imprint of Orion Books Ltd
Orion House, 5 Upper St Martin's Lane,
London WC2H 9EA

A CIP catalogue record for this book is
available from the British Library

ISBN 1 85797 122 1

Typeset by Deltatype Ltd,
Ellesmere Port, Cheshire
Printed in Great Britain by Butler & Tanner Ltd
Frome and London

To Brie Burkeman, with love

CHAPTER ONE

It settled into routine, like it always did, men hardened to violent death encountering it yet again, going through the procedures but thinking of other things, like a ball game or a bar or being in bed with someone other than their wives. It had stopped raining, which was something.

There were three patrol cars strewn haphazardly, their roof-bar lights still bouncing reds and whites off the puddled ground. The tinned voice of the dispatcher echoed unheard from inside the empty cabs. The crews and uniformed patrolmen were trying to move the curious on, saying there was nothing to see and that it was all over, which was a verbal part of the routine. There was the gore-splattered body to see, so it wasn't all over, and none of the onlookers moved. The yellow tapes, sometimes looped around the disused girders of the old overhead railway, marked off where it lay. The scene-of-crime technicians were inside the cordon under emergency arc-lights, each going through their preliminaries, forensic brushing and sifting, the examining coroner taking body temperatures and looking at the injuries.

'The Mafia comes to Washington DC,' declared Rafferty. There was a lot of blood and they couldn't make out all the wounds, but the most obvious was where the bullet had been fired directly into the mouth.

'They're everywhere else: why leave us out?' said his partner, Eric Johannsen.

'Wonder what he did wrong?' Michael Rafferty was a short, red-haired Irishman, with freckles and the hard-shell cynicism of a ten-year veteran of the homicide division. He and Johannsen had been counting down the minutes to the end of their shift when the call had come, and Rafferty was still angry at missing the Orioles game.

'We'll never know,' said Johannsen philosophically. He

was a big man, thick bodied as well as tall and with the white-blond hair of a proud Scandinavian ancestry.

The moment they'd seen the trademark mouth wound they'd recognised just how routine it was going to be. By now the professional hitman would be on his way to Alaska or New Mexico or California or Timbuctoo, the unmarked weapon already disposed of, the contract money already deposited and earning interest. All they could do was go through the motions, write up the reports, enjoy a little unofficial time off on supposed inquiries and commit the whole file to the 'unsolved' cabinet along with all the rest. And it wouldn't even reflect badly on their record, because no-one was expected to solve Mafia murders. That wasn't the way things worked. Ever.

The coroner stood, stretched and ducked under the tape. 'Want a closer look?'

'It's a body,' said Rafferty, with practised boredom.

'We've seen one before,' said Johannsen. 'Lots.'

The medical examiner, whose name was Brierly, was the odd one out in the murder team: after only three years he had some enthusiasm. 'White Caucasian. Male. Death was due to gunshot wounds.'

'You sure about that?' asked Rafferty.

Brierly ignored the sarcasm. 'Two to the body, one through the heart. Slugs were either hollow nosed or dum-dummed, flattening on impact. Took away most of his back on exit. There's some bone and flesh debris' – the man turned and pointed – 'about five yards from where the body is. I guess he was standing when he was first hit. No burn marks, so I'd say from about five or six feet.'

'What about the mouth?' asked Rafferty.

'That came later,' judged the medical expert. 'The lips are bruised but it's after-death damage. And externally it's comparatively slight. The barrel was pushed right inside before it was fired. Most of the back of the head's blown away: forensic will get the bullet from somewhere in the mess.'

'It'll be useless,' dismissed Johannsen, in a been-there-seen-it-before voice. 'The flattening destroys barrel marking.'

2

Rafferty gave his partner a what-does-it-matter frown. 'How long?' he asked.

Brierly shrugged. 'Two, three hours. The rain didn't start until around ten: we were driving home from the Kennedy Centre when it began. It stopped around ten-thirty. The ground under him is dry.'

'Age?' asked Johannsen, going through the list.

'Forty-five?' guessed Brierly.

'Anything more than the gunshot wounds?' pressed Rafferty. 'Beating? Torture? Stuff like that?'

'Nothing obvious,' said the coroner. 'I'll know after the proper autopsy.'

It began to spit with rain again.

'Guess that's all then,' said Rafferty, anxious to get somewhere dry. He'd had covered seats for the Orioles game.

Brierly looked back to the body. 'You think it's a Mafia killing?'

'We're running a book on it,' said Rafferty.

'Don't,' called one of the scene-of-crime technicians. He straighted from the body, holding already filled exhibit bags; separating one from the rest, he offered it to the two detectives.

The DC driving permit carried a picture of a plump, serious-faced man. The name was Petr Aleksandrovich Serov; the address listed – 1123, 16th Street – was that of the Russian embassy.

'Holy shit!' exclaimed Rafferty, the cynicism slipping.

'What's the captain going to do about that!' demanded Johannsen.

'He's going to get the fuck out of it, that's what he's going to do!' predicted Rafferty.

Just across the Potomac a man within a thread of being flashily dressed, which he should not have been, left the anonymous grey Ford at the far end of the National Airport car parking lot, hurrying to reach the New York shuttle terminal before the rain got heavy. The clothes were new and he didn't want to get them wet. He'd already assured himself there were no blood splashes. He'd enjoyed America. He wished he didn't have to go back so soon.

CHAPTER TWO

The alarms were sounded overnight, and by early morning the meetings were arranged at timed intervals in the Secretary of State's seventh floor office at Foggy Bottom.

The FBI was obviously first. Henry Hartz cupped the Bureau Director's elbow to guide him away from office formality to the dining annexe, where breakfast was laid.

'So what the hell have we got here?' demanded Hartz. 'A Russian diplomat, killed Mafia-style!'

'I wish to God I knew.' Leonard Ross was a carelessly fat, carelessly dressed man who had been a senior judge on the New York bench before accepting the appointment as FBI Director. After two years of Washington politics he regretted it, and promised himself he'd quit one day soon. Hartz was one of the professionals he got on with better than most.

'The Bureau will naturally handle everything,' declared Hartz.

Ross refused the covered food dishes, but poured himself coffee. 'You know Russia's got its own Mafia?'

'That's where I want it to stay. I don't even want to think what the media are going to make of this.' Hartz crumbled a Danish, mostly missing his plate and making a mess.

'Have the Russians said anything?'

'The ambassador is due at noon. What do we know about Serov?'

Ross made a doubtful face. 'Senior cultural attaché. Married. No children: not with him in this country, anyway. We never marked him as anything but a genuine diplomat . . .' He sipped his coffee. 'Only intriguing thing is his length of service. Seven years here. There have been two visa extensions . . .' Ross smiled. 'Both of which your people approved, without reference to us.'

'How big a task force will you put on it?' The early

4

sunlight reflected oddly off Hartz's spectacles, making him look sightless.

'Depends how it develops,' said Ross, refilling his cup. Too much coffee was something else he intended to give up. 'I'm not having an army, running around and getting in each other's way.'

'You going to appoint Cowley supervisor?' asked Hartz, expectantly.

'Head of the Russian Division at the Bureau is an administrative position,' reminded Ross.

'Horses for courses,' clichéd Hartz. Very occasionally the German birth and education that had ceased at the age of ten, when his family had come to America, still sounded in some word; it was evident now.

'I guess it's got to be him,' agreed Ross. 'The media will make a lot of comparisons about that, too.' He wondered if the contacts William Cowley had made in Moscow the previous year, on a combined Russian-American investigation ironically into the murder of an American diplomat at the US embassy there, would be of use this time.

'I've told the President,' disclosed Hartz. 'He doesn't like the Mafia connotation one little bit.'

'You think I do!'

'If we've got an organised crime connection in the middle of the Russian embassy, we've got ourselves one great big can of worms.'

'That's going to be the speculation,' predicted Ross.

'That's why I want the control to be between the two of us, to prevent it becoming a media circus.'

'How are the DC guys going to feel about that?'

'Maybe they'll be glad to get rid of it,' suggested Hartz.

The local police were, but the mayor was not so enthusiastic when, on their arrival, the Secretary of State announced the responsibility for the investigation would legally be that of the FBI.

'We'll cooperate in every possible way,' guaranteed John Brine, the police chief, with obvious relief. 'I'm sure we're going to work just fine together.'

'This is going to bring a lot of heat,' intruded the mayor, Elliott Jones. 'Washington, the murder capital of the World:

5

that sort of nonsense.' Jones was a second term civic leader, with ambitions for national office. In several interviews he'd admitted a willingness to be considered for the first black Vice President. He was still waiting for an approach from the Democrats.

'What's known so far?' demanded Ross.

'Not much,' admitted the homicide captain. Mort Halpern looked the detective he was, a big man in a blue suit shining from wear. 'It wasn't a mugging. There was still $76 in his pockets, and his watch and ring were untouched.'

'What about the mouth wound?' said Ross.

'Inflicted *after* death, according to the early medical examination,' said Halpern. 'Accepted Mafia trademark in the elimination of a stool-pigeon, of course. Every indication of it being a professional hit, too. The bullets were hollow nosed or scored to caused maximum damage. Nothing left for ballistics to work on . . .' He paused, looking at the Director. 'Everything is being bagged up for you already.'

'The scene of crime still secure?' asked Ross. 'I'd like to send some of my people to take a look – with your officers too, of course.'

'It's down between the canal and the river, in George-town,' said Halpern. 'Practically underneath the Whitehurst Freeway. Pretty easy to seal off completely. It was raining off and on last night: I had a canopy put over the whole area to prevent as much water damage as possible . . .'

'I went there last night, too,' said Brine, anxious for his participation to be known. 'I put uniformed officers on duty throughout the night. There are others there today. No unauthorised person has touched anything.'

'The two homicide detectives who initially responded are on standby,' added Halpern. 'I guessed you'd want them to liaise. And for them to remain part of whatever squad you set up.'

They *were* glad for someone else to carry the can, thought Ross. 'That's fine.'

'So what's the feeling?' said the mayor briskly. 'Is this a Mafia assassination of a Russian diplomat?' He smiled. 'That's pretty sensational, isn't it?'

'Too sensational,' said the Secretary of State, guardedly. 'There's going to be enough speculation, without our contributing to it. At the moment we don't have an official view of Mafia involvement. That understood by everyone?'

Elliott Jones frowned. 'I think we need to get some things clear. My office have already had a lot of media requests for a statement. Naturally I've held off until now, but I've obviously got to say something.' He was always immaculately dressed, usually in waistcoated suits and with a lot of jewellery. He looked good on television and knew it: his secretary had standing orders to video every appearance.

Hartz thought the handbook could be called Public Participation Without Political Problems: maybe he should write it himself. 'I'd like you to confine yourself to regret at the killing and your understanding that everything possible is being done to apprehend the murderer.'

'Is that all?' protested Jones, disappointed. 'I've got a lot of people who expect me to be up front with them.'

'I'm not telling you what to say: I know I can't do that,' sighed Hartz. 'I'm asking. And that applies to off-the-record briefings or conversations with particular media friends. That, perhaps, most of all. I want to keep as tight a lid on this as possible. By which I mean all statements that could be regarded as political coming from here, at State . . .' he nodded sideways, to Ross '. . . and anything about the investigation coming from the Bureau.'

'I see,' said the mayor, stiffly.

Hartz smiled a professional diplomat's smile. 'For my part, I would be quite happy publicly to link your name with anything from here. And I would naturally expect you to participate in any press conference.'

Recognising his cue, Ross said: 'I don't consider the Bureau to be taking over lock, stock and barrel. We will need your homicide people on the team. And that'll be made clear in anything we say, from the very beginning.'

'I'm happy enough with that,' accepted Brine.

'I think I can go along with it, too,' accepted Jones. There was still reluctance in his voice.

'I'm grateful,' said Hartz.

'But we will keep in touch?' persisted Jones. 'I'll know what's going to be issued *before* it's announced? I don't want to be caught out on something I don't know anything about.'

'My personal guarantee,' assured the Secretary of State.

After the city official had left, Ross said: 'The only way to keep the mayor quiet would be to shoot him in the mouth, too.'

'I'm not sure what's going to be more difficult,' said Hartz. 'The investigation. Or the politics.'

'I am,' said the Bureau Director, with feeling. 'It'll be the investigation. It's going to be a bastard.' Very briefly, he wished he hadn't waited this long before resigning.

The overnight rain had cleared the thunder. The day was already hot, and was going to get hotter, as it does in Washington in high summer. There was no overhead shade at the far end of the parking lot where the grey Ford had been left, and by ten o'clock it was already beginning to cook.

Just over 5,000 miles away Mikhail Pavlovich Antipov, the man who had abandoned it there, walked across the concourse of another airport, conscious of the looks his new clothes were getting. He saw Maksim Zimin waiting for him before Zimin noticed him, and waved to attract the man's attention.

The waiting BMW was in a prohibited parking area, but there was no penalty ticket. BMWs were the favourite of the Chechen Family, who considered Sheremet'yevo their undisputed territory: no police or airport official would be stupid enough to interfere with an obvious Mafia vehicle.

'Did you get the documents?' demanded Zimin, the moment they were in the security of the car.

'There was nothing in Russian or Ukrainian. He said he'd left it in Switzerland; that there was no reason to carry it to Washington. I brought back some things I couldn't read: French or German, I think. They might be it.'

'You frighten him enough, so that he would have handed it over if he'd had it?'

'I made him watch me kill Serov! How much more frightened could he have been!'

'So what's he going to do?'

Antipov frowned sideways. 'Do? He's not going to do anything. I killed him too.'

'*What!*'

'He was a witness to murder!'

'Which didn't achieve anything,' dismissed Zimin. It had all gone badly wrong. And it was going to reflect upon him, because he was supposed to have organised it.

'You said there had to be warnings,' reminded Antipov, defensively. He'd taken his jacket off and laid it in the back of the car, to prevent it creasing as he sat. He'd done the same in the Ford, with the man jibbering in fear beside him.

'We needed the documents!'

'Isn't there any other way?'

'I don't know,' admitted Zimin. He was going to look very stupid. He couldn't think of any way of avoiding the responsibility, either.

CHAPTER THREE

Dimitri Ivanovich Danilov prepared carefully because there was always the possibility others would be there – the Federal Prosecutor or someone high up in the Interior Ministry, perhaps – and he wanted to look right. He'd waited a long time, sometimes he thought too long, and he wanted his appearance to be correct in every detail. Danilov was professionally meticulous about detail, although the outward chaos in which he appeared to work hardly indicated that.

The Director had virtually promised Danilov the succession, before he'd gone to America the previous year during the joint murder investigation, and he'd shopped there with this sort of moment in mind, an occasion when he needed to look his best. He'd scarcely worn the shirt with the pin that fastened the collar behind the tie, which was also new. The shirt was more rumpled than he would have liked but it wouldn't be improved by Olga ironing it again, because she was hopeless at laundry, like she was about most household chores. The American sports coat was newer and held its shape better than either of his two suit jackets, but he chose a suit, the thinner one because of the summer heat. A sports outfit would be too casual.

Danilov dressed as quietly as possible to avoid disturbing Olga, who lay on her back, the sheets bundled around her, her mouth slightly open. The snore was irregular, rising and falling like a faulty engine. A shaft of early light was across her tangled hair, showing the greyness through the uneven brown tint. He hadn't noticed the varying shades until that moment – but then, they didn't look at each other that closely any more.

Danilov was genuinely sad about the way things had collapsed beween himself and Olga. Wrong word, he rejected at once. It had been more of an erosion, a wearing away through neglect and lack of interest until the shell of a marriage was left, with no substance to support it. They existed now in polite pretence, performing a weary charade, each waiting for the other to declare the last act. More his pretence than Olga's, Danilov corrected, refusing himself the escape. He'd been the one knowingly and cynically to prolong it, letting her think there was a chance of salvaging something long after he'd fallen in love with Larissa and no chance remained. And he'd cheated Larissa as well as Olga, making both wait until this moment, this day.

He'd be powerful enough after today to resist the possible embarrassment of long-ago compromises. Would Yevgennie Kosov disclose those compromises, when Larissa asked for the divorce, as he could now ask Olga? For a policeman as boastfully corrupt as Kosov it would be an act of suicide, because of the cross-accusations Danilov could make in return, but having known Kosov for as long as he had, Danilov guessed the man might be vindictive enough to pull the roof down on his own head if he felt his property was being stolen, which was how he'd think of Larissa leaving him – although the Kosov marriage was even more of a mockery than his own to Olga. So it had been sensible to wait until now: indefensible, by his much vaunted moral integrity, but sensible for the career culminating today.

Danilov's final, most careful preparation was to comb the fair, thinning hair over that part of his forehead where it had already retreated. It was an oversight, not to have had it cut: the threat of impending baldness wasn't so obvious, close cropped.

Danilov left the Kirovskaya apartment without waking Olga. There was a crush at the Kazan metro station, and he looked forward to having a permanent official car. He'd have to pressure the local Militia station to increase patrols around his block to protect the vehicle: it would be humiliating if the wipers or windscreen or wheels were stolen, which would happen if he didn't have it guarded. He'd have the power, as Director, to get it looked after: power for whatever he wanted to do. And he wanted to do a lot.

He tried to check the time, not wanting to be late, but his

watch – one of the few remaining tributes from his erstwhile grateful friends – had stopped again, so he had to wait for a station clock. He was ahead of time.

His elevation wouldn't be welcomed by anyone in the Organised Crime Bureau of the Moscow Militia. From the moment of his transfer, six years earlier, Danilov had regained an integrity that had lapsed when he was in uniform, and refused to get involved in the deals and the trading and the pay-offs. He'd been virtually the only one, apart perhaps from the Director. Danilov guessed that when his appointment became public there would be a lot of worried fellow officers who'd sneered and laughed and openly called him stupid over those previous six years. And they'd have every reason to be worried: under his director-ship the Organised Crime Bureau would stop being a rigged lottery, with every player a winner.

He wouldn't move too hurriedly. Or without proper consideration. If he purged it as quickly and as thoroughly as it deserved, there'd hardly be an investigator left, and he wouldn't be improving a bureau by wrecking it. In fact he probably wouldn't do anything about the past at all, except to use his awareness for the future. He'd let it be known, subtly but clearly enough, that the old days and the old ways were over: that under his command the back alley meetings and package-filled handshakes were gone. He'd move hard against those who disregarded the warnings, either transferr-ing them back into uniform or dismissing them entirely as examples to those who remained.

There was no-one else apart from General Leonid Lapinsk in the top floor office at Petrovka, and the Director did not rise from behind his desk when Danilov entered. Lapinsk had been showing his age in the last couple of years, but now Danilov decided the man looked positively ill, his face not just grey but cadaverous. Under stress the General had the habit of coughing, puntuating his words. He did it now, during the greetings, and Danilov wondered why: he couldn't image anything stressful about this encounter, virtually a meeting between friends.

'There are matters for us to discuss,' said the older man.

'Yes,' accepted Danilov. He supposed Lapinsk could make the announcement himself. Or perhaps they'd go on to the Federal Prosecutor's office on Pushkinskaya, or to the Interior Ministry, after Lapinsk had made clear how much he'd had to do with promotion.

'You brought particular credit to this department after the joint American investigation . . .' There was a burst of coughing. 'After which I gave you what amounted to an undertaking, about your future.'

Here it comes, thought Danilov. 'I appreciate the confidence you've always shown in me.'

Lapinsk looked down at his desk. 'Which has been justified by something rare here. But which frightens people. Honesty.'

Danilov was bewildered. 'I don't understand.'

'You are not to succeed me,' declared Lapinsk, hurrying the coughing words. 'The appointment goes to Metkin.'

'What!' Anatoli Nikolaevich Metkin was a colonel too, but lacked Danilov's seniority. And he headed the list of men to be warned in the clean-up Danilov had intended in the Bureau. A clean-up, he realised at once, that now wouldn't be happening.

'I've failed, in my promise to you: like I've failed properly to run this Bureau,' blurted Lapinsk, in sudden admission. 'I allowed certain practices, understandings, to go on. It's always been the way: policemen have to mix with criminals, to solve crime. I never intended it to become what it has, virtually a criminal enterprise. That's why I wanted you to take over: to put things back as they should be. I thought I had the power, even though I was retiring . . .' The old man gulped to a halt, near to breaking down. '. . . But it isn't just the Bureau. People here are protected higher up, within the Interior Ministry. And they're protected by others for whom they do favours in other ministries. Even by the gangs themselves. It's like a club, everyone looking after each other. I was blocked, in every way I tried to put you forward . . . In the end they've mocked me, mocked you . . . I'm sorry. So very, very sorry.'

Danilov tried to analyse what he was being told, examine it coherently. He'd been out-manoeuvred in a coup he hadn't

13

suspected by those who'd sneered and laughed but known what he would do if he gained control. There'd be a lot more sneering and laughing now. 'How are we being mocked?'

Lapinsk cleared his throat. 'Officially, I have been told that, such was your success over the American business, you are too valuable an investigator to be elevated into the administrative position of Director . . .'

'So I remain senior colonel, in charge of investigations?'

Lapinsk shook his head, unable to look straight at his protégé. 'You are to be Deputy Director.'

'There's no such position.'

'It's being created.'

The outrage physically burned through Danilov. It wasn't recognition. It was emasculation, removing him from the day-to-day work of a bureau as corrupt as the criminal organisations it was supposed to be investigating into a position where he could do nothing about it. He said: 'It's meaningless, professionally. There will be no power: nothing for me properly to do.'

'There'll be a car,' evaded Lapinsk. 'And a salary increase.'

'I could refuse.'

'They want you to,' Lapinsk warned him. 'If you do that, you'll have to accept whatever alternative you're offered. Or quit altogether.'

'Why can't I remain as senior investigator?'

'Your former position has already been filled.'

Totally emasculated, Danilov accepted. Any alternative would be the most demeaning that could be found: doubtless had already *been* found, in expectation of his rejection. He said: 'It's all been cleverly worked out, hasn't it?'

'You have enemies,' conceded Lapinsk.

'Who?' demanded Danilov. 'Give me names! I need the names!'

'Practically everyone here, in the Bureau.'

'Of course. But who in the Ministries?'

'I don't know.'

'Who do you think are honest, then?' asked Danilov desperately.

'The Federal Prosecutor, Smolin, maybe. Those at the very

top of the Interior Ministry: I could never get through to them. But I don't know who stood in your way, just below them.'

Danilov felt lost, totally exposed. In sudden awareness he said: 'A position didn't *have* to be created.'

'If you accept, you will remain in the building: people will know what you are doing. If you refuse, you could – and probably would – be downgraded on some invented disciplinary charge and relegated to the furthest Militia post, where you'd never be heard of again.'

If they wanted to know what he was doing, there had to be some apprehension about him. Despite the emptiness of the newly created position, Danilov wondered if he could use it to his advantage. It was a comforting thought. 'I don't have a choice, do I?'

'No,' admitted the outgoing Director.

He needed time to think: consider all his options. Perhaps first even to find one. 'If you need me to say it formally, I accept.'

'Just survive, Dimitri Ivanovich.'

'I wanted to do more than that!'

'You can't. And won't. Crime has won, here in Moscow. In the old days it was organised by the Party – Brezhnev and his gang. Now the gangs are on the streets: better organised even than then. And nobody cares, because nobody knows any other way. There *is* no other way.'

'I won't accept that.'

'You haven't a choice,' echoed Lapinsk.

Chillingly, Danilov realised the older man was probably right.

The Hertz computer at Dulles airport, where the car had been rented, automatically registered the failure to return the grey Ford at the expiry of its hiring date. There was no concern, because the charges simply went on accruing against the platinum American Express card issued to Michel Paulac, of 26, Rue Calvin, Geneva, Switzerland. It was quite common for tourists to miss their return date, forgetting to advise they were keeping a car for a longer period than they'd originally intended.

CHAPTER FOUR

'Looks like you're back on the road again,' greeted the Director. He was lounged behind his desk on the fifth floor office of the FBI building on Pennsylvania Avenue, gazing up towards the Capitol building, his jacket off, tie loosened.

'With a lot of differences,' said Cowley. The last time he had worked mostly in Moscow with Dimitri Danilov, investigating the murder of the niece of an American senator by a serial killer. It had never been publicly disclosed that the killer had been the resident FBI man at the American embassy there, now permanently detained in a prison for the criminally insane in North Carolina. Or, by the most bizarre of all circumstances, that the man had been married to Cowley's ex-wife.

Ross didn't pick up upon the obvious remark. 'There'll be protocols to be observed, official and otherwise. The Secretary is making all the formal requests; you'll handle all the embassy enquiries. You can have as much manpower as you need: the two DC homicide officers, naturally, are seconded to us. Everything the local forensic people collected has already been handed over. The area's still sealed: our own people are carrying out an independent examination.'

'What about the mouth shot?' queried Cowley directly. He was a bull-chested, towering man only just preventing the muscle of college football years from running to fat. It would soon, he knew, as it had begun to go when he was drinking, which he wasn't any more. Cowley wasn't embarrassed about his size: sometimes he even intimidated people with it to gain an advantage.

'The main concern, politically and otherwise, is a Russian Mafia connection right in their embassy,' conceded Ross. 'You got anything on Serov that isn't in the record?'

Cowley shook his head. 'I put a marker on him, after the

16

second visa extension. Came out squeaky clean. He was popular, on the party circuit. Spoke excellent English. Had a reasonable sense of humour: used to make jokes about his wife's name being Raisa, like Gorbachev's.'

Ross turned to look directly at his agent. 'You met him?'

'Once, at a reception for Yeltsin up on the Hill. For about five minutes.'

'Traditionalist or an advocate of the new order?'

'He was a professional diplomat,' said Cowley. 'Who knows?'

'We need to dampen the sensationalism as much as possible,' warned Ross. 'Information is being strictly limited, from the Bureau or through State. No leaks to friends in the media.'

'I don't have any friends in the media.'

'Good.'

'Who's in charge of the scientific stuff?'

'Robertson, here. There's a lot gone down to Quantico. Medical examiner is a man named Brierly.'

'Formal identification?'

'Someone from the embassy. No name yet. Take a DC detective with you to all the obvious things: I don't want any friction.'

'Who makes the collar?' asked Cowley.

'Let's find one first,' said Ross.

The preliminary report had come with the forensic material, and Cowley read it before the two homicide detectives arrived. As a division head Cowley had a suite, with a secretary in an outer office, and Rafferty entered exchanging how-the-rich-and-famous-live glances with his partner. Johannsen returned a mocking smile. Both shook their heads to coffee; they sat with exaggerated casualness.

'I hope we're going to work well together,' opened Cowley.

'You're the boss,' said Rafferty. It was a challenge.

'That a problem for you?' asked Cowley.

'Should it be?' Johannsen came in quickly.

'No,' said Cowley.

'Just point and whistle,' said Rafferty.

Cowley sighed, indicating their report on the desk. 'Fill me in on that.'

'Good place to kill anyone. Mostly offices all around. There's a jazz club, but there was a big band gig. No-one heard any shots. Same in the only bar that fronts on to the street.'

'How'd he get there?'

'No car that we can link to him so far.'

'The main Russian compound is at 1500 Massachusetts Avenue. Let's check all the cab companies for a pick up from there to Georgetown. Cover the embassy on 16th Street, too.'

'Yes, sir!' said Rafferty.

Cowley ignored it. 'Wisconsin Avenue runs right down to the river: how far from the end was the body?'

'About ten yards along, in the direction of the boat club.'

'There are a lot of apartment blocks below M Street,' Cowley pointed out. 'People would have been in, at night. They been checked?'

'No,' conceded Rafferty, wearily.

'According to this report' – Cowley tapped it – 'death could have been somewhere around seven or eight. Let's do every apartment, around that time tonight. And the garages beneath, for a car that might be Serov's.'

'Just the two of us!' protested Rafferty.

'We'll draw men from the Bureau's Washington office and you can call for additional help from your division . . .' Cowley looked to Rafferty. 'I'd like you to do the briefing. Anyone seconded, you included, goes on the Bureau budget.' He turned to Johannsen. 'I want you at the mortuary with me, for the formal identification.' Cowley spread his hands, towards them. 'Anything I've missed out?'

Rafferty looked at his partner before both shook their heads.

'You saw the body,' said Cowley. 'Was it a professional hit?'

'No doubt about it,' said Rafferty positively.

'Shit!' said Cowley.

★

'You said you were going to be made Director: I told people!'
Olga's accusing voice was muffled, and Danilov guessed she
had her hand over the mouthpiece: there was noise in the
background. Olga was a general typist at the Ministry of
Agriculture.

'It's internal politics.' Danilov wished he hadn't undertaken to telephone her. But when he'd promised he *had*
expected to get the job.

'But there's a car?'

'Yes.'

'And more money?'

'Yes.'

'Will there be official functions to go to?'

'Probably.' The charade was continuing. What about the
joint divorce, so that he and Larissa could marry, now there
wasn't the protective power of the directorship!

Ironically, Olga said: 'Is the rank of deputy director higher
than Kosov's?'

'Of course it is.' He hadn't known Olga was jealous of
Kosov: even his previous investigative rank had been
superior to that of a Militia division commander.

'That's something.' There were further muffled words,
away from the telephone. 'I've got to go.'

Danilov had to wait several minutes for Larissa to be
found, when he rang the Druzhba Hotel on Prospekt
Vernadskovo, where Larissa was one of assistant reception
managers. 'I didn't get it.'

'There's a room we could use, until seven o'clock.'

'That's not what I called for.'

'Just to talk. You need to talk.'

'I've lost,' Danilov said, hating the admission.

'Only if you allow yourself to lose. Fight!'

He never wanted to lose, Danilov accepted: so he
wouldn't.

'He could have lied to you!' Arkadi Gusovsky had a sick
man's pallor and when he became red with annoyance, as
now, he looked clown-like, contrasting red and white. The
ornate, heavily brocaded, smoky back room of the restaurant

on Glovin Bol'soj was full, because the Chechen leaders liked the protection of bodyguards, but no-one would have dared show any reaction to Gusovsky's strange appearance. Very early after assuming control Gusovsky had made everyone look on while he personally beat to death with a metal stave a man he'd imagined was smiling mockingly at him. It had happened in this same room. Gusovsky had insisted the body remain where it was while he ate rare steak.

'I made him watch what I did to Serov,' insisted Mikhail Antipov, nervously. 'He didn't lie.'

'He might not have understood Russian. The family was Ukrainian.'

'I asked him in both.' It was Antipov's knowledge of both languages that had made him ideal for the job.

Gusovsky, who was also unnaturally thin, threw the papers that had been taken from Michel Paulac's briefcase too hard on to the table between them; some fell off. 'You should have brought everything! These aren't anything to do with it. We need the original, to see the names that need changing.'

'You made a mess of it, didn't you?' Aleksandr Yerin had adjusted so completely to his blindness he was always able to appear to be looking at the person to whom he was talking. He asked the question of Zimin, the third member of the Chechen ruling heirarchy; there was no reply Zimin could find.

'I don't want anyone else making any more mistakes,' said Gusovsky generally.

Once more, no-one spoke.

CHAPTER FIVE

Cowley and Johannsen went to the mortuary an hour before the time set for the official identification: the enthusiastic Brierly hurried from behind his desk, hand outstretched, and when Cowley introduced himself said he presumed Cowley was taking over the investigation. Cowley wished he hadn't, in front of the DC detectives.

The detailed autopsy did not take anything much further than the preliminary report. Either body shot would have proved fatal: the heart had been shattered by one. There were no indications of a struggle and no skin particles or hair beneath Serov's fingernails to indicate he had tried to fight off his attacker: he'd bitten his nails anyway, so the chances of finding anything had been remote. There was an old abdominal scar, possibly from a hernia or an appendicectomy. He had eaten just prior to his death; the stomach contained undigested fish and what had obviously been an entrée salad, plus traces of alcohol. The massive damage to both the back of the body and the head by the exiting of the flattened bullets made it difficult for Brierly to be absolutely sure, but he'd found no evidence of any organic disease or illness. There was no sign of torture, either.

'Will the Bureau want its own autopsy, for DNA and stuff like that?' asked the young examiner.

Cowley nodded. 'But we're going to need more than science and technology to catch whoever did this.'

'I've packaged all the clothes up. I guessed you'd want them?'

'All part of the system,' confirmed Cowley. 'What about time of death?'

'Nine,' said Brierly. 'Maybe half an hour earlier.'

'How long before that had he eaten?' asked Johannsen.

'Perhaps an hour,' said Brierly.

'And Georgetown is full of restaurants,' reflected Cowley.

'He could have eaten at home and left immediately afterwards,' disputed Johannsen.

'Entrée salads aren't a Russian way of eating,' said Cowley. 'It's American restaurant style.'

'This investigation is going to wear out a lot of shoe leather,' complained Johannsen.

'Investigations do,' said Cowley.

Warning of the Russians' arrival came from the downstairs reception, which Cowley, Johannsen and Brierly reached as the foreigners entered. There were two men, only one of whom identified himself: his visiting card described Valery Pavlenko as a member of the cultural section of the embassy. Cowley, who over the previous five years, as Director of the Russian division, had supervised the assembly of the FBI files on Russian diplomats in the United States, recognised the second Russian as Nikolai Fedorovich Redin, supposedly in the embassy's trade section. He was, in fact, a member of the Russian external security service: when the man had been posted to Washington, four years earlier, it had still been called the KGB. A year after his arrival Redin had been positively identified trying to buy export-controlled computer base plates; Cowley had had the Department of Commerce ban the export, but argued against expelling Redin on the well established grounds that it was better to retain a spy they knew than discover who his successor might be.

There was a puff of white condensation at the temperature change in the examination room when Brierly withdrew the drawer. Some cosmetic effort had been made to pad a sheet around what remained of the head, and the face had been cleaned of blood; the same disguising sheet was arranged to cover the chest wounds. The coldness of the preservation drawer had whitened Serov's face, heightening the blackness of the bruising and powder burns to the mouth. Rigor had frozen it wide open, as if the man had died screaming. The eyes were closed. The identity label was tied to the big toe of the left foot, like a price tag.

'That is Petr Aleksandrovich,' said Pavlenko evenly.

22

There was no facial reaction from either Russian at Serov's disfigurement.

'We'd like to talk,' said Cowley, not wanting to lose the opportunity with a Russian away from the confines of the embassy.

The pathologist led them back along the corridor to a small room opposite the reception desk. As Cowley sat, Redin leaned close to Pavlenko and spoke: the grating of his chair prevented Cowley hearing what was said.

'We regret this incident very much indeed,' began Cowley. He'd served in overseas embassies, in Rome and in London when he had been a full-time field agent, and knew the need for diplomatic niceties.

'You are police?'

'Yes.' Cowley didn't intend openly identifying himself as FBI in front of Redin.

'You know who did this?'

'There's been no arrest yet.'

'Why was he shot like that, in the mouth? It is bestial.'

'We don't know,' admitted Cowley. He did not yet intend getting into a Mafia discussion, either.

There was another head-bent, whispered exchange between the two Russians. Again Cowley didn't hear what was said.

'Was he robbed?' asked Pavlenko.

'There is no obvious indication of that.'

'We would like his belongings,' announced Pavlenko. 'And the return of the body.'

'We are still making enquiries,' said Cowley, held by the sensation of *déjà vu*. The Russians had initially refused to release the body of the senator's niece or her effects, after the Moscow murder that had taken him to Russia the previous year. It had been one of several early disputes.

'What have your enquiries got to do with returning the body and the contents of Petr Aleksandrovich's pockets!' demanded Pavlenko.

'The investigation has only been under way a very short time,' pointed out Cowley. 'Everything will be released as soon as possible.'

Pavlenko was a thin-faced man. His features hardened now, in anger. 'We do not want this to become even more difficult than it is. A Russian national has been murdered!'

'And we're trying to find out who did it,' said Johannsen, close to rudeness. 'And why.'

Quickly interceding, Cowley said: 'Where did Petr Aleksandrovich live?'

Pavlenko hesitated. 'The Russian compound.'

'We need to learn his movements last night. We would like to interview Mrs Serova.' He instantly regretted demonstrating his knowledge of the language by his correct feminisation of the name, but the Russians appeared to miss it.

'She returned to Moscow on compassionate leave two weeks ago,' disclosed the diplomat. 'She has an elderly mother who is ill.'

'So Serov was living alone?' said Johannsen.

'Yes.'

'Does anyone at the embassy know what he was doing last night?'

Pavlenko shrugged. 'I have not asked.'

'We would like to be allowed to visit the embassy, to talk particularly to people in the cultural division, to discover if he had an appointment or an arrangement to meet anyone,' said Cowley.

'He said nothing to me,' replied Pavlenko.

'He might have talked to someone else,' persisted Johannsen.

'I do not think so,' insisted the Russian.

'Why not?'

'I was Petr Aleksandrovich's immediate deputy. The conversations were between the two of us.'

'He must have spoken to other people as well!' challenged Johannsen, and Cowley thought he detected the beginning of a policeman's belligerence at being given the runaround.

'Not yesterday. There were only secretaries in the office, apart from Petr Aleksandrovich and myself. He would not have talked about any social event with them.'

'Were you social friends as well as work colleagues?'

Pavlenko hesitated again. 'Yes.'

'So you would talk about social things?' said Johannsen.

'Not yesterday,' refuted the Russian.

'Would you have known if he was on an *official* engagement?' The homicide detective was still polite, but only just.

'There was nothing last night.' There was the faintest sheen of perspiration on Pavlenko's face.

Once again Cowley failed to hear all that passed between the two Russians, but he thought he caught Redin say *neel'z'ah* and wondered what it was Pavlenko had been warned he couldn't or shouldn't say.

'So there *is* an appointments diary?' pressed Johannsen. 'We'd like to see that.'

Pavlenko stopped just before the angry rejection, breathing deeply. 'It is unthinkable for you to examine official documentation belonging to the Russian embassy. I have told you there was no official function last night.'

'We would also like to examine the apartment at Massachusetts Avenue,' bulldozed Johannsen. 'There could be some indication there of where he went.'

'That's equally ridiculous!' refused Pavlenko.

Delicately, choosing each word, Cowley said: 'You have Russian staff responsible for the security of your embassy facilities, just as we have marines at our embassy in Moscow. Would it be possible for us to provide a list of questions to which we need answers – like, for instance, any diary entry or note at the Massachusetts Avenue apartment – for your own officials to answer for us?'

Pavlenko hesitated, glancing sideways at the other Russian, but without any muffled conversation said: 'No. I do not think so.'

'There are many routine enquiries for us to make,' said Cowley. 'Particularly around the Georgetown district in which he was found. It would help if you could supply a reasonably up-to-date photograph to be duplicated and carried by officers conducting street enquiries.'

'I am not sure any are available,' said Pavlenko.

Cowley sighed, careless of the frustration showing, no longer concerned at Johannsen's aggression. Pavlenko was being openly obstructive: standard Russian suspicion, or something more?

'A photograph was officially supplied for Petr Aleksandrovich's visa application,' he said. 'If there is none more current we will use that.'

Pavlenko's face twitched at losing the exchange. 'I will enquire of our personnel division.'

'There will be need for us to speak again.'

'Tomorrow,' insisted Pavlenko, trying to turn the demand against the American. 'To agree the release of the body and effects.'

'To discuss further co-operation between us,' corrected Cowley. The vaguest suggestion of an idea came to him. Just as quickly, he dismissed it. He was letting himself fall into nostalgia.

'Jesus!' exploded Johannsen, within seconds of the door closing behind the Russians. 'If they're all as awkward as that bastard, maybe we aren't dealing with a Mafia killing at all. Maybe whoever popped Serov just got fed up waiting for the son-of-a-bitch to say something that made sense! I thought we were all supposed to be on the same side now!'

'Some don't believe it as much as others,' said Cowley. 'I want you to do something. I'll get State to run a check on every diplomatic affair the night of the killing . . .'

'. . . So we can check every one to see if Petr Aleksandrovich Serov attended,' cut in Johannsen, in a groan.

'Right. And we'll trawl wider. He was the senior cultural attaché: there'd be invitations to all sorts of exhibitions and art events that wouldn't be on any State Department sheet. They'll all need to be checked out. According to our files, he enjoyed the party scene.' He could probably shorten the search by going over the Bureau monitoring log, even though Serov wasn't on any Watch rota: it was still automatic to flag the attendance of a Russian if one were identified.

'Why bother!' demanded Johannsen. 'Those guys don't give a shit about catching whoever did it. Why should we bust our asses?'

'I don't envy you guys,' said Brierly.

'I don't envy us either,' said Johannsen, with feeling.

They drove directly from the mortuary to the scene of the murder. As they turned off M Street on to Wisconsin, towards the river, Johannsen began identifying the unmarked cars of the detectives carrying out the house-to-house enquiries.

'Are they going to be pissed off, having to wait around long into the evening!'

'I wish there was another way,' said Cowley, meaning it.

Because the bottom of Wisconsin Avenue was sealed off, he parked against the tape and the stripped trestles. Cowley showed his shield and Johannsen automatically attached his badge to the top pocket of his jacket. There was a hard core of onlookers with a new street entertainment and some waiting-just-in-case journalists and photographers and two television crews. Cowley and Johannsen were through the barriers before they were spotted: they ignored the yells to attract their attention, and the one TV light that flared on.

An area about twelve square yards around where the body had been found was completely enclosed in protective polythene, creating a tent that concealed them from the media, occupied by about ten technicians, either in white or in light blue protective cover-alls. Two were manhandling a huge, generator-powered vacuum machine, sucking every-thing from the ground behind a squad carrying out an inch by inch visual search ahead of them. After the vacuum, more men were designating the area already scoured with rectangles of tape, like an archaeological dig. Cowley supposed in many ways it was. The chalked outline showing the position in which Serov's body had been found was unnecessary: a good half of the shape of the torso was marked with thick gouts of blood.

To one technician who appeared temporarily to be doing nothing Cowley said: 'Anything?'

The man indicated the vacuum. 'It'll take days to go through that. But we did find a shell casing, quite early this morning. That's already back at headquarters; Harry Robertson took it himself. You know him?'

Cowley nodded. 'Nothing else?'

'DC forensic retrieved a slug last night, under what was left of the poor bastard's head. Flat as a dime was the word.'

'Any tyre marks?'

The man gestured generally. 'Take your pick. At night this place is a goddamned parking lot. We've got more casts than General Motors.'

At the entrance to the makeshift tent Cowley hesitated, looking back to where the body had been, relating it to the nearest buildings. Overhead there was the constant thunder of cars along the freeway. A lot of detectives were going to waste their time long into the night, trying to locate anyone who might have heard anything.

A media reception committee was waiting immediately beyond the barrier. There were flashgun bursts and television lights and a babble of questions, to all of which Cowley and Johannsen shook their heads as they waded through. One reporter said to Cowley: 'Hey, don't I recognise you?' Cowley shook his head to that, as well.

It was awkward for Cowley to back and turn the car the way he had parked, and there were a lot more photographs before he could regain M Street. Before they reached the traffic lights Johannsen said: 'What about a drink? We've been six hours on the go and missed lunch, for Christ's sake!'

Johannsen's hostility had practically disappeared, and Cowley did not want to resurrect it. The decision was made for him as he turned right on to M Street and saw the vacant meter; they crossed back to Nathans before the lights changed.

'What'll it be?' invited Johannsen.

'Club soda. Lime wedge,' said Cowley.

Johannsen frowned. 'You don't drink?'

'Wrong metabolism,' evaded Cowley. There'd been a couple of slips since he'd gone dry, but it was rarely a problem any more. Oddly, it was now. He practically salivated at the thought of the taste, the taste of anything, beer or whisky, whatever would give that hit, that warm, comfortable, relaxing feeling spreading up from his stomach. He moved as far away from the bar as he could, to the ledge fronting out on to the street. The lime soured the soda Johannsen handed to him.

'You know something that surprised me?' demanded Johannsen. He was drinking Jack Daniels, straight, over ice: Cowley could smell it further along the ledge.

'What?'

'There weren't any questions from the Russians about it being a hit. Not serious questions. Pavlenko used the word murder and said it was bestial, but he didn't press when you said you didn't know why Serov was shot in the mouth. He just let it go.'

'The mouth wound doesn't have the significance in Russia that it has here.'

'They were being told the significance from dawn, on every radio station! And every television station. And every newspaper. Wouldn't you have expected them to be a damned sight more curious?'

'Yes,' conceded Cowley.

Johannsen took a long pull at his drink, and Cowley watched the other man's throat move as he swallowed. The detective said: 'I liked the way you fucked him over the photograph.'

'We're going to need the best we can get. With Raisa in Moscow, he pretty definitely ate around here somewhere.'

'Raisa? You got a file on them?'

'He was a genuine diplomat.'

'Who's been killed by the Mafia, like genuine Russian diplomats are killed all the time!' said Johannsen. 'Wouldn't it be good to screw Pavlenko further with a pocket diary among Serov's stuff, detailing lots of scuttlebutt!'

'I'd settle for a simple entry and a phone number.'

Johannsen finished his drink and put the empty glass pointedly on the ledge, Cowley had to wait several minutes in the crush at the bar, surrounded by people and glasses and the smells he remembered so well; he felt the perspiration prick out on his face.

When he got back, Cowley said: 'I think you're going to be proved right. It'll be a miracle if anyone heard anything down there: certainly not enough to take them to a window, to look out.'

'We as good as told you.'

'Routine to be gone through,' insisted Cowley.

'On the subject of which,' grinned Johannsen, 'I think it would be a Christian act if I volunteered a little assistance to my regular partner ringing doorbells in one of those apartment blocks over there, don't you?'

The man might instead tell Rafferty he'd just agreed it was a waste of time and call the door-to-door enquiries off, thought Cowley, but he was anxious to get out of the bar. 'I guess he'd appreciate it.'

The telephone monitor registered a call when Cowley got into the Bureau car. He returned it without starting the engine.

'Got something intriguing,' said Harry Robertson, the scientific co-ordinator. 'Looks like your Russian was shot dead with a Russian gun! How about that!'

CHAPTER SIX

There was no move to humiliate Danilov publicly until the day Leonid Lapinsk officially left. The old Director retired without any ceremony, merely touring the Petrovka building to say individual goodbyes. It was mid-morning when he reached Danilov's cluttered and over-flowing office, separate from the general squad room because of Danilov's seniority. Anatoli Metkin, the new Director, was at Lapinsk's side.

Danilov guessed a lot of the other investigators would be watching from the communal room further down the corridor. There was nothing for him and Lapinsk to say to each other. They shook hands and wished each other luck. Danilov told the other man he deserved his retirement and Lapinsk said he was looking forward to it but knew already he would miss the job. Danilov said he personally would miss the other man and immediately wished he hadn't when Metkin smiled, a gloating expression. Throughout the farewell, Lapinsk's nervous cough seemed more pronounced than usual.

Metkin made no attempt to move when Lapinsk backed out into the corridor. The man appeared to be speaking to both of them when he said Danilov's appointment represented an expansion of the Bureau, but Danilov took it as a confirmation of a larger audience he couldn't see.

Turning more towards Danilov, Metkin looked around the office in which it was difficult to move for files and folders and reference books and box containers, which made the place look like an animal warren but was in reality Danilov's own records system. He knew what every bundle and packet contained, and could retrieve material hours ahead of the proper basement archives. Metkin said: 'This will no longer be your office. Kabalin is senior investigator now.'

Vladimir Nikolaevich Kabalin had been Metkin's partner,

allegedly specialising in organised gang crime, and had been another on Danilov's now laughable purge list: Danilov wondered if Metkin would remain, with Kabalin, on the payroll of one or more of the gangs they were supposed to have investigated. There was no reason why they couldn't double or treble their income now; with Kabalin as senior investigator and Metkin in ultimate charge, the rackets could continue uninterrupted and unchallenged.

'Where will my office be?' he asked.

'It's a problem,' dismissed Metkin, enjoying himself. 'We'll have to find you somewhere. I want you in my office. An hour.'

The bastard was staging the performance to mock Leonid Lapinsk, whose protégé he had been, Danilov realised; the outgoing Director stood head bowed in embarrassment, just occasionally looking towards the squad room. Danilov said: 'So there's nowhere for me to put my things?'

Metkin almost over-stressed the sneer. 'Is there anything in this junk heap worth keeping?'

'Things that are necessary to keep,' insisted Danilov. How clever was Metkin: how *really* clever? This was juvenile.

Metkin shrugged. 'They'll have to be stored somewhere, until we can find accommodation for you. Don't forget: an hour.'

As he looked helplessly around the room, Danilov was sure he heard laughter from along the corridor. He got up and started tidying the files to be carried away, but the fury was shaking through him and he did it carelessly, so the fresh piles began toppling and slipping, creating worse chaos. Danilov stopped, forcing control. He could not allow Metkin to reduce him to unthinking, unco-ordinated anger by a few minutes of arrogant, childish pantomime.

He looked up curiously at another noise from outside, not knowing what to expect, then smiled, relieved. Yuri Mikhailovich Pavin had been *his* partner, whenever Danilov had been able to manipulate the shifts, a plainclothes Militia major whose heavy, slow-moving demeanour belied the astute brain that made him, in Danilov's opinion, the best scene-of-crime officer in the department.

'Hear you've got to pack up,' greeted Pavin. 'Thought you might need help.'

Danilov saw Pavin had several cardboard boxes – a rarity like everything else in Moscow – gathered in a ham-like grip. 'They can't have been easy to get?'

'Someone in stores owed me a favour.'

Pavin had never admitted how he supplemented his Militia salary, and Danilov had never enquired. Pavin moved towards the jumbled files. 'Any particular order? Things to be kept in sequence?'

'It's got to be done by noon: I've been called before Metkin then. Just dump them in as they come: I'll sort it out later.'

'I've still got the key to the store-cupboard we used as the evidence room for the killings last year,' said Pavin. 'They'll be safe there for a while. Not long, though.'

Danilov stopped packing, looking at Pavin in disbelief. 'You think anyone will bother to upset these things?'

'Yes,' said Pavin. 'You weren't expected to take the job. They don't want you here: you're an intrusive nuisance, so everybody is going to do what they can to make it as uncomfortable as possible. Besides, these boxes are worth having.'

'I'd be grateful for any warnings in advance,' said Danilov, tentatively, and quickly added: 'I don't want to cause you any difficulty.'

'I wouldn't want that either,' said Pavin honestly. 'If I can safely help, I will.'

They had packed, although badly, and already carried six boxes to the store-room before Kabalin arrived. It took the man too long to clear his face of the surprise at the empty room and Danilov was glad he'd blocked the doorway, keeping Kabalin outside for the disappointment to be witnessed by the other watching detectives.

'There's only one bulb!' protested Kabalin. The office was an inner one, with no window, so lights had to burn constantly: a wall socket and a desk lamp were empty, putting the room in semi-darkness.

'You'll have to get replacements from maintenance,' advised Danilov. The average waiting time for light bulbs in

Militia headquarters was six months, and then they could only be obtained for reciprocal favours. The bulbs hadn't blown: they were in one of the first packing cases now in the locked closet to which Danilov had the only key. The light sockets wherever he was put would be empty, which made taking those from his old room a practical precaution, though Danilov regretted matching the childishness with which he was being treated.

Anatoli Metkin had not had time to innovate any changes or even to become accustomed to the Director's suite, and Danilov decided the man looked the furtive interloper he was. Metkin was physically indecisive, neither tall nor short, fat nor thin. A crowd person, but for his face, which was criss-crossed and latticed with lines, and his mouth was bracketed by two deep grooves that began close to his eyes and curved the entire length of each cheek. His eyes were unusually light blue and unsettling because of it, and he didn't blink a lot, as if he were afraid of missing something.

'You're surprised at my appointment,' declared Metkin.

'I didn't have the opportunity earlier to congratulate you,' evaded Danilov. The hypocrisy stuck in his throat. How much more would he find difficulty in saying and doing, in the future?

'Lapinsk had promised the directorship to you, hadn't he!'

The former Director would not have admitted that. 'The appointment is the responsibility of the Interior Ministry, not a gift of an outgoing incumbent.'

'Exactly!' said Metkin, triumphantly, as if the reply had proved something.

Which Danilov supposed it had, hopefully for his own future protection, rather than Metkin's satisfaction. Who was Metkin's protector in the Ministry? There would be safety for himself, if he could find out. There were papers on the desk, and Danilov was curious to know if Metkin had written reminder notes for himself.

Fixing Danilov with an unbroken gaze, Metkin said: 'I do not intend any misconceptions between us.'

'I hope there won't be,' said Danilov. The man was

altogether too anxious, falling over himself to make his points and doing it badly. There was advantage to be taken here.

'Your appointment is provisional. Did Lapinsk make that clear?'

'No,' Danilov conceded. Had it been an oversight by Lapinsk? Or an admission of further failure the old man hadn't been able to concede?

Metkin smiled, crumpling his face further. 'If the experiment doesn't work, it will be reconsidered. For that reason, your promoted rank to Lieutenant-General is only *acting*, subject to confirmation.'

On what grade – his old or the temporary one – would his pension be calculated if he abandoned the whole stupid nonsense and quit the Militia entirely? 'There is a car?' He might as well get everything spelled out at the very beginning.

'Not personally assigned. Allocated from the car pool, and only when operational requirements permit.'

Which they never would, Danilov accepted. 'How do you see this new role being fulfilled?'

Metkin went at last to his reminder notes. 'Your function is to be administrative from now on. You will be responsible for all operational rotas and rosters. You will supervise and be answerable for all supplies and facilities throughout the building. You will control and administer all financial matters and prepare accounts and forward budgets, for presentation to the Finance Ministry. You will also liaise, where necessary, with uniformed Militia offices throughout the city.'

Danilov sat silent for several minutes, content to let Metkin believe he was overwhelmed by the catalogue of duties. Which *were* administrative, despite what Lapinsk had said, and *would* be overwhelming, if he ever tried to perform them properly, because they were the work of at least four men. But Metkin was failing to realise how the role he had just announced could be selectively manipulated. Hoping he was maintaining a look of shocked bewilderment, Danilov said: 'Have you officially notified every relevant department here at Petrovka?'

35

'The second thing I did after taking office.'

That would be an essential part of the ridicule, accepted Danilov. Which was the only aspect from which the idiot would have considered it. 'And the Ministry?'

'The first thing I did,' said Metkin. 'Both our own and Finance.'

He'd answered one of his earlier questions, Danilov decided. Metkin wasn't clever at all. The man was really remarkably stupid. Danilov was sure he could make Metkin look even more stupid. He was going to enjoy doing it.

It was regular commuters on the New York and Boston shuttles from National who became daily more offended by the smell from the anonymous grey Ford. Two noted the Hertz bumper sticker and complained to the airport office, on the third day.

The service attendant began retching when he was ten yards from the vehicle and backed off, believing he recognised the smell, although he wasn't sure. He was definitely sure he was paid to jockey cars and fix minor faults, not examine decomposing bodies. That was a job for the police.

The Hertz supervisor agreed, and dialled the 911 emergency number.

'Zimin was entrusted with briefing Antipov because he controls the bulls,' insisted Yerin. 'He should have gone to America himself, to see it went right: he likes seeing people hurt.'

Gusovsky had agreed to Zimin being excluded from the meeting at his house in Kutbysevskiy. They were alone in the study, the bodyguards relegated to the outer rooms.

'We didn't suggest he went,' reminded Gusovsky, lighting one of the thin cigars the doctors had prohibited when the shadow on his lung was first detected.

'He should have suggested it himself.'

'There's the other obvious way.'

'Who goes to Switzerland?'

'Stupar. The Swiss won't recognise his qualifications, though: he'll have to work through a local lawyer.'

'I think we should start limiting knowledge only to what people *have* to know. It's safer.'

'I agree,' said Gusovsky.

'And that should include Zimin from now on. He's only good at controlling thugs.'

Gusovsky didn't respond. If Zimin proved a liability, he'd have to be eliminated. Gusovsky decided against reaching a decision too soon: when it happened – if it had to happen – he'd make it an example throughout the Family, to prove no-one was safe, no matter how high in the organisation. A public execution, in fact.

CHAPTER SEVEN

Cowley supposed his identification was inevitable ('Hey, don't I recognise you?') once the Georgetown photographs were compared in the newspaper picture libraries. Just as it was inevitable the media would fill in the lack of real information with long references to his having been the first American investigator officially to work in Moscow. He still regretted the exposure. He'd missed the initial coverage, on the previous evening's TV news, but it was repeated on every morning channel and all the newspapers carried his picture at the scene the previous day and from the Moscow affair: some even had shots and lengthy accounts of the case. There was, of course, no identification of Pauline's second husband as the killer: according to the carefully concocted official records, the murderer was the mentally deranged Moscow labourer they had first – wrongly – arrested.

There were already three enquiries from FBI Public Affairs for interviews by the time Cowley got to his office. There was also a message from the State Department that the Russians were providing more up to date photographs of Serov. The embassy had also formally requested the return of the body. Cowley rejected the interviews, and telephoned the Director's office for a meeting that afternoon.

A list of what had been found on the body was already on his desk and Cowley at first skimmed it hopefully, remembering Johannsen's remark about a pocket diary. There wasn't one. In addition to the DC driving licence that had provided the original identification, there were locally billed MasterCharge and American Express cards, four house keys, $76 in cash, a pair of spectacles, in their case, American manufactured ballpoint and fountain pens, and a clean pad of reminder notes marked as undergoing forensic testing for previous page indentations. There had been a plain band of Russian-origin gold on the man's wedding finger, and a tie clasp and matching cuff-links of American make.

Cowley had just finished going through the list when Rafferty and Johannsen arrived. Even before he sat down Rafferty said: 'We didn't know we were with a celebrity! Do we give autographs when we're asked or not?'

There wasn't the earlier resentful edge of cynicism, and Cowley was glad. 'What about the house-to-house?'

'Zilch,' dismissed Rafferty.

'The captain wants to know if you need the scene to remain sealed. All your guys have gone,' said Johannsen.

'I'm seeing our scientific co-ordinator this morning. I'll check if it can be released. And there is something from the scene: a shell casing from a Russian gun.'

Both homicide detectives straightened slightly in their chairs, discarding the professional casualness. 'You think maybe he was killed by one of his own people?' queried Johannsen. 'That it *is* the Russian Mafia!'

'Could be a set-up, to make it look like that,' cautioned Rafferty.

'Let's wait for the evidence,' warned Cowley. He'd already made up his own mind what it proved, and he wasn't happy with the conclusion.

'If this is an in-house Russian affair we're not going to get diddly squat, judging from the co-operation of those two embassy guys yesterday,' said Johannsen.

'Maybe there'll be something we can pick up from the memo pad?' suggested Rafferty, studying the list Cowley handed him.

'The MasterCharge and American Express billing is local,' pointed out Cowley. 'Check with both: get the charge sheets, particularly if there were any on the night of the murder.'

'There would have been a counterfoil on him, if he'd picked up a tab,' argued Johannsen.

'Not necessarily, if he didn't want to put it against an expense account,' said Rafferty.

'Let's get the accounts,' insisted Cowley. 'If there's nothing for the night in question, they might still isolate a favourite restaurant. And restaurants are going to be today's enquiry. There are photographs of Serov coming through State, from the embassy.'

'It'll need to be done at night,' argued Johannsen. 'That's when he ate.'

'Done twice,' corrected Cowley. 'Some lunchtime shifts run over, into early evening. We could miss whoever served him if we leave it too late.'

Rafferty breathed out noisily but didn't protest. 'It'll need a squad again.'

'The taxi checks haven't been completed, but there's nothing so far,' reported Johannsen. Unexpectedly he added: 'The papers say you speak fluent Russian. You get anything of what they were whispering to each other yesterday?'

Despite the assumed nonchalance they were both good, Cowley acknowledged. 'When you pressed Pavlenko about social engagements, particularly on the night Serov died, the guy who wasn't introduced told Pavlenko he couldn't talk about it.'

'That all?' demanded Johannsen, disappointed.

'What I did get was incomplete. Just two words: "*You can't.*" They were taking a lot of trouble not to be overheard.'

'The papers also say you're head of the Bureau's Russian division, monitoring all Russian personnel in this country,' said Johannsen. 'You make the second guy, who wasn't introduced?'

Very good, thought Cowley. 'Nikolai Fedorovich Redin. KGB when it was the KGB. Now it's called an external security service.'

'What about Serov planning to defect?' suggested Rafferty. 'It's happened elsewhere, despite all the changes. Redin discovers it, knocks Serov off and throws in the mouth shot to blow smoke in our eyes . . .' The man paused, apparently unaware of the appalling metaphor. '. . . It would even be appropriate, if Serov were going to tell us things we shouldn't have heard. And the Russians do kill people who try to run: it's happened a lot.'

'In the past,' disputed Cowley. 'One, defectors invariably are intelligence officers, with something to offer: our files mark Serov as a genuine diplomat. Two, there's usually some approach, before they try to run. It's very rarely a walk-in: someone literally coming off the street. Three, I *am* head of the Russian division: if there'd been any prior contact, I'd know about it already. There wasn't.'

Both detectives looked unconvinced.

'Your files could be wrong,' said Rafferty.

'Maybe, rare though it is, he *did* intend to be a walk-in,' said Johannsen. 'You think the CIA would tell you if they had Serov about to jump into the bag?'

'Not necessarily,' conceded Cowley.

'Shouldn't you ask the Cousins at Langley?' suggested Rafferty.

It had been an impressive double act, admired Cowley: probably carefully rehearsed, like using the tradecraft word Cousins, which was coming close to going over the top. Cowley didn't think it would produce anything, but then neither had the house-to-house enquiries. 'Yes, we should,' he admitted. 'I hadn't thought of it, which I should have done. Thank you.'

Both detectives smiled, satisfied.

Harry Robertson was standing expectantly in his office, shifting from one foot to the other with the impatience of a dedicated specialist. He was a giant of a man who wanted to be bigger and was trying hard to achieve it. His hair was long, part secured by a coloured bandana in a pony tail and the rest matted into a beard that had never been trimmed and exploded in all directions to hang fully down to his chest, like a napkin. His stomach was enormous, encased in a lumberjack-check workshirt and bulging over corduroys held up by a death's head buckled belt at least two inches wide. The ensemble, predictably, was finished off by high-laced work boots.

Cowley decided Robertson had to be damned good to be allowed to get away with such determined affectation: J. Edgar Hoover would be corkscrewing in his grave. But then, the homosexual Hoover would probably be wearing a dress.

'Here's the little feller!' announced Robertson, with the pride of a conjuror producing the rabbit from an empty hat.

The shell casing was still enclosed in a see-through exhibit pouch. To Cowley it looked like an ordinary brass shell sleeve. 'How can you be sure it's Russian?'

'Size!' declared Robertson. He gestured towards a desk as dishevelled as he was. For the first time Cowley saw two handguns, side by side. They looked identical. There were bullets alongside each.

Robertson picked up the gun on the right of the desk, offering it for examination. 'Observe the Walther PP!' he invited. 'One of the most successful hand weapons after the invention of the bow and arrow. Developed by the Germans in 1929 as a police pistol, not to be confused with its smaller brother, the PPK, of James Bond fame and all that crap . . .' The man paused, to make his point. 'It is also the most copied handgun in the world, both with and without permission.'

Cowley shook his head against taking the gun. He supposed the theatrical presentation went with the man's appearance.

'Specifications,' itemised the scientist. 'It's 6.38 inches long and has a six-grooved, right-hand–twist barrel 3.35 inches long and an eight round magazine. Most popular chambering is known as a Short . . .' Robertson picked up one of the unspent bullets and held it forward for inspection.

Cowley looked, dutifully.

Robertson took up the second gun. 'The Russian 9mm Makarov,' he announced. 'It's 6.35 inches long and has a four-grooved, right-hand–twist barrel 3.85 inches long. And uses an eight round magazine . . .' He turned back to his desk, hefting the Walther again, making balancing movements with a gun in either hand. 'The Makarov is the unlicensed, unauthorised Russian copy of this . . .'

'So how can you be sure it was a 9mm Russian copy and not a 9mm German original that killed Serov?' demanded Cowley. 'Or any other 9mm copy?'

'Simple, dear sir!' said Robertson, pleased with the

42

question. 'I've already told you. Size. It can *only* be a Makarov because this shell' . . . he produced the spent casing in its glassine bag . . . 'won't fit anything *but* a Makarov. They modified the shell. It's fractionally larger than any other 9mm slug. You can't fire an ordinary 9mm round from a Makarov, and the Makarov will only fire a Russian-manufactured 9mm bullet.' He tossed the pouch up and down. 'And that's what this is. Guaranteed one hundred percent Russian.'

Reluctant as Cowley was to accept it, the ballistic evidence took them closer to a tie-in with the Russian Mafia. 'What about casing marks?'

'Pretty as a picture,' promised Robertson.

'So if we get a suspect weapon, we could make a match?'

'We'd testify right up to the Supreme Court,' assured the co-ordinating expert.

'The effects list mentioned a notepad being tested for impression from previous writing?' Cowley reminded.

'A blank,' said Robertson. 'We put it through every test, chemical as well as electronic. Not a register.'

'It was a new pad?'

'Half used.'

'Why didn't something show?'

'Because careful Mr Serov did not use a single piece at a time. The only way to keep the unused pages as clean as they are would have been to remove three or four leaves every time from beneath whatever he wrote.'

Which could also have been the action of an intelligence officer, accepted Cowley. 'Anything else?'

'We're taking the clothes apart, for alien fibres, dust, whatever we might find. And we scoured the ground cleaner than it's ever been: it'll take a while to go through that. We're not looking for anything specific, after all. Just something that shouldn't be there.'

'You still want that area sealed?'

Robertson shook his head. 'What we haven't got now we ain't never going to get.'

Cowley remembered the blood-gouted shape of Serov's body: before the covering tent was dismantled he'd advise the DC highway authority to clean it up, to prevent a macabre photograph appearing somewhere. 'Thanks for identifying the weapon.'

'Hope it helps,' said the huge man.

'So do I,' said Cowley, sincerely. For the moment, it compounded the problem.

Leonard Ross sat hunched forward over a yellow legal pad, making notes like the trial judge he had once been, not interrupting Cowley's briefing. Only when it finished did he say: 'You think we've finally got to face it's Russian Mafia?'

'I don't see how we can avoid it.'

'What about defections and spying?'

'I don't buy it.'

'Why not?'

'Instinct. Which is fallible and why we'll have to take it as far as we can.'

'Isn't there a significance in Redin being present at the meeting?'

'It was his job to be there, since the security changes.'

Ross nodded, accepting the qualification. 'I'll personally ask the CIA Director,' he decided. 'He'll still lie if he wants to – and he probably will if it's a cross-over that went wrong.'

'I'd hoped you would,' said Cowley honestly. The Director had a better chance than he did of being told something like the truth, if there was anything to tell.

'We'll give it another twenty-four hours before we make the Mafia connection,' decided Ross. 'And then only to Hartz. I don't want anything to go public, making it official, so don't mention it to the DC people in case it leaks.'

'From what's being published so far, the media don't need any official confirmation of it being Mafia.'

'Give me an opinion about the meeting with Pavlenko,' insisted Ross. 'Strict diplomatic formality? Or obstruction?'

Cowley hesitated, wanting to get the answer right. 'Bordering on obstruction.'

'You want me to bring pressure through the State Department for access to the embassy and Massachusetts Avenue?'

'That was my initial intention: why I wanted to speak to you before I got back to Pavlenko and tried for access at my level,' said Cowley. 'But I'm not sure it would achieve any practical purpose. They'll lie and conceal anything they don't want to come out and I won't have any authority to challenge them. And pressure from State wouldn't cut much ice, either.'

The FBI Director looked surprised. 'But you're telling me the investigation will collapse unless there's co-operation. So what's your point?'

'We need an official Russian investigator,' insisted Cowley. 'A professional who'll know what we want and doesn't buckle under officialdom.'

The Director shook his head, although not in refusal, looking quizzically across his desk. There was the vaguest of smiles. 'And you know just the guy?'

'If we're right, we're going to need him.'

CHAPTER EIGHT

The strongest surviving legacy of Russia's failed but struggling-to-resurge communism is the doctrine that nothing works – or will be allowed to work – unless there is a personal benefit between those who seek and those who provide: the what's-in-it-for-me philosophy.

Ironically for someone whose total honesty now made him an outcast, Dimitri Ivanovich Danilov was an expert at the system. He had begun his education as a personal-fine-on-the-spot beat officer with ambition, and had manipulated favour-for-favour and reward-for-reward on his way through the ranks to uniformed colonel in charge of a Militia district, where he had established the tribute-accepting reign he had abdicated to Yevgennie Kosov. Danilov had, however, operated by a strict code of personally acceptable morality. He'd never become involved in the protection of vice rings or drug dealing or gun running, or with the violent, sometimes murderous enforcement of some black marketeers. Indeed, he actually investigated and prosecuted as many as he could.

With a strictly Russian logic, Danilov had never considered himself truly corrupt; he'd believed instead he was being practical and pragmatic in an environment beyond improvement or change. He had never been a member of the Communist Party – which protected the most corrupt of all – nor did he ever accept its political ideology. Most of all he despised its obvious inefficiency: if the party couldn't provide, a man had to provide for himself, according to his own integrity. With the help, of course, of the always available entrepreneurs. The essential factor, Danilov's justification for the compromises he'd made, was that no-one got hurt or suffered in the arrangements he reached with the people who could obtain things other people wanted. If those providers made a profit and others – like Danilov – benefited

46

along the way from ensuring there was no official interruption, everyone benefited. It was simply a slight variation on the free market economy political leaders were today advancing as the salvation of the country.

Anatoli Nikolaevich Metkin's disadvantage was not knowing of Danilov's previous expertise and more particularly how Danilov could use the stultifying bureaucracy under which Metkin was trying to bury him.

The responsibilities Metkin had set out *would* have buried Danilov if he'd attempted to fulfil them absolutely. But they weren't if he combined another Communist inheritance with the first, building his own bureaucratic mountain and threatening an avalanche to engulf others.

Metkin's vagueness about Danilov's new accommodation had been part of the theatre. The man personally showed Danilov to a long, L-shaped room on the same floor as his own secretariat to convey the gloating impression Danilov would always be under his supervision. The room was internal again, with no natural light, and completely bare of furniture. There were no bulbs in any socket, but there were jack points in the walls, for telephones. But there were no telephones.

Danilov began his fight back within minutes of Metkin leaving him, giving the man just enough time to re-enter his own suite before descending to the basement garage. There were six unused cars in their bays. The office in one corner, with *I. A. Borodin* lettered on the door, was a hutch of a room, misted in cigarette smoke and with used stubs smouldering in an ashtray. Borodin, who was bent over a magazine displaying melon-breasted, splay-legged women, didn't look up.

'I'm looking for the manager,' announced Danilov. 'I want a car. That Volga outside looks good.'

Borodin, a dumpy man with grease-encrusted fingernails, snorted a laugh, bringing his head up from the pornography. '*I* allocate cars. Where's your authorisation docket?'

'You've had a memorandum from the Director . . .' Danilov stretched his copy across the desk, in front of the other man.

Borodin blinked down at it, then smiled up. 'So you're the new Deputy Director! Your having a car depends upon availability, I'm afraid. Everything out there is committed. Sorry.'

The instructions how he should be treated had permeated throughout every floor, literally from the top to the bottom, realised Danilov. 'You've also seen this?' asked Danilov, extending Metkin's order making him responsible for the supplies and facilities throughout the building.

Borodin nodded, not bothering to reply.

How well had he remembered the what's-in-it-for-me approach, wondered Danilov. 'The car pool, this garage, is a listed facility. All vehicle spares, petrol, the purchasing of new cars and the disposal of old vehicles is categorised under supplies. You are no longer allowed to order in your own name and under your own authority any parts, for any car. Nor will you be permitted to order a new car or dispose of an old one without reference and approval from me. All petrol purchasing will in future be by me. I will also want, weekly, details of all mechanics' work sheets and all overtime claims. I have also been appointed overall controller of finance: no money will be paid on any overtime claim unless I have countersigned it. I want all authorisation dockets, at the end of every week, detailing use on official police business.'

Borodin's mouth hung open almost as wide as the legs of the naked women he had been studying. 'I don't . . . I mean . . .' stumbled the man who had just heard the threat of every bribe-accepting, price-inflating racket being taken from him.

At a conservative estimate, Danilov reckoned Borodin stood to lose about twenty times his official salary: probably more. He waved the handful of instructions from Anatoli Metkin, because it was important the cause of the catastrophe be identified from the outset. 'The new Director is determined upon great change.'

'I don't want to get our relationship off on a bad footing,' said Borodin anxiously.

'Neither do I,' assured Danilov.

'You know anything about running garages? Cars?'

'Nothing,' admitted Danilov. 'I'll learn, in time.'

'It would be easier if we worked together.'

A motto that should be enshrined in stone over every official Russian door.

'I wouldn't want it any other way.' Danilov waved an arm towards the garage. 'Perhaps you'd let me have the order sheets, so I can see who those are going out to?'

Borodin made a half gesture of looking through the rat's nest of a drawer in his desk. 'I don't seem to have made one up yet. But I'm not sure, upon reflection, the Volga *is* committed. I think I could rearrange things to make it available.'

'I'd regard that as a favour,' said Danilov. 'Why don't you get it cleaned and valeted for me to pick up tonight?'

'It'll be waiting,' promised Borodin eagerly.

He hadn't forgotten a thing about how the system worked, decided Danilov happily. His meeting with the initially dismissive manager of stores and maintenance was a repeat performance; it took less than fifteen minutes to make clear to the man the benefits he had to lose, and be instantly promised next-day delivery of everything he needed for his empty office.

The Volga ran well and the valeting had been meticulous. Olga insisted on a first-time ride, demanding they go almost halfway around the outer Moscow ring road.

'This is better!' she said, head back against the seat. 'Like it was in the old days! About bloody time.' They had not had a car of their own for four years, since their old Lada had crumbled beyond repair. It had been one of the most expensive gifts Danilov had ever received, from a black marketeer whose convoys he had guaranteed through his Militia district for eight years. The watch that rarely worked had come from the same source.

Danilov glanced across at her. He couldn't detect the greyness through the tint, in the half light, but he didn't think he liked her hair quite as long. Apparently thinking a good appearance was necessary in a prestige car, Olga had put on her new coat, a brown tweed with a deeper brown felt collar. There was a button missing from the front. Olga was the sort

49

of woman from whose clothes buttons always seemed to be missing, even when they were new. She never appeared to notice.

'It is ours, isn't it?' she demanded, with sudden concern. 'No-one's going to take it back?'

'Don't worry about it,' said Danilov.

'I've invited Yevgennie Grigorevich and Larissa to dinner to celebrate your promotion,' she announced.

'That will be nice,' he said neutrally.

'You don't mind?'

'Why should I mind?'

'No reason.'

He was aware of her looking directly back at him across the car. 'When?'

'Larissa's going to call, to confirm a night. Now you've got the promotion and more money, I thought I could shop at the open market by the State Circus.'

'I'm not sure the increase will cover that.' He'd heard that prices in open markets, which were always groaning with produce and meat being sold by independent farmers and growers, were frequently ten times those in government controlled stores – although in government controlled stores the same items were rarely available. If there was a difference, it was that luxuries were no longer confined to the Party and KGB concessions. Ironically, the Party and former intelligence agents now had to stand in line behind their successors, the gangsters who had inherited the dollars and the power.

'We'll see,' said Olga, airily.

Danilov was careful to remove the wipers when he parked outside his apartment. He'd have to ensure, tomorrow, that the car was protected by the local Militia station. He wondered what he would have to offer in return.

All the office equipment was delivered the following morning, but when he went to the store cupboard by the squad room he found the contents of three boxes tipped over the floor in total disarray, although the door had been locked. The boxes were missing. The one in which the bulbs had been hidden was untouched, though, which was a bonus because he'd insisted on being supplied with bulbs along with everything else. Now he had spares.

He was aware of the sniggering attention of the other detectives as he ferried his belongings to and fro, to the upper floor. He genuinely tried to re-assemble his working area neatly, but almost at once it became the jumbled chaos of before. He still knew where everything was, if he needed it.

Danilov had been encouraged by his easy success with the garage and the supply manager. It gave him further ideas how to manipulate his specific orders. No-one in the squad room would be sniggering, very shortly.

Cowley had to concede the slight advantage in personal publicity when the call from the Alexandria police, across the Potomac in Virginia, came direct to him, without the delay of being routed through the normal FBI receiving and comparison system to link what had been found in the National Airport parking lot with the killing of Petr Serov.

'Just like yours, so I thought you'd be interested,' suggested the Alexandria detective, Hal Maine. 'Two in the chest and the third right in the mouth. And Christ, does he stink!'

It looked precisely the triumphal procession it was intended to be; a cavalcade of five BMWs, Gusovsky, Yerin and Zimin protectively in the middle vehicle, their minders in the others. They drove too fast along the central corridor which, until the collapse of Communism, had been exclusively reserved on the major Moscow highways for members of the Party. Now the Mafia considered if rightfully theirs, as the new rulers. No other cars impeded their progress. The GIA traffic police, in their elevated pods at the main intersections, controlled the lights in favour of the Mafia cars, as they once had for Party limousines.

'The Ostankino torched two of our airport lorries last night,' reported Zimin.

'How do you know it was them?' demanded Yerin. The Ostankino were the rival Family, jealous of the Chechen rule at airports, disputing all their territory.

'It's the word around,' said Zimin, which was sufficient.

'I'm not anxious for a war until we get the Swiss thing settled and make the arrangements in Italy,' said Gusovsky.

'If we don't respond it'll be regarded as weakness,' warned Yerin.

That morning's motorised tour was intended publicly to demonstrate their presence in their domain. Gusovsky leaned slightly forwards, to the driver. 'Make the left, on Ulitza Sadovaya,' he ordered.

'That'll take us on to Ostankino turf,' warned the man.

'Exactly,' smiled Gusovsky. 'Let's hope they take it as the warning it's meant to be.'

CHAPTER NINE

He did stink.

Few drivers had parked near the grey Ford for the past two days, so it had been easy to tape the area off, which Cowley thought hardly necessary because no-one was coming anywhere close to look. Four scene-of-crime technicians around the open trunk all wore respirators and gloves as well as protective overalls; the local officers, plain-clothed and uniformed, were well away from the car and carefully upwind. Cowley looked for Rafferty and Johannsen, whom he had alerted, but they hadn't arrived. Rafferty had said they'd found out where Serov had eaten the night he'd been killed, and sounded rebuffed when Cowley topped that news with the announcement of a second, matching murder.

As he approached the police group there was the now familiar burst of television lights and flash-gun bulbs from the penned-off media. The commotion alerted the watching police group. Hal Maine hoped he'd done right calling Cowley direct; conscious of boundary jealousies, Cowley warned the local man he'd asked the two DC homicide detectives to join him.

'You're welcome to this,' said Maine sincerely. He was a faded man in a creased suit and shirt; Cowley guessed he had about five years before retirement.

'What do we know?' asked Cowley.

Maine waved towards an open-doored, unmarked police car inside the cordon, where an overalled FBI specialist, a respirator discarded beside him, was sitting in the rear, transferring things from a crocodile briefcase into exhibit bags. 'The case was in the car, not the trunk, so there's not much smell. Swiss passport, in the name of Michel Paulac. Difficult to make a facial comparison with the photograph, because of the state of the body. Swiss driving licence in the same name, which matches that in which the car was rented from Hertz at Dulles, nine days ago. The rental agreement was in the briefcase, too. So was a first class return ticket, which should have been taken up four days ago, to Geneva. There's a wallet of visiting cards. Paulac's address is given as Rue Calvin, Geneva. There's quite a few documents in languages I can't read; looks like bank or financial stuff.'

There was another blaze of light from the media pack and Cowley turned to see two cars being allowed through the yellow tape by a uniformed patrolman. Rafferty and Johannsen were in the first, Brierly and Robertson in the second.

'Jesus!' said Rafferty, nose wrinkled, as he joined them.

Brierly was zipping up a protective all-in-one as he followed. He took a tube of highly mentholated emulsion from his examination bag, smearing it on his upper lip, directly beneath his nose, then offered it generally to the group. Cowley took some but the bear-like Robertson, who was wearing the same lumberjack workshirt of the previous day, shook his head. Rafferty said he wasn't curious enough to want to look and Johannsen said he wasn't, either.

Cowley had never before seen a body in such an advanced state of putrefaction. It was grossly swollen and the skin had split within the constriction of the clothing. Most of the face and hands were black. The body lay on its back, with the legs twisted sideways and the arms tightly above the head, to fit into the trunk. The smell began to get past the barrier gel and Cowley backed away, his stomach bubbling. He kept the white smear of emulsion under his nose, not caring if he looked ridiculous, although he pointedly kept his back to the cameras when he returned to the upwind group. Hal Maine had briefed the two DC detectives during his absence.

Johannsen said: 'First Russian, now Swiss. And all in America. Could be a job for a UN peacekeeping force.'

Cowley didn't join in the professional cynicism. To Rafferty he said: 'So where was Serov the night he was killed?'

'The French cafe near the Georgetown Mall,' announced the man. 'Waitress named Mary Ann Bell made a positive ID. Puts him there around six thirty, before the place properly filled up. Thinks he left around seven forty-five: she's pretty definite about that, because that's the time her shift ends and she handled the check.'

'Alone?' queried Cowley.

Johannsen shook his head, taking up the story. 'One other guy. Foreign accent, although not like Serov's. She remembers the second one better than Serov. The kid's working her way through college, like they all are. She's pretty: black hair and a tight ass. The guy came on strong and she was flattered. He promised to come back to see her again. She puts him around thirty, thirty-five. Says he dressed well: thinks it was a brown suit. Lightweight. Had a nice cologne. Good-looking guy.'

Cowley indicated the Ford. 'He's wearing a brown suit.'

'Pity about the cologne,' said Rafferty.

'Anything unusual while they were in the cafe?'

There was another head shake from Johannsen. 'When the second guy wasn't trying to hit on Mary Ann there was a lot of head-together stuff. She says they were serious.'

'Serov had eaten fish, just before he died,' reminded Rafferty. 'The special that night was scrod. They both had it.'

'With a bottle of Californian chardonnay,' completed Johannsen.

The huge scientific co-ordinator lumbered back from the Ford. Behind him Cowley saw the masked technicians manoeuvring a black body bag into the boot.

'Lookee here!' demanded Robertson, when he reached their group. The man held up a glassine bag with a brass shell casing in it.

'Makarov?' asked Cowley.

Everyone else looked between him and Robertson, without comprehension.

Robertson said: 'I'll tell you within an hour of getting back.'

Brierly followed immediately afterwards. He said the autopsy would be more difficult because of the decomposition but it looked like an exact copy of the first. Unless there were bone injury, it would be hard to find any marks of

55

torture or resistance. He'd try for fingernail scrapings, but he wasn't hopeful there, either. He'd do his best to help forensic get usable fingerprints but the best chance of provable indentification would be dental records, although the teeth were extensively damaged. The mouth shot had been inflicted in the car, which was how the shell jacket came to be in the trunk: the slug would be found, among the head debris.

Cowley went to the police car where the exhibit officer was packaging the recovered articles, and signed for the passport, managing to open it to the photograph by working on the outside of the plastic envelope. The parking ticket was in a separate sachet. The date automatically registered by the entry machine was the day Serov had died, the time 20-45. Cowley gave Rafferty the opened passport and told him to take the Key Bridge and return through Georgetown to confirm Michel Paulac had been the man with Serov.

As Cowley turned to Johannsen, the detective expectantly said: 'You'd like to know how many flights left National after eight forty-five? And to where?'

'And get the passenger lists and credit card slips for tickets that were bought that night,' completed Cowley. He stopped, looking around the assembled policemen. Trying as always to be diplomatic among different forces, he said: 'Anything else?'

'You're going to get your photograph taken again when we leave,' cautioned Rafferty. 'So you'd better wipe that shit from under your nose. Your look like Son of Hitler.'

Rafferty was thirty minutes behind Cowley returning to Pennsylvania Avenue, and arrived with more than confirmation of Michel Paulac being Petr Serov's dinner companion four nights earlier.

'Worked the visa pages open through the plastic,' he reported. 'Paulac's been here every month since the beginning of the year. Never for longer than one week, according to date stamps.'

'You've got the credit card number to work from,' said Cowley. 'He should have listed his hotel on the visa form.'

'On my way,' said Rafferty.

In his written report to the FBI Director, Cowley undertook fully to brief the protocol office at the State Department, before sending a detailed request for all possible information about Michel Paulac, of Rue Calvin, Geneva, to the Swiss police through Interpol.

Robertson was on the telephone precisely on the promised hour. The casing recovered from the car trunk was from a 9mm bullet of Russian manufacture for a Makarov pistol. Hammer markings were identical to those on the casing of the bullet that killed Serov.

Johannsen's was the last report, which he came back to make in person, leaving the rest of the squad at the airport. There had been sixteen departing flights after 8.45 p.m. on the night in question, three of them the last shuttles to New York and Boston. Four had been international – none direct or intermediate to Moscow – the rest internal. All credit card slips had already gone to the respective companies for payment, and flight manifests had also been filed. The airlines and the card companies had warned it was going to take a long time.

'And maybe get us nowhere,' pointed out Johannsen. 'Because Paulac's ticket was out of Dulles, we're assuming our killer drove out to National for his escape, right?' He raised his hands against interruption, wanting to finish. 'Why can't the Ford being dumped at National be a wrong steer, to send us in more circles than we're going around in already? Or if he flew *in*, he could have had a return ticket, or he might have bought his ticket with cash, so the credit card slips are going to tell us nothing. There's a passport check against ticket names for international flights, but there were only four of those. Any ticket for a flight *within* America could be in whatever name the guy wanted to use.'

'I don't need reminding of the problems,' said Cowley.

CHAPTER TEN

Danilov had caught a segment about the murder of Petr Serov on the previous evening's television news and seen – with difficulty, because the set was old and faulty and beyond effective repair – a brief shot of William Cowley emerging from a plastic scene-of-crime tent and walking, unspeaking, through a swarm of questioning journalists. There was no reference on Russian TV to Cowley's previous involvement in Moscow, or to Danilov, but there was, extensively, in the following day's newspapers. On his way to Petrovka, Danilov stopped the car and bought the papers, reading the near-matching accounts and briefly indulging himself in memories. On an inside page there was a group photograph taken at the time, of Danilov and Lapinsk and Cowley and the Federal Prosecutor. One headline described the investigation as a triumph of co-operation between Russia and the United States; another used the word 'brilliant'. Danilov carefully discarded the newspapers in a rubbish bin, not wanting to invite mockery by arriving at Militia headquarters carrying accounts of himself publicly described as the leading investigator in an Organised Crime Bureau from which he'd been deposed. But when he entered his office, every newspaper was on his desk, folded uppermost to demonstrate his previous importance. Games to play, Danilov decided.

Two fingered, he typed a memorandum to the Director asking what action he was expected to take upon the newspaper accounts of the killing of Petr Aleksandrovich Serov so obviously deposited in his office. Additionally he sent a note to the Foreign Ministry, asking to be informed what was happening in America, and made a copy for Anatoli Metkin with a covering slip assuming it was the sort of action Metkin would wish. He sent his communication to the Foreign Ministry at once, but to prevent it being interrupted he held back the message to Metkin.

By the time the creased-faced Director burst into his room, Danilov had typed invitations to the supervisors of the car pool and supply division, proposing meetings to decide their future working relationship, and written for display on the squad room noticeboard the news that he had been made responsible, on the specific orders of Anatoli Metkin, for all future work rosters, and also for the finance of the Bureau. Accordingly, he would in future need, in writing, each assignment of each investigator with itemised details of overtime being claimed; without such details, no payments would be authorised. He'd despatched copies of the roster arrangements to the Interior and Finance Ministries minutes before Metkin's arrival.

'What the hell are these!' demanded Metkin, waving Danilov's messages.

Danilov looked up, blank-faced: Metkin was very red. 'A request for guidance,' he said ingenuously.

'I don't know anything about any damned newspaper stories!'

'I assumed it was upon your orders. What reason would there be for anyone in the squad room to come all the way up here to leave them?'

Metkin made tiny, ineffectual flapping gestures with his hands. 'I don't want anything going to the Foreign Ministry.'

'I'm afraid it's gone. About two hours ago.'

'What?'

'I don't see the problem,' said Danilov. 'I might have misunderstood the newspapers, but shouldn't we be interested in the murder of a Russian diplomat?'

'Any request for information should have come . . .' Metkin stopped before completing the sentence, so Danilov did it for him.

'It will appear to have your authority, won't it . . . ?' He let Metkin stand there, nonplussed. 'Like these.' Danilov offered the other man copies marked for his attention but not yet sent, of the notes about work rosters and overtime payments.

Metkin's hands began to shake in fury. 'This is preposterous!'

'Why?' asked Danilov. It was Metkin's reaction that was preposterous: there couldn't be any logical argument against the proposed overtime supervision.

'I . . . It won't . . . Investigators will be spending all their time writing explanatory notes when they should be out investigating crime!'

'Fifteen minutes, at the end of every week. I can't see either Ministry finding fault with that.'

For the first time Metkin appeared to see everything was endorsed for distribution to the Interior and Finance Ministries. 'Don't send these!'

'They've already gone.' Danilov hesitated, wanting to enjoy twisting the knife. 'And I have never once tried to usurp your authority. It's made quite clear it's on your orders . . .'

Metkin looked steadily at him. His mouth moved very slightly, as if he were practising a challenge, but he did not finally make it. Instead he said: 'You have been extremely busy.'

'We've already agreed that I am going to be, with all the responsibilities you have given me.'

'Which you are taking extremely seriously.'

That afternoon a gaunt, sharp-faced woman who introduced herself as Ludmilla Markovina Radsic came unsmilingly into his office. 'I was told to report here as your secretary.'

'Temporarily?'

'Permanently.'

Danilov wished Metkin had at least imposed an attractive informant.

Olga shopped lavishly at the open market for the celebration supper with Yevgennie and Larissa Kosov. There was sufficient steak, vegetables both fresh and marinated, and cheese and fresh fruit to have thrown a banquet for four times their number. Because Danilov had no access to dollars she had had to pay in roubles: it had cost what was officially a whole month's salary. Danilov refused to compete, which he acknowledged to be a kind of inverted snobbery: the vodka

and brandy and champagne and the flat wine were all
Russian. When they went to Yevgennie and Larissa's apartment the Scotch was from Scotland – always Chivas Regal –
and the champagne and brandy and the burgundy was from
France.

'You could have got something else,' complained Olga,
when she saw him setting the bottles out.

Danilov did not, in fact, believe he could have done. 'I'm
happy with this.'

'I'm not. Neither will Larissa or Yevgennie be.'

'It'll be a new experience for them.'

'You told me you were superior to Yevgennie now.'

'I am,' confirmed Danilov. In empty rank but certainly not
in authority or power, he admitted to himself.

'They won't think so, when they see the sort of drink
you're serving.'

'Who cares what they think?'

'I do.'

The Kosovs arrived precisely on time, almost curiously.
Larissa looked spectacular – and knew it – in a clinging black
angora dress, topped by a white, three-quarter-length real
leather coat which had clearly not been fashioned in Russia.
Neither had the matching crocodile handbag and shoes.
Danilov had not seen any of it during their hotel or tucked-
away-restaurant assignations, and guessed she'd dressed for
him. Because it was virtually unavailable in Moscow, Kosov
usually dressed in cashmere. The jacket tonight was blue,
over tan trousers; his shoes were crocodile too. Danilov had
not seen the heavy gold watch before: there were jewels –
diamonds maybe – instead of numerals. His own had
stopped again that night. It was supposed to be a Cartier but
he knew it wasn't: the 'gold' surround had flaked a long time
ago.

There were effusive, both-cheek kisses, and Kosov
presented Olga with Belgian chocolates: when Danilov
kissed Larissa, she positioned herself so he would detect she
was not wearing a bra, smiling at him as they parted. Kosov
looked pointedly at the Russian label when Danilov poured
the champagne, but didn't comment. Danilov knew Kosov

would have done, if he had been drinking before he left their own apartment, as he normally did, and wondered why the man had abstained that evening.

'A toast!' Kosov declared, as usual moving to dominate. 'To Dimitri Ivanovich and his well deserved and well earned promotion!'

Danilov stood feeling foolish as the other three drank. He sipped his own wine, at the end. It was sharp. 'It doesn't mean a great deal,' he said, in gross understatement.

'Nonsense,' said Larissa. 'You're a star!'

'Of which we've been reminded,' said Kosov. 'See you were mentioned in the newspapers today.'

'History,' dismissed Danilov.

'Don't be modest,' chided Larissa. 'Aren't you proud of him, Olga?'

The idea seemed to surprise Olga. 'Of course,' she said, hurriedly. Her tan dress had a stain on the left sleeve and the shoes did not co-ordinate; she looked dowdy in comparison to the other woman.

'Thought you might have got the Directorship,' said Kosov. It was a question more than an opinion, a remark inviting a reply.

Danilov met the other man's look. 'It's an enlargement of the Bureau.' He wished he hadn't had to fall back upon Anatoli Metkin's empty insistence in the corridor the day Lapinsk had retired.

'A division of authority?' asked Kosov

'Yes.' Danilov was curious at Kosov's interest.

'You'll go on heading the investigative side of things?'

Danilov didn't think this was polite interest. It sounded like someone trying to pin down rumours – which would, among other things, account for Kosov's sobriety. 'It's interesting you should mention the newspaper references,' he evaded easily. 'I'm liaising with the Foreign Ministry about this business in Washington.'

'You're going to investigate that!' said Larissa excitedly.

Danilov decided she was very brave – or very confident – wearing a black wool dress: Larissa moved her head a lot but there was no stray blonde hair on her shoulders. 'We need to know all we can,' Danilov avoided again. He hurried around with the champagne: neither Larissa nor her husband had drunk very much.

'You get on well with Metkin?' persisted Kosov.

'There's a professional relationship,' said Danilov.

'Wasn't he junior to you, when Lapinsk was Director?'

Danilov saw both Olga and Larissa look at Kosov, then to him. Danilov said: 'We held equal rank.'

'Why didn't you get the Directorship, with Metkin as *your* deputy?' demanded Olga. 'You should have done, shouldn't you!'

Bastards, thought Danilov. Metkin was a bastard and those above him in the Interior Ministry were bastards and those who sneered in the squad room were bastards and Kosov, who'd clearly heard rumours if he'd not been openly told, was a bastard for making this scene in the middle of his living room. 'If I had been made Director I would have been removed from any investigative role. This way I'm not.'

'So you will continue as an investigator!' said Larissa.

'In certain, particular circumstances,' said Danilov, uncaring of his lie, wanting only to close off the inquisition.

Which it appeared to do. Olga bustled into the kitchen, taking Larissa with her, and Kosov switched to vodka and began to catch up on his alcohol intake. He made half-hearted attempts to get back to discussing Danilov's new role, but Danilov always managed to deflect him. Danilov had been unable to reach the commander of the Militia district covering Kirovskaya to get protection for the Volga, and had intended asking Kosov to fix it: now, that would be quite the wrong thing to do.

The steaks were excellent and the wine, which actually wasn't Russian but Georgian, was as good as any Danilov had been served by Kosov.

It was over coffee and brandy that Larissa whispered to Danilov she was working afternoon split-shift, with access to rooms throughout the week. He whispered back he would try. Larissa, in turn, insisted they had their future to talk about: he'd asked her to wait until he was promoted, which he'd now been.

After they left, Olga said: 'I thought Yevgennie kept on at you, at the begining of the evening.'

'I didn't notice,' lied Danilov. How much longer could he go on dodging the personal situation? Larissa had been right, of course; they had a lot to talk about. Danilov acknowledged, abruptly, that he was frightened: he was frightened of abandoning Olga, and he was frightened of trying to look after Larissa after the luxuries heaped upon her by Kosov, and now he didn't have the protective directorship he was frightened the uniformed colonel would try to use his past to cause as much harm as possible when Larissa announced whom she was leaving him for.

'Do you like Larissa?' asked Olga innocently.

'Of course I do. She's a friend.'

'I think she likes you. I saw the way she was looking at you tonight.'

Danilov had removed the wipers from the Volga. The following morning both wing mirrors had been stolen.

CHAPTER ELEVEN

Leonard Ross was an independently wealthy man and therefore completely sure of himself both publicly and privately, with no need constantly to play centre stage, so he was quite happy for Cowley, the Bureau expert, to present their suspicions. The Secretary of State stared throughout from the window of his seventh-floor office over the park and the very tip of the Washington monument.

'It's still speculation,' Hartz insisted, when Cowley finished. The hope was obvious in the man's voice.

'On known facts,' argued Ross. Somehow he'd rumpled the pure white hair and a part of it, near his forehead, stuck up like a surrender flag.

'Very *few* facts,' disputed the Secretary of State. 'Little more than that it's a Russian pistol and ammunition.'

At Ross's gestured invitation, Cowley said: 'We know in the Eighties the former KGB used world pressure for Jewish emigration from the old Soviet Union to infiltrate into this country a large number of professional criminals, to put as big a burden as possible upon our law enforcement. We even know where they predominantly settled, in Brighton Beach . . .'

'. . . And since the collapse of Communism, organised crime has literally exploded in Russia,' broke in Ross. 'It's taken the name of the role model it's copied from here – the Mafia.'

'I know about Brighton Beach! And the Moscow Mafia!' said the Secretary of State. 'What I want to know is the link with the Russian embassy!'

'We don't know that, not yet,' admitted Ross. 'Any more than we know why a Swiss financier was involved. And we're not going to find out by approaching the Russian embassy ourselves. They're blocking us, solidly.'

'What do the Swiss say?' asked Hartz.

Again the FBI Director deferred to Cowley.

'Not a lot, as yet,' conceded the Russian specialist. 'We've got to assume there was some financial involvement between Serov and Paulac. We're going to be blocked here, again, by the bank secrecy regulations, which we can't break into. Paulac was a bachelor. Thirty-eight years old, head of an international investment company, unknown to the police until now. No reason for thinking he's not quite respectable. As well as the office in Geneva there's an offshoot in Vaduz, Liechtenstein. It's the way these guys work, shuttling money between one bank secrecy country to another and back again, until it gets lost.'

'Often the profits from organised crime,' chipped in Ross. 'They rarely ask the source: that way their integrity isn't compromised.' He seemed to become aware of the dishevelled hair, smoothing it down. Cowley liked the improvement: Ross wasn't the surrendering type.

'The Swiss say they'll respond as best they can to any enquiry we make,' said Cowley. 'Problem is, we don't know the questions to ask.'

'You sure the Russians won't help?' queried Hartz, the long-ago accent sounding in his voice.

'Definitely not if the collusion is official,' said Cowley. 'Or, from their response so far, even if it's not. We're stymied, either way.'

Hartz shook his head, doubtfully. 'Could we have the Russian Mafia linking with the Cosa Nostra here?'

'Yes,' said the FBI Director brutally.

Without turning from the window, Hartz said: 'OK, we could invite Russian participation: we established the precedent with the senator's niece. But if there is official collusion, we'd get a programmed stooge, even if they agreed to come in on it.'

'It's a risk,' accepted Ross. 'And if that happens we're back to square one, and likely to stay there. So we need to do all we can to get the guy Bill worked with before and trusts: Danilov.'

'How could we do that?' demanded Hartz.

'You could feed the idea to the ambassador,' suggested the

Bureau Director. 'Present it as a formal invitation for them to participate fully, in recognition of their allowing us into Moscow like they did. Make it clear Cowley is our man again, which would suggest Danilov as the obvious partner. Press the point about how well it worked last time. And there's Danilov's ability to speak English, which I wouldn't think a lot of their Militia investigators can.'

'It's tenuous,' argued Hartz.

'There's also a practical argument about their being officially involved,' pointed out Cowley. 'There is an obvious need to talk to Serov's wife, in Moscow: we could reinforce the co-operation idea by asking for that to be done.'

'There's a lot of pressure for a press conference,' continued Ross. 'Let's organise one right after your meeting with the ambassador . . .' He motioned sideways. 'Put Cowley on, with whoever else you want to include. And announce the offer publicly. We could plant a few suggestions in advance, to guarantee the media speculate about the guy we want.'

'It seems a lot of trouble, for one man,' observed Hartz.

'A professionally honest one,' Cowley insisted. 'If we don't get that we might as well admit failure right now.'

'And it's not a lot of trouble if it gets us towards understanding all this,' asserted Ross. 'What if there *is* a nation-to-nation Mafia incorporation! You want to think about that? I don't!'

Still reluctant to acknowledge what he was being told, Hartz looked at Ross. 'The CIA are adamant they weren't running anything with Serov?'

'Emphatic.'

'What about the body?'

'It can be released as far as we're concerned,' agreed the Director. 'It'll be our gesture of co-operation. But I don't want to let go of the effects, not yet. Something still might come up that makes them material, although at the moment nothing's obvious.'

Silence enclosed the office once more. Hartz swung around from West Potomac Park and the unseen Lincoln Memorial. At last he said: 'I'm frightened this is going to unravel into one great, big goddamned mess.'

'I'm frightened it already has,' said Ross.

The lovemaking was incredible, like it always was with Larissa: it was one of her days to fantasise and she'd wanted to be a whore, even making him pay her. Danilov thought she would have made a very good whore, far better than the blank-eyed professionals outside in the hotel foyer.

'Satisfied?' She was sprawled over him, leaking his wetness.

'Completely.'

'I'm not.'

'I won't be able to.'

'Yes you will.' She raised herself slightly off him, moving back and forth so that her nipples caressed his. 'Yevgennie says you've been stitched up!'

'What makes him say that?' asked Danilov, immediately alert.

Larissa shrugged, making her breasts wobble over him. 'I don't know. It's just what he said. Have you?'

'Not as tightly as they'd like me to be.' He hadn't yet devised a way to use the spying secretary against them.

'What's it all about?'

'I won't do the deals.'

'Yevgennie says you're stupid not to do that, too. He says you did when you were in uniform.'

Danilov frowned. 'That was a long time ago.'

'Why make life difficult for yourself?'

'I want to work as I do now.'

'I don't want to go on being your whore. This is only a game.'

'I don't want it either.'

'You promised me we'd do something after the promotion.'

'It wasn't the right one.'

'What's that got to do with it!'

'What if Yevgennie files for an official enquiry into what I did in the past?'

'With what he's doing now? How can he?'

'He could feel cheated enough, by both of us, not to care.

68

Things are going to be difficult enough for you as it is – we could end up trying to live on your salary!'

Larissa smiled at him, saddened by his reluctance. 'I'd be happy enough. I love you. Don't you love me enough?'

'I love you *too* much,' said Danilov. Which he did. He felt complete with Larissa: fulfilled. If Larissa was prepared to risk whatever needed to be risked, why wasn't he?

Cowley told himself he was just going out for a walk, although he knew of course that he wasn't: even walking was part of it, a reason for leaving the car behind. He'd isolated the bar on his way home, on the edge of Crystal City, but hadn't realised how long it would take to get there on foot. He stopped twice, the second time half turning back. But he didn't complete the movement.

There weren't very many customers. The barman shifted, impatiently, at Cowley's uncertainty over his order. He chose beer: people didn't get drunk on beer. Not unless they drank a lot, and he didn't intend drinking a lot. Just stopped off for one, while he was out for a walk: the sort of thing people did, out walking.

It tasted good: damned good. Cowley sipped, enjoying the taste and the ambience: enjoying everything. The beer didn't affect him. Hadn't expected it to. No reason why he shouldn't have another.

Cowley made the third into a chaser, for a Wild Turkey on the side, feeling the mellowness move through him. But still not drunk. He could handle it now. Learned how to do it. Just too late, that's all: too late to convince Pauline. Wished it hadn't been too late: wished to hell she'd give it one more shot. Just friendship. That's all. Couldn't expect anything else.

One more whiskey, with a beer back. Then he'd quit. Still in control. Clear headed. Coherent. Not a problem any more. Wouldn't be, ever again.

Cowley did stop, after that drink. The barman said he'd see him again maybe and Cowley agreed maybe. He felt good, not just from the booze but because he knew he wasn't drunk. Proved he could do it. That he was OK now. Just a pleasant way of spending a pleasant couple of hours.

He'd been a coward, Lapinsk accepted. A coward when he'd been appointed to the Bureau – perhaps because the manipulators recognised him as weak – and a coward during his directorship and finally, most craven of all, a coward holding back from Dimitri Ivanovich whom he'd groomed to do what he had never had the courage to do. And who would not be able to do it, not now.

Absolutely to accept – without any excuse or mitigation – that you are a coward is possibly the worst thing a man can be called upon to confront.

In Russia those who ultimately control Families, their boards of directors, are called *komitet*, which means committee; it is the equivalent of the Italian Mafia *cupola*. For this gathering at Arkadi Gusovsky's home, the indulgently fat and perfumed Zimin had been included, because he'd had to be: he spoke Italian and English, both of which were important for the coming weeks.

'According to the lawyers, the Swiss formalities will take some time,' announced Gusovsky.

'Why don't we postpone the Italian meeting?' suggested Zimin, the appointed delegate.

'Because we'd lose face: show we're not ready,' dismissed Yerin, irritably. 'We're not going to do that.'

'We're sure of getting control,' said Gusovsky. 'We'll go ahead with the meeting: it'll take several weeks, to settle everything. But then there'll be no problem. Everything will be ours.'

CHAPTER TWELVE

The media manipulation was perfectly orchestrated. The State Department leaks stopped short of giving a reason for the meeting between the Russian ambassador and Henry Hartz, which built up speculation. The suggestion of Moscow being invited to join the investigation was given to selected journalists by the publicity-conscious mayor, Elliott Jones, after a detailed briefing from Hartz. The campaign got the name and photograph of Dimitri Ivanovich Danilov in every newspaper and news agency report and on every television screen. The State Department and FBI both refused to comment, but after letting the stories develop their own momentum the Bureau promised a press conference in which William Cowley would take part.

There was a totally unexpected fillip to the manipulation from the Russians themselves. The day before the Washington conference, the Interior Ministry in Moscow made an ideally low-key statement that the ambassador's summons to the State Department had been to discuss the murder of Petr Aleksandrovich Serov. What had been discussed was being considered.

That night Cowley considered going for another walk to Crystal City, but didn't. He hadn't suffered from a hangover after the previous occasion – one of the problems of the past was that no matter how much he'd drunk, he'd never felt ill the following day – but he thought it was better not to drink at all. The ease of the decision pleased him, as further proof he had everything under total control.

Cowley travelled to the State Department, where the conference was to be staged, in the Director's car: to achieve maximum effect they got out at the main entrance, picking their way through a white dazzle of camera lights. In an anteroom Elliott Jones was being powdered down by a make-up girl to prevent skin shine.

The FBI Director led the way into the conference room, the mayor following. Lights burst on and the noise began and Cowley had a feeling of an event re-creating itself: it was practically a mirror image of the murder press conference in Moscow, insisted upon by Senator Burden. Cowley had detested it then, and he was detesting it today. He felt his skin flush in the heat of the lights and thought maybe he should have had make-up after all.

Ross gestured for quiet, which he got almost at once. He talked in measured, even tones: Cowley decided the man must have been an impressive judge. Until that moment, the make of the murder weapon and the fact that the bullets had been of Russian manufacture had not been released. Ross made the prepared announcement, to guarantee the headlines, waving down the eruption of questions that followed. Once again he quickly regained command. Because the crime appeared to have those Russian links as well as to involve a Russian diplomat, it had been decided to invite Russian representation, just as Russia had invited the FBI involvement in an earlier case with which they were all familiar. As the Director of the FBI, he sincerely hoped Moscow would accept the offer. There were essential enquiries to be made in Moscow, but a Russian investigator would also be welcome in the United States and shown every assistance, just as William Cowley had been given all possible help when he had gone to Moscow.

The snowstorm of questions ranged over every possible theory, speculation and rumour, to hardly any of which they provided positive answers. The most concerted query revolved, in every conceivable way and manner, around the Mafia. Ross acknowledged there was a Mafia, even by that title, in Russia, but refused to postulate any connection yet with organised crime in either America or Sicily. They did not yet know why a Swiss financier had travelled from Geneva to meet a Russian attaché: that was one of the questions a Russian investigation might answer.

When his turn came to be questioned, Cowley accepted the circumstances were coincidental to the earlier Moscow case. He had enjoyed working there, and was sure the level

72

and extent of the co-operation he'd known then could be repeated in this case were he to be reunited with Dimitri Danilov. Here Cowley looked sideways, to Ross, and said he had officially praised the Russian's ability in written reports to the Director, at the conclusion of the earlier murder enquiry. If there were no Russian participation the case might be impossible to solve. He was sure the Russian authorities did not wish the investigation to fail and would do whatever they could to prevent that happening.

Cowley's only potential awkwardness came with a series of persistent questions about whether he thought an accredited diplomat at a foreign embassy was involved in criminal activities. Cowley's only reply, which echoed hollowly when he gave it, was that he had no reason to connect Petr Serov with any crime. The Director repeated it, for emphasis. That denial sounded hollow, too.

Back in the anteroom, afterwards, Rafferty said: 'The only way left to get Danilov here if that fails is to send in a SWAT team to kidnap him!'

'If they do respond but send a stooge, I guess we've got part of our answer, about collusion,' said Ross, reflectively.

'Then where are we?' asked Cowley.

'The same place as we are at the moment,' said the Director. 'Nowhere.'

The media coverage in Moscow was restricted in comparison to Washington only by the limitations of television channels and newspapers. The television at the Kirovskaya apartment faded halfway through the item, with Danilov's face filling the screen, sending Olga into a screaming rage. The following morning Danilov stopped and bought all the papers, as he had when the murder of Serov occurred; on this occasion he was featured on all the front pages. He stored them in the boot, for Olga to read that night. When he got to Petrovka there were no mockery-intended copies on his cluttered desk. He'd been there an hour when the summons came from Metkin.

'You have been ordered to the Interior Ministry,' announced the Director. 'We both have.' The man stopped, rehearsing what he had to say. 'Leonid Lapinsk committed suicide last night. Shot himself with his service revolver, which he hadn't surrendered.' Another pause. 'Through the mouth: blew his head off.'

CHAPTER THIRTEEN

Danilov recognised the Federal Prosecutor, Nikolai Smolin, from previous encounters, but needed introductions to Vasili Oskin, the Deputy Interior Minister in whose office they convened, and to Sergei Vorobie, the Deputy Foreign Minister. He was refusing to anticipate anything about the summons or to believe any of the newspaper speculation.

It was difficult anyway to focus fully in these initial moments, after the intentional brutality of Metkin's announcement. Danilov's instant reaction had been pity, for a sad, totally disillusioned old man who'd despised himself as a failure. But just as quickly the doubt came, the doubt of a trained investigator. Had Lapinsk really been sad and disillusioned, deserving pity? Or was there some other reason for taking his own life – if indeed he *had* taken his own life? He wouldn't be able to answer that sort of question until he'd at least read the full report. The preliminary, which Metkin had contemptuously shown him, had talked of clear-cut suicide. But there had been nothing to suggest a reason. He had to know why, before he could decide between pity and condemnation.

Danilov forced himself to concentrate. Lapinsk was dead, for whatever reason. He was alive, and without warning possibly propelled over the heads of his enemies. He had to take each and every advantage he could. An immediate impression was that Metkin's attitude was too effusively respectful for any of these three officials to be the man's unknown protector.

'We have to discuss the murder in Washington,' announced Oskin, a thin, balding, soft-voiced man. He looked briefly to the Foreign Ministry man before adding: 'It has been escalated into a political matter that has to be properly handled.'

'There's been a formal diplomatic invitation – a request, in fact – for us to assist,' said Vorobie. Danilov belatedly recognised him as one of the Russian ministers who had publicly denounced the 1991 coup from the steps of the Russian White House.

Oskin smiled briefly, towards Danilov. 'Your earlier communication showed sensible foresight.'

Danilov ducked his head at the praise, wondering what Metkin would later say to whoever had put the newspapers in his office, if it had not been his own idea. Turning the head movement towards Metkin, he said adroitly: 'We thought it was inevitably something which would extend to here.'

Metkin's reaction was exactly what Danilov had hoped. 'Absolutely inevitable. That's why I suggested it.'

Keep on being over-eager, thought Danilov.

'There's been a request to speak to Serov's wife,' said Vorobie. 'The Americans also want access to the embassy and to the man's home, to which we cannot agree.'

'Clearly not,' agreed Metkin, trying to convey an opinion by following one already expressed.

Idiot, thought Danilov: it was the time and opportunity to illustrate the professional gulf between himself and the other man. Danilov said: 'Apart from the access difficulty, are we going to take up the American approach?'

'Yes,' announced Smolin, entering the discussion. 'There are several practical advantages, apart from the obvious.'

'Aid being the most important,' said Vorobie. 'We can't risk the financial assistance from Washington. This is, indeed, an ideal opportunity to demonstrate full collaboration, like we did when the American politician's relation was murdered here.'

'Can we afford to do that?' asked Danilov quietly.

The question had precisely the effect he intended. All three officials frowned in bewilderment: Metkin's head moved like a spectator at a tennis match. Danilov continued: 'The published reports say Serov was killed American Mafia-style. The Swiss financier too. Was there any official connection between the two?'

There was a brief silence. Vorobie said: 'We have a positive assurance from the ambassador that there was no official knowledge of any meeting. Or reason for one.'

76

To the Interior Ministry man Danilov said: 'Was there any security reason for or knowledge of such an encounter?'

'None,' said Oskin at once.

'So our contribution can be quite open?' he persisted. Irrespective of any part he might or might not play, this was the moment when the rules were made.

'The method of killing *is* peculiar,' intruded Smolin. 'I think that question is one that can only be answered as the enquiry proceeds.'

'I agree,' said Vorobie. He was a plump but neat man, his face partitioned by a moustache almost too heavy for his features. A diplomat of the new order, he had the habit of hesitating before any sentence, thinking ahead about what he was going to say.

'It was an important point to raise,' conceded Oskin.

'We thought so,' said Metkin, anxious to contribute.

If he hadn't known Metkin's intention to drive him from the Bureau, Danilov might have felt some pity for the inadequate man. The conversation was between him and the officials, Metkin coming close to being ignored. Determined to keep it that way, Danilov said: 'Have the Americans been officially informed of our agreement?'

'Later today,' said Vorobie. 'After the ambassador has delivered our Note, we will issue a press statement.'

'There will be liaison between the two Bureaux in the first place,' decided Oskin. 'Close consultation between yourselves and the three of us. Priority will naturally be given to any facilities you may require.'

'Vladimir Kabalin is the newly appointed senior colonel in charge of investigation,' burst in Metkin. 'He's the officer to be assigned.'

'What!' said Oskin, face twisted beyond a frown in his surprise. Both Vorobie and the Federal Prosecutor looked similarly taken aback.

Metkin repeated Kabalin's name but hesitantly, discerning the reaction.

'Kabalin has no experience of joint international detective work, has he?' asked Smolin.

'No,' admitted Metkin.

'Does he speak English?' demanded Vorobie.

'I don't think so,' said the Bureau Director, lamely.

There were more frowning looks between the three men before Smolin said: 'There's no question who should lead this enquiry.'

'None,' agreed Oskin, decisively. 'It will be Dimitri Ivanovich.' He looked directly at Danilov. 'Your other duties and responsibilities can be rearranged or reassigned, can't they?'

'Quite easily,' assured Danilov. Despite his depression at Lapinsk's death, there was still excitement.

'Then it is decided!' declared the man.

'I am to liaise direct with the ministry?' questioned Danilov, teetering on the edge of insubordination but not really caring.

'That's what we want,' said Oskin.

But far more importantly, what Danilov wanted.

And that was what Vasili Oskin got, throughout the remainder of that first day.

Back at Petrovka Danilov filled in the time until the Russian response had formally been delivered in Washington by dictating to all departments in the building a flurry of copies-to-the-Ministry memoranda, redirecting for the personal attention of the Director the stifling administrative bureaucracy he had created. The first and most important note asked Metkin to circularise every department informing them of his secondment to the American enquiry and ordering his unquestioned right to any assistance he might demand. The second instructed Yuri Pavin to report to the top floor, on permanent assignment. He was to move in all the evidence-collecting material for a major crime, including a secure storage safe the combination of which would be restricted: there would be no difficulty getting one from the supply manager. Separately, by telephone to avoid a traceable record, Danilov asked Pavin for all details of Lapinsk's death.

In mid-afternoon Metkin used the excuse of personally handing over duplicates of every authorisation Danilov had sought to call Danilov to his office.

'You regard this as a victory?' demanded the Director.

'I don't believe myself to be in any kind of contest,' lied Danilov.

Metkin's wrinkled face was crimson. 'I was aware of everything going on back there this morning. Don't think I wasn't.'

Danilov said nothing: the petulance didn't deserve a response. But like much else that day there was something to learn from it: from Metkin's attitude, he was now quite sure none of the three men that morning were his protectors.

'When this is over you'll lose your special status,' threatened Metkin. 'You will be back under my unquestioned jurisdiction!'

There was the usual delay in the Moscow international exchange, and when it extended into the early evening Danilov was afraid he might have missed the man he wanted because of the time difference between Russia and the United States. But Cowley was still in his Washington office when the connection was finally made.

'We pressed for it to be you,' admitted Cowley.

'I'm glad you did,' said Danilov sincerely.

That night Cowley went for another walk to Crystal City. The barman recognised him and said it was good to see him again and Cowley said it was good to be back. He began with beer, as before, going on to Wild Turkey after a while. There really was cause to celebrate: it *would* be good, working with the Russian again. Would he still have the complex about losing his hair? Cowley hoped this time there wouldn't be the run-arounds they'd had before, neither at first trusting the other, each trying to outdo the other just that little bit. On the third drink he determined, positively, not to try any smart-ass stuff himself. At least, nothing that wasn't essential.

Because it was a celebration Cowley debated one whiskey more than the previous occasion, but in the end didn't order it, leaving the bar once again pleased at his self-control.

Whatever, he reflected as he made his way back to Arlington, his enjoyment of booze was not as bad as Pauline had insisted when they were together. Maybe he'd call her. He wasn't sure he'd know what to say, but he still thought he might try.

The official report into Leonid Lapinsk's death was unequivocal. The former Director had placed the Makarov against the roof of his mouth and pressed the trigger with his thumb, the print of which was on the trigger. His other fingerprints were on the butt and the barrel. There was no note or anything to indicate why he had done it. His wife, who had been in the apartment at the time and run to the bedroom at the sound of the shot, said her husband had been depressed in recent weeks. She believed it was because of his retirement from the Bureau.

Danilov was equally sure that wasn't the reason.

The news came in a hurried telephone call from the Petrovka headquarters of the Organised Crime Bureau, just as they were about to eat at the restaurant on Glivin Bol'soj. They impatiently sent the whores they'd chosen for that night outside the private salon, so they could talk.

'I don't like it!' protested Gusovsky.

'Metkin is still Director,' placated Yerin. 'We'll still know everything that happens.'

'There could be things we *won't* know!'

'Who's there to talk?' asked Yerin rhetorically. 'Any investigation will be a waste of their time.'

'What about the old fool's suicide?' asked Zimin.

'He didn't leave any stupid letters,' said Yerin. 'And what would have happened if he had? Nothing.'

Gusovsky nodded in agreement. Lighting another forbidden cigar, he said to Zimin: 'Call the girls back.'

Zimin hesitated, but only momentarily, then did what he was told.

CHAPTER FOURTEEN

Using the authority of Sergei Vorobie's name, which gained him immediate access to whomever he wanted at the Foreign Ministry, Danilov demanded the complete personnel file on Petr Aleksandrovich Serov. Through the ministry he also ordered the man's office at the Washington embassy to be sealed and to remain untouched until he arrived; he gave the same order for the apartment on Massachusetts Avenue. Knowing there would be a security service presence in the embassy, Danilov repeated the instructions about the office and the flat through the Interior Ministry for relay to Washington, well aware that in the past the old KGB, from which the new organisation had been formed, had regarded itself as beyond edicts from any but their own controllers. And sometimes not even them.

Throughout the telephone conversations Danilov was conscious of the scribbling interest of Ludmilla Radsic at the far end of the room, so when he finished he made it easy for her by dictating records of everything he'd done to create the beginning of Pavin's meticulous dossier and Metkin's spy file. Danilov decided the Director would by now be hating Moscow's direct telephone dialling system, knowing his calls would have been monitored through a general switchboard. From her strained but blank-faced attention during the previous night's conversation with Cowley, he knew Ludmilla did not understand English. While the woman was preparing the Ministry memoranda, Danilov quietly made his own flight arrangements to Washington and typed his own advisory note to Sergei Vorobie, requesting a final briefing. He did not send a copy to Metkin.

Again because of the attentive secretary, it was not until they were in the car on their way to Leninskaya that Danilov was able to speak openly to Pavin.

'This has confused everybody,' said the man, who was

81

driving. 'People aren't sure just how strong Metkin's position is: you caused a lot of upset with all those instructions and changes.'

'Have you been asked to inform on me?' demanded Danilov, with subjective cynicism.

'Kabalin was very friendly after yesterday's announcement: I'm expecting it to come. When are you going to Washington?'

'The day after tomorrow.'

'How long?'

'I don't know. I'll be liaising with the ministries but I'll come through you, as well, to maintain the records.'

'Metkin will demand them.'

'There'll be nothing he can't see.'

The Serovs' Moscow apartment was close to the Gagarin monument, in one of the last ornate and still exclusive blocks built for members of the disbanded Communist Party. The flat was on the top floor, with one of the best views over the city. The elevator worked and was clean. There was no graffiti.

Raisa Serova opened the door and regarded them curiously, someone whose inherent assurance was subdued: a new widow. She was an extremely attractive, even beautiful woman, heavy busted but slim, sheathed in a fitted dark blue wool dress. The patterned gold necklace matched the bracelet on her left wrist. Her deeply black hair was bobbed short and the lipstick matched the dark crimson of her nails. There was the suggestion of redness around her eyes, a hint she might have been weeping, but Danilov wasn't sure. Danilov guessed she was in her late thirties: it would probably be recorded on Serov's Foreign Ministry file.

The woman showed no surprise when they identified themselves, nor any reluctance to receive them. She seated them in an expansive living room, with a view of the obelisk-like tower commemorating the first Russian astronaut. She offered tea, which they refused.

'When is Petr Aleksandrovich's body being returned?' she demanded at once.

'We don't know,' said Danilov.

'Isn't that why you're here?'

'We're assisting the American authorities in their investigation.'

Her attitude changed slightly, into uncertainty. 'You think I can help?'

'Can you?'

'How?'

She moved to a low couch, directly in front of the window, and took a cigarette from a black malacca box on the side table, carefully fitting it into a stubby holder. Danilov saw the cigarette was American, like so much else in the room. The television and an extensive stereo system were imported, linked to the fluctuating Moscow electricity supply by heavy transformers: Danilov guessed the furnishings, the curtains, the rugs, and maybe even the suite and the tables, came from America as well.

'Your husband was murdered.'

'I know that. Shot.' There was the slightest tremor in the hand holding the cigarette, a hint of distress, but her voice was even.

'So was a Swiss financier. Petr Aleksandrovich dined with him, the night they were both killed.'

'I read that, in the newspapers.'

'Did you know your husband was meeting a man named Michel Paulac, on the 19th?'

'I have been here in Moscow for three weeks.'

'So you did not know of the appointment?' persisted Danilov.

'No.'

Beside Danilov, Pavin was recording every word: Danilov had always been intrigued by the quick neatness of the note-taking from such a large man. 'Did you know Michel Paulac?'

'No.'

'Your husband never spoke of him?'

'No.'

'Were you aware your husband associated with criminals?'

'What?' The woman's voice was angrily loud.

83

Danilov repeated the question.

'That's an absurd thing to ask me!'

'There are peculiarities about the killing.'

Raisa Serova stubbed out her cigarette but lit another immediately. Not looking at either of them, she said: 'Petr Aleksandrovich was a diplomat, performing a duty for his country. He was a respectable, honest man. My husband did not know criminals. Nor associate with criminals. I resent the question and I am offended by it. I shall complain to the Ministry about your impudence! Get out!'

Neither Danilov nor Pavin moved.

'I have come here with the knowledge of both the Foreign and Interior Ministries,' said Danilov. 'You can obviously appreciate the international implications of what has happened. It is not my intention to offend or distress you: I am merely asking questions that have to be asked . . . asked in the hope of arresting whoever killed Petr Aleksandrovich.'

Raisa Serova said nothing. Danilov sat, waiting, still making no move to leave. The impasse was broken by a muffled call from somewhere within the apartment. Without speaking, the woman left the room. Danilov and Pavin remained where they were, also silent.

When she came back she said: 'My mother is unwell. Terminally.' She wasn't outraged any more.

'Petr Aleksandrovich had been in Washington a long time?'

'Yes.'

'How did those extensions of duty come about?'

'Instructions from the Foreign Ministry here.'

'Petr Aleksandrovich did not not request them?'

She laughed at the naivety. 'Everybody tries to extend in America: there's no point in asking!'

'He liked it there?'

'He was popular. Did his job well: that's why he was kept on.'

Without the guidance of the Foreign Office personnel file, and still seeking a link between the two murders, Danilov said: 'Had your husband ever served in the Swiss legation?'

'No.'

'Anywhere in Europe?'

'Paris. It was his posting before Washington.'

Close enough, thought Danilov. 'Where else had he served?'

'Caracas.' She shuddered. 'Venezuela is not an agreeable place.'

'There must have been a lot of socialising, as a cultural attaché?'

'Yes.'

'Did you attend functions with your husband?'

'It is seen as a joint posting, although I did not have any official diplomatic status.'

Danilov thought she would have performed the role very well. 'So you and he discussed his work?'

She frowned. 'He would tell me of events coming up: warn me in advance when I might have to attend.'

'Did you keep matching diaries?'

Raisa Serova hesitated, looking directly at him. 'Yes.'

'Where is yours?'

The hesitation this time was longer, and Danilov guessed she was considering rejecting the inference of the question. But she got up and briefly left the room again, returning with a long but handbag-sized diary. Like everything else, it was American. She offered it to him without speaking.

The space for the 19th was blank: the only entries for a week prior and the period after related to her return to Moscow. There were two doctor's appointments listed.

'There was no purpose in matching our diaries when I was not in Washington,' she said, anticipating the question.

'How many diaries did your husband keep?'

'Two; one at the embassy, another at the flat. One was the duplicate of the other. Petr Aleksandrovich was extremely efficient.'

'Did you speak by telephone after your return?'

'Twice, I think. Maybe three times.'

'How did Petr Aleksandrovich seem?'

There was another frowning hesitation. 'As he always seemed. Quite normal.'

'He did not mention the intended meeting with Michel Paulac?'

'I have already told you, no!'

'You told me you did not know of an appointment,' corrected Danilov. 'Not that there had been no conversation about the man.'

'I said my husband had never spoken of him,' she reminded, correcting his correction.

Now it was Danilov who hesitated. 'Do you know . . . can you imagine . . . any reason why Petr Aleksandrovich should have met a Swiss financier? And why he should have been killed in the manner in which he was: in the manner in which they both were?'

The woman stared at him in open-eyed amazement. 'How could I!'

'You must be bewildered by it, then?'

'I am.'

'But you haven't tried to understand how or why he should have been meeting this man?'

'There is no way I can undersand. It's a mystery.'

'Please don't misconstrue this question,' warned Danilov in advance. 'But did your husband have friends or acquaintances you did not know about?'

'He must have done, mustn't he? I did not know of this man.'

'I meant others.'

'Do you mean women?'

Was he expressing himself badly, or was she making it difficult? 'I mean do you think, this having happened, that Petr Aleksandrovich knew and met people, male *or* female, whose acquaintance he kept from you?'

'It's possible. If I didn't know I *wouldn't* know, would I? There were things that happened at the embassy which would have involved people I had no right to know about.'

This was becoming a perpetual circle, decided Danilov. 'Will you be returning to Washington?'

She looked uncertain. 'I haven't thought about it. I suppose I shall have to, to close up the apartment.'

Which had been the point of his question: he wanted the chance to get into Massachusetts Avenue before Raisa Serova did. There had been outrage and protests from the

Americans at his entering the Moscow apartment of the politician's niece before them. The angriest outburst had been from the FBI man they'd eventually identified as the killer: they would never have proved it if the man had got there ahead of him. 'You haven't made any arrangements?'

'I thought the funeral would have been first.' There was a pause before she said: 'Have you had any contact with American investigators about this?'

'Very briefly.'

'What do they say? What do they think?'

'They don't have any theories.'

'The newspapers said you've worked with the Americans before?'

'Yes?' said Danilov, curiously.

'Are they good? This man they named, Cowley, is he good?'

'They have some extremely sophisticated methods of investigation, scientifically. Cowley is a very clever detective.'

Raisa Serova nodded, as if she were receiving confirmation of something she already knew. 'So they will find the killer?'

'I would expect so.'

'Will he die? Be executed, I mean.'

'I don't know,' admitted Danilov. 'The laws are different, from state to state.' And the District of Columbia wasn't a state anyway: he didn't feel it was necessary to qualify.

Appearing to retreat inside herself, the woman said: 'I loved him. Now I don't have him any more.'

The abrupt outburst surprised him. Danilov could not think of anything to say.

'Maybe, if I had been in Washington, he wouldn't have had the meeting that night? Wouldn't have died.'

Danilov was familiar with the 'what if' speculation of the bereaved. 'It happened,' he said, gently. 'He's dead.'

'Yes.'

Danilov handed her a card: he'd already handwritten on the back the direct number into his new office. 'If you think of anything, call me.'

Raisa Serova stared down at the card, then up at Danilov. 'There won't be anything.'

The Foreign Ministry personnel file on Petr Aleksandrovich Serov was waiting when Danilov returned to Petrovka. It was far more detailed than Danilov had expected. It confirmed, with the years listed consecutively, the postings to Caracas and Paris prior to the Washington appointment. He had married Raisa on 3 June, 1980, in Moscow's Hall of Weddings. From the dates of birth, Serov was nine years older than his wife: he had been born in 1948, she in 1957. The extensions of Serov's Washington service were noted, like the dates of the other overseas postings, but no reason recorded for keeping the man so long in America, although the four attached confidential assessments each praised Serov's work and performance. Three used the word exemplary. There were also two confidential assessments on Raisa. Exemplary was the word used again.

Danilov was still reading when the telephone rang. He let Pavin take the call, which was quite brief. Instead of announcing it from his own desk, Pavin crossed the room, so the exchange would be unheard by the secretary.

'You're to go to the Foreign Ministry,' said Pavin. 'Raisa Serova has complained.'

CHAPTER FIFTEEN

The chandelierd elegance was far grander than that at the Interior Ministry and Sergei Vorobie clearly considered himself very much in charge, at home in his own territory. Vasili Oskin was already there. Danilov at once registered the absence of the Federal Prosecutor, the one official Lapinsk had categorically named as an honest man. He supposed Oskin represented the law.

'There are things that have to be understood very clearly,' announced the Deputy Foreign Minister. 'And remembered at all times.'

The political lecture, supposed Danilov. 'I asked for this meeting to get guidance.'

'Did you become particularly friendly with this man Cowley on the earlier occasion you worked together?' demanded Oskin.

Danilov detected a difference in attitude from the previous day. 'I respected him, professionally.'

'The Americans exercised particular pressure for you to be the investigating officer,' said Oskin. 'How would you explain that?'

Danilov raised and lowered his shoulders. 'They knew me, from before.' This was *definitely* a different type of meeting.

'Reason enough for making it a personal request?' pressed Oskin.

'I can't offer any other suggestion,' said Danilov. Surely he hadn't escaped one oppressive situation immediately to encounter another?

'At all times your first priority *must* be the honour of Russia,' insisted Vorobie, close to pomposity.

'I have no intention of being manipulated!' said Danilov, wanting the irritation to show. *Couldn't* they manipulate him?

There was a momentary silence. Unabashed, Vorobie said: 'That is exactly what must not occur. We do not understand what's happened: we do not want – will not *have* – any embarrassment.'

'I thought that was made clear yesterday.' What had changed in twenty-four hours?

'It needs to be reinforced,' said Oskin.

'This is an American investigation, being conducted *in* America. I will have no authority or jurisdiction there,' pointed out Danilov.

'You will within the embassy: we've ordered it,' corrected Oskin. 'I want the closest liaison with us here about whatever you learn there . . .' He paused, for emphasis. 'In *advance* of any discussion with the Americans.'

Before Danilov could respond, Vorobie said: 'General Metkin is not with you?'

Momentarily the question off-balanced Danilov. Hurriedly he said: 'I assumed you would have summoned him, if you wanted him to attend.'

'Quite so,' agreed Vorobie.

'The liaison is to be direct between yourself and me at the Interior Ministry,' declared Oskin.

Did these two men know more about Metkin or about what Serov had been doing in Washington? And want the investigation strictly controlled: neutered even? That could explain why the Federal Prosecutor, the man who had formally to recommend a trial, had been excluded. Whatever, there was an opportunity to be seized. 'I have been ordered by General Metkin to channel all information through him.'

'I am countermanding that instruction,' announced Oskin. 'Metkin can receive copies. I want the initial information sent direct and immediately to me.'

Danilov recognised another victory but it didn't matter: he would, eventually, have to return to Petrovka, under Metkin's control. 'If the General is not officially informed it might appear I deliberately disobeyed an order.'

'I will tell him it's my decision,' undertook Oskin.

It would be necessary for Pavin to create his customary

immaculate files, whatever transpired in America. Should he talk about a second, duplicate copy of everything going to Pavin? Not necessary, Danilov decided: files had to be kept.

'There will be no independent decisions, taken without consultation with us,' insisted Vorobie.

It was ridiculous for them to imagine they could control an enquiry more than five thousand miles away. It would have been equally ridiculous for him to argue. Instead Danilov said: 'My authority has been established with the embassy?'

'Obviously we expect you to respect the position of the ambassador and his senior staff.'

'And the security *rezident*?'

'Yes,' said Oskin.

Restriction upon restriction, thought Danilov. The diplomatic staff would claim superiority of rank and the security officer would probably ignore him. 'I think I understand what I am expected to do,' said Danilov. What he understood was that he had been effectively trussed and gagged, made totally impotent: and that the public declarations of Russian open-handed co-operation were meaningless. *Their* understanding, determined Danilov: not his.

'On the subject of proper conduct,' picked up Vorobie. 'Serov's widow has complained you were rude and unsympathetic.'

'I was neither,' refuted Danilov. 'Every question was necessary.'

'What did you learn?' asked Oskin.

'Virtually nothing. She says she did not know of her husband's association with Michel Paulac.' Danilov looked directly at Vorobie. 'Why *was* Serov's tour of duty extended so often?'

'Proven ability,' said the Deputy. 'It happens occasionally. We take advantage of it.'

The vagueness intrigued Danilov, like so many other things about this meeting. He no longer had any feeling of euphoria. 'Anything else?'

'You will live in the diplomatic compound,' insisted Oskin.

Where he would be under effective supervision, Danilov

recognised. He was hardly going to be able to *conduct* an investigation.

'You will make no unauthorised statements,' continued Oskin. 'Any public announcements will come from here.'

'This is not going to be an easy assignment,' said Vorobie.

Not made any easier by this encounter, thought Danilov. Close to insubordination, he said: 'You haven't left me in any doubt about that.'

Pavin intercepted him at the office door, to warn him out of Ludmilla's hearing of Metkin's fury. 'I had to tell him where you were,' apologised the man.

'What else could you have done?' agreed Danilov.

'He's waiting.'

Metkin actually rose from his chair, as if he were going physically to attack, when Danilov entered the room, and for several seconds the man was unable to speak properly. When he did, the demand to know why Danilov had gone to the Foreign Ministry without telling him was disjointed and stuttered. Danilov insisted he'd expected Metkin to be summoned separately.

'Liar! I want to know *all* that went on: *all* that was discussed!' declared Metkin. The words were stretched by anger.

'I have to communicate direct with Vasili Oskin,' disclosed Danilov. It really didn't seem important any more to fight this man.

Metkin's apoplexy was absolute. His mouth opened and closed, without words: his body shifted and moved, unco-ordinated. 'You have to come through *me*!'

'Deputy Minister Oskin has countermanded that instruction. You are to be officially told of the decision. You are to receive duplicates, of course.'

'Why?'

'I don't know.'

'You manoeuvred this!'

'I did not.'

'Liar!' said Metkin again.

It *was* impossible for there to be any connection between

92

Metkin and the ministry official. Which removed one uncertainty but left everything else hanging in the air; Metkin's incandescent concern was surely more than simple anger about senior officials going over his head? 'You could take the matter up personally with Deputy Minister Oskin.'

Metkin's anger seeped away, as if a plug had been pulled. Quietly, invitingly, the man said: 'I think we should talk about things. Reasonably.'

It was his choice, Danilov realised. Metkin was seeking a special arrangement, wrongly believing he had influence he didn't possess: seeking the sort of accommodation almost everyone in the Bureau reached every day of their lives. The what's-in-it-for-me philosophy, on this occasion most definitely and hopefully for the absolute benefit and protection of Anatoli Nikolaevich Metkin. It could be easily manipulated, Danilov knew: sufficient to bring himself out of the wilderness of isolation. To what? Ever-smiling friends in shiny suits and real gold. Agreements reached in whispers. Easy access to everything he'd once had and for which Olga craved. Proper money: dollars, not lavatory-paper roubles. An easy life. A disease carrier among those already infected, everyone knowing the symptoms, everyone knowing there wasn't a cure because no-one wanted to be cured. He said: 'I don't think there is anything for us to discuss.'

Metkin's crumpled face appeared to collapse upon itself. 'Bastard!' he said.

It wasn't any longer an angry remark, Danilov recognised. Metkin was frightened. Which, he supposed, made two of them.

'What am I going to do while you're away?' Larissa had kicked the covering off the bed and was lying with her hands cupped behind her head, to bring her breasts up more fully.

'Stay faithful,' said Danilov.

'Will you stay faithful to me in America?'

'You know I will.'

'How long will you be away?'

'I don't know.' Danilov had already realised his trip to

Washington temporarily relieved the pressure with either Olga or Larissa.

She realised it, too. 'I want things settled when you get back.'

'Yes.'

'I mean it.'

'So do I.'

Olga was at the kitchen table when Danilov got back to Kirovskaya. She smiled up at him, offering a sheet of paper upon which she had been writing. 'My shopping list,' she announced. 'I'm glad you're going away.'

So was he, thought Danilov. But Larissa was right: as soon as he got back he'd have to settle everything. He was coming close to using the thought of Yevgennie Kosov lashing out vindictively as an excuse for doing nothing. Like so many other excuses, before.

'And this came, in the mail.'

The franking on the envelope showed the delivery had taken almost a week, fast by Moscow postal standards. It contained a single sheet of paper. On it were three names, none of which Danilov recognised: certainly they weren't people attached to the Organised Crime Bureau. Lapinsk had printed one word above his signature: *Prahsteet*. It means sorry.

'What is it?' asked Olga.

'I'm not sure,' said Danilov.

The ambush was perfectly staged. The three canvas-covered Chechen trucks carrying the looted word processors from the Domodedovo airport warehouse became separated on their way into the city because the traffic was unexpectedly heavy on the former Andropov Prospekt, even that late at night. The rear lorry was split from the convoy by at least one hundred yards when they turned off the Ulitza Masinostrojenij. It was a regular route – which was a mistake – and the Ostankino group were waiting at the darkest section.

The Chechen lorry was blocked, front and back, by two trucks that emerged from the side road near the bridge. Two

Chechen guards who tried to fight had their skulls fractured by iron staves. The attackers – a separate group from those transferring the word processors – occupied the brief time it took by breaking the legs of the drivers and the third guard. Before they left they set fire to the Chechen vehicles. The men with the fractured skulls were left lying too close and sustained second degree burns that disfigured them for life.

CHAPTER SIXTEEN

William Cowley was waiting at the immigration desk to usher Danilov out of the normal arrival line at Dulles airport to a side office. Inside they formally shook hands and informally examined each other, and Cowley just beat Danilov in saying how good it was to see him again. They spoke English. Cowley thought Danilov's hair had grown thinner, and that he had developed a slight paunch. Danilov thought Cowley had grown heavier, as if he were neglecting himself.

'Your people are waiting outside: this was the best way to talk, as soon as we could.' From the concealment of the main immigration office Cowley had already identified Nikolai Redin as well as Valery Pavlenko among the reception group: it would be interesting if Danilov later spoke openly of the former KGB man.

'What do we need to know?'

'Everything,' declared Cowley. He detailed the difficulties with the two Russians at the formal identification, and looked unconvinced by Danilov's assurance that both Serov's office and apartment had been sealed. 'Will they have been?'

'I don't know,' admitted Danilov honestly. 'I probably won't even when I start going through them.'

Pointedly Cowley said: 'How's it going to be between us, Dimitri?'

'Straight, I hope.' Danilov was reluctant even to hint at the restrictions imposed upon him, but unsure if the hesitation was motivated more by personal or professional pride. A combination of both, he guessed. 'How do you see it being handled?'

'The same,' promised Cowley. He didn't completely believe Danilov and knew Danilov wouldn't completely believe him. Just how straight *was* it possible for them to be

96

with each other? Not something to be determined this early. Testingly he asked about Raisa Serova, listening intently for any nuances to tell him Danilov was holding something back. He didn't detect that the Russian was, but he wasn't sure.

'Do you think she was telling the truth about Michel Paulac?'

Danilov made an uncertain gesture. 'We need to find something that doesn't fit before we can challenge her. She's a very controlled woman.'

Danilov's baggage arrived at the same time as his returned passport. The visa entry was for an indefinite period.

Cowley offered a card with all the FBI contact numbers. 'I'll wait to hear.' He smiled, ruefully. 'There's not a lot else I can think of *to* do.'

The third Russian waiting on the outside concourse was introduced by Pavlenko as Oleg Firsov, the senior embassy counsellor; the driver who took Danilov's case wasn't identified at all. Danilov was manoeuvred into the car between the two diplomats, with Redin in the front. Firsov, who was fat and perspiring and who was already smelling vaguely of body odour, moved to take instant charge. Everything had to be reported through him, before any communication to Moscow. That order included whatever Danilov was told by or learned from the Americans. It was potentially a politically awkward situation.

'Why?' interrupted Danilov, sharply, breaking the flow.

Firsov, who had been delivering the recitation staring directly ahead as if he were talking to an audience instead of just one man, frowned sideways. 'I don't understand the question.'

'Why is it potentially a politically awkward situation?'

'I would have thought that would have been obvious.'

'I don't take any inference as obvious,' rejected Danilov. 'Was Petr Aleksandrovich acting officially when he met Michel Paulac?'

'I have no information about that,' said Firsov.

Which was not an answer, identified Danilov. 'If you have no information how can you say it could be politically awkward?' he persisted.

Firsov sighed, in attempted intimidation. 'I was talking generally.'

'I don't investigate crime on the basis of generalities, either,' said Danilov, refusing the superciliousness.

From his other side, Pavlenko said: 'I don't think we should overlook seniority here.'

'Neither do I,' said Danilov. 'Before leaving Moscow I was personally instructed by Deputy Interior Minister Oskin, in the presence of Deputy Foreign Minister Vorobie, to communicate directly with him, without going through intermediaries. Has that order been rescinded? If it has, I wish to see the written message.'

Firsov's shift of annoyance released a fresh waft of odour. 'I do not believe Deputy Interior Minister Oskin intended the ambassador or any senior diplomat to be ignored!'

'I am not suggesting senior officials at the embassy should be bypassed. Neither was Minister Oskin. What I am saying is that my liaison with Moscow must be direct.'

'That point has been established,' said Firsov icily.

He wasn't making friends, Danilov recognised: but then, he'd hardly expected to. 'Liaison without interference or censorship . . .' He paused, expectantly. Firsov remained staring directly ahead, breathing heavily. '. . . unless, of course, something I might report would benefit by additional assistance of facts from any member of the embassy staff.'

'We assume you would like to settle in, after the flight?' suggested Pavlenko.

'No,' denied Danilov at once. 'I would prefer to go direct to the embassy and Petr Aleksandrovich's office.'

The silence froze inside the car. They were travelling along the sculptured highway towards the city: soon, Danilov remembered, they would be dropping through the Memorial Parkway beside the ribbon of the Potomac, where it would be possible to start picking out landmarks. 'There were specific instructions from Moscow about the office? And the apartment?'

'They have been followed,' assured Firsov.

'What was done to either, before that instruction?' asked Danilov, worried about the intervening time gap.

'Nothing,' said Pavlenko carelessly.

It was a guess, although a fairly safe one, for Danilov to direct his question to the front of the car, to the unspeaking Nikolai Redin. 'Then there was a serious security lapse, surely? Are you saying no member of the security division within the embassy examined the office or the living accommodation of a member of the embassy who had been murdered?'

Danilov got his confirmation of Redin's role from the way the man's neck and ears flushed. He turned to the rear. 'Of course they were examined!'

'What was removed from either?' demanded Danilov.

'Nothing,' said the security officer.

And if there had been, there was no way he would ever find out, Danilov accepted. The embassy limousine turned over the Key Bridge and Danilov recognised Georgetown, where he had spent time with Cowley on the last occasion. He hoped there would be the chance to do it again. He'd get his hair cut, too. Maybe buy a watch that worked.

It *had* been good to see Cowley again, although Danilov had been uncomfortable with the verbal fencing. Several times in the serial killing investigation they'd risked serious error from initial, matching mistrust. The danger shouldn't arise this time. They had been strangers then, thrust into a unique situation. Now they knew and admired each other. And he'd already decided to interpret the Moscow instructions his way. Had it been alcohol he'd smelled on Cowley's breath? There was no reason why it shouldn't have been, but he couldn't recall the man being a drinker.

At Lafayette Square, just before turning into 16th Street, Danilov looked sideways to the White House, thinking as he had the first time how small and inconsequential it appeared for the official home of the American President. The Russian White House was far more impressive. The protesting homeless were still bivouaced under plastic sheeting and boxes beside their complaining posters. He'd thought before how quickly such demonstrations would have been cleared from around the Kremlin by the KGB. Now the KGB was gone and the streets of Moscow had their own box-and-tent townships of tattered, threadbare people.

Inside the embassy, Firsov left Danilov with as much dismissiveness as he could achieve, and the reminder that the ambassador expected to see all communications to Moscow. Pavlenko led the way to the cultural section, Redin following. It was the security man who unlocked the door with an almost theatrical flourish, standing back for Danilov to enter. From the threshold Danilov saw a desk in immaculate order, pens and pencils in their holders, document trays bare, telephones neatly in line, and a pristinely white and unmarked blotter. A wastepaper basket alongside was empty.

Hopeless, he thought: they'd had the last, mocking laugh.

Momentarily Olga frowned into the telephone, not recognising the voice. Then she said: 'Yevgennie! How are you?'

'Didn't want you to become lonely without Dimitri,' said the man. 'Would you like to eat out one night?'

'Tell Larissa to call me, so I'll know what she's going to wear,' asked the woman.

'We'll have to see how her shifts work out. She might not be able to make it. But that would be all right, wouldn't it?'

Olga, who didn't want to spend time by herself at Kirovskaya, hesitated. 'I suppose so.'

'I'll telephone, in a day or two. Set something up.'

'I hope Larissa can make it.'

'You can trust me by myself.'

Kosov made another call immediately after disconnecting from Olga. 'It's all arranged,' he said.

'Good,' replied Arkadi Gusovsky, in the study of his Kutbysevskiy mansion. He turned to Yerin as he replaced the receiver. 'He's done what we told him to do.'

The blind man appeared surprised. 'Everyone does what we tell them to do. They have to.'

CHAPTER SEVENTEEN

Danilov was aware of the two men following as he entered the room. He turned, stopping them before they were fully inside. Remaining in their path, Danilov said: 'Thank you.'

'There may be something that needs explaining,' said Pavlenko.

'If there is, I'll ask,' said Danilov.

'I am the senior security officer,' said Redin. 'I will assist you.'

'I don't need help,' refused Danilov. He couldn't have staged such an open confrontation in the old omnipotent days of the KGB. He wasn't sure he could do it now. But Redin flushed, as he had in the car, twitching a look towards the cultural attaché, and Danilov knew he had won. 'Thank you,' he repeated, closing the door upon them as they retreated into the outer office.

Danilov turned, his back to the door, looking once more into what, under closer examination, scarcely qualified as an office at all. It was a cubicle created by hardboard screening from a corner of the huge, open room beyond, and so small it would have been almost absurdly overcrowded with three in it, particularly if one were carrying out any sort of search. So why had they tried to pack in behind him? Was it simply for a diplomat and a security officer to watch him, the intrusive outsider, at all times? Serov's workplace had obviously been searched. Had they wanted to watch him do it again because they'd found nothing and were anxious to see if he would do better? Redin was a professional intelligence officer, whose training included the craft of room scrutiny.

At once Danilov questioned his own thought. The training and expertise of a trained intelligence officer was different in one very important respect from that of a trained and experienced investigator. He would instinctively look to detect *and* to connect: Redin's search, he guessed, would have been more to locate the obvious.

Apart from the immaculate desk, there was a filing cabinet recessed between the windows and a half-glazed bookcase just inside the door. A padded office chair was neatly slotted into the leg space beneath the desk; a more basic visitor's seat fronted it. A polystyrene cup stood beneath the air-conditioning unit to prevent the drips staining the thin, brown cordweave carpet. On the windowsill there was a vase of atrophied tulips, their petals scattered on the sill and the floor below. After all the trouble sanitising the room, Danilov was surprised: rather than make the room appear untouched, the flower debris accentuated the fact that it had been examined.

Danilov began with the bookcase. The visible, glass-fronted part contained a selection of textbooks on American culture, although the very bottom shelf held tomes on Russian history and art. All were large, with a lot of coloured illustration. Guessing Redin would have done the same, Danilov held each by their spine, to shake free anything concealed between the leaves, and additionally rifled through the pages to double-check. There was nothing. The enclosed lower half of the bookcase was serried with shelves upon which were arranged, as neatly as everything laid out on the desk, carefully indexed records of Washington cultural events from the beginning of Petr Serov's posting. Danilov went through them as intently as he had the better bound books above, not wanting to dislodge any genuine but unattached document. He realised as he worked that the folders were further indexed with events Serov had attended, as opposed to those he had not, and in addition were marked to indicate those to which his wife had accompanied him. Each attendance, either separately or with Raisa, was also marked with names and sometimes telephone numbers or addresses of possible cultural contacts.

It took Danilov an hour to go superficially through the dossiers; he finished wishing he was accompanied by the painstaking Major Pavin, to whom he could have delegated the proper page-by-page task. There was nothing immediately to help the investigation but there was something to learn, nevertheless. Danilov didn't doubt the faultless perfection of the desk was the work of Pavlenko or Redin or both. But the folders before which Danilov now squatted *did* confirm that Serov was an obsessively methodical keeper of detailed records. And that being so, it was a more than reasonable assumption he would somewhere have kept records of an association with a Swiss financier named Michel Paulac.

But where?

Danilov rose and went finally to the desk, sitting in the chair in which Serov had sat, looking from closed drawer to closed drawer, unsure where to begin. The moment he did, there was fresh evidence of Serov's fastidiousness. The top right-hand drawer contained invitations accepted, the left those rejected, often because of a clash of dates. The right-hand drawer also contained an address book, which Danilov scoured avidly, trying every combination of letters to locate a listing for, or reference to, Michel Paulac. There was nothing apart from official diplomatic numbers. Danilov slumped back, accepting it had probably been too much to hope for but disappointed just the same.

The official appointments diary was desk size, too big to be carried except in a briefcase. Serov's handwriting was precise and legible, every word easy to read. Danilov went at once to the day of the murder. The only notation was a lunchtime reception for an exhibition of Native American art at the Smithsonian, marked as having been attended. Hunched forward over the desk, Danilov worked his way through every entry from the beginning of the year, forcing himself on until he reached the murder date again even though it quickly became obvious that it *was* an appointments diary, recording nothing else.

He put the diary aside and went just as intently through everything else in the desk. It was entirely devoted to the man's function and position at the embassy: there was nothing personal, not even a photograph of Raisa. There was a Xeroxed form of Russian embassy events, the diplomatic list of Russian embassy personnel, six official diplomatic year books of European legations each marked at their cultural sections, a bulldog-clipped collection of bills and dockets on top of empty expense claim forms, and two drawers devoted to embassy stationery.

Danilov replaced the contents of each drawer as he had found it before extending the search in the way he guessed Redin would have done. He extracted each drawer completely from its slot, running his hands inside the cavity for anything secured or taped to the desk frame. He repeated the examination around every edge and the bottom of each drawer before replacing it. He got down on his hands and knees, probing the knee space for any concealed item, and at the end had found absolutely nothing.

The filing cabinet was as unproductive as everything else. There were brochures of events, both past and for the immediate future, all inserted according to date. Two drawers contained material and documents for the not-yet-assembled records that would have joined the rest of Serov's career history on the shelves of the bookcase opposite. Two more contained correspondence stretching back over two years, annotated alphabetically. Recognising his own naivety, particularly after the failed attempt with the address book, he looked up P for Paulac and M for Michel before going on to F for finance and S for Switzerland. He even switched the combinations, in case Serov had filed European names under the designation of the Russian Cyrillic alphabet.

It *had* been naive to expect to find anything in an office that had clearly been cleansed as antiseptically as this. As naive as looking up initial letters in address books and filing cabinets, or imagining himself better trained in his art than Redin was in his. He'd given way to pride, Danilov accepted: he'd enjoyed the publicity too much, and too easily believed the media descriptions of his supposed ability. So he'd wanted to find within hours of his arrival in Washington the key that would unlock the entire mystery, like the English fictional detective who played a violin and wore a strange hat and solved crime in minutes, about whom a series was currently being shown on Moscow television. But he wasn't operating in a fictional setting. He was operating in real life, in hard reality, and his entire future depended upon his behaving like a proper detective.

Wherever that elusive somewhere was in which Petr Aleksandrovich might have left the secret of his association with Michel Paulac, it definitely wasn't here, indexed under letter heading.

Danilov slumped head forward against his chest, the momentarily unfocused appointments diary open before him, embarrassed with himself for expecting it to be so easy, pushing the personal discomfort aside by concentrating yet again upon the murder date. He saw the grouping of the words but he wasn't consciously *trying* to read them: seeing more the pattern than the construction of the spelling. Which was probably why the oddness abruptly and sharply registered: that and the fact that he had juggled with the script of two languages with different alphabets while looking at the address book and through the cabinet.

Danilov had read English at Moscow University, and learned it so well that his first intention, before joining the Militia, had been to become a translator and interpreter. He didn't need his expertise or fluency to be curious at what he was staring down at now.

Everything about what he had seen and read in this office told him Petr Aleksandrovich was a man of consummate attention to infinite accuracy. Yet the entry at which he was looking was inaccurate. The entry for the murder day read: *Exhibition of Native American Art. Smithsonian. Noon. Attend.* And Serov had written it in English. But the two 'R's in the phrase were written with the Cyrillic 'p', and the 'n' of 'exhibition' was printed with the Cyrillic 'h'.

Serov would not have made that sort of mistake. Danilov's conviction grew as he read the diary entries once more from the beginning, coming again and again upon the correct use of both letters. But there were exceptions: he found four dates, one in each of the preceding four months, when Cyrillic again intruded.

Carefully Danilov noted each date, stretching back into the chair as the fatigue finally washed over him. He was sure it was significant. Hopefully there was a way to find out what that significance was. It would also create a test, to see if Cowley really intended full co-operation. Danilov was uncomfortable at doubting the American, but supposed there would have to be such a test. He wondered if Cowley would attempt one with him.

'You've been in there a very long time,' said Redin, close to complaint, when Danilov emerged.

'I wasn't aware of a time limit,' said Danilov.

'Anything?' demanded Pavlenko, who was also waiting.

'After only four hours?' mocked Danilov, extending his rejection of the security man's remark.

'You haven't finished?' frowned Redin.

'Of course not,' said Danilov. Could there be a way for Pavin to dissect Serov's work files with his usual thoroughness? It would be something to consider tomorrow.

Danilov remained as vague when he telephoned William Cowley from the surprisingly spacious apartment allocated to him in the Russian compound on Massachusetts Avenue.

'When can we meet?' demanded the American.

'Tomorrow afternoon, after I've looked at Serov's home,' promised Danilov. 'I'll telephone.'

'How's it looking?'

'Too soon to say.' Unlike the telephone system in Moscow, calls here were routed through a central switchboard and he guessed the conversation, like any he had over the following days, would be monitored. It would be unsafe to initiate any discussion he did not want overheard from any Russian facility.

He collapsed gratefully into bed, curious whether he would find any more oddly spelled words in Serov's apartment the following day. And then discover what they meant, in the way he thought he could.

CHAPTER EIGHTEEN

There *were* wrongly spelled words. And on the same dates as those in the cumbersome office desk diary, although this time in a more convenient pocket version which matched the one produced by Raisa Serova in Moscow and which Danilov found in a bureau in the Serov apartment.

It wasn't an easy search. Oleg Firsov, the resentful counsellor, had insisted on accompanying him to the murdered diplomat's home, and Danilov had decided he couldn't oppose, as he had at the embassy. With Firsov constantly at his elbow, Danilov moved through the flat appearing to ignore a lot but missing nothing. He was sure it had been searched like Serov's office, but those before him had tried hard not to replace things *too* tidily, to maintain a lived-in impression. Danilov might not have realised the mistaken effort if he had not earlier been in the Serovs' sterile Leninskaya penthouse. It should have been the same here, despite Raisa's absence, because someone of Petr Aleksandrovich's neatness would not have allowed the indented seat cushions and dishevelled magazines and partially opened closet doors and drawers.

There were fewer personal or family photographs than he'd expected. There were four of Serov and Raisa by themselves in Russia or America and six of them with other people, four with the same elderly couple and two of Serov with a man. He overrode Firsov's protests against taking some away, packing them neatly in his briefcase.

'They're personal!' insisted the diplomat.

'So's being shot in the mouth.'

'I shall report this to Moscow!'

The only personal correspondence in the bureau was to Raisa Serova, always in the same wavering handwriting of an elderly mother bemoaning ill health. There were other complaints as well. Lawlessness had increased on the streets of Moscow since the collapse of communism. Economic reform and market economies had failed. Raisa was lucky to be out of it.

Bills were clipped together, as they had been in Serov's desk. There was a detailed accounts ledger, completed up to the day before Serov's death: in a pouch in the back, again clipped together and in numerical order, were statements from the Narodny bank. The joint account was ten thousand roubles in credit. Every listed transaction was doubly recorded in the accounts book, but here with a fuller explanation of income and expenditure. The income never varied, in any of the statements, neither did the source, in the audit book. Every deposit was listed as salary. Raisa was not shown to have any income.

To check the four particular dates without giving any indication to Firsov of his discovery in the embassy office, Danilov just rifled through the pages of the second diary initially, finding the confirmation he needed with the same double spelling on the same days. He felt an even greater jump of satisfaction than the previous day, knowing now the dates *were* significant.

Had he not been a diligent detective he might have discarded the diary at once, believing he'd learned all there was to find. But following the principle that crime was more often solved by dogged police work than by inspiration, he patiently went to the beginning of the year to read every entry, page by page. And was practically at once glad he did. There were far more frequent spelling variations here than in the office record, too many to copy and digest in front of an intrusive observer.

'I'll take this, too,' declared Danilov.

'A list should be kept of articles you're retaining.'

'It always is,' said Danilov patiently.

It took him until midday to complete his search. Afterwards, with Firsov close beside him, which he regretted, Danilov numbered the photographs on a duplicated list, one for himself and the other for the counsellor, and identified the diary by itemising its date.

'What do you intend telling Moscow?' demanded the man.

Danilov looked at him, surprised. 'There's nothing *to* tell.'

'So what are you going to do now?'

'Meet with the Americans.'

'Nikolai Fedorovich will accompany you,' announced Firsov.

Danilov felt the anger stir at the return of the patronising attitude. 'Nikolai Fedorovich Redin is not a member of the Militia.'

'He is officially accredited as a diplomat on the staff of the Russian embassy. It is essential you have a member of the embassy with you at all times.'

'You have such instructions from Moscow?'

Firsov's face began to colour. 'An instruction is not necessary.'

'I think it is.'

'Are you defying me?'

'I am personally answerable to the Foreign and Interior Ministries. As you have been officially advised. I don't need assistance, nor to be accompanied in my dealings with American investigators. Which I shall tell Moscow, if called upon to do so.' Danilov paused. Then, heavily, he said: 'I am a professional detective. How would you suggest we describe Nikolai Fedorovich to justify his part in an investigation?'

Firsov's colour deepened. 'You are insubordinate!'

'I am fulfilling the function I was sent here to perform and in which I will not be obstructed.' He'd probably gone too far, but it was too late to retreat now.

For several moments the two men remained staring at each other, Danilov expressionless, Firsov glowering. Impatient at the impasse, Danilov said: I need the names of everyone who knew Petr Aleksandrovich: someone must have known he was meeting Michel Paulac.'

'No-one did,' insisted the diplomat.

'You've already questioned people?'

'Upon the ambassador's instructions.'

'I would like to see your interview notes and your report to the Foreign Ministry.'

'I will seek authority from Moscow. And from the ambassador.'

'Why don't you do that!' said Danilov, exasperated.

There was a delay of two hours before Danilov telephoned Cowley, because he had a lot to do in the seclusion of his own quarters at Massachusetts Avenue. 'Where shall we meet?' he asked the American.

'Any objection to your coming here?'

'Suits me,' said Danilov. He guessed it would suit a lot of other people. Conscious of the open switchboard, he wondered how long it would take to report back to Moscow that he was about to enter the headquarters of America's Federal Bureau of Investigation.

CHAPTER NINETEEN

Cowley personally signed him through the admission procedure at the FBI building. Clipping the identity badge to his lapel, Danilov was aware of being an object of curiosity. He presumed, unconcerned, a record would be made of his presence, probably on film.

As they made their way through the restricted and monitored floors to the executive level, Danilov compared the gulf-like difference between the carpeted and comfortably upholstered modernity of FBI headquarters with the concrete-floored, plastic-buckled Petrovka block, space age against stone age. It was difficult to conceive it had actually been Russia which started the space era. Danilov continued his accommodation contrast inside Cowley's room, estimating his own office would have fitted inside it at least three times, with more space than they occupied already left over for Ludmilla Radsic and Yuri Pavin.

For several moments after sitting down, the two men remained looking at each other, smiling but not speaking, a reunion finally achieved. Then Cowley conceded: 'If the break's going to come, it'll have to be from your side. We're nowhere.'

'It isn't going to be easy,' warned Danilov. It had taken them much longer to get to this degree of openness before: he hoped it was an omen. Who'd be the first to renege? He might have to and accepted, realistically, that it might be forced upon Cowley as well. He hoped the testing time didn't last too long.

'We've been officially assured, Foreign Ministry to State Department, that your people didn't know what Serov was doing?' opened Cowley. How long would it take to gauge what Danilov could and could not do? It wouldn't be easy for the Russian: Serov had obviously had his hand deep in someone's cookie jar, so Danilov would have had the restrictions very firmly imposed.

'I was told the same.'

'True or false?' There was, of course, no hangover from the previous night but Cowley wished there hadn't been the sour taste in his mouth. He thought Danilov looked very good, although the hair was definitely thinner: he avoided an obvious examination, knowing the Russian's sensitivity.

Cowley was exploring, Danilov realised, unoffended: he'd done the same himself in Moscow, when the embarrassment was tilted more to America's disadvantage, and was doing it again now. 'Someone, somewhere, must know what was going on. Raisa Serova insists she did not know Michel Paulac, or of her husband's association with him. What is there from Switzerland?' If he was right about what he'd found in the diaries, Cowley was already holding back.

The American slid a folder across his desk towards Danilov. 'Your copy of all we know, so far,' he said. 'Paulac was a bachelor, thirty-eight, headed an investment group which, according to the Swiss, is highly successful. So he lived well. Rolls Royce as well as a Mercedes, apartment close to the lake. They've interviewed the two other majority partners in the firm. Both say they knew nothing about any association with Petr Serov and that there are no company records linking Paulac with Serov. That's possible, apparently: although they're partners they worked independently, each running their own portfolios.'

'What was found on Paulac's body?' One thing in particular that *had* to be there, Danilov thought.

'Keys, credit cards, $400 in cash, American, $300 in Swiss francs. There was a pocket diary with no entry referring to any meeting with Serov the day they both died. It's blank. So are the preceding days that we know, from the airline booking and the car rental, he was in this country.' He wondered if Danilov would pick up on what was missed out.

'That all?'

'A briefcase, inside the car. There were some company papers, pro-forma advertising stuff setting out the tax benefits of investing in Switzerland. There was a business address book but no listing for Serov. No note of any American number, in fact. A personal cheque book, three cheques missing, counterfoils showing total withdrawals of $2,500 but all the transactions were in Switzerland, before he arrived here. He rented the car on an American Express card. From the Amex records we know he stayed at the Mayflower Hotel: the date of his arrival tallies with the day he booked in. We've shown photographs of Serov to all the staff. No-one can remember him ever coming to the hotel. There were two other credit card counterfoils, for restaurants. Again, a blank on any connection with Serov. One was a Chinese restaurant downtown, near the old Post Office: a waiter insists Paulac ate alone.'

Danilov sat silently for several moments. 'You haven't mentioned the passport,' he challenged.

'It was found,' Cowley confirmed.

'How many times had Paulac been here?'

'So you found something at the embassy?' smiled Cowley, challenging in return.

Danilov didn't smile back. 'Why were you keeping it back?'

Cowley did not answer directly. 'We checked out every restaurant against which there was a credit card slip. There wasn't one single identification of Paulac with Serov. Only this last time. Paulac *always* stayed at the Mayflower, Serov never showed there.'

'So you didn't consider it significant?'

Cowley, discomfited, said: 'What sort of limitations have your people put upon you?'

'I'd guess about the same you worked under in Moscow. I intend operating properly, as best I can. And if I don't think I can, I'll tell you. I'm sorry you don't feel like doing the same.' He had little room for genuine anger, Danilov accepted.

'There was no sighting of him with Serov on the previous occasions!' repeated Cowley. He guessed he was visibly flushing. He nodded to the file still unopened in front of Danilov. 'The other entry dates are set out there. You'd have seen them when you read it!'

'I only had the one visit with which to confront Raisa Serova in Moscow. It could have been useful to have them all.'

It was a valid point, conceded Cowley. But he hadn't recognised how it might have helped the Russian. Which was an absurd oversight. Worrying, too. 'My mistake,' he admitted.

'There was no sensible reason!'

'I'm sorry.'

Danilov supposed he could send Pavin to see the woman again, but guessed she would swamp the man with her arrogance. He took the paper from his pocket, dictating the four other dates in the earlier months on which the misspelled words appeared in Serov's diary both in the office and the man's home.

'Paulac was here on every occasion,' confirmed Cowley, checking them off against his own copy of the dossier. He was still burning with embarrassment at Danilov's rebuke. It had been stupid, doing what he'd done: or been made to appear stupid, the way Danilov had caught him out. Worse, it *had* meant the man going ill-prepared into the interview with the wife.

He'd won the exchange, Danilov decided: there was nothing to be achieved maintaining an offended attitude. 'Serov never mentioned Paulac by name,' Danilov disclosed. 'He used a simple but quite effective code. On each day he also records attending an event in a public place – the Smithsonian, that sort of thing – where anyone could go.'

'You think he might have met Paulac at those places?'

'I think it's worth taking the photographs to the organisers and staff to check.'

'So do I,' agreed Cowley. 'What was the code?'

'Misspelling an English word with a Cyrillic letter.'

'That the only time he used it?'

Danilov hesitated. Practically all of the two-hour delay in coming to Pennsylvania Avenue had been spent trying to understand the purpose or function of the other misspelled words in the apartment diary, which was resting now in the inside pocket of his jacket. And which he had failed to do. Just as he failed to understand the purpose of the same code which Serov appeared to have used over the preceding years in a lot of the papers and files – although never the official embassy diary – in the shelved bottom cabinet of the office bookcase, which Danilov had specifically checked before leaving the embassy for the FBI building. A computer was a million times faster than the human brain, he thought. 'There were a lot of other occasions. But I don't think it connects with Michel Paulac.'

'Why not?'

'The duplication isn't in the office diary, which the Paulac meetings are. The letters appear in the diary he kept at Massachusetts Avenue, and link with the logs and archives of what he did over the most recent years he was here: he was a fanatical keeper of records. And in this case the letters aren't duplications, either.'

'I don't understand,' frowned Cowley.

'It's just a collection of separate letters. Could your scientific people programme a computer to play Cyrillic crossword puzzles? But without the clues to guide them?'

'I think they've been doing it for years,' smiled Cowley, glad that Danilov smiled back.

Danilov finally opened his dossier and held up the much enlarged photograph taken from the financier's passport. 'This Paulac?'

'Yes,' nodded Cowley.

'I've collected some photographs from the apartment, of Serov with another man. This isn't him.'

'We're not going to get that lucky!' said Cowley.

Danilov continued looking through the file. After a few moments he looked up and said: 'The briefcase was inside the car, not the boot?'

'Yes.'

'Locked or unlocked?'

Cowley smiled again, acknowledging the professionalism. 'Open. It's a combination lock that gave our forensic people a hell of a job: the two sets of numerals are separately programmed but only mesh when they're operated in unison.'

Danilov nodded, as if he were receiving confirmation of something. 'A Swiss financier whose entire professional life is governed by secrecy doesn't leave open in a car a briefcase he's taken the trouble to have fitted with an especially difficult lock.'

'I know,' agreed Cowley. 'I'd give a lot to know what was taken out.'

'Any indication Paulac was forced to give up the combination?'

Cowley gestured to the file in Danilov's lap. 'Look at the photographs! How could you tell, from that!'

Cowley saved Danilov the chore of copying the American dossier by offering a second set, which gave the Russian one for the Interior Ministry and one for Pavin. They agreed there was little purpose in setting the computer task for the Bureau's cryptology division with an incomplete selection of letters; Danilov thought he could get them all from Serov's folders the following morning. He gratefully accepted Cowley's invitation to dinner that night with the two local homicide detectives, and put Firsov and Redin out of their misery by announcing the outing as soon as he returned to the embassy on 16th Street.

Accepting he had to comply to some degree with Moscow's instructions, Danilov offered a briefing on his visit to the FBI. Firsov and Pavlenko blanched at the photographs of the decomposed body of Michel Paulac; Redin remained unmoved. Intent upon any give-away reaction from any of the three, Danilov disclosed it was probable the financier and Serov had met on other occasions, without mentioning the connection between the marked diary dates and the entry stamps on Paulac's passport. None of them showed any apprehension at the enquiry deepening the involvement of the embassy. Danilov then took Pavlenko through the earlier dates: the cultural official pedantically compared his own diary to the office version before insisting he'd known nothing of Serov's movements. Danilov thought he could spot a liar under questioning and decided Pavlenko was telling the truth.

'I will send this to Moscow tonight,' announced Danilov, with the file in his hand. He spoke looking at the security officer.

'Yes?' said Redin, curiously.

'I'd like to see the report you made to the Interior Ministry, after you examined Petr Aleksandrovich's office.'

Redin blinked. 'I'm not sure of your right to do that.'

'Then I'll ask for a ruling from Moscow,' declared Danilov briskly. Trying to guard against any alteration or editing, he said: 'My assistant can collect it from the Ministry, if there's any problem in your finding the original.'

'We'll wait for Moscow's ruling,' refused Redin, stubbornly.

Danilov recognised the name and the location of the cafe from his re-reading of the file, and was curious whose idea it had been to eat at the same place as Serov and the financier the night they'd been murdered. They weren't at the section served by Mary Ann Bell but Rafferty called over the girl who had made the positive connection between the two dead men and introduced her. Mary Ann, shy and still plump with adolescence, said she recognised Cowley and Danilov from the media coverage, and despite her awkwardness Danilov knew she enjoyed the moment in front of everyone else with whom she worked. He thought Rafferty was enjoying some fame by association, too, which surprised him. Both DC detectives were cautious at the beginning, listening and watching more than talking, making their judgments. What they did say was usually cynically hard-edged. Danilov wasn't uncomfortable under their examination. Were Rafferty and Johannsen on the take from someone, like most of the detectives at Petrovka? It would be interesting to see if a proper bill were offered and settled at the end of the evening. He wasn't sure how to offer his contribution – or if he were expected to. Cowley adopted the role of host, distributing menus and ordering drinks. Danilov noted Cowley only drank club soda and refused wine when it was passed around, and decided he'd made a mistake about smelling alcohol on the man's breath when he'd arrived at Dulles.

As they ate, Cowley told the two detectives they might have a lead to other times Paulac and Serov met, making it clear the information came from Danilov's enquiries at the embassy.

'Your people co-operating, towards one of their own?' demanded Johannsen.

'Not really.' Danilov welcomed the conversation. He didn't think he would have any difficulty being honest with the two detectives and wanted it to register with Cowley after the earlier disagreement.

'You know what I think?' said Rafferty. 'I think your guy was dirty.'

Danilov frowned at the expression, not understanding.

'Crooked,' helped Cowley.

'Probably,' accepted Danilov.

The easy admission surprised the detectives. Rafferty said: 'So what are we going to do if we prove he is?'

Now Danilov appeared surprised. 'I'm not sure of the technicalities of your system, but what I'd do is submit the evidence to the prosecutor. What would you do?'

'That's not what I meant,' said Rafferty. 'I'm talking cover-up.'

'I investigate. I don't cover up,' insisted Danilov. He'd had to go along with a compromise over the serial murders, after the FBI man had been found mentally incapable of standing trial. But that had not been his decision or even his wish. It had been political, Russia agreeing to American pressure to avoid the embarrassment of a law enforcement officer revealed as a multiple killer. Just as any compromise this time would be political, not of his making.

'What you're saying is, you're going to level with us on this?' pressed Johannsen.

'That's exactly what I'm saying.' Danilov addressed the reply to Cowley.

Cowley smiled, returning the look, understanding the Russian's performance. 'Dimitri and I have already decided the ground rules.'

The two murders were the only subject of conversation, which was what Danilov wanted anyway. He didn't learn anything he'd missed or had been omitted from the American file, but it fleshed out what he did know, giving him a perspective against which to set his own eventual judgment. He wasn't sure how long that would be: a long

118

time, judging from the progress so far. Rafferty and Johannsen relaxed as the evening and the drinking went on. Danilov, did, too, although he stopped drinking, still vaguely bothered by jetlag.

When her shift ended, Mary Ann Bell came over to say goodbye and that it had been nice meeting them, and when Rafferty, slightly befuddled, proposed a toast to their success Cowley finally allowed himself a glass of wine. Because they were so close to where Petr Serov's body had been found, it was agreed they'd detour that way running Danilov back to Massachusetts Avenue, for the Russian to get the location and the surroundings fixed in his mind.

But they never did.

Danilov was leading when they stepped out on to M Street, because the other three politely stood back for him, which was unfortunate because Cowley was following immediately behind so the waiting photographers caught both of them, side by side, in the doorway of the restaurant linked to both victims.

Behind them Rafferty said: 'Holy shit!' and barged past, ineffectually waving his arms – which he shouldn't have done, because the photographed protest was construed as trying to hide something important about the murders which had not so far been released. There were at least three reporters, as well as photographers, shouting questions that weren't answered and impeding their progress to Cowley's car, which they had left in a parking lot where vehicles are manoeuvred up and down on hydraulically elevated frames. All they could do was stand and wait, despite Rafferty and Johannsen's shouts to the attendant to move his ass, so by the time they got into the car the cameramen had enough photographs to stage an exhibition. Cowley and Danilov's refusal to respond to any questions practically became a farce.

There was no dissent when Cowley announced they'd miss the murder scene, because the photographers would follow them.

'Sorry about that,' apologised Cowley generally, turning on to Wisconsin Avenue.

'Who the fuck told them!' exploded Rafferty.

'The cafe, I guess,' said Johannsen. 'Maybe Mary Ann.'

'It's not really important, is it?' said Danilov. It didn't contravene his instructions against making any unauthorised statement.

'You haven't seen what our media can do with two cents' worth of fuck all!' said Rafferty.

They parted outside the Russian compound, Danilov agreeing to see Cowley at Pennsylvania Avenue the following day. On their return downtown, Johannsen said: 'Seemed quite a nice guy, for a Lieutenant General.'

'And a Russian,' completed Rafferty.

Back in the embassy compound, Danilov was unsure if it really had been someone from the cafe who had set up the media ambush. Rafferty had been very quick to hurry forward when the flash-bulbs exploded: almost as if he had expected it to happen.

CHAPTER TWENTY

Yevgennie Kosov agreed it was a pity Larissa couldn't alter her shifts but they were short-staffed at the Druzhba: it meant, of course, they'd have to eat out. Olga said she hoped Larissa wouldn't mind and Kosov wondered why she should. Olga said no reason at all. It was flirtatious and fun but not awkward: two old friends playing social games.

He refused to say where they were going but warned it would be dressy, which worried her because it was inevitable he would compare her to Larissa, who always looked like a model who'd stepped from the pages of a Western magazine. Olga laid out what she considered her better outfits and mixed and matched for the best effect. Everything looked faded and old and out of date: during one free-fall dip of despair she almost rang Kosov back to cancel. In the end she chose her black dress with the matching bolero, which was also her newest, and was extremely careful to iron it without making the material shine. She booked for her hair to be tinted but when she got to the hairdresser they'd run out of the deep auburn they'd used before and there was no way of telling when they might get any more. She accepted dark titian, which took unevenly, and didn't believe the girl's assurance that it looked like variable highlights.

Kosov was precisely on time. He was totally sober, immaculate in a blue suit that had a sheen, like silk, and presented her with another box of Belgian chocolates. Overlooking the fact that such luxuries had not been available in Moscow until very recently – and could still only be found if a person had contacts or knew the right free enterprise shops – it reminded Olga that Dimitri had never bought her special gifts like this, not even when they had been walking out. She hoped he'd remember to bring back from America all the things she'd asked for.

Kosov chastely kissed her, surveyed her at arm's length,

and declared she looked wonderful: Olga allowed herself to believe it. There was still some vodka from the Kosovs' previous visit but he refused it, saying they had a lot to do.

The car dumbfounded Olga. In the darkness she didn't recognise its shape as one she'd ever seen on the streets of Moscow before. The door clicked shut behind her, as if it were closing itself, and she couldn't hear the sound of the engine. The dashboard was a technicolour of different lights and dials, and there was a smell of polished newness.

'This isn't an official police car!'

Kosov laughed. 'It's German. A BMW. A new model.' He touched a dial and music filled the vehicle, from several speakers.

It was a Western tape, a romantic song: Olga didn't recognise the female singer. 'You *own* it?'

'Brought it in last week. Like it?'

'It's fantastic!' The soft warmth of the heater enclosed her.

'At least you've got the Volga now. When Dimitri's home, that is.'

Olga understood. 'Larissa can drive this car?'

'Of course.'

Kosov drove towards the centre of Moscow until the ring road, which he joined but then quickly left to sweep up towards the renamed Tverskaya Street.

'A hotel?' she guessed.

'Which one?'

Because of where they were she said: 'Intourist.'

'That whorehouse!' said Kosov disdainfully, unaware of Olga's visible wince at her mistake. 'We're going to a proper place.'

She thought she knew when Kosov went around the square to drive past the Bolshoi, but didn't suggest it to avoid being wrong again.

'The Metropole!' he announced. He hurried around to open the door for her and took her arm to guide her inside, halting curiously when she hesitated. 'What?'

'You haven't taken the wipers off.'

For the second time that evening, Kosov laughed in genuine amusement. 'That's *my* car. And it's known.

122

Already. Professional thieves know better, and Militia patrols protect it from amateurs. *Nobody* touches my car!'

Olga had never been inside the Metropole, not even before its refurbishment, nor been enclosed in so much unrestrained luxury. There were chandeliers everywhere, each with a million diamond-bright droplets scattering light in all directions: white and grey and black marble patterned the floors and walls: huge velvet drapes, curtains more enormous than she had imagined curtains could possibly be, covered windows and partitions; the carpets and floor coverings were grander and more extensive than the drapes, stretching away from her in every direction, like inviting fields to be walked through.

Kosov broke into Olga's daydreaming vision. 'Which bar do you prefer?'

Olga blinked. 'You choose.'

He took her arm solicitously again, guiding her towards the one off the central vestibule. It was a vault of a room, with more glittering chandeliers and with the upholstery of the chairs and banquettes toned to the carpeting. Kosov was recognised at once – Olga only just detected the identifying green of the dollar note exchanged during the effusive greeting handshake – and they were offered the choice of several banquettes. Kosov chose the most secluded, furthest from the main entrance.

The champagne, in its frosted ice bucket, arrived unordered. The glasses were crystal. 'French,' pointed out Kosov unnecessarily, as the bottle was poured. He touched her glass with his and wished her good health, and she said the same back. She felt light-headed before she drank anything.

'What's Dimitri Ivanovich think of it here?'

Olga hoped she was not blushing too much. 'I haven't been here before. He hasn't either.'

'What?' Kosov sounded disbelieving.

'He's been very busy,' she tried desperately. Using the only defence she had, Olga added: 'And now he's in America, of course.'

'Larissa and I come here quite a lot. We should do it together when Dimitri Ivanovich gets back.'

'That would be nice.'

'Have you heard from him?'

'I haven't expected to, not this soon.'

'How's the investigation going?'

'He doesn't talk about work.'

'He must say something!' Kosov topped up the glasses.

'Not a lot.'

'This assignment must be very important for his career.'

'I suppose it must be.'

'I would have expected him to say something.'

'He hasn't.' Olga thought all the women around her looked like models, as Larissa always did, and was glad the subdued lighting concealed the Russian cut of her dress and the colour differences in her hair. Most of the women glittered, she guessed from diamonds in their jewellery. Everyone seemed confident, sure of their surroundings and themselves. Once the jacket of a man at an adjoining table gaped, exposing what she thought was the butt of a handgun: it excited her, whether it had been a real gun or not.

'I really was very surprised he didn't get the Directorship.'

'He thought he would,' disclosed Olga.

Kosov made a show of pouring more wine, and looked expansively and obviously around the plush room. 'Ever regret Dimitri coming out of uniform? He seems to have changed a lot since becoming an investigator.'

'Things *were* different,' conceded Olga nostalgically. The Kosovs were their oldest friends, so she supposed it was obvious to them Dimitri didn't accept favours any more: all they had to do was spend thirty minutes in Kirovskaya, or compare the clothes they wore.

'You sorry about that?' persisted the man.

'Of course I am!' There was no reason to conceal the bitterness from a friend. She thought, nostalgic still, that perhaps their marriage would not have become the sham it was if Dimitri had stayed in uniform: but perhaps more importantly, had stayed on a payroll other than that of the State. 'Wouldn't you be? Wouldn't Larissa?'

'No doubt about it,' agreed Kosov sympathetically. 'I'll never understand why he changed. It was Dimitri who introduced me, in the beginning . . .' He looked conspiratorially around the adjoining booths, coming closer. 'It was one of them who got the BMW for me.'

'I don't understand it either.'

'Haven't you talked to him about it?'

'I've tried. He just says he feels better this way.'

Kosov covered her hand with his. 'You don't mind me talking like this?'

'No.' She didn't object to the hand-holding, either. The cologne he wore smelled pleasant; expensive.

'I just wish there was something I could do. Help, I mean.'

'So do I.'

He withdrew his hand, smiling broadly. 'At least you can enjoy tonight.'

They ate in the hotel. There was more instant recognition in the restaurant and another exchanging handshake. She thought several men in suits that shone, their tables well stocked with champagne bottles and Western cigarette packs, gave signs of recognising Kosov. Olga took Kosov's recommendation and had beef, which was imported and excellent, and agreed the French Volnay was far better than Georgian wine. He was a good dinner companion, constantly making her laugh with stories of police enquiries that had gone wrong and anecdotes she hadn't heard about government leaders and politicians.

Over French brandy he said: 'Have you heard of Nightflight?'

Olga stared back at him without comprehension.

Kosov gestured generally beyond the hotel. 'It's the newest nightclub in town: on Tverskaya, just before Pushkin Square.'

Olga, growing heavy-eyed from the wine, had imagined he would take her home at the end of the meal, but she was determined not to miss anything, believing she had missed too much already. 'I'd like to go there.'

The BMW was untouched, as Kosov had predicted, and the nightclub so close they could have walked: Olga wished they had, to clear her head.

She had only seen clubs like Nightflight in the Western

movies of which she was a devotee. The gloom, which again hid her faded dress and hair colouring, was pierced by strobe lights twisting and bouncing off revolving, many-faceted orbs suspended from ceilings, making her blink. There was a reflective, glass-backed bar, far to her left. In front, to music that throbbed like a heart-beat, a dance floor heaved with gyrating people. Olga felt a sharp twist of panic at the idea of Kosov asking her to dance, which she couldn't, but instead he guided her upstairs to a gallery, where it was quieter and where people sat clustered around tables. The lighting was stronger here, but still not enough to worry her.

They went along the balconied area towards a large, already occupied table: when they reached it Olga realised, surprised, that they appeared to be expected. The four men already there rose at their approach with unusual politeness, each reaching out to shake her hand and introduce her in turn to their female companions. All the girls were younger than Olga, but they were unreservedly friendly and she did not feel ill at ease, although their clothes and jewellery were far better than hers.

The first time she didn't properly get any of the names: which weren't complete anyway, just given names, sometimes not even the patronymic. As she was absorbed into the group, she picked up from conversations swirling around her that the most friendly brunette, to her immediate right, was Lena and the smiling woman opposite was called Ivietta. The man directly across from her, a fat, easily-laughing man who wore the same cologne as Kosov, was definitely Maksim. She was sure, too, the other man on the opposite side of the table was Mikhail.

There was champagne again, although Olga only took a token glass and scarcely touched it, because it was tasting sharply acidic. Maksim danced with Lena and another girl whose name Olga never identified and briefly, again, Olga feared he was going to ask her as well, but he didn't. An extremely thin man named Arkadi, who from his appearance was the oldest in the party and to whom everyone was very respectful, told her he didn't dance either but enjoyed seeing other people do it, and Olga said she was the same.

Kosov was everyone's friend and everywhere showing himself to be so. He moved from chair to chair around their own table and kissed all the girls – always in a companiable way, never lasciviously – and several times went to other tables nearby, where he was received with equal friendliness. Arkadi saw Olga watching Kosov's tour and remarked that Kosov was a good man, and Olga said she thought so, too; she waited for him – for anyone – to ask about Larissa, but no-one did. There appeared to be no curiosity about her relationship with Kosov and she was glad: there was nothing to explain, so she did not want to bother.

It was Kosov who returned with the club photographer, talking loudly of souvenirs. There were token protests from the women, Olga among them, that they weren't prepared, but eventually the pictures were taken, the men assembling around the seated females, the poses struck. Much later food was ordered – the best Beluga caviare, smoked and dried fish and hot meat, boar and venison – but Olga could not eat anything, after the dinner at the Metropole.

She was astonished, when Kosov finally suggested they leave, to realise it was three o'clock in the morning. There were handshakes and farewell kisses from the men as well as the women; everyone said they hoped to meet her again. Outside, the BMW remained untouched.

'You have a lot of friends. They were very nice to me.' Olga had known, obviously, the Metropole existed but had never imagined it being like it was. And Nightflight had been beyond *any* imagination. She knew no-one would believe her at work the following morning. *This* morning, she qualified. Maybe she wouldn't say anything. At once she knew she would: she wanted people to know. To be impressed.

'They're the sort of friends Dimitri Ivanovich should have,' said the man.

Olga had guessed what they were, but the confirmation still brought a flicker of surprise: excitement, too. 'It's not me you have to tell.'

'He's a fool.'

The criticism didn't offend Olga but it unsettled her: she still did not understand why Kosov had covered her hand as he had in the hotel. She said: 'I really think I should call Larissa tomorrow.'

'You worried I'm going to make a pass at you?' he challenged directly.

'Of course not!' Olga said, wishing the denial had sounded stronger.

He didn't speak for several moments. 'It wouldn't be right. Not considering our friendship.'

Olga did not know what to say: the warmth from the heater was making her feel very tired.

'I wouldn't have been surprised if one of the others had tonight,' continued Kosov. 'You're a very attractive woman, Olga. Beautiful.'

'You're embarrassing me!' she protested weakly.

'You think Dimitri Ivanovich would object to our going out?' demanded Kosov, as if the idea had suddenly occurred to him.

'Of course not.'

'He might not like your being with my friends.'

'Maybe not.'

'I don't think he's treating you like he should, Olga. I think he's being selfish.'

At Kirovskaya Kosov helped her from the car, escorted her to the door of the apartment and kissed her on the cheek as lightly as the other men in the nightclub had.

It took him thirty minutes to cross Moscow again, to get to his own apartment off the inner ring road. Larissa, who had not been working at the Druzhba that night, stirred but didn't properly wake as he entered the bedroom. He waited to see if she would say anything but she didn't, so he didn't speak either. They slept in separate beds so he did not disturb her when he settled down.

'She seemed a remarkably simple woman,' said Arkadi Gusovsky. 'Stupid, even.'

'For which we should be grateful,' suggested Maksim Zimin.

'Honest investigators should choose women with common sense.'

'Perhaps she's got qualities we didn't realise,' giggled Zimin.

'A woman that dull wouldn't be any good in bed,' judged Gusovsky.

CHAPTER TWENTY-ONE

Lingering jetlag woke Danilov early, so he was one of the first arrivals at 16th Street, in the cultural section ahead of Valery Pavlenko. Danilov emptied the bottom of the bookcase in the order in which it had been stored, but worked backwards from the most recent folders to the earliest. Knowing now what he was looking for, he was able to do the job quickly, scanning the words for the wrong letters without reading the context: he'd gone back through all that year and ten months into the preceding one before Pavlenko came through the door. Predictably, Redin was behind.

The desk was strewn with papers and files and documents, making it impossible for them to understand what he was doing: he said cursorily he was continuing the examination of Serov's office, deflecting them by demanding if the security man had been told by Moscow to make his earlier report available. From the expression on Redin's face, Danilov knew the man had and didn't like it. When Redin nodded, curtly, Danilov said he'd collect it that afternoon, when he re-interviewed everyone Firsov had already questioned. He told them both he still didn't need any help, pointedly waiting until they retreated from the room.

It was another hour before Danilov completed the search, but longer before he accepted it had ended. He reached the beginning of 1991 before acknowledging there had been no misspelled words over several months. He relocated the last entry, just past the middle of the year, and read more carefully through to January to confirm he had missed nothing.

He had numbered the odd letters as he isolated them: the count came to sixty-three. As he had the previous day, with the diary notes, Danilov tried to fit the characters into patterns or groups, switching back and forth from Cyrillic to

Roman spelling, but they remained meaningless. On impulse he juggled further in a series of numbered sequences calculated from the dates and months and years of the entries in the Western calendar in which they appeared, against how they would have appeared in the Russian Gregorian chronology. They still didn't make sense, and Danilov conceded a computer was the only practical way to understand what they represented. It would have been good to have worked it out by himself.

Cowley once more escorted Danilov through the admission procedure. In his office the American made a token study of the letters, shook his head in defeat and said the cryptology division were programming a computer in readiness: there was no reason for Danilov to know that despite all the changes and relaxations, of which their working together was a visibly prime example, the Bureau division monitoring Russian nationals temporarily residing in the United States maintained a bank of permanently adjusted machines operated by Russian-speaking specialists. Cowley knew, from CIA liaison, the Russian security service worked the same system in Lubyanka Square.

Danilov pointed out the abrupt stopping of the entries in the middle of 1991, and was annoyed not to have thought of it himself when Cowley remarked the first extension of Serov's posting dated from that year.

Cowley said the two DC detectives were checking the guest lists of events in Serov's diary which coincided with the financier's earlier visits to Washington. And then, saving the best until last, added: 'Something intriguing's come from Switzerland. Seems Paulac hasn't long been the family name. It was legally taken by his grandparents, after they fled the Ukraine in 1918. Before that it was Panzhevsky . . .' Cowley smiled at the look on Danilov's face. 'And according to his housekeeper, Michel Paulac was a fluent Russian and Ukrainian speaker: Russian books all over the flat. She also thinks he's entertained Russians there in the past. But his partners again say they don't know about it . . .' He paused once more. 'We checked the passport, obviously, for entry visas into Russia. There aren't any.'

Danilov seized the opportunity to recover from his oversight about the 1991 date. 'Russian visas aren't stamped *into* the passports of foreigners. It's a separate arrival and departure document taken out when the holder leaves.'

'So if he did visit, it could be traced in your Moscow immigration files?'

Danilov looked wistfully at the list of unintelligible letters on Cowley's desk. 'Which may not be on computer.' In the old days the KGB and Intourist, which they controlled, had maintained detailed and easily retrievable records of all foreign visitors. He'd never imagined mourning the former Communist control. But then, he'd never imagined working in America with an FBI agent as a partner.

'Somebody will have a lot of paper to go through?'

'Yuri Mikhailovich is working with me,' said Danilov. Pavin had been their scene-of-crime officer last year.

'It could be the opening,' urged Cowley. 'There'd *have* to be a link between anyone Paulac met in Moscow with his meeting Petr Serov, here.'

'There'd be a sponsor's name, on his visa,' agreed Danilov.

'Tell Pavin I'm sorry,' commiserated the American.

Danilov took over Serov's former office to write the Moscow report on Paulac's ancestry and set out the immigration chore for Pavin to attempt. He also asked the major to try to identify the unknown man pictured with Serov in two of the photographs he'd taken from Massachusetts Avenue and shipped back overnight. He said nothing in any message of the disparate letter collection which at the moment he couldn't explain.

Oleg Firsov produced the list of embassy personnel already interviewed. Redin's report gave a detailed account of the mortuary meeting with the Americans and of the near confrontation that had followed, but openly admitted he had discovered nothing from his search of the office or the Serov apartment.

Firsov's dispatch to the Foreign Ministry was as empty as that of the security chief, and Danilov realised why when he repeated the interviews. The denials of any awareness of

Serov's involvement with the Swiss financier were practically recited, like the insistence Serov had been a wonderful diplomat with a wonderful wife doing a wonderful job whose murder was inexplicable.

He was behind the desk in Serov's office, everything completed and not able to think of anything else to do, when the telephone jarred into the rooms, startling him.

'We've got it!' declared Cowley triumphantly. '*You* got it!'

'What?'

Cowley avoided the direct answer. 'I could manage a drink in the roof bar of the Washington Hotel. Fifteen minutes.'

Danilov made it in twelve: the FBI man was already there. 'Names,' Cowley announced. 'All Russian. Seven in total. Four are in our computers, for listed convictions or suspicion of involvement in serious crimes. One, Viktor Chebrakin, got a murder rap reduced to manslaughter in 1984: he was released two years ago. Another, Yuri Chestnoy, is suspected of two killings but the file is marked insufficient evidence. Each of the seven, according to State Department records, emigrated from the Soviet Union in the Eighties.'

'Where do we go from here?'

'The Russian ghetto,' replied Cowley, answering literally. 'I've already alerted the local force and our New York office. We'll go up on the shuttle tomorrow morning.'

'So Serov was a *d'ehdooshkah*,' said Danilov.

'It's Godfather, not Grandfather,' the Russian-speaking American corrected.

'Serov *was* dirty, wasn't he?' said Danilov, enjoying his new expression.

'Dirtier than a pig in shit,' agreed Cowley.

The dacha was in the wooded Lenin Hills, off the Medvedkovo road, and had been the weekend retreat of a senior Party secretary before Gusovsky took it over. The KGB had installed the alarms and protective fencing, which Gusovsky had disdained as totally inadequate: now the country house was completely enclosed by a high, electrified wall, with sensors seeded in the grounds, which men constantly patrolled with Doberman dogs.

It was an elaborate party, as Gusovsky's gatherings always were. Marquee-covered tables were bowed under goose and snipe and partridge and hazel-grouse, and there were other displays of beef and pork and chicken. There was a separate bar tent stocked with every sort of liquor and wine and a range of cigarettes and cigars, and waiters were in constant circulation. Many of the specially supplied girls were swimming naked in the pool or playing softball. There were a lot of men but no wives: some of the men were also naked in the pool. Some couples had already paired off.

Gusovsky and Yerin sat apart, side by side on the encircling verandah of the dacha, equal on identical chairs. Gusovsky counted aloud: 'Four ministries, two at Deputy level. Three judges, and senior officers from every Militia district.'

Yerin laughed. 'Fairly average turn-out, for midweek.'

Gusovsky waved at Kosov's approach. Encouraged, the man climbed on to the verandah. 'Great party. The girls are wonderful!'

'Take your pick,' invited Yerin.

'I will.'

'We need to have Danilov,' declared Gusovsky.

'I understand,' said Kosov.

'We want you to get him for us.'

'I can do it,' undertook Kosov, too eagerly. Danilov had been on a payroll before: he was sure, after the conversation with Olga, that all it needed was the right persuasion. He decided against telling the other two men why he was so confident.

'You sure?' pressed Yerin.

'Positive.'

Gusovsky nodded to the pool and the shrieking girls. 'Try the one with hair almost to her waist: she's very good.'

'Do you really think he can get Danilov?' asked Yerin, as Kosov hurried off towards the pool.

'We'll give him the chance: they know each other.'

'I'm really not sure about Zimin being the one to go to Italy,' said Yerin.

'It's always been the idea: he's got the language,' reminded

Gusovsky. Excluding Zimin from the party, at Yerin's urging, was the greatest concession Gusovsky had made so far to the blind man's antipathy to the third man who ruled the Chechen.

'He's weak,' insisted Yerin. 'We can't risk a weak man.' Their intention was to make the Chechen the strongest and most powerful Family in Russia: they were confident the link they were about to forge in Italy would achieve it.

'It would be difficult for you to go,' said the thin man. 'And for me.' As if on cue, Gusovsky began to cough; he stubbed out his half-finished cigar.

'I suppose there's no alternative,' Yerin capitulated. He was silent for several moments. 'Zimin thinks we should give the Ostankino a definite message. He's sure it was their people who intercepted our airport shipment. He knows the man who organised it, Ivan Ignatov.'

'If he's the man who did it, let's kill him,' decided Gusovsky, easily.

Danilov returned immediately to the embassy after his meeting with Cowley, apprehensively aware that the names of at least four recorded criminals, one a convicted killer, in Serov's possession created precisely the sort of problem the Deputy Foreign Minister had specified at the departure briefing.

He warned the Foreign Ministry the Americans knew Serov had the names and that the following day he would travel with the FBI to the last known address of one of the listed Russians. He attached to the Ministry cable his orders to Pavin, to go through all available Moscow records for the three names not in the American crime computer.

Danilov left a copy of everything for Oleg Firsov's arrival in the morning, stretching back in the chair at Serov's desk which he had commandeered as his own workplace. He wished it were possible to talk personally to Pavin, but given the time difference between Washington and Moscow, Danilov knew the major would not be at Petrovka. He looked at his watch, to calculate the exact difference, but it had stopped at seven o'clock. He supposed Olga would be at

Kirovskaya: then again, she might not. She spent a lot of evenings at the cinema with work-friends; sometimes it seemed that was all she ever did. He decided not to bother telephoning: he could not think of anything for them to talk about. There hadn't been anything for them to talk about for a long time.

Olga was at the apartment, at that moment looking down at the photograph in Izvestia of her husband emerging from the Georgetown cafe. She thought he looked frightened and bewildered, like an animal caught in the glare of a hunter's light. He'd been out enjoying himself. So she had no cause for unease at having gone out with Yevgennie Kosov. She hoped Yevgennie would call again, as he had promised. And that they'd go this time with Larissa, of course. She decided to pick out some clothes, just in case.

CHAPTER TWENTY-TWO

Cowley had delayed going to New York until the next morning so that he could brief the FBI Director. It also enabled Danilov to telephone Pavin at a Moscow time when he would be at Petrovka, and Cowley to get Rafferty and Johannsen's report on the cultural events in Serov's diary coinciding with Paulac's visits to Washington.

Neither Danilov nor Cowley was entirely happy with their respective results.

Pavin said he'd gone again to Raisa Serova's apartment on Leninskaya, and been turned away because he had not been accompanied by anyone from the Foreign Ministry. The major also warned that arrivals at Sheremet'yevo were not computerised; neither were they filed in any alphabetical, nationality or dated order. A slip-by-slip search for a visit by Michel Paulac could take months, even if the time frame were narrowed.

Danilov had just replaced the telephone when Nikolai Redin thrust into the room, demanding to know how the seven names had been discovered. Scarcely speaking – only saying "there!" and "there!" and "there!" – Danilov led the security officer through the dossiers, pointing out the incongruous letters which the computer had formed into identifiable names.

'The list should have been returned to Moscow! Computers there could have given us the same breakdown!' insisted Redin.

'The individual letters were there, for you to see, when you made your search,' returned Danilov. 'You missed them.'

Redin went quiet at the clear implication. 'You've told Moscow?'

'You've seen every message I've sent to Moscow.'

'Are you *going* to tell them?'

'I don't see any practical purpose.'

The vaguest suggestion of a smile hovered at the corners of Redin's mouth. Abruptly the man turned and left the office, without saying anything more.

Less than a mile away, on the fifth floor of the FBI building, Leonard Ross stared down at the Russian names and said: 'Looks like we've got that great big can of worms nobody wanted. The Secretary of State is going to be one very unhappy man.'

'Danilov says he's not getting any vibes that it's official.'

'I hardly expected he would: or that he would tell us, if he did.'

'He'd tell me,' insisted Cowley. He hadn't expected Rafferty and Johannsen's inquiry to turn out as it had. He decided against discussing it with the Director: they were talking about positives, not negatives. Not that it was strictly negative. More inexplicable at the moment.

'Right now I believe we've got unarguable evidence of the Russian Mafia operating out of the Russian embassy,' said Ross. 'And I don't like that one little bit.'

'How public are we going to go?'

'I shouldn't think Hartz would want to go public at all. There's no advantage to us in doing so, is there?'

'None.'

'Best left to the diplomats,' judged the Director. 'Any playback from New York?'

Cowley shook his head. 'It would be a miracle if there was.'

'A miracle is exactly what I'd welcome at the moment. Call me the moment there's anything.'

'I'd like to think it would be that quick,' said Cowley. He paused. 'But I don't.'

He looped up to the embassy to collect Danilov, who was waiting. On their way back to the 14th Street bridge, Cowley announced that the organisers and staff of every event Serov had marked as having been to on the occasions Michel Paulac had been in Washington were adamant the Russian had not attended. There had been sign-yourself guests list for four of them; Petr Serov's name did not appear on any.

'Is it essential to sign such registers?' asked Danilov, unfamiliar with the practice.

'No,' admitted Cowley. 'But there are always photographers. Our photographic experts have examined the contact sheets of everything that was taken, at every function. And not just for the obvious people in the foreground: every background, too. Serov doesn't show.'

'What about Paulac?'

Cowley shook his head. 'That's the intriguing thing. Two separate sets of people at two separate affairs recognise his photograph, although we've got to allow for the fact the man's picture has been splashed across every newspaper and television screen in Washington for the past week. But one of our photographic guys thinks he can see him in the background of one of the contact prints, although it wouldn't be strong enough to go to court with.'

'It doesn't make sense!' protested Danilov. 'Why should Paulac be at these things if Serov *wasn't*!'

'Don't ask me,' said Cowley. 'I just work here.'

As they approached National Airport, Cowley pointed out the lot where the financier's body had been found. Danilov allowed himself to be swept along by the walk-on, walk-off, write-your-own-ticket convenience of the shuttle, thinking of the shoulder barging, cancellation-without-notice chaos of Russian air travel. Aboard the aircraft he read several times the instructions for the apparatus on the seat back facing him to make sure he had not misunderstood before saying to Cowley: 'This is a telephone to make calls while we're in mid-air?'

Cowley missed the Russian's astonishment. 'You'll probably need an American-billed credit card . . .' He began to grope into his inside pocket. 'You can use mine if you want to make a call.'

'No,' refused Danilov, glad the other man hadn't detected his naivety. 'It can wait.'

From his window seat, he gazed down through the puddled clouds, wondering what were the names of the occasional neatly arranged townships and even more occasional smoke-belching industrial sprawl. A lot of the houses had the azure-blue postage stamp of a swimming pool in their gardens, and every built-up area displayed its white-painted church with a needle-point spire thrusting upwards to where God was supposed to be. Danilov supposed there were dachas with swimming pools in Russia – probably in the hills above Moscow, where the former Communist élite had played at being Tsars – but he'd never seen them from the air on the rare times he'd flown out of the city. And few Russian churches were white, and all had squat, fat-breasted towers not really indicating any upward direction at all. Perhaps in Russia even the clerics weren't sure where God was supposed to live. Or maybe the churches of Mother Russia were supposed to have breasts.

The announcement that they were approaching New York came over the public address system before Danilov could see it, because he was sitting on the wrong side of the aircraft on its approach. Then the plane banked and the city that most people – certainly most Russians – thought to *be* America all by itself lay set out below, a packed-together jumble of snag-toothed skyscrapers and tower buildings, everything overlaid by a thumb-print smudge of purple-brown smog. As the plane descended it was just possible to see the tight, joined-up lines of toy cars and lorries, so there had to be roads, but Danilov's impression of Manhattan was of a solid mass, a sharply carved or weathered cliff in the caves and gullies of which people presumably lived.

The FBI's New York supervisor, Hank Slowen, was a neat, compact, slightly built man. He wore rimless spectacles, his fair hair combed precisely from an arrow-straight parting. Cowley had only ever known the man wear blue, as he was today, the jacket unrumpled, the trouser creases sabre-sharp. Slowen's neatness was accentuated by the appearance of the man beside him: the Brooklyn detective, a lieutenant introduced as Wes Bradley, was a burly, bulging man whom nothing seemed to fit. The waistband of his trousers was lost beneath the roll of his stomach and the check sports jacket perched on his shoulders, with no chance of being fastened across the ample midriff even if there had been a button on the front, which there wasn't. The shirt was fresh but already surrendering, the open collar tips turned up by the knot of a tugged-down tie.

Bradley directed them towards a dented, paint-dull Ford, badly parked in a prohibited area, the attachable but unlit police emergency light prominent on the dashboard. Danilov knew men like Bradley all over Moscow, detectives who used police authority as a passport to where no-one else could go. The interior of the vehicle was as neglected as its owner, overflowing ashtrays spilled on the floor, among the take-away food wrappers; the upholstery on the driver's seat had parted in protest along two seams. The engine was slowly choking to death.

Over his shoulder, Bradley said: 'So what can I tell you?'

Answering the question in kind, Cowley said: 'Who killed a Russian diplomat and a Swiss financier. That'll do fine for starters.'

Bradley regarded him sourly in the rear-view mirror. 'We got two addresses, both at the Beach. After he got out of the slammer Chestnoy lived for a few weeks over a shop actually on Brighton Beach Avenue. Last known address was just off Riegelmann boardwalk. We gotta sheet on another of your names, Igor Rimyans. No prosecutions or convinctions. Lotta chatter about connections with the Colombians. That's the growth industry, drugs. They do a cocaine speciality here, like crack. Called "ice".'

Danilov was in the back of the car, by the window, listening but looking out as they zig-zagged through the streets, presumably towards the unseen and unsuspected sea. He was surprised, shocked almost, by what he was seeing. So far, his experience of America had been restricted to the triumphant boulevards of Washington and its smaller but well-maintained, well-kept streets in the downtown area and around Georgetown. The only suggestion of social deprivation had been from the protesters huddled under their tarpaulins around the White House and he'd thought that theatrical, as protests always were to some degree.

What he was seeing now wasn't staged. There were exceptions, sometimes whole streets of well preserved clapboards with tended garden patches. But far more were sagged and collapsing, broken windows cardboarded over, wooden slats curling away from their framework. The roads were clotted with cars, all decaying like the houses: a lot had been vandalised, lopsided on bricks or metal crates where wheels had been stolen, doors gaping to show dashboards and seats ripped out, hood and trunk lids stretched open, like the beaks of hungry fledglings. There were hoardings and brick walls of offices or small shopping complexes, too, and all were wreathed and filigreed with graffiti – sometimes aimless whorls, sometimes the philosophy of the mindless in whose vocabulary fuck was the only verb.

Bradley said: 'We got people out on the streets. But don't get too hopeful.'

'I'm not,' said Cowley.

Slowen was travelling in the front. He twisted back and said: 'It's a ghetto. Closes up like a clam shell when the water ripples . . .' He was so soft-spoken it was difficult to hear above the noise of the distressed engine.

'How well organised?' asked Danilov.

'Well enough,' said Bradley. 'Started off pretty ragged. Guys selling forged driving licences and credit cards; stolen gas from hijacked tankers. They're still running that, but they've moved on to extortion and running hookers. And like I said, drugs, everyone's entry to the good life.'

'What about positive connections with Russia?' asked Danilov.

He saw Bradley's shoulders go up and down in a shrug. 'Organised connections, we don't know. Never come across a trail so far. But everyone at Brighton Beach's got family in the old country.' He stretched backwards, offering a folder. 'Guess you probably got them already, but there's our sheets on Chebrakin, Chestnoy and Rimyans. Mug shots, too. All we've got on your fourth guy, Valentin Yashev, is a suspect file, and we're not sure if the photograph really is him: it came from an informer who probably wanted the twenty bucks to score a coke bag. Yashev's supposed to be an enforcer, heavily into extortion: muscle right up through to the top of his head.'

'A man who would kill if he were told,' said Slowen, thoughtlessly.

'Shit, man!' exclaimed Bradley. 'All these guys will kill, sometimes just if they feel like it. You know what Chebrakin said when he was questioned . . . questioned by some dumb fuck who hadn't read him his Miranda Rights, so we couldn't produce it at the trial . . .? He said he shot this liquor store owner because the man had waved him away dismissively. Not shown the proper respect. From that, some mother-fucker defence lawyer made a case for self defence man-slaughter, can you believe! What it was was Chebrakin sticking a thirty-eight in the poor bastard's face and pulling the trigger because he hadn't paid his dues.'

'Was that how he *was* killed, shot in the face?' seized Danilov at once.

'Sorry,' apologised Bradley. 'Just a way of talking: it was actually a body wound.'

'Is there any ritual, about the way they do kill?' asked Cowley.

Bradley's eyes came up in the rear-view mirror again. 'We've asked around about mouth shots. No one's come across that before, not among the Russians. Looks like a first.'

'I ran the same check with the same result,' said Slowen. 'None of our people had come across it outside the Sicilian or American Mafias.'

Bradley came into Brighton Beach from the north, driving parallel with the ocean. Danilov saw that boardwalk meant exactly what it was, a very practical planked thoroughfare stretching out over the seafront from which sand could easily be swept between the palings. A lot of advertisements and cafe and shop names fronting the water had the word 'Moscow' in them.

'Welcome to Little Odessa!' said Bradley.

'Odessa's in the Ukraine,' said Cowley.

'Give the man a present from the back shelf!' said Bradley. 'That's where most of these immigrants come from: more Ukrainians than any other ethnic group.'

143

Bradley hefted the police emergency globe back on to the dashboard, and halted the car beneath a sign prohibiting parking on Brighton Beach Avenue. He got awkwardly from the vehicle, slowed by his bulk, and said: 'Let's go hear the word.'

There was an alley from the avenue, leading to the boardwalk. A black in jeans and basketball shoes was leaning against a wall at the far end. When they got closer, Danilov saw the T-shirt slogan read 'Jesus for President'. Bradley hesitated, leaving the contact to the other man, who shrugged and came up to them immediately.

'There ain't no secrets here,' he said. 'I might as well be in uniform in a black-and-white with the siren going.'

Bradley introduced him all around, just as Wilkes, before saying: 'Well?'

'You're not going to believe this,' said Wilkes. 'No-one knows nothing about nothing. The last address we had for Chebrakin is a no-call. It's over a laundry: was two rooms that were let up until a year ago. Now it's the laundry store-room. Full of washing powders and ironing flats and shit like that.'

'Shown the pictures around?' pressed the lieutenant.

The black detective nodded. 'Covered all the bars for three streets back from here: few on the side as well. Brought in the entire night shift last night and four guys today. Zilch . . .' He smiled towards Cowley and Danilov. 'You guys shouldn't have bothered to leave home.'

Cowley said to Bradley: 'What about regular informers?'

It was Wilkes who responded, nodding seriously. 'Your guys are here somewhere. One or two of them, at least. I know that because of what we're *not* getting. The word's out, OK? By now there should have been something coming back, even if it was bullshit: guys trying to rip us off for a few bucks. It happens every time we raise a red flag, promising reward for results. This time we got nothing. Which tells me our snitches know they're going to get their peckers nailed to that boardwalk over there if they even so much as acknowledge the existence of the people you want.'

Cowley sighed. 'Somehow I wish you hadn't told me that.'

144

'What do you want to do?' asked Bradley.

Cowley wished he knew: he'd hoped the local PD would have had leads, things to follow up, by the time they arrived. He looked at Danilov.

'Let's start with the laundry,' suggested the Russian.

Just he and Cowley went, the others going with Wilkes to meet Brooklyn detectives still on the streets.

Both men in the laundry were wearing Jewish yarmulkes; one was much older than the other, and Danilov guessed they were father and son. When they produced the photograph of Chestnoy the younger man said someone had already asked and they didn't know where the man was: they hadn't seen him for more than a year. The older man continued working at the steam-press, wisped in white mist. He started, visibly, when Danilov repeated the enquiry directly at him in Russian – the younger one looked surprised, too – but repeated his son's denial, in that language. When Cowley, also in Russian, asked about re-directed mail, the younger man said Chestnoy's mail had stopped, months before. When there had been some, the man had called to collect it, not given a forwarding address. They didn't know any magazine or periodical to which he had subscribed when he had lived there; they didn't know any of his friends or any of his favourite places in Brighton Beach, either. They also didn't know if he'd had a girlfriend or a wife. He'd never paid his rent by cheque, always cash, so they didn't know which bank he used, if any. There hadn't been a telephone connected upstairs and he'd never asked to use theirs, so they hadn't overheard any conversations.

Danilov and Cowley accepted the offer to look at where Chestnoy had once lived. Danilov went determinedly through both rooms, looking for anything that might have been left behind, even scanning the walls and scattered newspapers on the floor, upon which the man might have written a reminder note or a telephone number. He got dirty and dusty doing it, and found nothing.

They worked their way shop by shop, bar by bar, cafe by cafe along the boardwalk and then moved back into adjoining and parallel streets, constantly speaking Russian, which did not always work: sometimes people replied in Ukrainian, which neither Cowley nor Danilov spoke. It was well past lunchtime when they stopped at the Moscow restaurant, fronting the sea, and had borscht and boiled sturgeon. Danilov insisted on paying. They delayed their questioning here until they'd finished eating. No-one admitted ever having met or known Yuri Chestnoy or anyone else on their list.

The FBI local supervisor and the Brooklyn detectives were waiting at the pre-arranged rendezvous, the alley where they'd met Wilkes, when Cowley and Danilov returned in mid-afternoon.

'None of my guys came up with anything,' reported Wilkes.

'I'll buy the beer,' announced Cowley, nodding back along the avenue towards a bar adorned with less graffiti than any of the surrounding buildings. No-one protested they couldn't drink on duty. Everyone did order beer except Bradley, who asked for Black Label scotch, and Cowley, who hesitated and had soda with a lime wedge.

'You know the heat there is on this,' Cowley reminded, gazing around the table. 'We're at government-to-government level, questions being asked for which a lot of important people want answers that make sense. So far . . .' he nodded sideways, towards Danilov, '. . . we have not been doing very well providing them. I don't want to go back to Washington to tell the Director in person that people we want very much to talk to – people whose names were listed by a murdered Russian diplomat – are somewhere here in Brighton Beach but we can't find them. I want the entire population of this little town to think the pogroms of Stalin and the Nazi invasion have started all over again, in tandem. I'll get as many extra men as are necessary drafted in and I'll have the Director personally tell your department the Bureau will pick up the tab for all the overtime. I don't want a dealer selling a dime bag to any screaming addict. I don't want a bet placed on a number or a horse or anything else. I don't want a hooker turning a single trick. If a seagull shits on the boardwalk, I want it arrested and charged. I want Brighton

Beach to be squeezed dry and I want it known why it's being squeezed dry . . .' He looked at Wilkes. 'Tell your snitches and tell them to tell everyone else: Brighton Beach is out of business and out of bounds until we get a steer towards Chebrakin or Chestnoy or Rimyans or Yashev. Everyone sweats until I get cool. OK?'

'Sounds like fun,' said Bradley.

The contract had been given to Mikhail Antipov, who had carried out the Washington hits, because Yerin had said it was important the murder was identical, although it had to be a different Makarov. They met to hear how it had gone in the totally secure club on Pecatnikov Street. They'd allowed Antipov the brief bravado and congratulated him on his choice of an opposing hitman in the Ostankino and paid the bonus. The others on the Chechen *komitet* were surprised when Yerin, the long term thinker, insisted Antipov leave the gun with them.

'This shouldn't just be a killing,' decided Yerin, after Antipov had been dismissed.

'What?' asked Gusovsky expectantly.

'Kosov might not succeed in getting Danilov. So we should take out insurance.'

'What sort of insurance?' questioned Gusovsky.

'Something that will permanently get rid of Danilov if he won't play,' declared Yerin.

'Kill him as well?' anticipated Zimin.

'Of course not!' said Yerin impatiently. 'Something far better than that.'

When Yerin finished explaining Zimin said: 'It's a brilliant concept. But I can't believe it will work: it's too complicated.'

'Leave the clever thinking to me,' smiled the sightless man, superciliously. 'You just worry about managing your killers.'

CHAPTER TWENTY-THREE

The time difference between Washington and Moscow worked better in reverse, because it enabled Pavin to send to America as much as was known about the murdered Ivan Ignatov before Danilov left the embassy the following morning. Quite obviously, in such a short period, the extent of that information was still limited to official, available records, but what there was offered another ill-fitting piece for the incomplete jigsaw. Ivan Ignatsevich Ignatov had a criminal history ranging from pimping, violence – one victim lost an eye, another was permanently crippled from a shattered kneecap – to foreign tourist mugging and larceny from Customs-bonded warehouses at Moscow's Domodedovo Airport. By far the most interesting and connecting fact, however, was that the man's crime sheet identified him as a member of the Ostankino Family, one of the Militia-acknowledged clans making up the Moscow Mafia.

His body had been found near the permanent exhibition area for international trade, by the river loop. It was possible the killer or killers had hoped it would be washed downstream, but instead it had lodged on a just-submerged mud bank. Like the Washington victims, he had been shot three times: the complete autopsy was yet to be carried out, but the scene-of-crime preliminary examination suggested the mouth shot had been the last: an earlier bullet, directly into the heart, had been the cause of death. The bullet to the mouth and what was believed to be its casing had been recovered. It had come from a 9mm Makarov pistol. There was no evidence of robbery or torture.

Cowley read the single-page report quickly. 'Back in your territory?'

'It always had to be there, at some time and in some way,' said Danilov.

'How public are these Families?'

Danilov considered his answer. 'We don't have the resources – or the official urging – properly to move against them. And a lot of people don't want them curbed anyway. The Mafia provide what can't be obtained.

'Chicago, 1920s,' compared Cowley.

'The role model,' agreed Danilov.

'But they *are* known people?'

'It's not been my section,' apologised Danilov. Organised gang investigation had supposedly been the responsibility of Anatoli Metkin, before his elevation to Director. Could that be the reason for the man's near-hysterical interest in the Serov killing, even though it had been 5,000 miles from Moscow?

'So we could shake the trees and maybe make a few apples fall?'

Danilov frowned, unaccustomed to Cowley speaking like so many of the other detectives but glad he understood: quite often over the last few days he had had to struggle to keep up. 'We could try.'

'Let's hope with more success than Brighton Beach.'

'Let's hope,' agreed Danilov, sincerely. It might prove even more obstructed, this time, with officialdom added to the difficulties.

'So we're going back,' said Cowley.

He didn't want to, Danilov acknowledged: so much so that since Pavin's call the previous night and the cables that morning he had consciously avoided thinking about it, which was ridiculous. And then he fully realised what Cowley had said – *we're* going back. In Moscow, even with the uncertain support of the deputies in the Foreign and Interior Ministries, there would still be the intrusion and obstruction of the resentful Metkin, whom he did know, and others, whom he didn't. But not if Cowley were there as well. 'Back we go again,' he agreed.

'I suppose we do,' agreed Cowley.

That was certainly what Leonard Ross expected, when Cowley met the Director an hour later. The man agreed at once to a Task Force to blitz Brighton Beach and that Hank Slowen could supervise from the New York office. The Director also promised personally to brief the Moscow embassy, through which Cowley had to communicate daily. Remembering the gulag-type living conditions of the American residential compound, Cowley hurriedly said he'd prefer to live this time in an hotel, which Ross accepted without question.

Back in his own office Cowley ensured he and Danilov were booked on the same flight and cabled the FBI station at the embassy, asking for a reservation to be made at the Savoy.

At the Russian embassy on the other side of the White House and Lafayette Square Danilov sat at Serov's desk, listening to his own telephone at Kirovskaya ring unanswered. He put it down, deciding he would have to return unannounced. He had a hell of a lot to do before leaving Washington the following day. And he still hadn't had his hair cut, which they did so much better here than they did in Moscow.

It was at the request of the Secretary of State that Leonard Ross invited the Washington mayor, the police chief and the chief of detectives to the Bureau later that afternoon for as full a briefing as possible.

When Ross finished, Mort Halpern said: 'You think we got a whole new Mafia organisation, stretching from here to Russia? Or a tie-up between our Cosa Nostra and theirs, somehow connected through the embassy?'

'We don't know, not yet,' admitted the FBI Director. 'But it looks like it. And if we have, it's the most serious development of organised crime I can think of.'

'Either scenario worries the hell out of me,' said Halpern.

'Of us all,' agreed Ross.

'We going public on this?' asked Elliott Jones.

'No!' said Ross adamantly. 'Under no circumstances! This stays wrapped for as long as we can keep it that way.'

'What about warning the public?'

'Warning them of what?' rejected Ross. 'The only thing

that would come of releasing it at this time would be panic and more headlines that we could handle.'

The whole intention of the briefing was, ironically, to prevent any leak percolating out to the media: by sticking to their understanding to keep the City officials informed, Ross and the Secretary of State expected them to maintain theirs and make no statement, public or otherwise, about the case.

It showed surprising, even naive, trust.

CHAPTER TWENTY-FOUR

The arrival at Sheremet'yevo was disorganised, the airport clogged by its customary chaos, and Danilov was embarrassed at the comparison with his smooth, considerate reception in Washington. He had advised both ministries as well as Petrovka of their flight details, but there were no arrangements to ease them through the official formalities. A surly uniformed immigration officer took an inordinate time studying Cowley's American passport, visa and entry form: finally Danilov tried to pull rank, identified himself and told the man to hurry, which was a mistake because the officer truculently did the opposite, which Danilov should have anticipated. It took almost a further forty-five minutes for their luggage to appear on the carousel, and when it did Cowley's case had a deep score down its side.

There were two groups waiting for them outside on the concourse. Anatoli Metkin, in his full general's uniform, was with Pavin, who looked visibly uncomfortable: one of the three men in the American embassy group held a photograph from which to identify Cowley. There was a confusion of introductions, and a momentary impasse over which car Cowley would occupy driving into Moscow. The American solved it by announcing he wanted to be briefed as soon as possible: he would travel in the embassy vehicle but in convoy to Petrovka, for an immediate arrival conference.

'What is there from America to bring me up to date?' demanded Metkin the moment Danilov entered their limousine. It was Metkin's official Volga, with his personal driver. Pavin rode next to the man in the front seat, Metkin in the rear, alongside Danilov.

'There's nothing you haven't already been told.'

'What co-operation was there?'

Danilov was determined to retain the independence

granted him by the Deputy Interior Minister. Which made it inevitable he would antagonise Metkin. 'You'll obviously get a copy of my report to the ministries, like you've seen everything else.'

Metkin's lined face tightened into a mask. 'I asked you a question!' He spoke with exaggerated quietness, trying to intimidate.

In front of him Danilov saw Pavin staring rigidly ahead. He supposed the driver would gossip, although it was hardly a confrontation. In fact, Danilov decided, it had been a mistake to oppose Metkin so quickly and upon something so inconsequential. 'They were extremely co-operative.' Metkin would regard it as capitulation.

'What about our own embassy?'

That was very much a matter for the Foreign Ministry, not Metkin. 'I was able to work satisfactorily.'

'Where did you obtain the names?'

Ahead, Danilov could just make out the still shrouded skyline of the city, and wished it was closer, sparing him this inquisition. 'From among Serov's belongings. I explained that from Washington.'

'What about other names?'

Not an inconsequential question, decided Danilov. 'I did not discover any more.'

'What has happened to Serov's belongings?'

'They are being shipped back to the Foreign Ministry.'

Metkin turned directly across the car. 'Why the Ministry? It is a Militia enquiry. Police evidence.'

'They are technically Foreign Ministry documents. I have separated those that contain the names, for easy identification if we have to call for them as evidence. I can't, at the moment, see we will need them. I've also asked that they are all kept available for us to examine further.' Danilov was curious to know if Metkin were a good enough investigator to guess or realise why he was returning the Serov dossiers this way. He hoped he hadn't wasted his time: it had taken him the entire afternoon at the embassy, after discussing the killing of Ignatov with Cowley.

Metkin nodded towards Pavin, in the front of the vehicle.

'I have read the duplicates you sent back: all that was sent to the ministries.'

'It was intended that you should,' said Danilov cautiously.

'What about the rest?'

Danilov frowned sideways. 'Rest?'

'Did you have any communication with either ministry of which I am unaware?'

'None whatsoever,' insisted Danilov.

'I have your absolute assurance of that?'

'You asked me a question,' said Danilov. 'I have answered it.' He'd never been there – and didn't want to go – but Danilov guessed the chill inside the car was roughly comparable to Siberia in deep winter.

At Petrovka there was more brief confusion as Cowley told the Americans he would make his own way to the hotel and the embassy. Metkin's head darted back and forth during the exchanges, which were in English. As the embassy officials got back into their car, Metkin, speaking slowly and enunciating each word, asked if Cowley were comfortable in Russian; the American, unaware of the tension between Metkin and Danilov, said he was but if a problem arose Danilov could always translate. Metkin's face closed, and he stumped into the Militia building without speaking further.

The gathering was in Metkin's office, which Danilov accepted to be an improvement over that adapted for him, but it was still far short of the comfort in which FBI executives worked. There had been some changes since Danilov's last visit. There was a glass-fronted bureau displaying neat racks of books that hadn't been there before, and a more extensive range of telephones on a new, separate side table. Metkin busied himself as the host, seating Cowley in a ready-placed chair before going to yet another new range of low cupboards near the window to disclose an array of bottles. He appeared disappointed when the American refused the offer, which was not extended to either Danilov or Pavin. Danilov's dismissal by his Director became even more obvious the moment the discussion began: Metkin's concentration was entirely upon Cowley, with no attempt to include the other two men. Danilov forgot the irritation that had begun in the car, more interested than offended. He had expected Metkin immediately to bring them – or Cowley, at least – up to date about the murder of Ivan Ignatov. Instead Metkin persisted with questions about the Washington killings, so much so that at one stage Cowley actually looked away from the Militia Director to frown curiously at Danilov.

It was thirty minutes before they got around to the shooting of the Russian gangster. As he talked, Metkin produced photographs of where Ignatov had been found, both including and excluding the body, and some mortuary pictures of the dead man. Cowley studied each one before pointedly handing it sideways to Danilov.

The Russian spent more time looking at the mortuary shots than those of the river, then leaned sideways, quietly asking Pavin a question while Metkin talked. At once, the Director stopped and said: 'What was that!'

'I was asking if the autopsy confirmed the sequence of the wounds,' said Danilov. And stopped. He decided Metkin was making himself look foolish, as he had at the ministry encounter.

'Why?' demanded the man.

'I would have thought it significant, wouldn't you?'

Metkin blinked, appearing to realise he was exposed in front of an American he was trying to impress. 'In what way?' he was forced to ask.

'Why there was a mouth shot, if that wasn't what killed him,' said Danilov, with forced patience. 'We know Ignatov belonged to one of the Moscow Mafia Families: why the copying of the American or Italian trademark, unless it was for a boastful reason?'

The Director looked confused.

'It could show a link between our organised crime groups in America and yours here, in Russia,' offered Cowley helpfully. 'We'll be very worried if it does.'

'Quite so,' agreed Metkin hurriedly.

'The pathologist thought it was the final shot, when he was already dead,' said Pavin.

'Like ours,' said Cowley, talking more to Danilov than the Director. 'They want it to be understood.'

'By us?' asked Metkin, anxious to keep up.

Cowley frowned again. 'Our experience in America is that the Mafia send messages to each other, not the enforcement agencies.'

'I understand,' said Metkin.

Danilov wasn't at all sure Metkin did understand. He was witnessing the Director's performance with growing astonishment. 'What do we know about Ignatov's movements, prior to his being killed?' Danilov spoke generally, although he meant the question for Pavin. When the major didn't reply, Danilov looked directly at him: Pavin, in turn, was staring at the Director.

'We're making enquiries,' insisted Metkin, but badly, weak-voiced.

Surely the preliminary groundwork had been started, thought Danilov, growing more shocked. 'What's the early forensic report say?'

'We're still awaiting it,' said Metkin. 'We're searching both river banks, upstream, to find where the body went in.'

'We haven't a forensic report after more than forty-eight hours!' Metkin *hadn't* properly organised the investigation! It would explain why he had tried to close him out of any discussion and asked more questions than he'd offered answers: the incompetent fool didn't have anything *to* offer!

'I've demanded priority,' Metkin shrugged and looked with exaggerated apology to Cowley, inviting professional sympathy. 'Why is it that scientists always complain of overwork?'

'Has the area where the body was found been dredged?' pressed Danilov relentlessly.

Metkin's face was blazing. 'There was difficulty getting a suitable vessel. It's beginning today.'

Why had the idiot insisted on getting personally involved, so blatantly exposing his inadequacies! Danilov's contempt for Metkin had until now been more for his suspected compromises and corruption than for the level of the man's intelligence. On this showing Metkin didn't possess either intelligence or cunning. Danilov felt oddly discomfited. Which *was* odd. Why should he feel any sympathy –

discomfiture most of all – for Anatoli Nikolaevich Metkin? Certainly not *for* Metkin. His feeling was for a department he should have been heading and which, if he had been its director, would not be displaying this sort of ineptitude.

Nodding to the American, but speaking to Metkin, he said: 'Mr Cowley has to report back to Washington. We don't have anything *official* – no scientific assessment apart from the wound sequence – to offer? Is that right?'

Metkin's colour had not subsided. 'It is being prepared. It will have to be translated into English, of course.'

Despising himself – although not much – for manipulating the American's involvement, but determined to gain the maximum advantage over someone he knew would have shown him no mercy, Danilov said to Cowley: 'Do you want a translation? Or would you prefer the original?'

'The original,' replied Cowley, as Danilov knew he would.

'That should speed things up, shouldn't it?' persisted Danilov.

'I will send as much as possible to the embassy before the end of the day,' undertook the crumple-faced Metkin.

Speaking to Cowley, and very obviously taking over control of the encounter, Danilov said: 'I might bring it myself.'

Metkin didn't object or argue. Instead, appearing anxious to escape, he said: 'I think we've covered everything, up to date.'

There was an almost visible collective relaxation when the three men reached Danilov's elongated room, further along the corridor. Danilov asked Ludmilla Radsic to find a third chair for Cowley – for a brief moment believing she was going to refuse to leave the room – but didn't immediately speak when she went out, unsure exactly *what* to say.

It was Cowley who spoke first. 'I don't understand what was going on back there. I don't want to know, necessarily: it may be none of my business. It only becomes my business if the investigation is endangered.'

'I hope it won't be,' said Danilov, deciding against any

further explanation. As the woman re-entered with the chair he reverted to English. 'If I feel it might, we can discuss it.'

Cowley hesitated. Then, pointedly, he said: 'The *moment* it becomes a problem, OK?'

'My word,' assured Danilov.

Presciently, looking between the two Russians, Cowley said he guessed they had things to talk about and he had to touch base at the embassy and would stay there until Danilov called. Seeing the opportunity, Danilov insisted he and Pavin would check the American into the Savoy first. Neither tried to get out of the car when they got there, and Cowley didn't seem to expect it.

'What the hell's going on?' demanded Danilov, when he was finally alone with Pavin. 'That was a farce in Metkin's office!'

'It's been a farce from the beginning,' complained Pavin. 'When Ignatov's body was found, Metkin summoned everyone to a conference in the squad room. But *no* decisions were made. He had me give a verbal report of what had come back from America – he's convinced you're withholding things, incidentally – but virtually none of the normal procedures for a murder investigation was started. After the conference, Metkin stayed for hours in his office with just Vladimir Kabalin. The first day was lost. There is a rumour in the squad room there was a call from the Interior Ministry, but I don't know from whom or what was said. But it was only afterwards that any sort of proper investigation began. Kabalin was appointed investigating officer: he's using Aleksai Raina as his scene-of-crime officer. Nothing has come for me to co-ordinate with what we've got from America.'

Danilov snorted, gesturing Pavin to pull in to the side of the road. 'I still don't understand why Metkin exposed himself like that. It was ridiculous.'

'We only had a few hours' warning that Cowley was coming back with you. That seemed to change everything.'

And could explain a lot more. If he had returned from America by himself, the obvious failings of the investigation could very easily have been manipulated to make him the incompetent. As it was, Metkin had became ensnared in his own trap. 'He still shouldn't have risked it.'

'He'll have realised that by now. It would have been better left with Kabalin: made him look the fool.'

Danilov twisted in the seat, to face his assistant. 'You think Metkin could know something about the Serov business? This is where it all begins, here in Moscow. It *has* to be!'

Pavin considered the question seriously, slowly shaking his head, although not in outright rejection of the idea. 'I can't see how. Not with Serov in America. About Ignatov . . .' He shrugged. 'I doubt it would be a personal knowledge of the man himself. About the Ostankino Family, it's possible. In Moscow anything's possible, if it's illegal.'

'Those rumours in the squad room, about the call from the Interior Ministry? What about a name? Rank even?'

Pavin shook his head again. 'No ministry name. But it's generally accepted he's got special friends outside: the inference is obvious, from the way he and Kabalin specialised before the promotion, that whoever they are, they're high in some organisation. Again, no names.'

'Not even a suggestion of a Family?'

'Not even that it *is* a Family. My own guess is that it must be, so why not the Ostankino?'

He had to guard against being misdirected by his personal feelings. 'Maybe I'm looking too hard.' Accepting it was a task roughly similar to trying to find Paulac's entry documents if he'd visited Moscow, Danilov nevertheless offered Pavin the single-sheet note Leonid Lapinsk had mailed before blowing his head off. 'None of these three names have surfaced so far. I don't know their significance, but they must mean something. Try criminal records first, then government employment registers. Don't put them into the files: they're not part of the investigation.'

'You find them in Washington, too?'

Danilov remained silent. If he disclosed the source and the three were later found to be criminals, a dead Director whom he'd admired would be tainted by association. 'I just want them checked.'

'*Did* we get copies of everything you sent back to the Ministries from America?' demanded Pavin.

'Absolutely,' insisted Danilov.

'Why send Serov's things direct to the Foreign Ministry?' queried Pavin. 'I would have thought they would have justified a closer examination back here than it was possible for you to make while you were there.'

Danilov smiled. 'It took me most of my last day in Washington to photocopy the entire collection of documents in which Serov hid the names: photocopies I've personally brought back. We're going to ask the Foreign Ministry for the originals to be returned: say we want to examine them further. Which we do, to compare *everything* I've got – the complete set – with what comes back from the Ministry. If there's anything missing, we'll know there's something official they don't want us to see, won't we?' Danilov was sure it was a worthwhile precaution: one, probably, he should continue now he was back in Moscow. He decided, at that moment, that he would.

'You think something *will* be held back?'

'I want some way of knowing how independently Serov was operating from Ministry control. Which we might get if the material is incomplete. Serov was five thousand miles away: he *had* to have a link back here.'

Back at Petrovka, Danilov began dismantling the barriers erected against him. He sent memoranda to both deputy ministers that he was resuming command, with a carbon copy to Vladimir Kabalin to reinforce his authority to receive what had so far been assembled on the Ignatov killing. He added that he wanted Kabalin and Raina to remain part of the murder squad, which would need extra manpower. Trying to ease Pavin's workload, he ordered them to take over the scrutiny of Sheremet'yevo airport entry visas, for any reference to Michel Paulac. He advised the Foreign Ministry he wanted to interview Serov's wife again, for them to appoint an observer if they wished, hoping they wouldn't consider the woman's complaint sufficient to do so. He decided against telling Pavin that he was making additional photocopies of everything: it came close to being a paranoid precaution.

It was not until the very end of the day that any of the promised material on the Ignatov murder arrived, a preliminary autopsy report delivered to Danilov by one of Metkin's secretaries, with an assurance a duplicate had been sent direct to Cowley. Danilov thought Metkin's effort pitifully inadequate, like everything else, but he was glad he did not have to go to the American embassy himself. He had the woman carry back to Metkin copies of all the instructions he had issued, guessing the man would already know from Ludmilla Radsic: she had left the room several times after finishing the typing.

Ivan Ignatsevich Ignatov had been a well-nourished male, aged forty-nine, with no indication of organic disease, although his medical file recorded treatment for syphilis. The medical report confirmed the mouth-shot had been post death. There was no water in the lungs, so Ignatov had been dead before going into the river, and there was no water damage to the body, so it had not been immersed for any length of time. Cause of death had been a direct bullet wound to the heart. There was evidence of previous, non-fatal injuries: what were judged to be three stab wounds to the left arm and shoulder and another, which could have been far more serious and would probably have required hospital treatment, to the lower right-hand side of the body, near the liver.

Before leaving the Militia building Danilov ordered Pavin to assemble – and copy for Cowley – all available archival material on the known Mafia Families of Moscow, particularly the Ostankino with whom Ignatov had been linked. When he telephoned Cowley, the American said he was going to hit the sack, too.

Danilov was later unable to remember anything of the drive to Kirovskaya, his recollection beginning with being in the apartment trying to explain to Olga that he'd attempted to warn her of his return from Washinton the previous day but that she hadn't been there to take his call.

Olga smiled hopefully towards the suitcase. 'Do I have presents?'

'Perfume. Armani,' said Danilov. He'd bought it in-flight, during the duty-free distribution.

Olga frowned. 'I gave you a list!'

'I came back in a hurry. There wasn't time for shopping.' He had forgotten all about her damned list, but there really had not been time.

'I don't believe you!'

'I was working! Not on vacation!'

'I saw a photograph of you coming out of a restaurant! Was that work?'

'*Yes*,' he said emphatically.

'A normal married man would have found time!'

A normal married man probably would have done, he conceded. But he didn't consider himself to be normally married, not any more. 'I'll be going back,' he said, without thinking, wanting only to deflect the diatribe.

'You'll get them all then?' The hope was back in her voice.

'I promise.' He'd promised Larissa he'd resolve their situation when he returned to Moscow.

Olga followed him into the bedroom, talking all the time but disjointedly, verbally giving him a shorthand account of what she had done while he had been away. She went into minute detail about her dinner at the Metropole Hotel with Yevgennie Kosov and of going afterwards to the most popular nightclub in Moscow, having decided there was no reason not to tell him because it had all been entirely innocent. But by then Danilov was deeply asleep, and didn't hear anything she said.

Cowley had more difficulty getting to sleep than Danilov, lapsing into half slumber but then coming abruptly awake in the darkened hotel room, his mind too busy with the events of the day.

The courtesy visit to the embassy had been predictable and uneventful. No-one he'd met on the previous visit appeared still to be there. The First Secretary was a beaming Texan named Jeplow who seemed uncomfortable out of cowboy boots and promised the ambassador was available whenever Cowley felt like saying hello. The resident FBI agent was a chain-smoking New Yorker two assignments distant from Barry Andrews, but who apparently knew the story of Cowley's first visit, because the man's initial greeting had been that whatever happened it was going to work out better this time. His name was Stephen Snow. He hadn't come out to Sheremet'yevo because he didn't want to make himself too obvious to the Russians, even though it was now two to a bed and everything was hunky-dory. Cowley, who couldn't remember the last time he'd heard the expression, assured the man he understood. Snow said, naturally, he was there to do anything Cowley asked.

A recurring reason for Cowley's wakefulness was the bizarre encounter with the Militia Director. Cowley didn't think he'd ever witnessed a depth of antipathy between two men as obvious as that which seemed to exist between Metkin and Danilov, which – as he'd said immediately afterwards – wasn't any of his business. His concern was how long it could remain none of his business, if it was going to wash over into their professional relationship, which it had clearly done that morning. It was a long way from being a situation to bring officially to the notice of the Bureau or the State Department, but it was something he had to keep very much in mind. It might have helped if he'd had some idea what it was all about. Did he know Danilov well enough openly to ask? Something else he did not have to decide right away.

The meeting was again in the Pecatnikov club, where they felt most secure: Alexandr Yerin was particularly familiar with the surroundings, because he lived in an apartment two floors above.

Mikhail Antipov frowned across the table at the *komitet*, not sure how forcefully he could protest but deciding he had to, because he was the one exposed to all the risk. 'I won't have any defence, if anything goes wrong!'

'Nothing will go wrong,' soothed the blind man.

'How do we know we can trust them to do it right?'

'They've got to do it right,' said Gusovsky. 'They've got to do everything we tell them: they're ours.'

'A new Mercedes and $5,000,' reminded Yerin.

'Just laugh at them?' queried the killer.

'That's all. Just laugh at them,' agreed Gusovsky.

After the man left, Maksim Zimin said: 'No-one expected the American to come back.'

'That won't be a problem,' said Yerin. 'In fact, I don't think he should be left out.'

'What are you suggesting?' asked the thin-bodied Chechen leader.

'I don't have an idea at the moment,' admitted Yerin. 'But I will. We'll fix Danilov and we'll fix the American.' The man smiled. 'Before the year is out, we'll virtually be running Moscow: we're practically doing it already.'

CHAPTER TWENTY-FIVE

The available material on Mafia Families in Moscow lacked any of the detail official police dossiers should have contained. It was predominantly newspaper clippings, giving the impression the city's freed press had better access to information on organised crime than the police department supposedly responsible for gathering it, which Danilov guessed was probably true. Although the input to the records had been Metkin's responsibility until recently, and therefore the man's failing, Danilov prevented it being obvious to the American. He had Pavin prepare a verbal instead of a factually written presentation.

Pavin identified six Mafia clans in the capital, each with links to major cities throughout the former Soviet Union: the connections with St Petersburg were particularly strong. The Ostankino, with which Ivan Ignatsevich Ignatov was linked, was not reckoned to be the largest or the most powerful. The strongest and best organised was the Dolgoprudnaya who, under the freedoms of the new market economy, were already suspected of large-scale involvement and investment in legitimate businesses.

'Just like the mobs in America. And in Sicily,' interrupted Cowley. When he had been married to Pauline, Cowley had served at the Rome embassy: his later posting to London, where his marriage had collapsed and Pauline had met Barry Andrews, had been a reward for Cowley's part in breaking a major Mafia drugs cartel.

Relaxing and becoming more assured, Pavin said the Chechen were the chief rivals to the Ostankino. Pavin used the Western phrase, calling territorial battles turf wars. What the Americans and Italians called capos were leaders in Russia; enforcers were bulls; gangs were brigades. Those who controlled them were therefore Brigadiers, not God-fathers, although Brigadiers were thought to operate under higher authority for which there was no colloquialism. Each Family imposed entry fees upon anyone wanting to become a member, but each commanded a casual, transitory army of small-time thugs. Here Pavin used another street word – *lokhi* – which strictly translated as amateur.

The Chechen concentrated upon Moscow's four airports – mostly upon Sheremet'yevo, the international receiving terminal from which the most valuable Western articles could be stolen. They raided passenger luggage and freight, sufficiently able to bribe or intimidate security guards that they freely brought lorries right up to the warehouses to haul away what they stole. Their knowledge and control of the airport involved them in the shipment of drugs from the south, where there were big growing areas for marijuana and the poppies from which heroin was refined.

The Chechen appeared to work in reasonable harmony with the other large-scale drug traders, the Assyrian Family. With their hordes of street bulls, the Lubertsy brigade's single most important income was from extortion, from small business up through to joint-venture companies with Western, overseas connections who considered it easier to pay off than officially protest. The Ramenki extended their running of prostitutes around the main hotels to exacting tributes from the hotels themselves, which again found it easier to pay than protest. The Ostankino, who had been the quickest to see the potential of spare and discarded weaponry following the disbandment of the former Soviet military machine, were the armourers for all the other Families, and because of their access to every sort of gun, grenade, shell and explosive device were frequently the most violent, especially in their turf wars with the Chechen.

It took Pavin almost an hour to make the presentation: the man was croaking, dry-throated, when he finished. Danilov thought Pavin had done brilliantly with what little had been available, and wished there had been a proper higher authority from which he could have got an official commendation, beyond the personal congratulation he intended later.

166

'What about specifics?' demanded Cowley worryingly.

'Not enough,' conceded Pavin, at once but not apologetically. 'They've divided Moscow, like your five Families have carved up New York: the Lubertsy, for instance, are overlords of the south-east of the city, the Dolgoprudnaya have the north-west. A lot of Western copying, here. They meet in restaurant and nightclubs; particularly in nightclubs, with the new freedoms. We've got some locations but they change: by the time we get there, it could be a place of the past. And the fear is absolute. No-one is going to tell us that theirs is the restaurant or club where anyone meets. At worst they'd be killed, their premises bombed. If they escaped physical harm their drink and food supplies would cease: what customers remained would be met at the door and turned away.'

'The old ways are still the best,' remarked Cowley.

Pavin did apologise in advance for the limited number of known identities. He produced a total of fifteen, spread throughout the Families: some were incomplete, lacking patronymics and none, Danilov noted, were those on Lapinsk's brief letter, or had appeared in Serov's code.

'What about overseas links, to either America or Sicily?' he asked.

Pavin shook his head. 'Not a thing.'

'So we've got ourselves a first,' said Cowley reflectively.

'That we know about,' qualified Danilov.

The murder file already created by Pavin on Ivan Ignatsevich Ignatov was far more comprehensive than any on the organised crime Families. Ignatov was thought to have been forty-nine years old at the time of his death, although the date of birth in Kiev, in the Ukraine, was uncertain. There was no date, either, for his arrival in Moscow or record of the permission to live in the city that had been a legal requirement under the old Communist system, so he had been permanently breaking the law until five years earlier. Each time, there had been a sentence for the residential offence in addition to the verdicts on eight of the ten separately listed criminal convictions. Five had been for physical violence, the others for larceny, burglary and running prostitutes. He'd served a total of eight years in various prisons, two in the Ukraine, the rest in Russia. Apart from extra jail terms for illegal residency, there had always been enforcement orders for the man to be returned to the Ukraine at the completion of each jail term.

Ignatov had been linked to the Ostankino Family during his last arrest. It had been for violence, for smashing the arms and legs of a breadshop owner on Ulitza Ogarova during an extortion demand, for which he had been jailed for three years. The baker had named the Ostankino as a crime syndicate to which he had been paying protection money: Ignatov had been the collector, demanding side payments for himself. In court Ignatov had denied any knowledge of any gang. Eight months after the trial at which the Ostankino Family had been named, the extortion victim, who had just started to walk again, had been knocked down in a hit-and-run accident and was now permanently crippled, confined for the rest of his life to a wheelchair.

Court records provided three different addresses in Moscow – one a brothel operated by three *shalava*, sleeve-snatching street whores unable to get foreign clients because of age or feared disease, reduced to charging visiting peasants less than a hundred roubles a time. No-one, at any address, admitted any knowledge of the dead man. His occupation was variously given as a labourer and a porter, never with any workplace or employer. So far no friends or acquaintances had been found, nor any record of his having been married or permanently involved with any woman.

'A man who didn't properly exist,' said Danilov. Holding up the last pages, listing the arrests and court appearances, he said to emphasise his point: 'And stupid. Every arrest at the scene of a crime, convicted because he was taken straight from police detention to a court. What's that tell us?'

'Small time,' agreed Cowley. Enjoying the new word, he said: 'A *lokhi*.'

'So what's the connection between a street-level pimp and thug and a murdered Soviet diplomat? OK, we've accepted Serov was dirty. But surely Ignatov was *too* small time!'

Pavin answered the telephone when it rang, listening

without interruption. At the end of the one-sided conversation he put his hand over the mouthpiece and said: 'A uniformed Militia search party has found a gun, close to where Ignatov's body was recovered. It's a 9mm Makarov.'

'Leave it where it is,' ordered Danilov, as he got up from his desk. Exhausted or not, it had been a mistake not to have gone to the scene the previous night.

'It don't make sense!' protested Bradley, probing for beef in the stroganoff before him. He chomped, open-mouth, and said: 'This really isn't bad. Great, in fact.' He gulped at some red wine before he'd emptied his mouth. 'You should have had it.'

Hank Slowen had already pushed his pork aside, deciding it was too rich roasted with plums: he was convinced he had an ulcer, although two examinations hadn't discovered any medical evidence. 'It's early days yet.'

'All the druggies in the fucking place should be pleading for mercy by now!'

'They are,' pointed out the FBI supervisor. 'We've got hospital registers to prove it. They're screaming.' They'd chosen the Gastronom Moscow, right on the Brighton Beach boardwalk, making themselves very visible, like the rest of the Task Force throughout the area.

'For methadone or whatever other shit substitute they can get!' dismissed the detective. 'They're not screaming what we want to hear! Neither are the hookers or their pimps or any other bastard. It's like a monastery under a vow of silence out there!'

'Too early,' repeated Slowen. He wondered if Bradley knew whether it was monks or nuns who lived in a monastery: probably not.

Bradley finished his stroganoff: he missed a grease blob on his chin with his napkin and the FBI man couldn't bring himself to point it out. 'Not too early,' argued Bradley. 'Too fucking scared. And if everyone in Brighton Beach is that scared, they've got something to be scared *about*. Like we've got something to worry about, because it means we're wasting our fucking time.'

Sergei Ivanovich Stupar believed himself a lawyer whose time had finally come. He had a brilliant, analytical brain which he'd known was being wasted in the former Soviet Union, mourning his inability then to quit for the West, where he knew he could have made a fortune.

He had been forty-five years old when Communism died, which was too old for a man seeking long-delayed rewards to study for any postgraduate degree in a foreign law school. Which Stupar, who was also a conceited man, decided he didn't have to do anyway. International law – particularly international financial law – was subject to interpretation from both sides of a no longer divisive barrier. Stupar, who had spent the beginning of his career manipulating the doubtful laws of Communist finance, blended perfectly into the milieu of adjusting and fashioning financial arrangements between East and West. Legitimate negotiations were, however, poorly paid.

The Chechen, on the other hand, promised to make him very rich, even paying him in dollars. He had initially been excited about the Swiss assignment, because it was precisely the financial environment in which he wanted to become involved. He decided he needed to exaggerate the problems he'd encountered in Geneva, to preserve his professional mystique and also because he was frightened of this man to whom he was reporting and wanted to impress.

'I've found a lawyer who will act for us,' he said, which was true. 'But not as long as there are police enquiries into the American murder of Michel Paulac.'

'The police have discovered the corporation?' demanded Yerin.

'They won't,' assured Stupar, also exaggerating his knowledge of international law and, more particularly, country-to-country treaty agreements. 'Switzerland is a complete bank secrecy country. But the Swiss are cautious. The lawyer won't move immediately.'

'How quickly could there be a transfer?' asked Gusovsky. He was unsure about excluding Zimin from this encounter.

'All it needs is a replacement Founder's Certificate and a nomination of new directors.'

'So we can go ahead,' said Gusovsky, to Yerin. 'We don't need formal control before the meeting. We know we can take over whenever we like.'

'It's important to keep to the schedule,' agreed the blind man.

CHAPTER TWENTY-SIX

The previous investigation had been in the winter, everything wrapped in a half-light of smothering greyness, sometimes fog, and Cowley had thought of it as a city with a blanket pulled over its head. In summer the greyness was still everywhere, unbroken by the faded green of the river-bordering trees. The streets were grey and the river was grey – except where the dredger was working, where it was black with churned mud – and the unsmiling people all around were grey. The uniforms of the street Militia were even officially grey.

And the murder scene was beyond professional belief.

Until that moment – based upon the police photographs – Cowley had imagined the alarm raised from above, from street level over an unbroken river wall. But the wall *was* broken, with steps leading to a concrete base beyond which floated a slat-board pontoon for passengers to board cruise boats and ferries: from where the dredger was working, he assumed the body had jammed on a mud-bank directly against one edge of the jetty, where it abutted the wall.

There was no taped-off cordon keeping the street clear for forensic examination, as there would have been in America. Onlookers were shoulder-to-shoulder along the wall on both sides of the entry to the river, littering fingerprints everywhere and foot-shuffling into oblivion any possible evidence. The pontoon steps were crowded with more milling, evidence-trampling sightseers and police and officials connected with the dredging operation.

'For Christ's sake let's clear these people away!' Cowley exclaimed. 'This is a goddamned shambles!'

'Too late,' said Danilov, as angry as the American. He still had Pavin locate the uniformed Militia major to clear the pontoon and the immediate street above.

'I can't believe this!' said Cowley, quiet-voiced in fury. 'I simply can't believe it! I'll have to tell Washington! And not to save my ass. They *should* know.'

'I think you should,' agreed Danilov again. What about his ass? Safe, he decided. Pavin's? There'd be efforts to side-step the responsibility. But a general, which Metkin was, or the senior investigating colonel, which Kabalin was, couldn't dump it on someone of Pavin's rank. Abruptly, a far more sinister realisation came to him. His safety had nothing at all to do with his being 5,000 miles away when Ivan Ignatov had been found. If Cowley had not returned to Moscow with him – which no-one had expected – all this staggering ineptitude and inefficiency would have been blamed upon him. Danilov hoped at least the Makarov had stayed in place and not been passed around between any interested hands before they'd got there.

It was difficult for the dredger to operate so close to the landing stage jutting sideways to the swirling current. The engine roared constantly between forward and reverse to keep it steady. Its bow-mounted scoop lifted and received mud so fine it looked like black, oily slime. It stank, of sewage and rot and filth, so badly that the three crewmen wore bandanas across their mouths and noses. Cowley thought it wasn't quite as bad as the hire car at National Airport, although he would have welcomed some mentholated salve beneath his nose.

There were two uniformed Militiamen and three river officials remaining on the pontoon. The policemen, near the river wall, reacted curiously when Cowley, obviously not a Russian but someone who could speak the language, asked if boats and passengers had gone on using the pontoon after Ignatov's body was found. When the older of the two, seemingly the more surprised by the question, said of course, Cowley physically had to turn to stare downriver, his mouth clamped shut against an outburst. He did not turn back until the arrival of the Militiaman who had found the gun.

The man was extremely young, the uniform still stiff with newness, the boots not yet scuffed. He seemed unsure what to do when he confronted Danilov. He half raised his arm to make a salute, but did not complete it. There was a suggestion of a blush.

'Udalov,' he announced, rigidly to attention. 'Aleksandr Vasilevich. Militia Post 22.'

One of the lucky army conscripts who'd managed to get into the police service after the dismantling of the Russian military, guessed Danilov: how long before the kid got involved in side-street kickbacks and compromises? Danilov said: 'You found a gun?'

Udalov pointed to where the two other Militiamen were standing. 'We were told to leave it where it was. There.'

The pistol was on a ledge less than a metre above the waterline and perhaps a metre from the furthest edge of the pontoon. Turning back to the young man, Danilov started to shout: 'Did you . . . ?' but then stopped, completing the turn to the river officials. Gesturing to the bellowing dredger, he said: 'Can you close that down?'

'Police orders were to dredge the area,' insisted an official.

'These are new police orders,' said Danilov. 'Take it out into the river until we've finished.' It was several minutes before the fat-bellied ship reversed away.

'Did you touch it?' Danilov resumed.

'No sir!'

'Our message said it was a Makarov,' came in Cowley. 'How did you know that if you didn't examine it? It's not very distinct that far away on the ledge.'

'I was in the Army until nine months ago,' confirmed the man. 'The Makarov was the gun I was trained to use.'

'It hasn't been touched or moved?' persisted Danilov.

'I didn't touch it,' said Udalov.

Both investigators recognised the qualification. 'Who did?'

'I do not know that anyone did.'

'Get the major down here,' Danilov said sideways, to Pavin. When the officer in charge arrived, Danilov pointed along the ledge and said: 'I want to know if anyone touched that gun. I either want an admission right now, or I will have everyone in your squad – you first – fingerprinted for elimination. Which will be an irritating waste of time, about which I will complain directly to Deputy Interior Minister Oskin . . .' He allowed time for the threat to settle. 'So, did anyone take that gun from the ledge?'

'I did,' admitted the major. 'We didn't know it *was* a proper gun until we looked.' He was a pock-faced man, ragged voiced with uncertainty.

Cowley felt the anger spread through him again. 'What part did you touch?'

'The top, near the hammer. That was the part nearest.'

'Nowhere else?'

'No.'

As frustrated as the American beside him, Danilov said to Pavin: 'Fingerprint him.' He looked suspiciously at the two men guarding the Makarov. 'Fingerprint them all!' Pointing to Udalov, 'Him last; I want to talk to him. And find out why a photographer and forensic aren't here yet.' Both departments had been ordered out before he'd left Petrovka.

Cowley leaned forward from the edge of the jetty. Over his shoulder he said: 'There could still be something on it: the watermark doesn't get that high.'

To the remaining Militiaman, Danilov said: 'Was there any rain in Moscow since the body was found?'

'I don't think so,' said Udalov doubtfully.

'No,' came the positive assurance from someone in the group supervising the dredging, who were now their audience.

Still to the young man, Danilov said: 'Tell us how you found it?'

'It was just there,' said Udalov simply. 'We all had to assemble this morning, a lot of us from different Militia stations, to search along this section. For anything that looked odd. I was told to come down here to see if anything came up in the dredger . . .' He smiled, shy but gaining confidence. 'It wasn't very interesting. And the smell was bad. After about an hour I looked along the inside of the river wall. And there it was, on the ledge!'

'You knew immediately it was a pistol?' said Cowley.

The man shook his head. 'I *thought* it was, but I wasn't sure. I was at the far end of the jetty when I first saw it. I *was* sure, when I came to where we're standing now.'

'Is it now *exactly* where it was when you first saw it? Or was it lying differently?' pressed Danilov.

Udalov stared along the ledge. 'That was how it was, the hammer the closest part to us: that's why the major got hold of it there.'

'As near to the edge as it now is? Or further in, nearer the wall?' demanded Cowley.

'Maybe a little closer to the wall. But only a millimetre or two.'

There was the clatter of descending footsteps as the scientific team clumped down the walkway.

Cowley said: 'It was good of them to come.' Even more pointedly, quoting the uniformed policeman, he went on: ' "We all had to assemble *this morning*, a lot of us from different Militia stations, to search along this section. For anything that looked odd." '

'What have I said wrong?' pleaded Udalov, recognising the words. 'I've told the truth!'

'*You* haven't said anything wrong,' assured Cowley. 'It's other people who haven't been telling us the truth.'

'It's beyond incompetence,' said Danilov. 'It's intentional obstruction.' He was convinced now that was exactly what it had been.

There was a silence between the two men, for several moments. Then Cowley, in English, said: 'I can't tell you how pissed off I am!'

In English, too, Danilov said: 'How do you think I feel? This was supposed to reflect upon me! Maybe it still will.'

Cowley shook his head but didn't say anything.

Danilov directed the nervously bewildered Udalov to be fingerprinted and for several minutes afterwards stood beside Cowley in matching silence, studying the gun and the ledge and the pontoon, positioning everything in his mind before stepping back for the technical experts. He decided the uncertainty with which the photographer assembled his camera and lights was quite understandable if he were the same man who had taken the earlier, totally inadequate sequence which had misrepresented the scene.

The far end of the jetty, to which they had to withdraw for

the technicians to work, seemed to catch more of the smell from the disturbed river bed.

'He went into the water here,' suggested Danilov, starting a professional to professional discussion.

'And the gun with him,' agreed Cowley.

Cowley walked part way back to where the forensic team was working. 'No blood anywhere on the pontoon.'

'Or up on the street, which there would have been if he'd been killed there.' Now Danilov paused, longer than the other man. 'Bloodstaining that would still be evident, even after people walking all over it, from the sort of wounds Ignatov suffered.'

'Too much *for* them to walk over,' accepted Cowley. 'The blood itself would have caused an alarm, even before the body was found.'

'So he was killed elsewhere?'

'And thrown from street level, over the parapet: not brought down here and tossed in,' expanded Cowley. 'If the body was dumped from this pontoon, the gun would have been tossed in, too. And *gone* in the water. It's on the ledge because it was dropped from above.'

'According to the notice at the top of the steps the last ferry uses this pontoon at eight at night,' said Danilov. 'There would still be a lot of people on the streets after that, though. According to the pathology report, Ignatov had only been in the water a matter of hours. I think we can assume he came over the wall, already dead, around midnight the day before his body was found. And the gun right after him.'

'Careless,' judged Cowley. 'Why not dispose of the murder weapon miles away? It's a hit, obviously. But it's not a very professional one.'

'Careless?' echoed Danilov questioningly. 'Or conceited? People – or a person – so sure of themselves they didn't imagine they had anything to worry about if the gun *was* found?'

There was movement near the wall as a forensic man finally scooped the Makarov off the ledge with what looked like a small fishing net and transferred it, without any finger contact, into a plastic exhibit bag. For the first time they both saw Pavin had returned to the jetty and was supervising the technical examination. Pavin personally took possession of the plastic-enclosed pistol.

'That'll have to go through our laboratories first,' said Danilov. 'Afterwards I think it should go through yours, as well.'

'So do I,' said Cowley. 'The sooner the better.' He turned to look fully at the Russian. 'I wasn't making any threats, to you personally, when I said I'd have to tell Washington what's happened here. There's no way you can be blamed.'

As it was intended I should be, Danilov thought. 'I know it wasn't personal . . . won't be.'

'You positive there won't be any fall-out to affect you?'

'Absolutely.' Because I intend to see there isn't, determined the Russian.

'So you want to use me?' guessed Cowley.

'Not in any way to cause you problems. Or difficulties.'

'But still using me, Dimitri Ivanovich?'

'If you're offended, I'm sorry.'

'So it's big internal problems?'

'I'm not really sure how big.'

'Can you win?'

'I don't know,' answered Danilov honestly. 'I hope so.'

The American seemed to be making a decision. 'Use me – and my presence here – as much as you want. Just warn me first.'

'Make the protest as strong and as official as you can.'

'I hope you know what you're doing, Dimitri Ivanovich.'

'So do I,' said Danilov.

Apart from taking the second series of photographs and retrieving the Makarov pistol, there was little for the Russian scientists to do, so their examination was soon over. The shipping officials told Danilov the dredger had already collected two containers of detritus. Danilov ordered them to collect a third before switching to the other side of the pontoon, hopefully to bring up anything that might have been carried downstream, away from the body, after it went into the river. They dropped Cowley off at the American embassy on their way back to Petrovka.

'As strong and as official as you like,' reminded Danilov.

He ignored his waiting messages, wanting to despatch his own first. They were very brief and, as required, were jointly addressed to both deputy ministers, with courtesy copies to Metkin. The FBI official was appalled, Danilov warned, at the incompetence of the Russian investigation. William Cowley intended formally complaining to Washington, who would obviously pass the criticism on to the State Department. Incalculable evidence had been lost by the failure to secure the area where Ignatov's body had been found or properly to search it. And what technical material had been produced, particularly photographs, had been entirely misleading: part of the American's report to Washington would doubt the standard and ability of Russian criminal science investigation. Danilov concluded by suggesting the complaints were precisely the type of embarrassment that had been discussed on the eve of his departure to Washington.

When he finished dictating Danilov expected Ludmilla Radsic to leave the office to fulfil her true function before typing the memoranda, but she didn't. She went immediately afterwards.

By then Danilov had read his messages. The first summoned him to the Foreign Ministry for a conference with both Sergei Vorobie and Vasili Oskin. Vorobie added that Oleg Yasev, a senior Foreign Ministry official, would attend the intended interview with Raisa Serova. The second note, from Anatoli Metkin, approved the attachment of Kabalin and his assistant to the murder squad: any further, additional manpower was available.

Danilov made his private, protective record of everything.

Elliott Jones shook hands with the Metropolitan Editor of the *Washington Post* with a politician's hearty enthusiasm, and said he was glad the man had been able to make lunch at the Four Seasons: it was his favourite restaurant. It was the mayor's invitation and he had decreed the discreet table. The editor said it was his favourite, too. Both further agreed they were glad they'd finally been able to get together again. For most of the meal the conversation was about politics, with the editor agreeing how helpful the *Post* could be if Jones ran for higher office. Not until the coffee did the talk get around to the Mafia-type murders. When the editor said he couldn't understand the virtual news blackout, Jones suggested maybe the story wasn't in Washington any more and maybe William Cowley and Dimitri Danilov weren't either. When the journalist wondered what would be important enough to take the investigators out of town, Jones asked if the *Post*'s resident correspondent in Moscow had reported the stool-pigeon type killing of a known member of the Moscow Mafia. The editor said he didn't think so.

'When am I going to meet him?' demanded Olga. 'I didn't last time.' She warmed to her idea. 'We could make a party of it, with Larissa and Yevgennie. He was very good to me when you were away.'

Olga clearly wanted an audience for the reflected importance of entertaining an American investigator, Danilov saw. Why not? He'd enjoy impressing Larissa and he hadn't forgotten Kosov's gloating doubt after his deputyship had been announced. 'How was Yevgennie good to you?'

'He took me to the Metropole. And a club, the Nightflight: it was wonderful. I told you!'

'With Larissa?'

'She was working. And he's got a fabulous new car. Lots of dials in the front that all light up.'

Why would Kosov choose a night when Larissa was working? 'What did you talk about?'

'How you were getting on in America. I said I didn't know because you hadn't phoned. Can we invite them, too?'

'Yes,' agreed Danilov. This time he wouldn't have the reluctance he usually did, going through the subterfuge of social politeness with a man he was cuckolding. This time he'd be curious.

CHAPTER TWENTY-SEVEN

It took Cowley three hours to transmit a full account of the Moscow débâcle, helped by Stephen Snow who ferried the cables up to the secure embassy rooftop communications shack. Afterwards he accepted Snow's invitation in the other direction, to the basement social club.

He recollected it vividly from the last time, with Pauline and the then unsuspected Barry Andrews, present and past husband trying to appear civilised, each over-compensating, each ill at ease. Little had changed. The marines who formed the security detachment were still as anxious to get as close as possible to the secretaries and the female staff who remained aloof during working hours, and the music sounded the same, scratched and vintage sixties. Hamburgers and ribs on disposable grills were an innovation and the beer was being kept cool now in a small refrigerator and two plastic cold boxes, instead of floating in a garbage bin of melting ice. Cowley recognised several people from his previous visit, although he couldn't get their names. The recall was better on their part, understandably: he was an oddity, someone briefly appearing from outside their insular environment, the Man from Mars.

A trestle table was bowed under the weight of gallon jugs of PX hard liquor, all of which Cowley refused. Instead he made a beer last while he renewed old acquaintances and made new ones, determinedly vague about the reason he was back there, talking generally about an enquiry connected with something that had happened back home. Without exception, everyone with whom he talked asked at some time how long he'd have to stay in Moscow.

Cowley excused himself early and got a cab within minutes by using the street-wise advice of his previous visit, flagging down passing vehicles with a packet of Marlboro cigarettes displayed in his cupped hand. The driver tried for ten dollars in American currency but accepted five without argument.

Having got there, Cowley wondered why he had been in such a hurry to get back to the hotel: at least at the embassy there had been other Americans to talk to, even if he had found them dull. There seemed nothing better to do than go to the bar.

He was on his fourth Chivas Regal when, for the first time, he properly noticed three or four professional girls dotted around the side tables. One smiled openly at him, but he did not respond. Once it would have been different, but he wasn't bothered any more.

'This is unexpected! Dangerous!' Vladimir Kabalin was a tall, long-necked man upon whom shirt collars didn't properly settle. The sleeves of his jacket were too short, increasing the giraffe-like awkwardness.

'It's a bonus!' argued Metkin.

'It will make the rest more difficult. We should demand a meeting.'

'*Demand?*' queried Metkin.

'Ask,' corrected Kabalin.

'It's only one man,' said Metkin.

'Two,' insisted Kabalin. 'And it's the American who's the problem.'

'Soon there won't be any problem at all,' said Metkin. He considered Danilov had beaten him once. The man wouldn't do it again.

CHAPTER TWENTY-EIGHT

The suggestion came from Wilkes, the black detective who thought at street level, but was initially rejected by Hank Slowen, who said you didn't uphold the law by breaking it. Wes Bradley asked since when: a forest blaze could be put out by burning a firebreak in its path and no-one got pissed at the firemen. How many more Russian Mafia murders did Slowen want? At the end of the week the impatience was obvious from Washington and Slowen floated the thought past the two Washington homicide detectives with whom he kept in daily contact. Both thought it was a great idea.

The choice was left to Wilkes.

The hooker was dull-eyed but painted professionally to attract attention with glistening make-up that hadn't had time to smudge. She wore long boots that came up over her knees but were still far short of the micro skirt that only reached her crotch. The long-sleeved T shirt was short-waisted to expose a lot of bare stomach and tight for the nipples of her heavy tits to bulge through. Carla Roberts was one of several names she used: in blue movies she was known as Pouter Pet. When Wilkes announced that alias to the waiting detectives Carla grinned and said they all better believe it. The print-out showed fifteen previous prostitution convictions; there were also sentences for larceny and receiving.

'What the fuck's going on?' she challenged, immediately aware of the change from a normal vice arrest when she was led past the charge room cages into an interview room.

Bradley indicated a chair. Hesitantly she sat down but pushed it away from the table. Bradley picked up her sheet from it. 'Ten arrests in the past year, Carla. You training to fuck for America when it becomes an Olympic sport?'

'Average,' said the girl, professionally. She crossed her legs, professionally again, not tightly, so her see-through underwear stretched over her crotch.

Bradley said: 'Nice!'

Slowen, against the wall, thought how glad he was he'd chosen the Bureau and not the police force. He knew the arrest record gave the girl's age as twenty-three: he would have given her another ten years.

Carla smiled at Slowen, embarrassing him. 'You guys got something special in mind? A little party, maybe? I quote rates.'

'Maybe,' said Bradley. 'You know, with a record like yours a concerned, Christian-minded prosecutor could recommend a custodial sentence. Care and rehabilitation. Show what a caring society we are. And you'd be with an awful lot of dykes, so that pussy you're flashing at me wouldn't heal up. Wouldn't get paid for it, though. Still, you could be saved . . .'

'What the . . . ?' Carla uncrossed her legs, putting both feet firmly on to the ground. 'Why don't you stop jerking me around and tell me what this bullshit is all about!'

'It's about co-operation, Carla,' said Bradley. He reached across to where she was sitting, grabbing her left arm before she could stop him and yanking the sleeve up above the elbow. There was a line of track marks along the vein in the crook of her arm: one was scabbed and looked septic. 'Old hits. You finding difficulty scoring recently?'

The girl snatched her arm away and dragged her sleeve down to cover the evidence of her heroin addiction. 'Why don't you fuck off!'

'That's what we're offering to do,' said Wilkes.

'Providing the exchange is right,' said Bradley.

'You help us, we help you,' agreed Wilkes.

Slowen thought it was like a double act, the sort of routine comedians used. He didn't consider this version funny.

'We could make a case for rehab, putting you before a court. And get it,' insisted Bradley. 'Shitsville, with smoke-stacks. And there'll be the dykes, of course.'

'. . . Or you could learn to love us,' came in Wilkes, on cue. He took something Slowen didn't immediately identify from his jerkin and dropped it on the table.

Carla's eyes locked on to it. A nerve twitched, by her

mouth and Slowen thought her hand moved, instinctively, to reach out.

'Lotta happiness in that baggie, Carla,' promised Bradley. 'It's good stuff. Could be eighty percent pure, not like the cut-down crap. Enough there for a month, unless you binge . . .'

'. . . And we know there ain't nothing out there on the streets 'cos we've stopped all the traffic lights at red,' said Wilkes. 'Which is how they're going to stay. Seems to me you're still pretty much together, so I guess you had a little stash going for you. Sensible girl. But it's going to run out soon. Then what you gonna do, Carla? You ever been really strung out? Screaming for it but there's nowhere to go get some? That's what it's going to be like for you, in a day or two. Screaming. Hurting . . .'

'. . . Or this,' said Bradley, pushing the heroin closer to where she sat. 'Feel it, Carla. Feel the weight of it. Imagine how good it would be . . .'

'. . . All you gotta do is tell us where we can find Viktor Chebrakin or Yuri Chestnoy or any other of these connected Russian guys,' took up Wilkes. 'You do that you walk with our grateful thanks and that little present there, all to yourself . . .'

'. . . Or we gotta tell the courts about the dealing,' said Bradley.

'What fucking dealing . . . ?'

'That baggie there,' said Bradley. 'That's what Detective Wilkes found on you, after arresting you for soliciting, Carla. I know he did. He's already told me.'

'MOTHERFUCKER!' screamed the girl.

Slowen felt sickened. But the Bureau had done enough entrapments and deals in the past. And would in the future.

'So what do you say, Carla?' invited Wilkes.

For several moments the hooker sat staring at the generous sack of heroin, hypnotised by it. The twitch became more pronounced and she swallowed a lot, tongue coming out over her tight-together lips. 'I don't *know* where those people are! If I did, I couldn't tell you.'

'You're not hearing me right, Carla,' said Bradley.

'Fuck you!'

Wilkes, the man who knew his way in dark alleys, said: 'It's as bad as that, is it?'

'Don't know what you're saying.'

'They couldn't get you, if they were inside.'

'I don't know! And it's not just one or two names, is it? It's groups. Organised.'

The girl shook her head. Slowen noticed for the first time the sheen of perspiration making her face even shinier, threatening the sharp lipstick and mascara lines.

'We'd make it look right,' promised Wilkes. 'Bring more girls in, run them through the courts so you couldn't be singled out. Make a dealer bust, too. Lotta guys, so no one person would stick out as someone you'd fingered . . .' He picked up the bag, tossing it up and down in his hand. 'I bet you never had this much stuff at any one time in your entire life.'

'Promise?' mumbled the girl.

'Our word,' assured Bradley.

'I get the bag?'

'And less heat from now on,' guaranteed Wilkes. 'Just enough to convince them you're not a special friend.'

'Peter,' she said, a mumble again.

'Peter who?' seized Wilkes.

'Peter the Pole. Don't know any other name.'

'*Is* he Polack?'

'How the fuck do I know! Speaks English like he's got a rock in his throat.'

'Where do we find Peter the Pole?' asked Bradley.

Carla shrugged. 'Around.'

Bradley put an enclosing hand over the heroin. 'Better, Carla.'

'He usually uses the Adam and Eve bar, on Columbus. But not now the heat's on.'

'Where's he live?' asked Wilkes.

'I'm not sure.'

'We take guesses.'

'There are rooms over the amusement arcade on Atlantic.'

'We want you to look at some mugshots, see if you can pick out Peter the Pole for us, OK?'

186

'I get the bag?' Carla persisted.

'You *got* the bag,' assured Bradley.

As the girl left the room with Wilkes, Slowen said: 'That wasn't very pretty.'

Bradley said: 'What's pretty got to do with it?'

Leonard Ross had lunch served in his private dining room, Maryland chowder followed by New England lamb.

'We've got to accept we've caught the Russians running a criminal enterprise from their embassy,' insisted the Secretary of State. 'There can't be any other reason for the way the investigation is being handled in Moscow.'

'Cowley doesn't go that far,' reminded the FBI Director.

'But he expects us to protest officially?'

'I asked specifically. He says yes.'

'You got any thoughts about withdrawing him?'

'None,' said Ross. 'I've got two murders to solve. Cowley stays until we understand the connection.'

'I've summoned their ambassador for an explanation,' disclosed Henry Hartz. 'I'm damned if we're going to have a Mafia office on 16th Street!'

'Seems like one's already there,' warned the Director.

The doubtful Yerin had again persuaded Gusovsky to meet the two Organised Crime officers without the third member of the *komitet*. Gusovsky had agreed to Zimin's exclusion because he still trusted the blind man's judgment in all things, but he would have liked to feel more confident about Yerin's entrapment idea. The meeting had been in the Glovin Bol'soy restaurant, in a private rear salon where the policemen had eaten discreetly while they finalised the move against Danilov and Cowley.

'I liked the confidence Metkin showed,' remarked Gusovsky, after the two other men had left, both with their dollar bonuses safely pocketed.

'No reason why he shouldn't be confident,' insisted Yerin.

'There'll be an enquiry at the highest level. There'll have to be, to make it look right officially.'

'We've got all the influence we need.'

'I hope we won't be called upon to use it,' said Gusovsky.

Yerin had a blind's man sensitivity to nuance. 'You nervous?'

'I'd like more guaranteed control.'

Yerin closed his hand in a grasping gesture. 'We've got the Organised Crime Bureau, the Interior Ministry and the judiciary! It would be hard to have *more* control!'

'That should be enough,' conceded Gusovsky, annoyed now he'd let the uncertainty show.

'All Antipov's got to do is laugh.'

Danilov and Cowley laughed initially, though. But wrongly.

CHAPTER TWENTY-NINE

Danilov did it first, aloud, within minutes of Yuri Pavin entering the Petrovka office. Even the normally dour man was smiling. He held the plastic-enclosed Makarov in front of him like a trophy.

'A positive fingerprint match!' announced Pavin. 'Mikhail Pavlovich Antipov. One of the names on a Mafia list. The Chechen Family!'

'Ballistics?' demanded Danilov, just before laughing aloud.

'The bullets recovered from Ignatov's body definitely came from this gun,' assured Pavin, completing his announcement.

Cowley laughed as well, when Danilov reached the American at the hotel, although very shortly. Pain was banded around his head, so that he had to squint against the light. He'd never had a proper hangover before. 'This is how it happens sometimes. Let's hope all the rest starts falling into place! I'll be with you as soon as possible.'

Danilov was too preoccupied to detect the sluggishness in the American's voice, thinking ahead: he was reluctant to tell Anatoli Metkin, although he knew he had no alternative. But Metkin received the news far more calmly than Danilov had anticipated, doing little more than nod, and making no reference to the earlier warnings of the American complaints. He agreed every available investigator in the Bureau should be seconded to the hunt for Antipov, and that uniformed Militia be brought in if necessary. When Danilov said Cowley was on his way to Petrovka, Metkin invited the American to attend the general briefing which he, as Director, would obviously give.

Cowley made no comment when Danilov passed on the invitation. Danilov thought the American's face was puffy, and there seemed to be a lot of redness in his eyes.

They were the last to enter the squad room. There was a stir at the appearance of Cowley, who smiled and nodded generally: Vladimir Kabalin, lounged in a chair in the forefront, responded to the smile, extending it to Danilov. Beside him Aleksai Raina, who had acted as Kabalin's scene-of-crime man and whose direct responsibility it would have been to seal the river area, didn't make any greeting. He appeared quite relaxed but then, reasoned Danilov, he might not yet know of the criticism.

Everyone stood politely when Metkin came into the room. He waved them down with a gracious hand. Although it was unnecessary he formally introduced Cowley, who was acknowledged with more nods.

Metkin's briefing continued to be formal. He outlined the irrefutable scientific evidence linking the Chechen gangster with the Ignatov killing and said the man's criminal record was being run off, for every detective to receive a copy. There was no known address for the man. An arrest was urgent, so uniformed Militia as well as airport police would be alerted, to be on standby if necessary. First news of an arrest had to be given, day or night, to Dimitri Ivanovich Danilov, who was heading the investigation and would co-ordinate all information.

'What brought about that transformation?' demanded Cowley, back in Danilov's office.

'Your presence, most probably.'

'There's quite a flap in Washington. I was asked if I wanted it to be official. I said yes.' The American had followed Danilov's lead and was speaking English. At the far end of the room, Ludmilla Radsic was frowning, unable to understand.

'I've been summoned to the Foreign Ministry.' Before which he could see Larissa, if she was working the day shift at the Druzhba: there was insufficient time before the afternoon appointment to do anything practical in the investigation.

'If Antipov gets picked up it'll take all the heat out of any protest,' Cowley pointed out.

'I know,' accepted the Russian. He was glad professionally, but disappointed personally.

'What about another meeting with Raisa Serova?'

'Why don't we try tomorrow?' suggested Danilov. He'd have to contact the Foreign Ministry escort, he supposed. He frowned and then remembered: Oleg Yasev. Reminded by one new name, he thought of the other three Lapinsk had given him. Pavin would have exhausted criminal records by now. He'd have to ask what progress there was with the ministry personnel registries.

He walked Cowley from the building, to phone Larissa from a street kiosk out of Ludmilla Radsic's hearing. Larissa, who was working days, wasn't sure if a room were free. He wanted to lunch, Danilov insisted.

Although there genuinely was no time for anything else, Danilov remained uneasy about intruding his personal affairs into the middle of a day. Pavin's obvious surprise, when he said he was making a private enquiry but would telephone before going to the Ministry, didn't ease the feeling. Pavin didn't know of Larissa, of course, but Danilov was sure he guessed there was another woman.

Another of the reception managers who shared the same vacant room arrangement as he and Larissa recognised Danilov and smiled conspiratorially as he entered the hotel. He would, Danilov decided, be glad when all the deceit was over. Larissa was waiting beyond a curve in the reception area. She walked towards him head high, bringing her breasts up and with her hips undulating, and several men in the lobby turned to enjoy her progress.

'You trying to tell somebody something?'

She laughed at him. 'Only what you're missing. There isn't a room.'

'I said I wanted to eat lunch with you.'

She took his arm as they went towards the restaurant: over Larissa's shoulder he saw the other reception manager smile at them. Because Larissa was managerial staff and recognised they were seated and given menus at once, and the wine Danilov ordered was served within minutes. Russian favour-for-favour philosophy working on automatic pilot, Danilov thought: it seemed a long time since he'd frightened the garage and supply managers at Petrovka. They'd be praying for the murder investigation to last for ever: but then he did not really want it to end either.

'You look fantastic,' said Danilov. It wasn't empty flattery. Unlike Olga, he'd never seen Larissa untidy or uncared for: the clothes always appeared just to have been put on – even after the times they'd practically torn them off – her hair was always perfectly coiffeured, her make-up never blurred. Wrong to compare the two: unfair, as well. Olga didn't know there was a comparison. Larissa did.

'How was America?'

'OK.'

'Solve the crime?'

'No.'

'Saw in the papers you were enjoying yourself.'

It would have been the same photograph of him leaving the Georgetown restaurant to which Olga had referred. He said: 'What shifts did you work, when I was away?'

She looked at him curiously. 'Days. Why?'

So Larissa wouldn't have been working when Kosov had taken Olga to the Metropole and on to a nightclub. 'I just wondered.'

'You going to be jealous of me when we're married?'

'I'm not jealous.' What was it he'd felt watching the other men look at her in the lobby?

'You blushed and looked guilty when Natalia smiled at you from the desk. I saw you!' she teased.

'I didn't,' he denied, pointlessly.

'She thinks you're nice,' disclosed Larissa. 'Everyone knows who you are, after what was in the newspapers and on television.'

'I'll be taking the American out while he's here. Socially.' He stared down at the blubbery pork that was placed in front of him, knowing he'd made a mistake.

Larissa looked up at him questioningly. She'd been more sensible, ordering fish.

'Olga thought it might be nice if we all went out together: her and you and Yevgennie,' he went on.

'I'd like that,' Larissa said at once. 'So would Yevgennie: it would make the asshole feel important.'

'I thought the Metropole, perhaps?'

She pulled another face. 'Very impressive!'

'You been there before?'

'A few times. Yevgennie likes it. He can show off.'

'Olga liked it, when he took her.'

Larissa stopped eating, her fork poised half way between her plate and her mouth. 'You're joking!'

'Didn't you know?'

'No!' She shook her head, disbelievingly. 'You're not serious, are you?'

'Olga said the Metropole was wonderful: told me about Yevgennie's new car with dials in the front that light up.'

Larissa pushed her plate aside. 'Wouldn't it be the funniest thing! Olga and Yevgennie . . . !' She giggled. 'Who's going to tell them we don't mind, you or me?'

He didn't like Larissa dismissing it as a joke, which he at once accepted was absurd. After his hypocrisy there would be an almost natural justice in Yevgennie Grigorevich and Olga having an affair. Could they be? Of course they could. Should he mind? Whether or not he should didn't enter his reasoning. He *did*. The thought of Kosov making love to Olga offended him and the thought of his making love to Larissa offended him, although Larissa insisted it didn't happen between them any more and hadn't for a long time, years in fact. 'I don't understand it.'

'*Does* it matter?' she asked seriously. 'I thought we had decisions to make when you got back? So? You're back.'

'I can't do anything now. Not right in the middle of this case! That's unreasonable and you know it!' He hadn't intended to sound so indignant.

'When's it going to end?' She sounded indignant in return.

'I don't know. It could be soon.'

'As soon as it's over?'

'As soon as it's over.' Danilov had the feeling of having said the same words before: but he was sure that if he had, Larissa would have challenged him about it.

'I've decided how we'll do it,' she declared. 'At the same time. We'll choose a day and you tell Olga and I'll tell Yevgennie.' She smiled, sympathetically. 'It'll be easier for me. Yevgennie doesn't care: he's been fucking everything including knot-holes in wood since the day we got married. Olga doesn't suspect anything, does she?'

'She made some remark, a long time ago, that you and I seemed to get on well together. I don't think she meant anything by it.'

'It would be nice if we could stay friends, afterwards. With Olga I mean. It probably won't happen, but it would be nice.'

'I'd like that,' agreed Danilov. 'I won't say anything to her, about her and Yevgennie. She told me, after all, so it can't mean anything.'

'I'm not interested enough to ask Yevgennie,' dismissed Larissa.

Danilov's own words echoed in his head. It might not have meant anything to Olga, apart from a rare outing to places she didn't normally go, but he belatedly remembered Olga telling him Kosov had asked about the Mafia investigation. 'Yevgennie said anything else about me? About the job?'

Larissa examined him over her wine glass. 'You think that's why he took Olga out? Trying to find out something about you?'

Larissa was remarkably astute as well as being beautiful. 'I don't know,' he avoided.

'He's taken me to places . . . restaurant and clubs . . .' she offered slowly. 'There have been people there he's friendly with. I don't like them.' The movement didn't amount to a shudder, but it came close.

'What's the new car like?'

'German. Very luxurious.'

'From his friends?'

'Who else?'

None of the black marketeers to whom he'd introduced Kosov had ever been grateful enough to offer him a limousine, reflected Danilov. Thinking of how he *had* been rewarded, Danilov looked at his watch. Distrusting it, he checked with the restaurant clock and saw, surprised, that it was registering the correct time. 'I have to go.'

'Arrange the evening, with the American,' said Larissa.

She allowed a gap. 'I'll tell you, if Yevgennie says anything. About you.'

'I want you to.'

'I think he's jealous of you,' she said. 'It's nothing more than that.'

'I'm not sure he's jealous,' said Danilov. He thought Kosov was altogether more than that.

There was nothing new when he telephoned Pavin, at Petrovka.

Rafferty and Johannsen had rarely had it so good and were determined to keep it that way. They were beyond the reach of their own precinct, on permanent secondment to the Bureau. And with Cowley in Russia things were on hold, although both were far too clever to let that become obvious. They worked out of an anteroom to Cowley's office, which enabled them to appear constantly surrounded by illustration boards and annotated folders and exhibit lists. They maintained case records in immaculate order, creating a separate section for what Cowley sent back from Moscow. They used the telephone a lot, particularly when anyone looked into the room, direct dialling personal calls: Johannsen spoke to relatives in Stockholm he normally only communicated with in a card, at Christmas. Rafferty confidently got tickets for baseball games, knowing he could always make them. They harassed their DC colleagues two or three times a day for any progress at street level on the two murders, despite being told to go fuck themselves, and made friends with the security staff at the Swiss embassy, through whom anything might emerge concerning Michel Paulac. The interesting photographs came from there in the middle of the second week.

'Now lookee here!' said Rafferty, as they drove away. Johannsen was at the wheel. They'd decided to lunch at a seafood place an FBI agent had recommended up on the bay shore, near Annapolis.

'You want me to crash the car or you going to tell me without my having to look?' asked Johannsen.

'Three pictures,' announced Rafferty. 'According to the

covering note, Swiss security think they show our man Paulac with three men who could be Russian.'

'Serov?'

'Nope.'

'They look Russian?'

'What's a Russian look like, for Christ's sake! Baggy-pants days are over: these guys are into Gucci and Ralph Lauren now.'

'Where do the photographs come from?'

There was a rustle of paper and turned-over prints as Rafferty shuffled through the package. 'Private party, hosted by Paulac, at some restaurant overlooking the lake . . .' He was silent, reading for a moment. '. . . Somewhere around October, 1991.'

'Looks like a comparison run past every Russian picture the Bureau have on record,' said Johannsen. 'We should start tomorrow.'

'And if we blank out, we send them to Cowley in Moscow. There's only about a hundred million Russians. Should be a piece of cake for him to get a match.' The previous day they had told Cowley there were no police or FBI records on any of the Moscow Mafia names he'd supplied.

'What about asking the Swiss to go through their entry files for incoming Russians, for say September, October and November, 1991?' suggested Johannsen.

'Christ, you're a clever detective!' mocked Rafferty.

'I fancy shrimp,' said Johannsen. 'Shrimp and then a nice big crab. You think there's crab available at this time of the year?'

'Smart detective like you should be able to find one,' said his partner.

CHAPTER THIRTY

Danilov saw at once that Metkin was not there. But Nikolai
Smolin was: Danilov was still curious at the Federal
Prosecutor being excluded from the departure briefing. At
once he announced the identification of Mikhail Antipov
from the recovered murder weapon, conscious of the
palpable relief that went through the other three men. But it
was limited, by objectivity. The Deputy Interior Minister
said: 'Getting a name isn't getting the man.'

'All available officers from the Bureau are being supplemented by uniformed Militia wherever and whenever necessary,' assured Danilov.

'Do the Americans know?' demanded Oskin.

'Cowley attended the briefing at which the search was
organised.'

Sergei Vorobie frowned. 'Which brings us to the original
purpose of this meeting, the formal protest Note handed to
our ambassador in Washington. The identification of the
killer greatly mitigates the problem, but it is *exactly* the sort
of diplomat embarrassment we wanted to avoid. And
warned you about. Why *did* the American tell you in advance
he was making a complaint?'

Danilov decided at once why Metkin wasn't present.
These men regarded him, the recognised officer leading the
investigation, as the man responsible for the fiasco. Limiting
himself to the question, Danilov said: 'I regarded it as a
matter of courtesy.'

'Don't you also regard it as arrogant of the man to raise it as
high as he did? Making it official like this?' asked Vasili
Oskin.

Danilov hesitated. 'The mistakes were serious, at the time
endangering the entire investigation. And couldn't be
rectified.'

'Why *were* mistakes made?' said Smolin.

He *was* being blamed! It was easily defensible and he was going to have to rebut the accusation, but he had wanted any internal enquiry at least begun independently of himself, so there could not be any later charges of a vendetta or personal animosity. 'I can't answer that. I was not here when the body was found: when the investigation was started.'

'Who could answer?' demanded Oskin, unusually loud voiced.

Why were they forcing him to name the Director, from whom it was obvious the answers had to come? And why wasn't the man here, either at his own request or at their demand? From the call he'd made to Pavin from the Druzhba hotel he knew Metkin hadn't made any enquiry about the investigation during his absence: that didn't make sense, either. 'Anatoli Nikolaevich Metkin is the Director.'

'Who supervised the initial enquiry?' persisted Oskin.

'Senior investigating colonel Vladimir Kabalin,' supplied Danilov. This encounter wasn't going at all how he had expected: at that moment he wasn't sure *how* it was going. Despite his intended determination specifically to avoid the role, they were making him the accuser: and isolating themselves from any damaging fall-out by doing nothing other than properly reacting as their official positions might later require. Communism had institutionalised everyone, Danilov decided: made everyone frightened of offending an unknown higher authority.

'Tell us, in absolute and precise detail, what *wasn't* done,' insisted Smolin.

First accused, then accuser, now the prosecutor. Throughout the litany of failures, a recitation of beginning-to-end facts from the moment of their arrival at the river bank, the three men sat regarding him impassively. At the end Vorobie said: 'That's appalling. Inconceivable.'

With me as much a victim as Ivan Ignatsevich Ignatov, thought Danilov.

'If we arrest Antipov, and from him understand the connection between the killing here and those in Washington, we might be able to avoid giving the explanation the Americans are demanding,' suggested Smolin.

'According to the ambassador, the Americans think an organised crime group is operating out of our embassy with the tacit awareness if not the positive encouragement of the Russian government!' declared Vorobie. 'The fact that Antipov is a proven gangster is a virtual confirmation.'

'We can deny *official* knowledge,' insisted Smolin.

'We already have!' said Vorobie irritably. 'How the hell can we be believed when an accredited, murdered Russian diplomat *provably* had the names of Russian gangsters secretly in his possession? I wouldn't believe any denial myself! No-one would!'

Someone had to know what the names were doing there, thought Danilov. Who? Was it one of these two ministers, calmly lying, sure of remaining undiscovered because they were on the inside of the investigation, aware of everything that was happening?

'The Americans should not have been allowed to know of the names,' said Oskin critically.

'I didn't know they *were* names,' defended Danilov. 'They were meaningless letters until a computer made sense of them.'

'The whole thing has been a shambles,' said Smolin.

'It has *not* been a shambles!' protested Danilov. 'I was not responsible for the American protest.'

No-one knew for several moments how to continue. Then Oskin said: 'We *must* get Antipov! And quickly. Why don't we bring in the Security Ministry, too?'

'A manhunt that wide would leak,' cautioned Danilov, careless of the obvious inference of corruption throughout enforcement agencies. 'If Antipov learns of it he'll cross into any one of the former Soviet republics and be safe. I can't pursue him there, not any more.'

There was another brief silence, broken again by Oskin. 'If we don't get him quickly – a week at the outside – the Security Ministry will be brought in.'

'Definitely no more than a week,' endorsed Vorobie.

Smolin's nod made the suggestion unanimous.

Danilov decided he had not emerged well from the encounter.

'Let's hope there's nothing else to harm relations between us and Washington before we get him,' said Oskin.

It was a forlorn hope.

The following day's story given by the mayor to the *Washington Post* detailed everything down to the Mafia identities being found in Serov's papers, and named Ignatov as the third victim. But to protect Elliott Jones as the source it carried a Moscow dateline, giving the impression the news came from a Russian informant.

The media circus everyone had wanted to avoid cranked into gear.

CHAPTER THIRTY-ONE

The man who opened the door to Raisa Serova's apartment was tall and straw-haired, aged about forty. Surprisingly deep black eyes were shielded behind rimless, medically tinted spectacles. The suit was well cut, conservative grey. When Danilov introduced Cowley, Oleg Yasev said: 'I was not told an American was to be present!'

'There was no reason for you to be told,' said Danilov. He hoped the autocratic attitude was not going to set the tone of the encounter, but feared it would.

For a brief moment Yasev remained in the doorway, barring their entry, but then he stood aside.

Raisa Serova was on the same couch she'd occupied during Danilov's previous visit, legs elegantly crossed. She wore a black dress cut more for its style than to indicate mourning. The heavy linked bracelet matched the single-strand gold necklace at her throat. Everything was as neatly sterile as before. Raisa frowned at Cowley, too, recognising him as a foreigner. 'Why are you here?'

'Your husband was murdered in America: it's an American investigation,' said Cowley. This wasn't going to be easy, he guessed.

The woman looked questioningly at Yasev, who shrugged. Raisa gestured towards the man and said to Danilov: 'I am told you entered my apartment in Washington? You had no right!'

'I had every right. I was accompanied by an official from the embassy. A list was made of everything I took as possible evidence.' Who was supposed to be interviewing whom?

'You *took*!' Raisa uncrossed her legs, coming more upright in her seat. 'What did you take?'

Pavin was carrying everything in his briefcase, so she'd see soon enough. 'A diary. Some photographs.'

'I want everything returned! Immediately!'

'Mrs Serova,' intruded Cowley, as professionally calm as Danilov. 'How long had your husband known and associated with gangsters?'

Her arrogance slipped. She began: 'I don't . . .' but Yasev cut across her. 'I really don't consider that is a proper question to ask!'

Danilov turned fully to face the man. 'You are not here to decide what is or is not proper. You are here in support of Mrs Serova, nothing more. If you interfere or in any way obstruct this interview I will contact your ministry and have you removed . . .'

'. . . and I will have an official protest made from Washington,' endorsed Cowley. He must remember later to tell Danilov it was an empty threat, just made to get this asshole off their backs.

Yasev's face flamed beneath the yellow hair. 'My instructions are to protect Mrs Serova.'

'What does Mrs Serova need protection from?' seized Danilov.

'Protect her interests,' added Yasev.

Danilov jerked his head towards the telephone near the entrance to the living room. 'Call your ministry,' he ordered, intentionally demeaning.

Yasev stared at him tight-lipped, hands clenched by his sides in frustration. He shook his head, retreating slightly behind Raisa, as if physically standing guard.

Acknowledging their victory, Cowley said: 'I asked you a question, Mrs Serova.'

'Which was preposterous. My husband knew no criminals.'

'Not a man named Viktor Chebrakin?' took up Danilov, intent upon the slightest reaction. He was aware of Cowley, beside him, concentrating just as strongly.

'No.'

'Or Yuri Chestnoy?'

'No.'

'Igor Rimyans?'

'No.'

'Valentine Yashev?'

'No.' Throughout Raisa showed no facial response what-soever to any of the names.

'They were listed in your husband's handwriting, with others, in documents in your husband's office,' said Danilov.

'I know nothing of it: I don't believe you.'

'It's true.'

Danilov had told Pavin before their arrival how he wanted things produced. He reached sideways for the diary he had taken from the Massachusetts Avenue apartment. The pages containing Serov's coded records of Michel Paulac's Washington visits were tagged with yellow paper slips. 'Is this your husband's?'

'You know it is.'

Danilov crossed to where Raisa was sitting, flicking through the marked entries. 'He misspelled words, to identify the dates of Michel Paulac's trips to America.'

'That's ridiculous! And I told you I don't know anyone named Michel Paulac.'

'Were you and your husband very close?' took up Cowley.

Yasev shifted slightly. Danilov looked at him warningly. The man said nothing.

'That is an impertinent question!' protested the woman.

'What's the answer to it?' persisted Cowley.

'Of course we were! Why?'

'He kept a very great deal from you, didn't he?'

Yasev went from foot to foot.

'That remark does not deserve a reply,' dismissed Raisa.

'When we met last time you showed me your diary,' reminded Danilov.

'Yes?'

'Can I see it again?'

'Why?'

'I want to compare the Paulac entries in your husband's diary against yours,' admitted Danilov openly.

'This is not right . . .' started Yasev, but in front of him Raisa raised an imperious hand, stopping the protest. She got up, left the room but was back within minutes, dismissively handing Danilov the black-bound book.

Danilov took his time. He checked entry against entry and

prolonged the examination by passing both diaries sideways to Cowley. There was no tally between the two.

'Satisfied?' she demanded.

It was Cowley who answered. 'Your husband was murdered. Horribly.'

'Yes?'

'We are trying to find his killer. Or killers.'

'Yes?' she questioned again.

'Why are you so resistant, Mrs Serova? Don't you *want* the murderer caught?'

Raisa Serova stared up at Cowley for several moments: briefly her impassive face twisted, close to an expression of anguish. 'All you have done – every question you have asked – makes out Petr Aleksandrovich was a criminal!'

'Wasn't he?' demanded Cowley remorselessly.

'No! He was a kind, loving man dedicated to the job he did! He cried for joy when Communism ended here! And again when the coup against Gorbachov failed!'

'He knew criminals!' insisted Danilov.

'I DON'T KNOW THEM! OR ABOUT THEM!' The screaming, near-hysterical outburst startled them all: Pavin, less prepared than anyone because he was head-bent over the notebook, actually gasped in astonishment, jerking up towards the woman.

'This is disgusting! Disgraceful!' protested Yasev. 'I insist it stops!'

Again both investigators ignored him. Danilov reached out again for the photograph of Serov with an unknown man. 'Who is this with your husband?'

Raisa remained gazing down at the picture so long Danilov was about to prompt her when she spoke. All the hard, supercilious control had gone. She was wet-eyed and her lips were trembling. 'My father,' she said, broken-voiced. 'He died two years ago. Of exactly the same cancer that is going to kill my mother, whom I took into hospital three days ago: less than two months, the doctors say. In the bowel, so they suffer a lot. And in between Petr Aleksandrovich has been murdered. Which leaves me with no-one . . .' She looked towards Cowley. 'Is this better, now I am crying . . . ?'

There was a loud silence.

Cowley said: 'I am not trying to make you cry, Mrs Serova. I'm trying to find your husband's killers. And the reason for his being killed. And how he came to know the people he apparently did.'

'Don't you think I'd *tell* you, if I knew! Don't you think I *want* them caught and punished; gassed or hanged or however it is you execute people in America!'

'You knew nothing at all?' said Cowley, less aggressively.

'Nothing!' She indicated Yasev again, behind her. 'So unless there was some official reasons that I don't – you don't – know, I lived with a man who kept secrets from me. A man I didn't know at all, but thought I did. So I don't know now what sort of marriage I had.'

Danilov looked sideways, enquiringly, at Cowley who shrugged back, no questions left.

Sensing the embarrassment of both investigators, Yasev said: 'Are you satisfied?'

Danilov retrieved from Pavin the final photograph, that of Serov with the elderly couple, offering it to the woman without the need to ask the question. Raisa glanced at it and said: 'Petr's parents. They live at Kuntsevo: they were very proud of him.'

Cowley was disappointed. He'd actually been encouraged by Raisa Serova's initial arrogance, believing from the psychological sessions at the FBI's Behavioral Science Unit at Quantico he recognised a barrier behind which she was hiding and which could be broken down: that was why he had been so hard, showing no sympathy. It *had* been a barrier, he supposed: one behind which she had every reason to crouch, in her grief. He was disgusted with himself, without needing any accusation from the pompous asshole of a ministry official. Cowley's head ached, too, and his stomach was sour. He made a resolution to go easier in the bar tonight.

'Can I have the photographs?' asked the woman. She was practically pleading.

Danilov handed them to her, along with her diary.

'What about Petr's diary?'

'I need to keep that,' refused Danilov. 'I need to understand the marked entries.'

There was no protest this time. Raisa said, more to herself than to anyone else: 'The funeral's on Wednesday. At Novadichy . . .' Then, as if there had been some doubt, she went on: '. . . his parents are coming.'

Danilov welcomed the dismissive gesture from Yasev, moving towards the door ahead of Cowley and Pavin. In the car – in Russian for Pavin's benefit – Danilov said: 'That got us nowhere.'

'It could have done,' said Cowley.

At Petrovka, on the far side of town, Metkin smiled up at his former partner. 'All set?'

'An apartment on Ulitza Fadajeva,' said Kabalin. He still wasn't as confident as the other man.

'Make sure it's recorded in absolute detail.'

'Of course.'

'The Foreign Ministry have asked for a full explanation of what happened at the river. There's to be an enquiry.'

'Everything in place?'

'It will be. Antipov will complete it.'

Every official ministry and investigation branch in both Moscow and Washington was inundated by media demands after the *Washington Post* exclusive. The American State Department liaised with the Russian Foreign Ministry, each denying any knowledge of the source and each promising an enquiry to discover it. A joint, confirmatory press statement was issued in both capitals.

Cowley learned about it when Washington demanded if he had had any contact with the press – which he immediately denied – and caught Danilov at Petrovka to warn him.

'Part of our ongoing problem with your people?' asked the American.

'It could be. It certainly wasn't Pavin or me.'

'Now we'll have cameras over our shoulders all the time. Fame again.'

'Fuck fame,' said Danilov. It was a better obscenity in English.

CHAPTER THIRTY-TWO

The arrest of Mikhail Pavlovich Antipov was perfectly co-ordinated, even to the hour. It was carried out by a squad of plainclothes and uniformed Militia officers under the command of Vladimir Kabalin. They smashed their way with sledgehammers into the Ulitza Fadajeva apartment at four o'clock in the morning, when the man was in bed asleep. He was with two girls who later turned out to be mother and daughter: the daughter was fifteen years old.

The surprise was so absolute there were three officers with pistols drawn and trained upon him before Antipov properly awoke. He tensed, beginning to move his right hand behind him, but stopped when he saw the pistols: after he and the girls, without embarrassment, got nakedly out of bed one of the uniformed men found a 9mm Stetchkin pistol beneath the pillow.

'What's this about?' demanded the man. He remained naked. The girls were also taking their time getting dressed: the fifteen-year-old giggled openly at the ogling policemen.

'Murder,' announced Kabalin shortly.

Antipov laughed. 'Who did I kill?'

'Ivan Ignatsevich Ignatov,' identified Kabalin formally. One of the plainclothes officers was taking note of the exchange.

'I didn't kill anyone.'

'We know you did,' sighed Kabalin. 'We've all had enough time to admire the size of your prick. Get dressed.'

Antipov started to, but slowly. Nodding to the girls, now fully clothed, he said: 'What about them?'

The apartment block had been under surveillance from early the previous evening, which was how they'd known Antipov was there, but the girls hadn't entered with the man and Kabalin was uncertain what to do with them. 'They're coming too.'

Antipov stopped dressing, smiling again. 'They almost killed *me* last night: nearly fucked me to death!'

The girls laughed.

'Remember it,' advised Kabalin. 'Could be a long time before you get it again.'

As well as putting on clothes – a knitted sports shirt beneath a deep brown chamois jacket that matched the Gucci loafers – Antipov slipped a gold wristwatch on his left arm, a gold bracelet on his other wrist and took his time selecting rings, a platformed gold band for his left hand, a silver one with an onyx centre for the right.

'You look beautiful,' said Kabalin.

From the main room Antipov looked at the smashed-down door. 'Who's going to pay for that?'

'It's all being recorded,' assured Kabalin. A photographer was already taking pictures of the interior of the apartment. Kabalin indicated his scene-of-crime officer, Aleksai Raina: the man was putting the Stechkin pistol into an exhibit bag. 'Everything taken for examination is being recorded.'

'Have you got the legal right to remove things?'

'Probably not. You going to complain?'

'Probably not.'

'What about our time?' demanded the elder prostitute, taking her lead from Antipov. 'Who's going to pay for that? Everyone got a good look!'

'Think of it as advertising,' suggested Kabalin.

'On a Militia salary, none of you could afford to buy what's on offer,' said Antipov.

'Put your arms out,' ordered Kabalin.

'What!' For the first time Antipov showed anger.

'Manacles,' said Kabalin.

'Fuck off!'

'I don't care if you want to be chained forcibly. Suit yourself.'

Antipov extended his arms, wincing slightly when Kabalin snapped the handcuffs shut. The photographer took several exposures of the formal arrest.

At Petrovka, Kabalin let the two prostitutes share a detention cell and put Antipov in the holding cage adjoining the interview room. The arrested man had recovered his insolent disdain: he carefully removed the chamois jacket before stretching out full length on the narrow bed, hands cupped behind his head.

Kabalin telephoned Metkin from the Director's own office. 'Perfect,' he reported.

'I'll come,' said Metkin.

Dimitri Danilov was told by the desk officer as he walked into Petrovka to report at once to the Director: the man already had the telephone in his hand, announcing the arrival.

'It was all done while you were asleep,' Metkin announced, as Danilov entered the suite.

He took his time recounting every detail of the arrest, even showing Danilov the already processed photographs of the chained and glowering Antipov. A full account had already been sent to both the Foreign and Interior Ministries, with the suggestion that a full press communiqué be issued both to assure the American authorities of the standard of Russian investigations, after the recent criticism, and to satisfy the media clamour after the disclosure of the link between the killing of Ignatov and the Washington murders. Danilov didn't have to bother contacting Cowley about the arrest, either: Metkin had already informed the American embassy.

'It seems to have all worked out very satisfactorily?' offered Metkin.

'Yes,' agreed Danilov. It was like being back at the beginning, sure about nothing, understanding nothing. 'When was it discovered where Antipov was?'

'Some time last night. Why?'

'I would have expected to be told, as the officer in overall command.' It sounded like whining petulance. But he *should* have been told: taken part in the arrest.

'Concerned about headlines, Dimitri Ivanovich?'

'Concerned about the efficiency of the operation after the problems we've already had,' said Danilov.

Metkin tapped the photographs in front of him. 'Everything has been done correctly . . .' He smiled. 'Now all you and your American friend have to do is interrogate the man and extract the confession.'

Why, wondered Danilov, was the questioning being left to him? Was the need to include Cowley sufficient reason?

Antipov's arrest was not the only early-hours seizure in connection with the three matched killings. The Brooklyn Task Force had begun the promised, informer-concealing round-up of hookers and drug dealers the afternoon that Carla Roberts appeared before a judge to be fined $50 and released. By the end of the second day they had a surname and a description for Peter the Pole, who wasn't Polish but Ukrainian and whose full name was Petr Zubko. Records produced a rap sheet with two small-time drug-trafficking convictions and three for aggravated assault. And a mug-shot.

Bradley set up a round-the-clock stakeout on the Adam and Eve bar on Columbus and got a virtually positive ID on the third night: to make sure, they followed Zubko home to the amusement arcade on Atlantic Boulevard, picking out the room above when the light went on. The Americans didn't wait as long as the Russians, three hours later and 5,000 miles away. It was only one in the morning when the SWAT team smashed in the door: the plywood was so flimsy the lead man was carried by the force of his first sledge-hammer strike halfway through the hole he made. They were able to laugh about it afterwards: Zubko had already injected and was on the nod, too far gone to react. If he hadn't been shooting up he could easily have killed the spread-eagled officer with one of the two guns later found in the stinking, dishevelled squat. Neither of the guns was a Makarov.

It wasn't until mid-morning, long after the interrogation of Antipov had begun, that Zubko was fit enough to be questioned. As with Carla Roberts, Wilkes and Bradley did the questioning, with Slowen the uninvolved observer.

'You're in shit, Peter. Deep shit,' began Bradley.

'What you want?'

The hooker had been right, Slowen thought: the man did

speak as if he had rocks in his throat. He had the neglected thinness of an addict who rarely ate, nerves tugging near his left eye and in his cheek. The shake was beginning in his hands, and he was using both to scratch away the skin irritation there sometimes was coming down from a heroin plateau.

'To make the world a better place,' said Wilkes. 'It's our reason for living.'

'Don't know what you mean.'

'We mean ridding the streets of vermin like you,' said Wilkes.

'We're going to send you away to a very bad place and you're going to stay there for the rest of your life . . .' The lieutenant stopped, pretending the need to consult the man's criminal sheet. 'Says here you're forty-three. With the shit we found stashed in that rat-hole where you live, we got ourselves a major trafficking indictment here. And you're an already convicted trafficker. A recidivist . . .'

'. . . And there's the guns,' said Wilkes.

'The guns!' exclaimed Bradley, tapping his forehead. 'I forgot the guns. You know, we can't find a licence record anywhere for that Smith and Wesson and that Beretta . . .'

'. . . You got a permit for those, Peter . . . ?'

'. . . Sure as hell won't look good if you haven't,' said Bradley. 'The one thing judges hate more than a major drug trafficker is a major drug trafficker who goes around with a loaded piece, prepared to kill people . . . You kill people, Peter?'

'. . . Twenty-five years, I'd guess,' came in Wilkes. 'And there's no parole for drug convictions, so you're going to serve every one of them . . .'

'. . . Which will make your sixty-eighth birthday pretty special, 'cos that's the first one from now you're going to enjoy outside the slammer . . .'

'What you talk about?'

'Courts don't like big time, Grade A operators,' said Bradley. 'And that's what you are. How else could you describe a trafficker with maybe more than a kilo of sixty or seventy percent shit in his room when we come calling?'

'What you talk about?' repeated Zubko. 'Don't have no kilo!'

'Found it myself, under your bed,' insisted Bradley.

'Saw him do it,' confirmed Wilkes.

'No true!'

'Gonna swear on oath,' said Bradley.

'Me too.'

Slowen hadn't heard anything about a kilo of heroin until that moment.

'You plant it!' declared Zubko.

Solemnly the two detectives looked at each other, then back at the Ukrainian. 'That's a grave accusation,' said Bradley. 'Courts don't like lies being told about the police.'

Zubko was scratching himself more vigorously, the shaking was worsening, and there was a patina of sweat on his face. 'Why you do this?'

'Tell us about Viktor Chebrakin,' demanded Bradley.

'And Yuri Chestnoy.'

The man brought his shivering hands up to his face, as if physically to stop himself talking.

Wilkes said: 'We're not hearing you, Peter.'

'How about Igor Rimyans?' persisted Bradley. 'He's pretty big on the drugs scene in Brighton Beach, isn't he?'

Zubko remained with his hands to his face, hunched over the table.

Wilkes said: 'We're still not hearing you!'

'Don't know these men.'

'That's a lie,' said Bradley.

'I'll tell the court what you did to me. Put heroin in my place.'

'Who do you think they're going to believe? Us? Or you? Think about it,' urged Wilkes.

'What you want?'

'Where would I find Viktor Chebrakin or Yuri Chestnoy or Igor Rimyans . . . ?' said Bradley.

'. . . Or Valentin Yashev?' completed Wilkes.

The lowered head shook, in refusal.

'Twenty-five years,' said Wilkes.

'No parole,' said Bradley.

'There's a warning,' mumbled the man.

'We know,' said Bradley.

'We do deal?'

'We want addresses. *Right* addresses,' said Bradley.

'Then you not lie, about the heroin?'

'Names. Addresses,' insisted Wilkes.

'Rimyans,' mumbled the man.

'OK. Rimyans,' accepted Bradley.

'Queens,' said the man, voice scarcely above a whisper, still refusing to look up. 'The corner house at Junction Boulevard and Elmhurst Manor.'

'The Jackson district!' identified Wilkes, the man with local knowledge. 'We're a long way from Brighton Beach.'

'Airport,' said Zubko, simply.

'Supply points,' breathed Bradley. 'A spit from La Guardia, not much further from Kennedy.'

'You never tell it was me?'

'Of course we wouldn't.'

'And you not lie about the heroin?'

'Let's see who we find in Jackson,' avoided Bradley.

'I tell truth.'

'We're going to be very upset if you aren't,' warned Wilkes.

They held an immediate conference in Bradley's office, accepting the Washington edict that Slowen remain as supervising controller of the investigation spreading wider and wider throughout the New York boroughs. Before driving out to Queens Slowen had a long telephone conversation with the precinct captain in the Jackson district, who wasn't offended at the suggestion that Bradley and Wilkes, with their knowledge and involvement of the case, accompany him. Wilkes drove.

'You going to do a deal with Zubko if the address he's given us is kosher?' asked the FBI man.

Slowen was aware of Wilkes' expression of astonishment reflected in the rear-view mirror. Wilkes said: 'Deal with a motherfucker like him?'

Bradley said: 'He kills people. Kids.'

'You know where he trades?' demanded Wilkes.

'Schoolyards. Gives kids little samples without payment, like a supermarket loss leader, until they're hooked. Catching up with Zubko is the first positive benefit that's come out of this whole goddamned thing!'

'So the answer to your question, Mr Slowen, is no; we are not going to deal, whatever we come up with at Jackson.'

'With more than a kilo – and the two guns – it probably will be a long sentence,' said Slowen.

'The longer the better,' said Wilkes.

CHAPTER THIRTY-THREE

Cowley was waiting when Danilov got to his office after the encounter with the Director. So was Pavin. The scene-of-crime officer was subdued instead of being excited, which Danilov found strange.

The American wasn't. 'This looks like it at last!' greeted Cowley. He'd held himself to three whiskies the previous night, refused wine at dinner, and felt fine.

'It could be,' agreed Danilov. He saw there were duplicate photographs of those he had seen in Metkin's office and several obviously new folders banked up on the exhibit table. Some had overflowed to rest on top of the closed safe.

Seeing Danilov's look, Pavin said: 'Everything's complete, including the statements of those involved in the arrest. It's immaculate.'

Was Pavin jealous of someone else being able to correlate evidence as meticulously as him? It was difficult to believe, but it could be a logical explanation for the other man's attitude. Danilov told him: 'We'll need the gun. And the fingerprint sheets.'

While Pavin was unlocking the safe, Cowley said: 'You want the interrogation any special way?'

'Let's play it according to how he reacts,' suggested Danilov.

'I'll follow your lead,' accepted Cowley.

Danilov looked to Pavin. 'Let's make an audio recording, as well as a written note.'

'Already arranged,' assured the exhibit officer.

For a few seconds after entering the interview room, until he saw the earphoned technician, Cowley stared at the archaic recording apparatus in genuine curiosity, unsure what it was. A separate table had been brought in for Pavin's additional note-taking. There was only one chair on either side of the other table, for a one-to-one confrontation:

another chair stood by the door, put there because whoever had arranged the room hadn't been sure where else to leave it. Cowley was content with its position: with Danilov settled facing him across the table, Antipov would constantly have to switch from one interrogator to the other to answer their questions. It would form a psychologically disorienting triangle, to their advantage.

Cowley and Danilov, professionals both, instantly recognised another professional from the other side of the divide when Antipov swaggered into the room. He wore the chamois jacket slung around his shoulders, the sleeves hanging loose; it made look bigger shoulders that didn't need enlarging. His hair was greying and crew cut, although to create a rugged-man style, not for the disguising reasons Danilov wore his that way. It reminded Danilov he still had to get his cut. Antipov's face was tight skinned, stretched over angular cheekbones and jaw, stubbled from lack of a shave. He wasn't manacled, and the two uniformed warders stood back for the man to come through the door. Cowley's impression was more of their being courteous escorts than watchful guards to a shoulder-rolling mafioso.

Antipov stopped short of the table, hands nonchalantly in his pockets, exaggeratedly surveying the room. He halted at Danilov. 'Who are you?'

'Sit down,' Danilov ordered, dismissively waving towards the chair opposite.

Antipov took his time: he kept his hands in his pockets, extending his legs fully in front of him.

'I am charging you that on or about the fourteenth of this month you murdered Ivan Ignatsevich Ignatov,' announced Danilov. He nodded to the recording apparatus and to Pavin, alongside. 'Whatever you say will be taken down, for presentation at your trial.'

Antipov snorted a laugh. 'Why don't you fuck off?' He turned towards Pavin. 'Make sure you get that.'

'We've got the gun we can scientifically prove fired the bullets that killed Ignatov. It's got your fingerprints on it.' Danilov held it up, in the protective exhibit bag.

Having tried a laugh, the gangster yawned, hugely.

'Didn't get a lot of sleep last night, with one thing and another.'

Danilov said contemptuously: 'We've all seen the American movies. You're not doing it very well.'

Choosing his moment, Cowley said: 'No good as an actor and no good as a thug.'

Antipov had to turn, as Cowley had known he would: for the first time there was interest on the man's face. 'Russian crime so serious they've got to import help?'

'Why don't you tell us about Russian crime?' invited Danilov.

Antipov spread his hands innocently, palms upwards. 'What do I know about Russian crime?'

'It wasn't from a movie you got the idea of shooting Ignatov in the mouth, was it?' said Cowley. 'That was intended to mean something . . .'

'. . . What did it mean?' completed Danilov.

Antipov yawned again, more artificially than before.

Danilov held the exhibit bag up again. 'It's an automatic conviction. Which means the death penalty. You want to die, shot like you shot Ignatov?'

'I've never seen that gun before. Don't know anything about a man called Ignatov.'

'Don't be stupid!' sneered Danilov. 'He was an Ostankino bull. And you killed him.'

'Is there a gang war going, between the Ostankino and the Chechen?' demanded Cowley. 'They're your main rivals, aren't they?'

'I don't know what Ostankino or Chechen means.'

'What's your rank, in the Chechen?' said Danilov, setting the Makarov on the table in front of the man, where he could constantly see it. 'You a bull?'

'Or just a *lokhi*?' queried Cowley, taking up the sneer, trying to penetrate the veneer.

Antipov shook his head in contempt, not denial.

'Probably a *lokhi*,' jeered Cowley. 'In America the worst soldier wouldn't dump his weapon with the body.' Arrogant men often cracked under ridicule.

'What was Ignatov going to say about the Chechen?'

resumed Danilov. 'That's what the mouthshot is for, isn't it? A warning to stool-pigeons? You've copied that from America, like a lot else.'

'Why ask me?' There was a heavy shrug.

'Or do the Moscow mobs have different rules?' said Cowley, in growing desperation. 'You have different titles, after all.'

'I told you, I don't know anything about mobs or titles.'

'Maybe you're telling the truth,' said Cowley. 'A *lokhi*, too small time to know anything . . . a punk. Means you're shit. That's you, isn't it? Shit.'

'How long you going to keep this up?' said the man, holding the anger.

'As long as it suits us,' said Danilov. 'You're ours now. We can hold you as long as we like, how we like, where we like . . .' He snapped his fingers. 'We do that and you jump.'

'Go fuck yourself,' said the mafioso again.

It was looking increasingly as if that was exactly what they were going to have to do, decided the American. He couldn't at the moment think of an approach that might have been more successful with the man, but their supercilious performance certainly hadn't succeeded. 'You know what that double fuck was you had last night?' said Cowley, knowing the circumstances of the man's arrest from Kabalin's already prepared report. 'The last ever. Sure hope it was good for you.'

That failed like the rest. Antipov feigned masturbation. 'It was fantastic. You want their address? They're very expensive but worth every dollar . . .' He turned more fully, to Cowley. 'You could probably afford it. You'll have the money, being an American . . .' He nodded between Cowley and Danilov. 'Why not do him a favour, treat him to the fuck of the century?'

Thank God they could hold him as long as they needed, thought Danilov: it was going to be a long haul to break this bastard. 'You read newspapers? Watch television?'

'Sometimes,' shrugged Antipov.

'Two men were killed in Washington, just like Ignatov: shot in the mouth. One was a Russian diplomat.'

218

'Didn't hear about it,' said Antipov. 'I'm a businessman! What do I know about crime?'

'What sort of business?' pounced Cowley.

'Import–export.'

'What do you import and export?'

'Whatever I can. Nothing special.'

'Where are your offices?'

'I don't need offices. I buy one place and sell another. I'm a middleman.'

'You're a little thug,' said Danilov. He reached down by his side again, bringing up the old and new fingerprint sheets. He held out the first and said: 'The file that goes with these has two convictions for violence . . . two more for theft . . .'

'. . . It's a risky business . . .' broke in the man. 'Have to protect myself sometimes.'

Danilov paused beyond the interruption, suddenly thinking Antipov was actually enjoying the fruitless interrogation. Holding out the second sheet, he said: 'These came from the butt of the gun. That'll convict you. Put you before a firing squad . . .'

'. . . Wouldn't it make sense to try to help yourself?' pressed Cowley.

'How?'

The simple question, free at last of any arrogance, encouraged both investigators. Danilov said: 'With the evidence we've got, a death sentence is automatic. Co-operate, and I'll intervene with the Federal Prosecutor. See he doesn't demand the death sentence at your trial . . .'

'We're offering you life!' urged Cowley.

'Wish I knew what it was you wanted,' sniggered Antipov.

Cowley only just suppressed the exasperation, glad he was able to deny the cocky bastard the pleasure of knowing how deeply he was getting under their skins. He saw Danilov looking at him over Antipov's head and lifted his shoulders, helplessly.

'Don't be a fool,' said Danilov, standing but leaning across the table. 'You haven't got a defence. And we *can* do what we like with you. We'll talk tomorrow, and the day after that, and the day after that. For as long as it takes. Think of the choices. You going to choose to die? Course you're not! Only a fool would do that . . .' He nodded to the waiting detention guards.

Antipov took as much time standing as he had seating himself. 'Some things were taken from me, when I got here this morning. Rings. A watch. A gold identity bracelet. You'll see they don't get stolen, won't you? I don't trust the Militia, uniformed or otherwise. No-one does.'

No-one spoke for the first few minutes after Antipov was escorted from the room. Cowley crossed to take the interrogation chair at the table. Danilov gestured for the tape to be stopped.

'He should have snapped, being ridiculed,' insisted Cowley, sure of the psychology. 'That was the way to do it.'

'He hasn't had time to think it through,' suggested Pavin. 'It will be different when he realises he *is* going to die.'

Cowley shook his head, not completely convinced. 'He's got a long way to go before he becomes a frightened man.'

'But no real choice in the end,' insisted Danilov, confidently.

By the time they got back to Petrovka, the decision had been made to issue a press statement announcing the arrest. Vladimir Kabalin was named as the arresting officer: the point was emphasised that it had been an entirely Russian operation, although American participation was continuing with the ongoing investigation. A photograph of Mikhail Antipov was released.

The Jackson address was openly recorded in the housing register and in Post Office computers as being that of Igor Rimyans and his wife Irena. It was a clapboard, two-storey house with an attached garage and a well tended garden. There was a child's bicycle discarded by the verandah swing seat. The lace curtains were cross-looped, corner to corner, a woman's decoration. It looked deserted from the moment of their arrival, and there was no obvious movement throughout the afternoon. They put a van with two-way observation glass on Mill, and an hourly-changed car squad much further back along Elmhurst Manor. Quite close, on Junction Boulevard, a supposed sewer maintenance squad set up home beneath a canvas tent. The house remained in darkness throughout the first night.

The following day, Slowen was authorised to put a tap on the telephone. No-one called. He obtained the telephone records and had a headquarters team go back through every outgoing number dialled for the preceding four months: none led to anyone named in Petr Aleksandrovich Serov's documents. Slowen followed up the telephone tap with a search warrant, and a locksmith opened the door to Rimyans' house. It wasn't double locked.

It showed little sign of a hurried departure, apart from the bicycle in the garden. All the beds were made. A cot in a child's bedroom was burdened with toys. The closets in the master bedroom were still full of men's and women's clothing. The refrigerator was well stocked, the milk not soured. The bureau in the den contained neatly itemised bills and some correspondence in what Slowen guessed to be Russian; he took it all, for translation in Washington, and made a random selection of the photographs on display, for comparison against the pictures assembled as part of the case records. From the Rimyans' prints, they discovered the child to be a girl, aged about thirteen. Nowhere, in any address book or on any paperwork, did any of the names in which they were interested appear. The garage was empty, apart from a chest freezer as extensively stocked as that in the kitchen. From some of the paid bills in the den, vehicle service receipts, Slowen knew the car was a 1991 Ford, and its registration number, so he issued a search-and-find bulletin: conscious of his oversight in not extending their original Brighton Beach enquiry to surrounding districts, Slowen over-compensated, marking the circulation of the car alert nationwide. Sniffer dogs were taken in to go through the house from loft to basement, out into the garage and throughout the garden. No trace of drugs was found.

The house-to-house enquiries spread along both sides of Junction Boulevard and Elmhurst Manor, and into three adjoining streets. The Rimyans were a quiet, unostentatious couple. No-one quite knew what he did, but the consensus was it had something to do with the airports. The child, Marina, sang in the school choir. They did not invite neighbours into their home, nor accept invitations to visit.

'What now?' demanded Bradley.

'We scale down the surveillance, but keep it in place,' decided Slowen. 'Likewise the telephone tap. And we go back to Brighton Beach and start all over again. We widen the public records search for our names, throughout the entire borough of Queens and Brooklyn. Make a Social Security check, too.'

'We ain't going to get diddly squat,' guessed Wilkes. 'And the Rimyans ain't ever going to come back to their comfortable little nest here. I've never known the word go out more definitely than it has over this thing: nor be obeyed so completely.'

One unproductive interrogation followed another, to the impatience of Washington and the respective ministries in Moscow. On the fifth day, Danilov received the curt summons to postpone the following morning's session with Antipov: a further enquiry into the inefficiency criticism had greater priority.

That was the day arranged for Cowley, in the evening, to go out with Danilov and Olga and Yevgennie and Larissa Kosov. Cowley had rigidly limited his drinking to three whiskies for several nights now.

It was also the day Rafferty and Johannsen sent the Geneva photographs to Cowley in Moscow, with a note that they hadn't matched with anything in the FBI picture files. The package went off in the diplomatic bag to Moscow before the arrival of everything taken from Igor Rimyans' house in the New York borough of Queens.

Which was unfortunate.

CHAPTER THIRTY-FOUR

The dispute with Olga began with Danilov insisting upon taking Cowley to an authentic Russian restaurant instead of the Metropole hotel, although he agreed to a drink there first. It continued over his two initially suggested restaurants, so he didn't bother to discuss the third. Her usual tint was still unavailable at the hairdressers; the substitute took badly again and she blamed him for the uneven colouring, which he thought was irrational and said so. She couldn't find anything new to wear and turned her annoyance on Danilov, complaining he hadn't given her sufficient money to buy what she wanted. Danilov gave her more. Olga bought the first suit she'd tried but rejected as too small, which it was, so she had to alter the buttons on the skirt which made it hang awkwardly. He tried to maintain peace by telling her it looked fine when she showed him, and she accused him of lying. He lost his temper in the quarrel that ensued and agreed Larissa would probably look better than her because Larissa usually did, which he bitterly regretted the moment he spoke. It did at least make him think before he spoke again, so when Olga said she was unhappy and thought they had a shitty marriage Danilov didn't reply. They drove in hostile silence to Cowley's hotel.

The American was waiting in the bar, as arranged. The whisky in front of him was the first, and he'd decided not to have more than two after that. Danilov chose Scotch as well, and hoped his surprise didn't show when Olga ordered a martini, which as far as he knew she'd never drunk before. Cowley wondered why Danilov looked uneasy.

Kosov's new BMW was parked very obviously outside the Metropole when they got there. Olga led familiarly into the hotel, going at once towards the chandeliered bar, where Kosov and Larissa sat in one of the better lighted booths. After the newspaper and television publicity Danilov was aware of several identifying looks, and guessed Kosov had intentionally chosen the most prominent banquette. He decided he was right from the exuberance with which Kosov greeted the American, as if they were old friends. They'd only met briefly during Cowley's first investigation in Moscow: the Russian had been wrongly arrested in Kosov's division. Kosov had enjoyed the brief notoriety: and because of the cover-up he had never known about the mistake. There was a bottle of French champagne already open in a pedestal cooler beside the table, and before the greetings were completed Kosov made a performance of pouring, ahead of the hurriedly approaching waiter.

Cowley thought he recognised Kosov as the sort of policeman he'd occasionally encountered, usually in small, Southern-State towns they believed they owned and probably did, although perhaps they were not quite so obvious as the Russian. Their earlier meetings had been entirely on an official level, and Kosov hadn't behaved like he was behaving now. Cowley would not have expected a friendship between such a man and Danilov, which he at once acknowledged to be none of his business.

It was fortunate the two women were seated on opposite sides of the table. The jacket of Olga's suit was strained too tightly into creases from bust to hip and the overhead light wasn't kind to her patchy hair; she shouldn't have worn the amber bead necklace so close to the blue stone lapel brooch, either. Larissa looked stunning. Her blonde hair was perfectly looped just short of her shoulders, shown off against the bright red dress with which she wore only a single-strand necklace of irregular black coral.

Kosov worked hard to dominate the conversation, going into elaborate reminiscences of their earlier encounter, insisting Cowley agree the serial killing investigation had been one of the most difficult he'd ever conducted. Cowley did agree because it had been, although Kosov would never know why.

'I never thought you'd come back like this!'

'Neither did I,' said Cowley.

'And now you've got your man again!'

'Looks like it.'

'You must have a massive confession by now!'

'This is supposed to be a social evening, Yevgennie,' said Danilov. It was a gentle rebuke, which he felt he should make, but he was intent upon the interest Kosov was showing in the murders.

'The sort of work we do is interesting to everyone, isn't that so?' demanded Kosov, speaking to both women.

Olga nodded.

'I'm fascinated,' agreed Larissa.

Determinedly vague, Cowley said: 'Investigations take their course. This one's doing that.' There'd been another protest from Washington that evening at the failure of the interrogation.

'But you know which way to go? Where to look?' persisted the division commander. 'Are there going to be any more arrests here in Moscow?'

'I always keep an open mind until the very end,' said Cowley.

Kosov looked genuinely surprised when he was told they were not eating at the hotel, insisting the Metropole dining-rooms were the best in the city: Danilov half expected the man to add that they were also the most expensive, but he didn't. Cowley helped by saying he'd prefer a Russian restaurant: Danilov looked at Olga, who ignored him. Kosov paid for the champagne from a thick wad of dollar bills he ostentatiously counted out on the table top, adding a ten-dollar tip.

Outside the hotel Kosov said it was unnecessary to take two cars, bustling the American towards the BMW. Larissa appeared almost as possessive as her husband, hurrying Cowley into the back and putting Olga and herself on either side. Danilov got into the front. When Danilov announced they were eating at the Skazka, Kosov sighed in unspoken disdain. He put a Tina Turner cassette into the tape deck, which was tuned too loudly. As he drove off, Kosov waved his arm around the vehicle and said to Danilov: 'What do you think?'

'Very nice,' said Danilov. Olga had been right about the array of dashboard illumination.

'One of the newest: hardly any like it in Moscow.'

Danilov was tempted to ask the uniformed colonel how he could afford it, but didn't bother.

In the rear of the car Cowley was making polite conversation, telling Olga to persuade Danilov to bring her to Washington for a vacation so he could show them around. With no alternative – and hoping the idea would never be taken up by them – Cowley said of course he and Larissa were included in the invitation when Kosov asked.

It was easier than Danilov expected to park on the Tovarishchevsky Pereulok. He was clearly not known there so Kosov did not attempt one of his favoured-customer entrances, which increased the effect of what happened when they did go in.

Danilov had made the reservation days before – necessary, as he intended paying in roubles – and had called in earlier that day to confirm the table was being kept for him. The first indication the manager recognised him from the publicity of the case came when the man asked if he would be bringing the American detective. It was the only occasion Danilov had experienced the benefit of fame and he enjoyed it: it was much easier than the usual Russian necessity to guarantee service, suggesting favour for favour. And seemed to work better. Their table was waiting, already set with *zakuski* –hors d'oeuvres – that included smoked salmon, sturgeon, caviar and individual salads. The manager greeted Danilov like a regular customer, shaking his hand and saying it was good to see him again, and gained the hoped-for introduction to Cowley in front of everyone else in the restaurant.

The candlelight against the dark wood gave the Skazka a genuine Russian ambience, heightened by the gypsy musicians. They ate *bliny*, filling each pancake themselves with caviar, and *pelmeni*, dumplings floating in sour cream. There was pork served two ways, in a mushroom sauce and roasted with plums, and lamb shashlik. Danilov ordered both red and white Georgian wine.

Cowley enjoyed the evening. He made everyone laugh with anecdotes of investigation mistakes that were legendary and most likely apocryphal in the FBI, which encouraged matching stories from the other two policemen: Danilov told his tales better than Kosov, who was showing signs of getting drunk. Olga's words, when she tried to speak which wasn't often, were slurring by now, too. Even Larissa attempted a contribution, telling of bedroom mix-ups and unusual assignations at the hotel. Cowley was conscious of her seeming to address Danilov when she told them, as if he would be more interested than the rest of them. Kosov made two more attempts to talk about the investigation, both of which were easily evaded.

It was Olga, over Armenian brandy, who eagerly suggested they all go on to a nightclub, looking expectantly at Kosov. But the man didn't respond as she anticipated: he didn't give any reaction at all, in fact, and she was about to repeat the idea, imagining he hadn't heard, when Cowley said maybe another time.

Kosov insisted it was no trouble to drop the American off at his hotel: at the Savoy Cowley invited them in for a nightcap, allowing himself a final brandy, but still didn't take up the nightclub idea. They parted noisily with promises to get together again sometime.

In the Volga, going home, Danilov decided the evening had been saved, socially, by the Skazka. And that Kosov had been blatantly over-interested, even for a policeman, in the Mafia murders. He'd known Kosov to be dirty, he thought, calling up the new English word: but not this dirty. Which was not part of his current problem. Or was it?

'Why didn't you kiss Larissa goodnight?' Olga demanded, breaking into his reflections.

'Forgot.' Danilov thought he'd almost gone too far in the other direction, ignoring Larissa as he had, although it was how they'd agreed to behave when they'd spoken by telephone that afternoon. She'd practically been too obvious ignoring him, as well.

'She looked beautiful tonight, didn't she?'

'I didn't notice.' He'd have to stop lying soon.

It was not raining that night, so it was not until the following day – when it was – that he discovered the windscreen wipers on the Volga had been stolen while it was parked near the Metropole.

CHAPTER THIRTY-FIVE

The ministry summons was extremely specific, almost legally detailed. Danilov was ordered to bring with him the complete and interlocking master file on all three cases and to be accompanied by Yuri Pavin, whose assistance would have been necessary anyway because there was so much to transport. Expanded by the Washington and Geneva material referenced and indexed to the Moscow murder, the files occupied five bulging dossier boxes. A special table had to be brought to the Deputy Foreign Minister's chamber to accommodate it all.

Everyone had assembled in advance of their arrival: Danilov's impression was that a conference had been held between the two ministers and the Federal Prosecutor in advance. Chairs were set for him and Pavin at a small table, already in place, and Danilov's further impression, from the first question, was of hostility towards them.

It came from Vasili Oskin, who rose to go to where all the dossiers lay but selected only one, the master record. 'Who is responsible for this comprehensive file?'

'As the officer in charge of the investigation, I am,' accepted Danilov. It *was* a tribunal. But why!

'You are aware of its full contents?' demanded Nikolai Smolin.

'I have read what it contains,' said Danilov. 'Quite obviously, with the volume there now is, I need to remind myself of individual items from the index or referencing.'

Vorobie looked at Pavin. 'Formulated by you?'

Pavin, who had recognised an inquisition as quickly as Danilov, stumbled the start of his reply and had to begin again. At his second attempt Pavin said: 'It's the system I customarily use, on all serious crime investigations.'

Smolin replaced Oskin at the table during the exchange. No-one spoke while he flicked through the master dossier, and Danilov guessed some rehearsal had gone into this encounter. The Federal Prosecutor looked up and said to Pavin: 'It is arranged chronologically in order of date and discovery?'

'In this case – these cases – the file begins with the American murders, in dated sequence,' agreed Pavin. 'The Ignatov killing has a separate dossier, annotated where there are provable links with those in America: the names of known criminals in Serov's papers is the obvious illustration. Those annotations are picked up by cross-referencing, one dossier to another, and additionally held in the full index. That way, by daily maintaining the system, it is possible to move in sequential order through each separate file it controls. The master also contains all ministry and inter-departmental communications.'

The two government officials appeared to have withdrawn, leaving the questioning to the trained lawyer. Danilov was uneasy at the prosecutorial questioning. Why? he thought again. He had the sudden fear Pavin was being edged towards a concession, but couldn't think what there was to concede.

Smolin went briefly back to where he had first been sitting, picked up several sheets of paper, and carried them back to Danilov and Pavin. 'These will be indexed, like everything else?'

Danilov had never seen any of them before.

The sheets were all dated on the fifteenth of the month, the day Ignatov's body was found in the river. The first was a memorandum from Vladimir Kabalin, acknowledging his appointment as senior investigator into the murder of Ivan Ignatsevich Ignatov and suggesting to the Director that because of the man's existing knowledge and involvement, Major Yuri Pavin be seconded as operational scene-of-crime officer at the river bank, in addition to Aleksai Raina, to organise all the necessary and essential routine. There was a reply, signed by Metkin, agreeing. A third sheet, from Kabalin to Pavin, contained detailed instructions that the entire area be sealed for scientific examination.

Danilov felt satisfaction, the first of a switchback of emotions he was to experience that day, sweep over him.

He'd taken just the right precautions, without knowing why, to expose this whole charade as the evidence tampering it was. He remained utterly impassive, handing page after page to Pavin in the order in which he'd read them. Danilov knew Pavin was apprehensively respectful of authority, and would be awed in the presence of ranked officialdom, being questioned by the Federal Prosecutor; he ached for a way to let the man know there was no danger.

Pavin was red with confusion. He looked helplessly at Danilov, then back to the three officials. Stumbling again, Pavin said: 'This can't be. This never happened. I don't understand . . .'

Much as he wanted to, Danilov decided he couldn't intervene yet, not until he'd fully gauged the manoeuvre against them.

Smolin was back at the table, standing by the dossiers like a conjuror behind boxes from which inexplicable magic would be produced. 'These are your files, brought by yourselves today. Come . . . !' He beckoned Pavin, imperiously. '. . . Each memorandum is numbered. Locate it in the index. Then find its cross-reference . . . !'

Pavin stood but hesitated, and Danilov agonised at the appearance of the man physically holding back. When he did move, it was reluctantly. As he made the examination, the head-shaking bewilderment grew and he looked helplessly again at Danilov. '. . . It's properly done! As I do it! But I *didn't* do it! I was never ordered to seal the area: work with Colonel Kabalin and Raina. These orders, these messages, never came to me . . . !'

'You received orders you did not carry out,' accused Oskin, re-entering the discussion.

'The ill feeling between yourself and some members of the Organised Crime Bureau is obvious,' said Vorobie, speaking to Danilov again. 'We have conducted a lengthy enquiry with Director Metkin. He believes – as we believe – that because you were passed over for the directorship, you gave telephone instructions from Washington to ignore essential routine to create precisely the sort of embarrassment that arose, to discredit your department and him . . .'

It was a much cleverer and much more devious effort than they had tried before. Would this be all Metkin had fabricated? Or would there be more? He'd been excluded from the arrest of Mikhail Antipov, then entrusted with the so-far failed interrogation, which didn't make complete sense. Danilov decided to limit his defence until he was sure there was nothing else. It would still be a staggering counter-accusation to make.

He cleared his throat, not wanting to appear uncertain. 'Your accusation – the accusation of Director Metkin – is entirely without foundation or substance. The files in this case have been fraudulently tampered with, altered to include documentation invented to conceal either total incompetence or an attempt to discredit Major Pavin and myself! All of which I can categorically prove . . .'

He welcomed the utter astonishment of the three men facing them. Further awareness came to Danilov. This *had* to be the make-or-break confrontation between himself and Metkin: if he was going to survive, he had to make the rebuttal utterly devastating. He pointed to the stacked table.

'Those *are* our files. And because we were given no warning of what to expect this morning, you will accept we had no opportunity – or reason – to change them to support any defence we might make. They don't, in fact, support us: they damn us . . .'

'What's your point?' broke in Smolin. The lawyer's voice had lost its attack. It was neutral, less sure than a few moments earlier.

'Retain them until I produce a true copy.'

'You have a copy . . . ?' broke in Smolin, again.

Before Danilov could reply, Vorobie demanded: 'Why?'

The moment of positive commitment, Danilov recognised: there would be no retreat, no place of safety if he got anything wrong. He wouldn't disclose his duplication of Serov's documents, which still had to be tested. If he'd believed in God Danilov would have thanked Him for the decision, that first day back from Washington, to safeguard himself the way he'd devised there.

'Anatoli Nikolaevich Metkin should *not* be the Director of

the Organised Crime Bureau. He is incompetent, promoted beyond his capability . . . someone prepared to falsify and lie to remain in office and try to destroy others he regards as a threat . . .'

Astonishment stayed on every face, even Pavin's.

'The start of the investigation into the Ignatov killing was chaotic, completely disorganised and completely justifying the American complaint,' resumed Danilov. 'I believed a cover-up would be attempted, which is why, unknown even to Major Pavin, I have maintained duplicate records of every official communication in this case . . . I consider an enquiry should be held into the actions of General Anatoli Metkin' – Danilov allowed a final pause – 'both during his directorship, and as a Militia colonel of investigation before that.'

Both Sergei Vorobie and the Federal Prosecutor were looking at Oskin, the man representing the ministry to which the Militia was answerable. 'How long will it take for you to produce your evidence?'

'An hour,' promised Danilov.

'Time to summon Director Metkin,' said Oskin.

'I suggest senior Colonel Vladimir Kabalin also be included,' said Danilov.

In the car, returning to Petrovka, Pavin said: 'Where have you kept the copy memoranda?'

'Among all my other files that irritate you so much, because of the mess.'

'It won't be there,' predicted Pavin gloomily. 'They'll have gone through everything!'

But it was. Danilov looked up triumphantly at Pavin, who had gone to his exhibits. The man was standing by the open safe.

'The gun,' said Pavin, his voice choked with disbelief. 'It's not here! It's gone!'

The surveillance by the New York Task Force was kept on the house near La Guardia, but no-one returned. The telephone tap heard nothing. The public records search through the boroughs of Queens and Brooklyn did not

233

produce any of the other names Petr Serov had coded, in his Washington office. None of them had been accorded a Social Security number.

'I'm damned glad we're not up there,' said Rafferty. 'It's turning out to be one great big dead end. Harsh words are going to be spoken and ability questioned.'

Unaware of what was going to erupt in the next twenty-four hours, Johannsen said: 'It ain't going any better in Moscow, either. The only lucky guys are us, in this nice little backwater.' He looked up, curiously, at Rafferty's failure to reply.

The other man was standing at the table, the photographs that had been taken from Rimyans' living room laid out before him. He looked up at last, frowning. 'I think we're missing something,' he declared seriously.

'What?' demanded Johannsen.

'If I knew that we wouldn't be missing it, asshole!'

The summons from the Interior Ministry had been made by telephone, and the two men had left the Bureau headquarters before the return of Danilov and Pavin.

'The reaction is too quick!' insisted Kabalin. He was driving because they wanted to talk out of the presence of a driver.

'What was there to take any time?' said Metkin. 'The documents are unchallengeable.'

'Why both of us?'

'You were the officer in charge.'

'Acting on your instructions.'

Metkin frowned at the man. 'Don't do or say anything foolish, will you, Vladimir Nikolaevich?'

CHAPTER THIRTY-SIX

It was Danilov's first intention to say nothing about the missing Makarov, to allow time for a proper internal enquiry and search. Just as quickly he realised, like he realised a lot of other things, that the gun would never be found. And watching their initial frantic hunt and then insisting she had seen no-one open the safe was Ludmilla Radsic, who, if questioned by others which she undoubtedly would be, would provide the precise time he had discovered the gun had gone to prove he had withheld the information. The momentary concentration upon the woman prompted another thought and he almost asked her a quite different question, but stopped himself until he was sure.

'What are we going to do?' demanded Pavin. The normally unshakable man was white with bewilderment, moving around the room without direction, touching and shifting things as if he expected suddenly to find the missing evidence.

'Go back to the ministry,' said Danilov calmly.

'But this means . . .'

'. . . that everything's collapsed.' It was as much a remark for the woman's benefit – and satisfaction – as to stop Pavin blurting out something Danilov didn't want her to hear. Danilov was thinking even further ahead now, itemising what could be salvaged. A lot, he decided. Not everything – and not by far the most important thing – but a lot.

Pavin was still too confused fully to agree when Danilov tried to talk through the implications of the missing Makarov on their way back to the ministry. He wasn't able to provide an answer to Danilov's query about Ludmilla Radsic, either.

'It's all or nothing,' Pavin complained.

'It's that anyway,' Danilov said. 'It always has been.'

'It's the system to accept, unquestionably, the word of the superior officer.'

Just survive. Lapinsk's words, remembered Danilov. Now he was sure he could. He said: 'That's just it! That's the way Metkin and Kabalin think: their mistake. That's *why* we can win!'

'Only if the others will hear you out.'

'They'll have to, whether they like it or not,' insisted Danilov. 'It can't be kept internal; swept away. The Americans will have to be told the gun has vanished.'

'It was in our custody,' said Pavin miserably. '*My* custody.'

'I can do it!' Danilov said adamantly.

Despite its lavishness, Vorobie's office was inadequate for the enlarged meeting. Metkin and Kabalin were waiting in a larger conference room, with the Federal Prosecutor and the two government officials.

'I hope there's good reason for keeping us waiting?' demanded the Interior Ministry man.

'There is,' announced Danilov at once. 'The Makarov found by the river, with Antipov's fingerprints, has disappeared.'

Smolin's mouth actually fell open and stayed like that for several moments: Vorobie turned to look at Oskin, as if he'd misheard and expected the other man to correct the misunderstanding. Kabalin frowned. Any facial movement from Metkin was lost in the already creased features.

'What!' managed Smolin, finally.

'Major Pavin checked the evidence safe, while I was collecting this,' said Danilov, gesturing with his true copy of the communications register. 'The gun has gone.'

'That can't be!' said Oskin weakly.

'It is,' said Danilov. He had to anticipate every move and counter-accusation likely to come from the other two Militia officers. He wanted them confused, making mistakes in their eagerness to make their charges.

'The evidence exhibits are your responsibility,' intruded Metkin at once.

Good, thought Danilov: from the fatuous exchanges on the day of their return from Washington, he knew the more Metkin tried to advance an unsound argument, the more he exposed his weakness: the man's reasoning and manoeuvring *was* too deeply embedded in the past. 'I accept that: as I accept the dossiers are entirely my responsibility.'

The apparently full admission caused the baffled curiosity Danilov wanted. This time Metkin's frown was discernible.

'You admit it?' demanded Vorobie.

'I want it *understood*,' qualified Danilov. 'Like I want it understood that is why the written records have been altered and the gun has disappeared. To discredit me and bring about my dismissal.'

'I don't know anything about records being altered,' said Metkin. 'Those records prove without question either incompetence or insubordinate refusal to follow others. I don't need to describe to anyone here what the loss of the murder weapon means.'

'Without the gun, Antipov can't be charged: brought before a court,' said the Federal Prosecutor anyway, as if he couldn't believe what he was being forced to say. 'The gun, with unarguable fingerprints, *was* the evidence.'

'Which the Americans will have to be told,' agreed Danilov. 'It's difficult to imagine their reaction to this. Proof, if any more were needed, of official complicity, to prevent a proper police enquiry . . .' Time now to switch, to bury the bastards under the weight of their own misjudgements. '. . . The enquiry into the Ignatov killing was deliberately mishandled, at its outset. Since then every effort has been made by the Director of the Organised Crime Bureau flagrantly to obstruct it. There should be a thorough and complete enquiry into that determined attempt to disgrace and discredit the department, together with myself and Major Pavin.' Had he left anything out? If he had, it was too late now. The abyss was yawning before him, bottomless. He wasn't frightened. He supposed he should be.

This time the reponse was splintered. The higher officials lapsed into further head-turning bemusement, seeking an inquisitor. Metkin had to speak, although not as the inquisitor, more the prosecutor, the role Danilov was sure the man had rehearsed. Come on, thought Danilov: over-extend yourself. Make the most important mistake of all.

The Director rose, making what he was going to say formal and official, a declaration. 'I refute utterly these outrageous accusations, which are totally without foundation, the ramblings of a desperate man. The horrendous shortcomings and the even more horrendous failures are those of Dimitri Ivanovich Danilov, who should be removed at once from an enquiry he has so bungled, from its inception, it cannot now continue . . .'

It would once have worked, Danilov accepted: as little as four years ago, any attempted defence would have been ignored and higher authority would have sided with higher authority, obeying the Communist favour-for-favour principle, and he would have been as good as dead. Now . . .

Metkin turned, sure of himself, confronting Danilov face-to-face. 'The responsibility for picking up what is left of this miserably failed investigation will be mine. And that of senior Colonel Investigator Vladimir Kabalin . . .' He went back to the assembled, tight-faced officials. 'The decision upon the failings of Dimitri Ivanovich Danilov and his assistant must be yours. My official recommendation is that the enquiry be an internal, criminal one, for gross dereliction of duties, which is provided for under the Militia statute . . .'

Got you! thought Danilov triumphantly: old ways, old reasoning. Just like they'd miscalculated how to – or *not* to – set up the Ignatov case. Beside him Pavin came close to a physically separating movement, which didn't offend Danilov. The repeated cough was to attract attention more than to clear his throat and he stood, matching Metkin's stance. 'The suggestion there should be an official enquiry was mine,' he reminded. 'And its sentence upon anyone found guilty of negligence or misconduct should be as severe as possible, under both the law and internal regulations . . .' The pause was entirely self-indulgent, Danilov savouring the moment. 'But it can't be internal, within the Militia. This is a joint investigation, between America and Russia. And now we can't proceed with a murder prosecution. Which we have to announce not just privately to the Americans but publicly, because of the international publicity that has been generated. To satisfy the Americans and the public in general

238

of our official integrity and professional ability, any enquiry must be entirely independent of the Militia . . .' Danilov caught the look Kabalin attempted to exchange with Metkin, who refused to respond. Abruptly another idea came to him, which gave a gap for Oskin to break in.

'I don't think there is any doubt of the need for a fuller hearing,' began the Deputy Interior Minister briskly. 'I propose this meeting be adjourned for more detailed consideration of all the points that have been raised . . .'

'Not all the points *have* been raised!' interrupted Danilov, annoyed at himself for allowing the intrusion. 'This meeting has already been adjourned once today: I have not yet been able to answer the accusation I was brought here to explain . . .' It had broken the sequence he was trying to present, making his case more disjointed than Metkin's. Talking directly to the deputy, Danilov said: 'The independence of a very necessary enquiry will have to be under the aegis of the Interior Ministry, at least. With officials of other ministries co-opted . . .' He chanced the slightest of pauses, thinking of another bombshell he could lob, unreal though he knew the concept to be. 'Possibly, even, including American participation: full exchange of evidence and findings at least . . .'

Metkin did answer Kabalin's look at last: the colour was beginning to seep into the Director's face.

He'd risked insubordination, thought Danilov: could he get away with arrogance as well? 'An essential remit of any enquiry must be the attitude of Mikhail Antipov . . .' They weren't going to cut him off: they were frowning, but in interest, not irritation any longer. '. . . You have all seen the transcripts of the interrogations of this man: entirely pointless, unproductive questioning . . . Why? Why has a man – a man arrested by senior Colonel Kabalin – remained contemptuous and patronising, knowing, because I told him at the first interview, that his fingerprints were on the murder weapon: knowing a conviction that carries the death penalty was inevitable? That's inexplicable, even for a hardened criminal like Mikhail Pavlovich Antipov . . .'

'. . . This is unfair!' erupted Kabalin at last. '. . . I am not being given an opportunity to explain . . .'

239

Danilov could hardly believe the interruption. More quickly than anyone else, he said: 'Explain, then!'

Kabalin was even appearing awkward. He'd half risen, but not completed the movement; now he was neither sitting nor standing but at a crouch, as if he were about to run. Danilov guessed the other man would have probably liked to do just that.

Kabalin said: 'There is a clear inference being made, entirely unsubstantiated by any fact. I reject it!'

This time Smolin got in first. 'What inference?'

'That in some way Antipov learned from me the gun would never be produced.'

'Did he?' asked Oskin directly.

'No!'

'Something that may be possible to prove, either way,' re-entered Danilov, abandoning any reservation on how far he might go. 'Antipov was due to be questioned again today, although long before now. That interview, like all the others, will be fully recorded. He would suspect something if I *wasn't* the person who accompanied the American. How much would his attitude change if I told him his protectors – his *protectors*, not naming anyone – had failed to dispose of the gun . . .'

'This is preposterous!' exploded Metkin. 'I am being accused – !'

'You've already been accused, by me!' Danilov shot back. To the three men sitting in judgement, he said: 'Let me be accompanied by a ministry official, to authenticate everything that occurs: everything that will also be authenticated quite separately by the tape recording.'

'The entire thing could be twisted!' persisted Metkin.

'Like other things have already been twisted,' scored Danilov.

'It would not be independent!' said Kabalin.

'Would you accept my independent integrity?' demanded Smolin.

'You!' blinked Metkin.

'If I were the official present at today's interview? And I conducted it, and were the person to announce to the man that the gun *hadn't* been disposed of?'

'Of course,' mumbled Metkin, with no choice.

Smolin had been identified as an honest man by Lapinsk, remembered Danilov.

'Then it is settled,' said Oskin.

Not yet, thought Danilov urgently. 'There are other factors to be considered. Apart from myself and Major Pavin, only three other people were authorised to know the combination of the evidence safe. One, obviously, was the Director. The second was senior Colonel Kabalin. The third was his scene–of–crime officer, Major Aleksei Raina . . .'

'This is intolerable!' tried Metkin again. The man was extremely red-faced now, seemingly finding it difficult to remain still. Beside him Kabalin remained ashen, looking nervously from speaker to speaker.

'It *is* a factor to be considered,' judged Vorobie.

The communications register, remembered Danilov. 'It is possible someone else might be able to help in the enquiry. There is still the matter of falsified documents.'

'What falsified documents?' demanded Metkin.

Uninvited, Danilov crossed to the table where the forgotten dossiers lay, allowing himself the briefest of checks before smiling up, satisfied, at the signature he wanted to find. He picked the register up and carried it to where the three men sat, putting it open at the relevant pages in front of them. Alongside, he set his nightly maintained photocopies. 'The duplicates are the true record. The memorandum ordering Major Pavin to seal the scene of the crime, and those between the Director and Colonel Kabalin, have been added subsequently and the entire numbering sequence, referencing and indexing also changed, to cover their attempt to discredit . . .'

'. . . Ridiculous!' blustered Metkin, aware for the first time there was an accurate record. Groping desperately, he said: 'Why should he have made a copy, other than to protect himself from the justifiable charge that he and his assistant failed to obey my orders!'

Danilov let the other man's question hang in the air. 'If I intended altering the communications register, why would I have made copies showing the message as *not* on file but let the originals remain? That just doesn't make sense. Wouldn't I have removed them and had the dossier falsified my way to erase *all* traces?'

'You knew I'd have *my* secretarial copy!' said Metkin, unthinking now in his panic. 'That's how I've exposed you!'

'Then there would have been no purpose in my trying to change anything in the first place, would there?' deflated Danilov. He was supremely sure of himself at last, confident he was beyond any further attack. He returned to the officials. 'It's the system that any document received and put into any record is signed for, as a receipt. You'll see the signature on all the disputed slips is that of my secretary, Ludmilla Radsic. I would suggest her evidence, of how – and when – they came to be in the register would form an important part of whatever enquiry is set up.'

Oskin gave the verdict. 'Pending that enquiry, supervision of the Organised Crime Bureau will be transferred to my personal directorship at the Interior Ministry.'

Metkin, thick-voiced, said: 'What does that mean for my position?'

'It is suspended,' declared Oskin.

A good homicide detective with a hunch like a burr under a saddle blanket knows when the time for cosy relaxation is over. Rafferty was a very good homicide detective. And Johannsen respected his partner's hunches.

They went through everything assembled in America and everything shipped from Moscow and Geneva, and cross-checked each other's re-examination. When that blanked out they tried to refine the scrutiny to the stages of the investigation, working backwards instead of forwards, from the first moment of Rafferty's intuitive feeling. Which had been directly after they'd received the shipment from the New York Task Force of the items taken from the abandoned home of Igor Rimyans.

'Got it!' announced Johannsen triumphantly. He held up one of the photographs taken from the Rimyans' home, waving it like a flag, then offered it to Rafferty. 'Look in the

242

background, beyond the group being snapped! See the guy, almost out of the frame?'

'What about him?' asked Rafferty, staring down but seeing nothing of significance.

'There he is again!' declared Johannsen, proffering a second print. 'Third from the left in one of the pictures the Swiss police sent us: pictures of Russian guys who'd been entertained in Geneva by our late lamented Michel Paulac!'

'Eric, my son, I've said it once and I'll say it again. One day you're going to make a great detective. And on that day your country is going to be as proud of you as I am.'

'And my life will be fulfilled,' said Johannsen.

The blind man took the call, because the attempted entrapment had been his idea. He talked Metkin down, impatient with the incoherent babble. 'Who knows about the gun?'

'Me. Kabalin.'

'So nothing can be proved, providing you both insist you know nothing about it.'

'Kabalin is shaky.'

'Tell him if he tries to do a deal – causes us any problems – we will kill him. Make sure he understands. But we'll kill his wife and his children first. One by one. Make sure he understands we mean it. Because we do.'

'It hasn't gone right, has it?' gloated Zimin. 'In fact, it's gone very wrong.'

CHAPTER THIRTY-SEVEN

The interrogation of Mikhail Antipov did not resume the day of the confrontation, nor for several days after. The Russian Foreign Ministry offered the American State Department an expanded apology at international diplomatic level, and the Federal Prosecutor invited William Cowley to Pushkinskaya and talked of personality clashes and internal jealousies to be examined by an immediately convened tribunal. Washington agreed not to make any public disclosure, accepting Moscow's argument it could further impede an already interrupted investigation, with no practical benefit.

Ludmilla Radsic told the tribunal that upon the Director's personal instructions, following the original American protest, she had signed receipt of memoranda she had not been permitted to read. She'd had nothing whatsoever to do with the compilation of the register and did not know its contents. She had been personally briefed by the Director prior to her appointment as Danilov's secretary to make separate notes and report back to him on everything that occurred in his office. She'd been told to listen to every telephone conversation and to every conversation in Russian between Danilov, Pavin and Cowley. She'd had to write down the exchanges in as much detail as possible: once, entering the Director's office, she'd heard him relaying something about the unsuccessful interview with Raisa Serova to someone on the telephone. She did not know the combination of the exhibit safe, nor what had happened to the Makarov. She'd had to surrender every reminder she'd made, so she had no written evidence. Each of Metkin's secretarial staff testified they had not prepared the disputed messages.

Metkin and Kabalin continued to deny falsification, insisting the memoranda were genuine, or any knowledge of the missing murder weapon. Metkin also categorically denied ordering Ludmilla Radsic to spy for him. The woman's circumstantial evidence was judged enough to continue the suspension of both men but insufficient to bring any formal, criminal charges of conspiracy to impede the course of justice.

Danilov regarded that as a cover-up, to remove a problem but prevent a public government humiliation, and Cowley agreed with him. Their disillusionment worsened when the questioning of Antipov re-started.

Although directorship of the Bureau remained with Oskin, the day-to-day supervision was passed to Smolin, who conducted the session as he'd undertaken. Antipov still swaggered, lolling sideways with one arm lodged over the chair back: by now he virtually had a full beard and he smelled badly, from not washing. When Smolin identified himself Antipov laughed in Danilov's direction and said: 'He so bad you've got to do his job for him?'

Smolin was too experienced a lawyer ever to feel irritation. 'It's all gone wrong,' he said. 'They were caught, trying to get rid of the gun. *That's* why I'm here: this is official. We've still got the gun and it's going to put you in front of a firing squad. And we have their confessions, too.'

'Congratulations!'

'It's everyone for himself now. That's all they're interested in, saving themselves. As you should be.'

'Who's they?' demanded Antipov.

'You tell me,' said the prosecutor, possibly his only mistake.

'No!' refused Antipov. '*You* tell *me!*'

'Metkin. Kabalin.'

The Mafia man pulled a face, turning down both corners of his mouth. 'Never heard of them. Like I never heard of anyone named Ivan Ignatov. Or something or someone called Chechen or Ostankino.'

That was the moment Danilov and Cowley – and Smolin – knew they'd lost. The Federal Prosecutor persisted for almost a further hour, until the repetition risked becoming farcical.

'Metkin and Kabalin weren't his only protectors!' decided Danilov in the conference that followed, careless in his frustration at making the accusation to a government minister in the presence of the American.

There was no disapproval from Smolin. 'Which would have to mean someone within the Interior Ministry.'

'Or the judiciary,' added Danilov.

'Which might also account for the decision not to proceed with criminal charges against Metkin or Kabalin!' suggested Cowley, emboldened by Smolin's easy acceptance of what Danilov had said.

'That was taken on my advice,' corrected the Federal Prosecutor, although still with no resentment. 'There wasn't enough, legally, to proceed.'

'When *will* there be?'

'When there is a mistake that can't be covered up,' insisted Smolin.

Danilov hoped there was still the possibility of finding one, but didn't tell Smolin. He'd insisted upon a replacement secretary. She was a hopefully smiling woman named Galina Kanayev, who had a dumpling face on a dumpling body and whose first job, under Pavin's guidance, had been to correct the falsified communications dossier. She welcomed the relief of typing Danilov's official request to the Foreign Ministry for a re-examination of all Petr Serov's material returned from Washington. Prompted by being told of the comparison he was going to have to make, Pavin said the three names Lapinsk had provided had not shown up in any criminal record: he was about to begin on the records of government personnel.

Danilov told Cowley that night, in the Savoy bar, he had finally initiated the search. 'It's a possibility,' accepted the American doubtfully.

'Any other suggestions?'

'What about surveillance on Antipov, when he's released?'

'We'll try,' agreed the Russian. 'He'll expect it, though.'

'What about bugging his apartment, before you release him?'

'I'll suggest it,' said Danilov.

246

Cowley remained in the bar after Danilov's departure. By now he had an accustomed place in the corner furthest from the door. He saw, the moment she entered, the darkly attractive, short-haired girl who'd established an equally accustomed place at a side table, just inside the entrance, for over a week now. He guessed she was a professional, because there were a few of them regularly around, but he'd seen her reject quite a few approaches, so obviously she was extremely particular. He smiled almost without thinking, in the way of bar regulars, and she smiled back: worriedly he wondered if she might have misunderstood and make an approach, but she didn't. He smiled at the girl as he finally left the bar and she shifted slightly, smiling up expectantly. But he carried on alone to his room.

'The man was head of the Organised Crime Bureau!' protested Maksim Zimin. 'We knew how the investigation was going! Now we don't! It was a totally unnecessary mistake!'

It was the first time that one of Alexandr Yerin's intricate proposals had collapsed so badly, and he didn't like the failure or the criticism. 'They weren't our only source, close to what's going on.'

'They were the best! Kosov doesn't have any *inside* access,' persisted Zimin. 'And we can't intercept what's going to Oskin!' He thought this more than balanced the Washington error.

'There's no benefit in looking back,' intervened Gusovsky, although he agreed with Zimin. 'The link-up is far more important. We are going to get the company details legally assigned soon now.'

'We're not going to delay the meeting?' queried Zimin, the delegate, hoping his reluctance didn't show. He was uneasy operating outside the guaranteed safety and protection of Moscow.

'Definitely not,' insisted Yerin. 'We've got to maintain their confidence.'

'There's no way we can be blocked, getting the money. You can make all the agreements: they won't expect you to be carrying it with you,' said Gusovsky.

'We won't have the investigation monitored!' said Zimin, not wanting to relax the pressure on the blind man.

'Kosov will have to work that much harder,' said Gusovsky.

'What about Metkin and Kabalin?'

Yerin gave a waving gesture, like someone disturbing an irritating insect. 'They're no further use to us.'

'They *know*!' insisted Zimin.

'And if they talk they go to jail for the rest of their lives! They know that, too. Stop pissing your pants!'

'I need to know everything about Switzerland,' said Zimin.

'Just make the contact and convince them we can set up the deal,' said Yerin.

CHAPTER THIRTY-EIGHT

The funeral, at Novodevichy cemetery, of Petr Aleksandrovich Serov provided the news-starved media with the first public event since the activity around the scenes of the American murders: what little there had been at the Moscow river bank had ended before the Ignatov killing had been leaked by the Washington mayor. The swarm of international journalists, cameramen and TV crews hugely outnumbered the tiny group of mourners.

Danilov and Cowley did not attempt to join it. Instead, glad of the tight-together clutter of gravestones and portrait-adorned vaults, they remained initially unrecognised outside the mêlée. That, in turn, hid the Militia photographer. It had been Cowley's idea to get police pictures, which Danilov had acted on without reference to Smolin. It had been a mistake proposing the electronic eavesdropping on Mikhail Antipov's apartment on Ulitza Fadajeva. The prosecutor had said there was insufficient time for the installation before the man was released. Smolin had seemed uninterested in any surveillance in depth, which had unsettled Danilov.

It was an overcast day of low, scudding clouds, the few trees rusting with approaching autumn. It was cold, too, although Raisa Serova did not wear a coat: her suit was an appropriate mourning black, without any visible jewellery. Twice, while they watched, she spoke sideways to Oleg Yasev. Danilov had not expected her to be accompanied by the Foreign Ministry official, but Raisa kept her hand linked through the elbow-cupped arm of the fair-haired Yasev, while being constantly attentive to Serov's elderly parents, on her other side. The old lady, bowed as much by arthritis as sorrow, was crying, needing her husband's arm around her shoulders as well as Raisa's help to get to the graveside. There were only three other mourners, all men. Danilov didn't recognise them, but got the impression they were officials from their dress and demeanour.

It was an American television cameraman, panning to follow Raisa Serova from the grave to her car, who recognised Danilov and Cowley from the earlier publicity. Raisa became aware of the sudden switch of attention and glared, particularly at Danilov. There was another head-together exchange with Yasev, who appeared to nod in agreement with what she said, as Danilov and Cowley were engulfed by the pack, like they had been outside the restaurant in Georgetown.

Now, as then, they refused every question, shouted in Russian and English: Danilov used the American's bulk, following in the man's wake as Cowley shouldered his way towards the waiting Volga. The press determination to get some comment matched that of Cowley and Danilov not to give it. A solid barrier formed between them and the car, refusing to give way, and Pavin, who had remained in the driving seat, had literally to add his weight from the rear to complete the path Cowley was trying to form. Someone got his hand trapped in the door, yelling with pain as Danilov slammed it closed. For no obvious benefit, apart from still more photographs, the pack remained thronged all around the car. Pavin had to edge forward inches at a time to reach the cemetery gates.

'Jesus! said Cowley, as the vehicle reached the main highway.

'I should have had some uniformed officers.' Would Smolin have vetoed that, too?

'Those three guys mean anything to you?' Cowley had marked the three unknown mourners as officials, too.

'We can ask Yasev.'

'I'd already decided to ask him.'

'Surprised he was there?'

'I suppose it was understandable.'

The police photographs were printed at once, to maximum enlargements, and compared to every picture so far gathered on the three cases. There was no match. Danilov had just finished dictating the official request to Oleg Yasev for their identities when the call came from Smolin that the widow had already complained, through Yasev, about the media presence at the funeral. She blamed the Russian investigator personally for releasing the time and location to the press. Today's protest had also repeated the demand that her husband's still-retained diary be returned. Smolin saw no reason why that should not be done.

The rebuke finally made Danilov's mind up how to operate in the future, which was not, he didn't think, the way Nikolai Smolin intended. Danilov concluded he had been freed from the restrictive interference of a corrupt director to have it replaced by the restrictive interference of a group of government officials more interested in satisfying diplomatic than legal requirements. And then, he further qualified, only if the replacement group *were* honest.

Danilov shared every message with the American. Cowley said: 'He know about going through Serov's stuff from the embassy again?'

'No,' said Danilov. 'And he isn't going to.' He was going to have to rely greatly upon the American, if they ever found a way in Russia to move the enquiry on.

Cowley's seat in the corner of the bar, near the television set showing CNN for the benefit of the Western tourists, was waiting for him: before he reached it the barman was pouring the Scotch.

She arrived an hour and two drinks later, smiling across at him from her established seat near the foyer. There had been two other regulars setting up positions ahead of her and they'd smiled, too, but he hadn't responded. This time he did. There was obviously an arrangement between the bar staff and the girls, who often sat without drinks unless they were bought by prospective clients.

Cowley intercepted the enquiring look between the barman and the girl, and said: 'On my tab.' The girl chose crème de menthe and smiled at him again, more openly this time, edging the second chair slightly away from her table, in invitation. Why not? What was wrong with just talking? He hadn't talked with or been in the company of a woman since the night out with Danilov's wife and Larissa. He carried his own drink from the small bar. As he approached she pushed the chair out further.

'I am Lena,' she said. Her voice was surprising deep, almost mannish. It was the only thing that was. The check wool dress was too well cut to be Russian, tight enough – but not too tight – to accentuate a perfect, ample-breasted body. The dark hair was short, the make-up discreet, certainly not so garish as the other girls in the bar.

'Bill,' he said.

'I wasn't sure it would ever happen.' Her English was good, not hurried, which was a usual Russian mistake.

'Nothing has, yet.'

'I think it's might, don't you?'

'We don't have to use English. I speak Russian.'

'I want to practise.' There was no *double entendre* in the remark.

'English then,' he agreed.

'You've seemed lonely.'

That was practically a stock phrase, but Cowley didn't take it as such. He *was* lonely. Cowley had been with quite a few hookers, certainly before his marriage to Pauline and occasionally afterwards, when he'd been away or abroad on protracted trips and still hadn't sobered up, in all ways. His immediate impression was that Lena would be one of the better ones. If he became a client, that is: he still didn't have that intention, despite her confidence. Her appearance wasn't surface thin, as it all too often was. Her nails were perfectly manicured, her hands well kept, and the smell was of perfumed freshness, not artificial fragrance of the previous day's scent. In the West she would have been sophisticated enough to have worked through a discreet, high-class agency, not ply openly in hotels. Been a model, even.

Lena did not overdo the sexual innuendoes, and easily followed in whatever direction he led the small talk. She did not even attempt to hustle drinks, usually a requirement of establishments allowing a hooker to operate, but on two occasions even refused when he beckoned for more.

Cowley always had one, though.

Later – too much later – Cowley's recollections were splintered, not even in the order in which things probably unfolded. He remembered agreeing without argument to $100 in American currency. There was the grandiose gesture of having champagne sent to the room. He had no memory of getting there. She'd undressed for him, languorously, but the imagery was hazy; tits bigger than he'd expected, a pubic thatch tantalisingly close to his face, before being pulled away, hips gyrating, then thrusting, letting him know the pleasure that was to come. There'd been no awareness of getting undressed himself: just of her helping but not clumsily, easing things erotically away from him. There'd been a cold reminder that he was naked, when he spilled champagne upon himself. That was about the last thing he could even vaguely call to mind: from then on it became completely disjointed, things that had to have happened, like her going down on him, her hair covering his crotch, mingled with an impression of their being among other people, which had to be from the earlier part of the evening, in the bar.

Cowley awoke feeling dreadful, the worst of the newly experienced hangovers there had so far been. His entire head seemed encased in a tightening shell. His throat and mouth were raspingly dry, like they had been when he'd been anaesthetised for a cartilage operation after a college football accident, and when he stood he began to heave and had to stumble to the bathroom, although when he got there he couldn't be sick.

Lena was gone, but everything was wrecked by what they had done together. The half drunk bottle of champagne was lodged haphazardly in its cooler, slowly dripping what remained of its contents over the small table. Two glasses lay on their side, the bowl of one cracked. Bed covering, sheets and pillows, were strewn everywhere, his clothes among them. With enormous difficulty, his head squeezed by the pain, Cowley sorted through, retrieving everything he had discarded the previous night. Towards the end, as coherent thought returned, Cowley started both to hurry but at the same time concentrate, remembering Lena's profession and frightened by what she might have stolen before leaving.

253

She'd taken nothing.

Which left him with only one uncertainty. He didn't know whether he'd used a condom the previous night: if they had fully made love he was sure Lena would have ensured they were protected, as much for herself as for him, a first time, unknown client.

He supposed he could always ask her, tonight. And perhaps tonight he wouldn't get so drunk, so he could enjoy it more the next time.

'We don't want Antipov near any of the places,' decreed Gusovsky. 'We'll get a message to him – no telephone – to keep away until the surveillance is lifted.'

'Shall we brief Kosov together?' asked Zimin.

'I think we should,' decided Yerin. 'Make the bastard understand that he's got to earn his money: he's taking too long to do what we tell him.'

'What about the other business?' asked Zimin. The previous night another lorry convoy had been hijacked, and they had lost an entire consignment of Scotch whisky.

'It's a direct challenge,' agreed Gusovzky. 'We've obviously got to respond just as directly.'

'And hard,' said Yerin. 'But try to limit the killing. I think we should try to avoid too much public attention.'

'We should cost them money,' reflected Gusovsky.

'I'll organise it,' offered Zimin, who enjoyed violence. He already had an idea in mind.

CHAPTER THIRTY-NINE

When the moment came for Danilov to work with the total independence upon which he'd decided, he was stopped by a last moment of doubt: after all the outside attempts to destroy him he was knowingly inviting his own destruction, like a lemming rushing towards the cliff edge. It was a brief hesitation. Someone or some group in an official position *had* to know what Serov had been doing, how he was doing it and why he was doing it. So for him to go on duplicating memoranda to ministries and officials like the hare in a paper chase was telling the very people he needed to search out and confront how to evade and hide.

It was the meticulous and methodical Pavin who found what Danilov had missed in Washington. The reserved, puffy-eyed Cowley called it a breakthrough but Danilov, more cautiously, suggested it was no more encouraging than the rest. When Danilov added he had no intention of telling anyone, the American said: 'You could be putting the rope around your own neck, before kicking the chair away.'

'We *need* to do it. If we don't you might as well go back to Washington and I might as well mark the whole thing unsolvable.'

'You're the one who's got everything to lose,' warned Cowley. He, by comparison, had everything to gain.

Reminded of the other endangered person, apart from himself, Danilov said to Pavin: 'If there is ever an enquiry I will testify you acted upon my specific orders: that you had no choice.'

Pavin considered the undertaking. 'It wouldn't save me, not entirely. If I disagree I should go over your head.'

'*Do* you disagree?' asked Danilov.

'No,' said the man. 'I think this is what we should do.'

There had been a section missing from Petr Serov's original records when they were returned to Petrovka from the Foreign Ministry, an apparently innocuous account of a week-long visit to the Kennedy Centre in May, 1991, of a Nigerian dance group. Intermingled in Serov's English written report were ten Cyrillic letters, which Pavin, knowing the code to follow, had formed into the name Ilya Nishin.

'I think this name is particularly important,' said Pavin. The man was clearly flattered at being included in a planning meeting, enjoying the praise for locating another name. 'All the others appeared in the autumn of '91. This one is the first.'

'We haven't tried to connect the names against the dates they were concealed,' pointed out Danilov. 'Why don't we do that, starting with this one hidden in May, 1991? If it doesn't turn up on your criminal computer, let's run it through your immigration records, for the entire month.'

Cowley nodded to the idea. 'We could take it further: give the name, month and year to the Swiss to see if they've got any trace.'

All Danilov's doubts had gone. His only feeling now was satisfied excitement at having something positive to pursue.

'We've got more than one curious name,' reminded Pavin. Stultifying Russian bureaucracy required that the returned Foreign Ministry documents carry the signature of the official approving their release. The authority had been that of Oleg Yaklovich Yasev.

'He has been assigned to Raisa Serova, both for the interview and the funeral,' Danilov pointed out, trying to remain objective. 'There's a logic in his handling the document request as well.'

'I don't believe in coincidences,' said Cowley.

'Neither do I. He's an executive officer: reasonably powerful. And he's been using that power, with all the complaints . . .' To Pavin he said: 'I want to know everything you can possibly find out about him.'

Cowley said: 'I've got a gut feeling about this. Things are going to start happening now. Just you see.'

It was a casual aside the American did not later remember, so he never realised the bitter irony of the remark.

Cowley was back at the embassy by mid-afternoon. It took him less than an hour to transmit the newly discovered name and set out the complete checks he wanted made, and with time on his hands he agreed to a drink in the embassy mess with the chain-smoking Stephen Snow. He limited himself to two, still not feeling completely recovered from the previous night.

The resident FBI man had read the cable traffic, so the conversation was obvious. Cowley repeated he had a detective's instinct it was going to take them somewhere.

Cowley used the Marlboro trick to get a taxi outside the embassy, and slumped in the back, thinking of Danilov. The guy was taking a hell of a risk. But he was an adult, sane and over twenty-one, so he could make up his own mind. Cowley accepted it convincingly answered all his early uncertainties about the openness of Danilov's co-operation. The guy wasn't just co-operating now: he was virtually working with America and closing out his own people. A hell of a risk, he thought again. Although from all that had happened he had a pretty good idea, Cowley conceded he couldn't properly guess the sort of shit Danilov had had to wade through in the beginning. Not just the beginning: up until just a few days ago.

Cowley smiled expectantly at the receptionist, the expression becoming a frown when she handed him the package with his key. It was a stiff-backed manila envelope, about 10" by 8", made thick by its contents. The only marking was his name, scrolled with the stiff difficulty by someone unaccustomed to forming Roman lettering.

He made no attempt to open the envelope in the lobby. Instead, with the proper caution of a trained investigator handling a Mafia enquiry, he carried it to his room to examine and feel it minutely, fingering for anything solid, squinting from every angle for any detonating wire or thread. He still opened it from the bottom, gently pulling against the glue to ease the flap open.

The contents were as explosive as any bomb could have been.

There were twelve prints, all professionally lighted, all

professionally sharp, all perfectly developed. Every one completely identified him, apparently taking part in every sort of sexual act. His closed-eyed semi-consciousness when Lena had performed fellatio looked like an expression of ecstasy. So it did with her vagina at his mouth for the feigned cunnilingus. Lena had put herself into three different positions of supposed sexual intercourse. There were two photographs of him completely naked, her hand on his limp genitals. In both he was smiling drunkenly, a tilted champagne glass in his hand, the FBI shield they had taken from his jacket open in its wallet on the bedside table.

Cowley swallowed against the bile, gripping the shake away from the hands that held the photographs. He went through them several times, turning each one to look for any inscription. There wasn't one, on any. He looked carefully back inside the envelope for a message. It was empty.

For a few brief moments he remained uncertainly by the bed – the bed so clearly shown in the pictures now laid out upon it – striving to think rationally, coherently. He finally assembled the photographs and put them back into their envelope, which in turn he put inside his briefcase: never once did it occur to him to destroy them, which would have been pointless because they were prints, not negatives from which as many other prints as were wanted could be developed.

Aware in advance his next action would be equally pointless, he still descended the four flights to the bar, halting directly inside the door. The barman nodded the nightly greeting, starting to pour the Scotch unbidden. Two of the regular girls smiled up, hopefully. Lena, of course, was not there. There wouldn't, he knew, be any purpose in asking where she was.

Cowley turned, going back to his room. He retrieved the photographs, going carefully through them once more, gaining nothing from the renewed examination. He finally replaced them in the briefcase before sitting down, staring between the case and the telephone.

How would it come? he wondered. With what demand? And what would he do, whatever that demand was?

The despair finally engulfed him. 'Dear God,' he said, aloud. 'Dear God, help me.'

The location came from Yevgennie Kosov, a restaurant on Ulitza Moskina, quite close to the Kunstler Theatre, from which it drew a lot of its clientele; like the Western counterparts they copied so assiduously, the Moscow Mafia enjoyed a show business ambience. It was an established Ostankino haunt.

Zimin took six bulls with him. They saw the Ostankino group go in and allowed half an hour for them to settle, unsuspecting, before bursting in. The surprise was absolute. Only one Ostankino bull had time to try any effective defence but his Stetchkin shot wide, embedding its bullet harmlessly in the wall. The Chechen had guns but did not use them. They carried wooden and metal staves and crowbars with which they broke arms and legs and in two cases fractured skulls, matching identically the Ostankino attack on the Domodedovo convoy. Completing the mocking comparison, they torched the restaurant as they left.

Zimin supervised the attack but took no personal part in it. He liked watching. It was better for him than sex.

FORTY

There'd been no warning from either Olga or Larissa, and Danilov stalled because their evenings were nearly always arranged in advance. His thoughts see-sawed. Larissa had talked of announcing their decision together. But Kosov wouldn't be as friendly as this. He would if he didn't know what was coming. Larissa wouldn't do something like this without telling him.

'Just as you are,' urged Kosov. 'A few drinks, some cold meats. Just sitting around, chatting about things.'

Olga fussed for an hour, undecided between two dresses, eventually choosing the first she'd selected. He tried to reassure himself, while he waited. There *had* been unplanned occasions before – he'd initiated a few himself in the first flush of his affair with Larissa – but not for a long time: certainly not since he'd been at the Organised Crime Bureau. Larissa wouldn't try to force his hand like this, impatient though she might be: he knew she wouldn't. If he called back to make an excuse, Larissa would think he wasn't sure. Which he was.

'How do I look?' asked Olga, parading.

'Very pretty.' He'd have to find a way of telling her about all the different colours in her hair: it looked as if she had an old rug on her head.

Danilov looked with curious apprehension at Larissa when they arrived: unseen by anyone but Danilov, she raised her eyebrows in an expression he didn't understand but hoped was matching curiosity at the unexpected invitation. She wore Armani jeans that Olga could not have risked, and the sweater was inevitably cashmere. He hadn't seen her wear either before: she looked sensational, and he decided he was as anxious as she to get some permanence into their relationship. He didn't want to go away tonight, leaving her with someone like Kosov.

'This is a surprise?' invited Danilov, still seeking guidance.

'I wanted the American to come, but he wasn't at the hotel when Yevgennie telephoned,' said Larissa.

Cowley wouldn't have been included if this were going to be honest declaration time! Danilov began to relax.

Kosov went into his usual performance with French champagne, flustering them, glasses in hand, into chairs and saying it really was like old times and they should do things on the spur of the moment more often. Olga said she thought so, too. Danilov let the small talk swirl around him. He and Larissa managed uninterrupted looks several times.

Danilov expected Kosov very quickly to raise the subject of the investigation, but he didn't, not immediately. Instead, showing a depth of argument that surprised Danilov, he started discussing the increasing strength of the resurgent local-level Communist cadres, demanding Danilov's opinion on whether it was an unstable reaction to the failure of supposed democracy, or whether Danilov believed it would be enough to reverse the fragile reforms and still uncertain changes. Danilov replied that the dismantling of the former order had gone too far to be turned back, and that it was unthinkable any of the newly independent republics would now consider anything more than the loosest of trade links. He added he was worried about the political frailty of Russia itself, which he was.

Both women became bored by the conversation – Danilov wondered if that hadn't been Kosov's intention – and started to gossip between themselves, and when Larissa talked of preparing the meal Olga volunteered to help. Kosov sent them off with refilled champagne glasses, switching to whisky himself.

'I think the old ways are too ingrained,' declared Kosov, resuming their debate. 'I agree there will be changes at the political top but it will all be cosmetic, to impress foreign financiers. *Real* things aren't going to alter. There are too many people who don't *know* any other way: don't want to know any other way.'

Danilov recognised the familiar favour-for-favour argument. 'It would change – not quickly but eventually and inevitably – if people demanded it.'

'But they *don't*,' insisted Kosov. 'People only know the one way things work . . . understand it. That's how they want it to go on . . .'

It was a bigoted, fallacious opinion, decided Danilov. 'Work for some people. Not for all: not enough. Which was, after all, what the revolution was supposed to be all about.'

'Starry-eyed ideology,' sneered Kosov.

The man personified all that had been wrong in the past, Danilov thought: and now, in the present. Kosov had even joined the Communist Party to get this apartment and whatever other privileges were available to members, not from any political persuasion. 'It'll come, in time.' He wished the women would come back, no matter how inconsequential their conversation.

'Too late for me to benefit. Or you. Not that you benefit enough: not like you once did.'

Danilov now bitterly regretted following the inviolable rules in his uniformed days. It put him at a disadvantage with the other man: let Kosov know that despite his new-found and despised honesty, he'd operated like everyone else in the past. Was stained like they were stained: the same as them, which he didn't want to be, ever again. 'What's that mean?' he demanded directly.

'Just a remark,' shrugged Kosov. He topped up Danilov's glass, adding whisky to his own.

'It sounded as if you were making a point,' pressed Danilov. He wasn't drinking any more.

Kosov came back to him, smiling. 'You're missing out on a lot. I don't have to tell you that.'

'So why *are* you telling me?'

This time there were no words with the shrug. Kosov sat, seeming to find something of interest in the glass he cupped in both hands, swirling the drink around and around. He wasn't actually drinking, either.

'Is it *you* telling me?' Danilov persisted. 'Or are you expressing the views of other people you think I should take seriously?' He was being approached! By whom? For what?

The shrug came again, like the automatic reflex of a boxer warding off a clumsy blow, but with no proper answer.

Instead there was a question. 'You really think you're going to solve your famous crimes?'

'Yes,' Danilov exaggerated. How to keep the man talking? That's all he had to do, keep him talking.

Kosov shook his head. 'Don't be so naive, Dimitri Ivanovich! I'm your friend! Trust me!'

'Perhaps I would, if I could understand what you're saying.'

'You survived at the Bureau, when you weren't supposed to: won, even. The directorship could unquestionably be yours, like it should have been the first time, if people were sure of you.'

That reply didn't help Danilov. Who was Kosov speaking for? One of the Mafia Families, or someone within the government operating in collusion with organised crime? The Ministry confrontation and the tribunal enquiry hadn't been disclosed, yet Kosov was showing knowledge far beyond rumour. That awareness didn't help answer the question either. But it suddenly made Kosov a very important person, although not for the reasons the man would have welcomed. 'So I'm getting a message?' Come on! thought Danilov, anxiously.

'A personal opinion.'

Bollocks, thought Danilov: wrong to try too soon for specifics. He had to keep the conversation general and try to find the path to follow. 'I can't compromise on this. There's the American involvement: the need to satisfy outsiders.'

'Cowley follows where you lead: he doesn't *direct* the investigation. What can't be solved can't be solved.'

What had there been so far positively to understand? He hadn't been expected to survive Metkin's attack. But he had. So now they – whoever *they* were – were worried: seeking that special sort of Russian agreement to prevent the inquiry into Ivan Ignatov's murder reaching a legal conclusion. Why this approach so quickly? Had he or Cowley or Pavin missed something? Was there evidence they'd overlooked demanding to be recognised? What more? Kosov himself. Danilov knew the man had taken the favour-for-favour lifestyle of a Militia district commander far beyond the hand-over introductions he himself had made: at the level of those introductions there weren't horse-choking wads of dollars, cocktail cabinets full of imported liquor and brand new BMWs with neons of dashboard lights. But he'd never imagined Kosov ascending to this echelon, speaking on behalf of the Mafia or high officials in government or both. Remembering Kosov's enjoyment of flattery, Danilov said, without too much hyperbole: 'I am impressed, Yevgennie Grigorevich.'

Kosov gave a self-satisfied smile, sipping his whisky at last. 'It's important, to have influential friends. Like I said, it's the system everyone knows how to use.'

'So you were asked to make an approach?' suggested Danilov, risking directness again.

Another shrug. 'The friendship between you and me is known.'

Danilov shifted, momentarily uncomfortable. What about his friendship with Larissa? 'You know you can trust me, Yevgennie Grigorevich? That this conversation won't be repeated to anyone.'

'What conversation?'

'Quite so,' accepted Danilov. Trying to keep his tone conversational, he said: 'Tell me about them: about the Chechen and the Ostankino? About all the Families.'

There was an immediate frown, and Danilov angrily recognised he'd gone too far. Kosov shook his head, either in denial or refusal, and said: 'You *could* be director, you know.'

'I haven't thought about it,' Danilov encouraged. 'Too much has been happening.'

'With certain additions, at the top,' said Kosov.

Danilov believed he knew what the other man was implying, but the proposition was so preposterous he refused to assume it, wanting Kosov to say the words. 'Additions at the top?'

'Don't you think we'd make a great team?' invited Kosov.

It *was* preposterous. An absurd, ridiculous, preposterous joke! Danilov could not think of anyone with whom he would less like to be linked, professionally. At once came a sobering realisation. Was it so absurdly ridiculous? If Kosov had the government influence suggested by this conversation, couldn't the man be *imposed* upon the Bureau: become its director, even! He said: 'It's never occurred to me.'

'I think it's time I moved on,' insisted Kosov, his voice matter-of-fact, as if the decision had already been reached. 'I've been in charge of a district a long time.'

With Kosov at Petrovka, the Bureau would become entirely organised *for* crime. 'Have you discussed it, with anyone else?'

The head shake came once more. 'All this business has to be resolved . . .' Heavily, Kosov added: 'Resolved *properly*. Time enough to talk about other things after that.'

Danilov was abruptly seized by a fierce anger, concerned it would show in his face. What right had this fucking man – this arrogant, bombastic, crooked man – to sit and patronise him like this, virtually telling him what to do, practically with a fingersnap! Almost at once, objective man that he was, Danilov brought in the balancing thought. They'd made a mistake, like putting the buried-in-the-past, inefficient Metkin in charge of the Bureau. But this time it was a much more serious error. They'd declared themselves, through Kosov, given him and Cowley the opening for which they had been looking. He'd have to cultivate Kosov, like the rarest plant in the greenhouse. Honestly, Danilov said: 'You've given me a lot to think about.'

'I'm glad.'

Any further discussion was prevented by the women's return, for which Danilov was grateful, because he could not think of anything more to say at that stage. Larissa got him into the kitchen on the pretext of carrying something in while Olga was setting the table and Kosov was opening wine.

'You looked terrified when you arrived!'

'I thought you'd said something.'

'I'm going to, soon.'

'We both are,' promised Danilov.

'I'm working split shifts next week. Free every afternoon.'

'What about evenings?'

Larissa frowned. 'Not until the very end of the week. Why?'

'We were supposed to be doing something with Cowley again.' He had already thought of a possible way to use Kosov: ironically, it was prompted by what he hadn't been allowed to do earlier.

'I was thinking about the two of us!' said Larissa, offended.

'I was thinking about seeing you twice,' escaped Danilov.

Danilov suggested going out with Cowley again when they were all around the table. Kosov agreed at once and Olga said she'd like it, too. Pointedly, she added this time perhaps they'd go to a nightclub, and Kosov agreed to that, as well.

On their way back to Kirovskaya Olga said: 'It was a good evening, wasn't it?'

'One of the best I can remember,' said Danilov.

Cowley had not slept at all. For a long time, not until nearly dawn, he didn't even undress, repelled by getting into the bed featured in the photographs. Which he finally accepted as infantile, eventually lying down to rest at least. By that time his mind had stretched to the outer reaches of every emotion, from astonishment at how easily he had been trapped, through abject shame, to the inevitable, unavoidable consequence. He was destroyed. His only course now, to leave the splintered investigation with any sort of integrity, was to give Washington the fullest humiliating account, pouch the compromising photographs personally to Leonard Ross, and tender his immediate resignation before the blackmail demand was made.

That remained his intention for several hours, until the word sacrifice began to recur in his mind. He would, of course, have to resign. But if he did it at once whoever had set him up – which had, obviously, to be a group or a person fearful of everything being solved – had won, probably destroying not just him but the whole two-nation enquiry.

He wouldn't let that happen.

The determination burned through Cowley, the most fervent vow he ever made. He would destroy them as they destroyed him: bring them down with him. He'd make himself the knowing bait, pressing on with the investigation,

266

getting closer and closer until they became worried enough to make their demand. He could do it: *had* to do it. He'd supervised three blackmail cases during his career, before specialising in Russian affairs, and got convictions in every one. He knew the bargaining and the ploys, when to force the strong arguments and when to appear to capitulate. And he would always have an advantage. They would believe themselves superior, dealing with a man terrified of exposure and losing his career. Which he had already decided was lost anyway. It would be a final if pyrrhic victory.

CHAPTER FORTY-ONE

Danilov telephoned Pavin from Kirovskaya that he was making an enquiry on his way in, impatient to get to Cowley's hotel. His enthusiasm faltered at the sight of the American, who was grey-faced; the skin sagged under his eyes, which were vague, without focus. He looked distracted, exhausted.

'You don't look well.'

'I slept badly.' Cowley knew exactly how shitty he looked and didn't need to be told.

'You sure that's all it is?'

'You said you had something important,' urged the American.

Danilov's excitement took over. He bustled Cowley into the Volga, picking up the inner ring road but without any destination. Danilov tried to keep the account coherent, interspersing the actual conversation of the previous night with his impressions, but several times the American had to intrude with a question, fully to comprehend. Towards the end Cowley forced aside the eroding depression and the aching fatigue, recognising this possibly to be the biggest break so far, and one they certainly needed.

'It was obvious Kosov was on the take,' Cowley agreed.

'But not to this extent,' qualified Danilov. He hadn't admitted that at uniform level he'd also been a willing player. He didn't intend to, if he could avoid it: he very much wanted the American's professional respect.

'What's your guess?'

'I don't want to guess. I want to find out, definitely. And I want you to help me.'

'How?'

'You broke a New York Family with some impressive bugging, particularly in cars. That car is Kosov's status symbol. He'll do business from it: maybe enough for us to go further forward.'

'You still don't intend telling everyone officially?'

'More determined than ever not to.'

'It's your neck.' Cowley slightly lowered the window, for air.

'You said that already.'

'We had a hell of a Task Force, on the New York operation. With local police back-up. We couldn't create an organisation like that here. Definitely not if we're working virtually solo. Which we are.'

'We could do the car, surely?' insisted Danilov.

Cowley nodded, but doubtfully. 'We couldn't guarantee the reception unless we established a permanently close tail. Which we can't. So the strength of the signal will vary enormously. We wouldn't get everything.'

'I don't want everything: just enough!'

'We could connect the transmitter to a receiver in the embassy,' suggested Cowley. Deciding their co-operation was sufficient, he added: 'There's a man there who could monitor.' It would provide something more practical for Stephen Snow to do than relaying messages.

'I've already suggested another evening. Kosov's bound to insist we use the BMW.'

'We'll be fucked if he doesn't.'

'We'll keep on until he does,' said Danilov, refusing to be put off.

'The Bureau have a hell of a range of equipment,' offered the American. 'If I ask for it today we should get it by tomorrow's pouch: allow an extra day, just in case there's a difficulty. So fix the evening any time after that.' If the eavesdropping had any practical success, whoever had the photographs would hit on him with the blackmail. How long before the ignominious disgrace? A week? A fortnight? As long as a month? To whom would the pictures be released? The embassy was an obvious guess; the Bureau in Washington, as a long shot. Either would be contained internally, certainly after his instant resignation. What about a public leak, to newspapers? There were enough permanent American bureaux in Moscow, all listed in the telephone book. And the censor-free Muscovite press. Cowley didn't think any of the pictures could be published, but they wouldn't have to be: they could be described in print in sufficient detail and innuendo. So he would become a public as well as a private laughing stock. Pauline would hear or read what had happened: know he hadn't changed in any way. He hated the idea of Pauline knowing most of all. He'd been drunk and tricked by a whore and was going to be destroyed by it. And it was no-one's fault but his own.

'How about Friday?' suggested Danilov. 'We'll need to familiarise ourselves.'

'Friday's good,' agreed Cowley. He was silent as Danilov made the connecting loop, to return them along the peripheral road. Then he said: 'Kosov's your friend. Larissa, too?'

Danilov darted a quick look across the car. 'He replaced me, when I got out of uniform. Things kind of grew from there.' Only because of Larissa, he thought.

'It's never easy, turning in a dirty cop. Particularly if he's your friend.' Why had the Russian jumped like that?

'No,' agreed Danilov. He hadn't thought yet of the personal implications, but he started now.

'Maybe something could be worked out. If he's not definitely involved – just a conduit – maybe it could be dealt with discreetly? A quiet retirement.' Which was the best *he* could hope for, realised Cowley. He was thinking more about himself than about a corrupt Militiaman.

Everyone goes for compromise, accepted Danilov. 'He's more than a conduit: messengers don't drive brand new German cars. At the least, he might be withholding information about a murder.' So Kosov would have to be arrested and charged, unless it were stopped by higher authority. Wasn't it obvious Kosov would try to bargain with accusations about his own past? And it wasn't just the criminal investigation. What would Kosov do when he and Larissa made their announcement? The euphoria Danilov had felt began to leak away.

'It's going to seem a long time until Friday,' said Cowley, more to himself than to the Russian.

★

But it didn't.

The first intriguing – although still inconclusive – development confirmed Pavin's prediction that the undiscovered name had more significance than the others in Petr Serov's belongings.

With an approximate date to put through their computerised immigration records, the Swiss authorities traced an entry into Geneva of an Ilya Iosifovich Nishin on 22 May 1991. American immigration located the arrival of Nishin at Dulles airport five days later, on 28 May. Michel Paulac's passport – and another immigration check – showed Paulac on the same flight. Both men, on their visa forms, gave the Mayflower Hotel as their Washington DC address. FBI records did not have Nishin criminally listed.

In the same diplomatic pouch with that information Cowley received from the FBI's Psychological Behavioral Unit at Quantico, to which he had sent every tape of the Mikhail Antipov interrogation, confirmation that their approach to the man had been the right one. Detailed analysis of the tapes had failed to detect any stress peaks, which was inconceivable confronted with the irrefutable evidence, at that time, of the murder weapon.

'He knew the gun would disappear,' said Cowley.

'Thanks for going to the trouble, but I didn't need a psychologist to tell me that,' said Danilov.

It wasn't the end of the name discoveries. On the Thursday, Danilov finally received a reply from Oleg Yasev to his query about the identities of the three unknown mourners at Petr Serov's funeral. One, Valentin Lvov, had known the murdered diplomat from their joint posting at the Paris embassy. The other two, Ivan Churmak and Gennardi Fedorov, had officially represented the government.

'Fedorov!' identified Pavin at once.

Danilov had already recognised the name as one of the three on Lapinsk's list. It took an hour to identify him as the senior representative on the permanent Interior Ministry executive.

'And there's another link,' disclosed Pavin. 'Oleg Yasev also served in Paris during the same period as Petr Serov.'

'You haven't given me these names before,' accused Cowley.

'I didn't think they had any part in the case,' said Danilov. 'I thought they were given to me as a personal warning.'

'It's a hell of a coincidence, isn't it?' questioned Cowley.

'They represented the government,' reminded Pavin.

'Which is concerned over potential embarrassment about a criminally-linked diplomat,' completed Danilov.

'Kosov bullshits,' decided the blind man. 'We should go ahead, not wait to see if he can deliver Danilov.'

'I'm the one who'll be exposed,' protested Zimin.

'Frightened?' goaded Yerin.

'For the success of an operation that is going to make this Family one of the most powerful in the world: certainly in Russia!' returned the indulgently fat man.

Gusovsky was concerned the animosity between the two men was going to end in disaster. Objectively, he thought again, it would have to be Zimin who was removed. 'We already know we have to wait. But we don't need to produce the money. So we can get the control transferred at our leisure.'

'Do we go ahead?' persisted Yerin.

'No,' decided Gusovsky. 'We wait a little longer to see if Kosov *can* get Danilov. It's worth the delay.'

'It would be a double bonus if he does. It would mean we were back where we were before with the Organised Crime Bureau,' pointed out Zimin.

'The man won't produce,' insisted Yerin emphatically.

CHAPTER FORTY-TWO

The American equipment arrived with specific installation and reception instructions. There were several microphones, of different shapes and sizes – some little larger than a pinhead – and with a surprising variety of attachments, together with suggestions of how and where they could best be concealed. The monitoring equipment was more elaborate than Danilov had expected. That, too, could be used in different ways, either manually operated or voice activated, without the need for an operator.

They devoted a substantial part of the Friday, in advance of that evening's outing, testing everything as realistically as possible. They tried the bugs out in various positions in the Volga and drove throughout Moscow to assess the standard of reception and learn what sort of conditions risked the worst interference. They did a lot of the experimentation in and around Kosov's Militia district. Only then did Danilov realise the area Kosov commanded – and of which he himself had once been in charge – was convenient to two of the city's four airports, the operating territory of the Chechen Family. It should have occurred to him before.

Body pressure and movement overlaid conversation if a microphone was attached to the fabric of a seat. Aware of the impressive tape and radio deck in the BMW, they both worried that the music would drown anything less than a shouted exchange, reassuring themselves that if Kosov had the sort of discussion they hoped, he was unlikely to play music. Bridges and underpasses – even the tunnel quite close to the American embassy, where the receiving equipment was installed – made talk inaudible.

By mid-afternoon they had decided to plant two micro-phones, both in the front of the BMW on the logical assumption Kosov would always be driving: neither could recall sufficient detail about the interior layout to choose a precise location. They agreed to arrange themselves as before, giving Danilov the front passenger seat and the responsibility for fixing the devices.

'Let's hope it'll work,' said Danilov. He was disappointed there wasn't better clarity on the tape, which they'd further agreed should be voice activated and therefore live at all times of day and night.

'Let's hope,' echoed Cowley, with anything but hope in his voice, although Danilov missed it. The reluctance was introspective. A week or a fortnight or a month? he wondered again.

Cowley's entry into the Savoy bar, leading the rest of them, was his first since his entrapment, although he'd looked in from the lobby every night in the desperately empty hope of locating Lena, all the time knowing she would not be there. He forlornly searched for her that night, at last deciding he should stop making himself look stupid in his own eyes if not those of everyone else in the hotel.

Kosov quickly tried to impose himself – waving away Cowley's intention to reciprocate Danilov's earlier hospitality – and Danilov and Cowley made only a token protest, content to let him play the grandiose host any way he wanted.

Everything worked to choreographed perfection, with an additional advantage they hadn't expected. Danilov's making directly to the front of the BMW ensured the intended seating arrangements, and as he settled Kosov apologised for the restricted leg-room caused by the car phone, intentionally to draw attention to the new addition to the vehicle. Danilov allowed himself to be overly impressed, unclipping the instrument from its dashboard holder to examine it. He fumbled replacing it.

Kosov had clearly put a lot of thought and effort into the evening, even taking account of Cowley's stated preference for ethnic restaurants. They went to the traditionally Georgian U Pirosmani, with its spectacular view from Novodevichy Proyezd of the sixteenth-century convent on the other side of the river. There were violin music and

274

Georgian specialities, but not as many questions from Kosov about the investigation as either Danilov or Cowley had expected. They were careful to be as vague as they'd always been about those he did ask, because it would have been a mistake to have responded differently.

Larissa manoeuvred herself next to Danilov and separate from the others as they walked from the restaurant to the car. 'We're going to need somewhere to live, aren't we?'

'I suppose so.'

'One of the receptionists knows of an apartment that's becoming vacant soon, out in Tatarovo: her sister's getting married. Shall we look at it?'

Danilov felt a sink of uncertainty at making a positive commitment. 'If you like.'

'What would *you* like? You don't sound very enthusiastic!'

'We'll look at it,' he said, more positively.

'We'll need to bribe, because we're not on the housing list,' said Larissa, matter-of-factly. 'I'll ask my friend how much she thinks it will cost.'

Danilov guessed from her familiar entry that the Night-flight had been the club to which Kosov had taken Olga, while he was in Washington: Kosov was greeted with the recognition he enjoyed and allocated a table at once. Because Olga did not dance there was no problem about the number of times he did, with Larissa. She was excited about the apartment, which was large by Russian standards, with two bedrooms as well as a lounge: Danilov thought it sounded expensive. Olga believed she saw some of Kosov's friends from the earlier visit but they made no greeting and he said nothing, so she decided she was mistaken. Cowley danced twice, for politeness, with Larissa, but spent some time circulating around the club more than was really necessary, looking at a lot of girls. Lena was not among them. There were a lot of men in suits that shone, smoking Marlboros: as they probably owned the Mercedes and BMWs outside, they wouldn't need to keep the packs to attract a cab. They ended the evening with renewed promises to go out again soon: Danilov initiated the discussion.

He had to wait until Olga went to bed back at Kirovskaya before he could telephone Cowley, as they had arranged.

'Where?' asked the American.

'The smaller one, with the magnetic base, behind the telephone mounting on the dashboard. The other on the seat strut.'

'Now it all depends on American electronic technology,' said Cowley.

'And Kosov talking a lot,' added Danilov.

He did.

CHAPTER FORTY-THREE

They were surprised, although they shouldn't have been, that the recording started from the moment Danilov attached the microphones on their way to the U Pirosmani, making the initial intercept that of themselves, as well. Everyone sounded drunk after the nightclub, although Danilov and Cowley certainly hadn't been. There was a lot of Olga's nervous, please-agree-with-me laughter. Within minutes of Larissa and Kosov being alone, on their way home, Larissa described Olga as dumpy, with hopeless dress sense, and wondered why Danilov stayed with her, which Danilov despised her for saying. Kosov insisted Danilov and Cowley had hopelessly mishandled the murder investigation from the beginning, so that it was now a lost case: that was obvious from the way the American looked, like shit. Danilov smiled: Cowley didn't.

The clarity of the recording was good that night – Cowley thought it might have been because it was *at* night – but deteriorated afterwards. It was frustratingly intermittent the following day, when Kosov was alone, but almost at once encouraging. The initial deafening American jazz prevented their hearing the beginning: by the time Kosov turned the music system off, the car-phone exchange had begun. Even then things were lost, entire sentences broken or too faded, even when they wound the tape back and tried again with the volume at maximum.

Kosov began the exchange, from which they assumed he had initiated the call. If there had been any greeting, it was lost in the few seconds before the music was turned off. There was no identification.

'. . . *thought you'd be interested.*'

'. . . *have been dangerous,*' responded the fainter voice. '*You tell him?*'

'*Made it clear,*' said Kosov.

There was a rumble of static. The only audible word was *understood*; the tone made it a question.

'*Course he understood*,' assured Kosov. It was cocky, I'm-on-top-of-everything talk.

The static recurred, losing at least an entire sentence from whomever Kosov was talking to. The next voice was Kosov's. '*Other ways?*'

'. . . *shouldn't interfere* . . .' came from the other end, with abrupt clarity.

'. . . *It's their job!*' Kosov's remark was greeted with guffawed laughter from both ends.

'. . . *want* . . . *wrong* . . .'

'*Nothing will go wrong*,' came Kosov's voice, enabling the demand to which he was responding to be inferred. It was an eager-to-please assurance, like Olga's pitter patter laughter, earlier.

The reception was suddenly so good they had to turn the volume down. '*You sure you can get there?*'

'*Quite sure.*'

Danilov moved to speak but Cowley shook his head against the interruption.

'*How's the car?*'

'*Fantastic.*'

'*We want it to work. And I don't mean the car.*'

'*I've told you it will!*'

'*Think of the car: the sort of gratitude there'll be.*'

'*Don't need to think. I know.*'

'*We're relying on you, Yevgennie Grigorevich.*'

Danilov nodded to Cowley, at the introduction of an identifiable name.

'*I wouldn't have thought you needed confirmation by now.*'

'*We always want confirmation. Three people are dead because we wanted confirmation.*'

The silence was so long both Cowley and Danilov thought there had been a complete break. Then Kosov said: '*You didn't need to say that.*'

'*Don't take it personally.*'

'*What other way is there to take it?*'

'*You're being melodramatic.*'

278

'*I told you it's all going to work!*' Kosov's voice was subdued.
'*I heard you.*'
'*We'll go on using this line.*'
'*If that's what you think is best.*'
'*Safest,*' said Kosov, finding a better word. '*Anything else for us to talk about?*'
'*Just do what you've got to.*'
'*What about the rest of it?*'
'*All covered,*' guaranteed the other man, the strength of the signal fluctuating again. '*Not your concern.*'
'*I need to know!*' The protest was still subdued.
'*You will, when it's necessary.*' The contempt leaked over the telephone link.
'*What, until then?*'
'*Stay in touch.*'

The reply was lost. So was any farewell. There was a high-pitched whine, '*That's right*' from Kosov, and then the deafening music again: Billie Holliday singing 'Melancholy Baby'.

'We're right there, in his office!' declared the American. Flat voiced, he quoted: ' "We'll go on using this line." How else is he going to do business but from the guaranteed security of his car phone!'

Danilov found it hard to believe how easy it had suddenly become. 'Not anyone official.' It was essential to analyse.

'Definitely not,' agreed the American. In further, belated agreement he added: 'It could have been about the discussion you and Kosov had.'

' "You sure you can get there?" ' echoed Danilov. 'That could refer to Kosov thinking he can transfer to the Organised Crime Bureau.'

'We shouldn't over-interpret,' warned Cowley. 'The conversation can be made to fit, but I don't think we should be too positive yet.' Was the reluctance professional objectivity, or personal unwillingness to accept the inevitable?

'I'd liked to have heard more about "other ways",' said Danilov. 'I can't guess what that meant.'

Cowley had isolated the remark, too, linking it with what followed about interference, which had caused both speakers so much amusement. 'There can't be any doubt about the three people who died to provide confirmation. But confirmation of what?'

Danilov took the question further, not able to provide an answer. 'It was a threat to Kosov. The three who died had their mouths blown away. So Yevgennie Grigorevich *knows* what it's all about: he could tell us!'

'Not until we're a greater threat,' stressed Cowley. 'Nobody's frightened enough of us yet, either here or in America.'

'And they're hardly likely to be,' said Danilov, cynically.

Cowley said: 'I won't pass any of this on to Washington, not yet. It might have meaning for us. For anyone else it just raises more questions than it answers.'

'Maybe we won't have to wait much longer,' said Danilov.

They didn't.

Over the succeeding days they eavesdropped on Yevgennie Kosov's car adequately enough to understand approximately eighty-five percent of every conversation. Sometimes they listened to activities inside it, too.

There were a lot of command briefings to Kosov's subordinates in his Militia division, usually bullying and demanding. There were outings with Larissa, during one of which she protested she didn't like the people they were going to meet and Kosov told her to shut up and be pleasant because they were the providers of a lot of the 'good things' they enjoyed. Danilov and Cowley played that tape several times, to extract every nuance, and listened intently to the homeward journey in the hope of hearing a name, which they didn't. There was a telephone conversation with someone named Eduard, with a peremptory insistence upon a wine and Western spirit delivery within a week, upon which Danilov particularly concentrated because an Eduard Agayans was a black marketeer to whom he'd introduced Kosov: Danilov was unable to decide if it was the same man from the faintness of the intercepted voice. There was an incoming call, probably the most difficult to decipher, which they decided was an instruction to Kosov to guarantee the unimpeded passage through his district of a fleet of six trucks, coming up from the south. Throughout the exchange Kosov showed the respect of the first overheard recording, but the reception this time was too bad to be certain if it was the same man: Cowley said if they turned the tapes over to the technicians at Quantico, a positive voiceprint could be made. There was no indication during the conversation what the lorries contained.

That afternoon Kosov dialled someone they *were* sure was the man of the first day. It was an extremely brief exchange, Kosov asking if there was anything he should be told, which there wasn't, and the man asking the same in return and receiving the same reply. Cowley thought it possible when they made the tape available to Washington, other Quantico specialists would be able to extract a number – from which in turn they could get an address – from the electronic variations in the dialling. There were two clumsy, sexually intimate conversations with women, quite soon after one of which a girl audibly entered the car. Fifty American dollars was agreed, for fellatio, which was performed to a lot of grunted pleasure from Kosov.

There were recordings of three other passengers in the car, all male, one obviously another Militia officer. That journey was the day after Kosov received his instructions about the lorry convoy, which he passed on in specific detail to the unnamed policeman: three days later there was a call of thanks from the man who had sought an unhindered journey. Another passenger was a fence, paying a bribe of $500 for the right to operate on Kosov's territory. They were not sure about the third. The man said very little and what he did say was spoken in a quiet voice, so not everything was picked up, even though he was sitting literally on top of one of the microphones. A lot of it was also intentionally ambiguous. It was not until Kosov talked openly of a ministry – although without stipulating which one – that Danilov guessed at a government official. They prepared a written transcript of the entire encounter, paring away the double meanings finally to agree Kosov was establishing himself as the man's supplier – 'anything you want, all you've got to do is ask, you know that,' Kosov said at one point.

And on the eighth day they heard – not completely, but far more than they had dared hope – what they had been listening for.

'*Gusovsky*,' announced a rasping voice, maybe that of a heavy smoker, the moment the receiver was lifted.

'*Arkadi Pavlovich!*' greeted Kosov.

'Chechen,' identified Danilov at once.

'Pavin called him a leader,' remembered Cowley. He smiled, half disbelievingly, at the Russian.

'. . . *gone quiet?*' asked the caller.

'. . . *told you they were getting nowhere*,' came Kosov's stronger voice.

'*I need to be absolutely sure: we're ready to go.*'

'*You can be. Dimitri Ivanovich is my friend.*'

'Me?' queried Danilov.

'Who else?' agreed Cowley.

Static snowed the line, blotting out Gusovsky's response and the beginning of whatever Kosov said.

'. . .*waiting to hear from you, before I spoke to him again.*'

'. . . *want a definite assurance*,' said Gusovsky.

'*I can get it.*'

'. . . *worth his while.*'

'*I'll tell him.*'

'*What about you?*'

'. . . *suggested it.*'

There was more interference. All they caught of what Gusovsky said was: '. . . *going personally.*'

'*Who?*' asked Kosov.

There was a gap, which they later decided had been a pause of uncertainty. The reply was broken, when it came.

'. . . *Zimin . . . Zavorin. . .*'

'*Rome or Sicily?*'

'*Sicily . . . all arranged . . .*'

'*When?*'

'. . . *soon.*'

'. . . *not going to be any more trouble?*'

282

'. . . *got the message. They know they've lost it.*'

'*Any more killing would attract too much attention,*' suggested Kosov.

'*There won't be, if there doesn't have to be.*'

The line blurred, the sort of interference that had come from their road tests when they drove through an underpass. 'Shit!' said Cowley vehemently.

'. . . *no problem with the other one,*' returned Gusovsky's voice.

'*Are you sure?*' asked Kosov.

'. . . *whenever we want to. And he knows.*'

Danilov was curious at the way Cowley shifted beside him, as if he were uncomfortable. The American did not answer his look.

'*So what do you want me to do?*'

'*Speak to him again. They won't go until I'm sure.*'

'*They couldn't have found out: haven't found out.*'

'*I won't take the risk, not this close.*'

'*Shall I call you?*'

'*This number.*'

The line abruptly went dead, the intercept filled at once by the Billie Holliday tape. Cowley snapped off the machine, looking expectantly at Danilov.

'We needed luck,' said the Russian quietly, as disbelieving as the American. 'We've got it!'

'It *has* to be about the conversation he had with you,' said Cowley, beginning their analysis. Mentally continuing it, he thought, *No problem with the other one . . . and he knows.* Soon, Cowley supposed: very soon. It was like slowly bleeding to death.

'It'll be proved definitely, if he makes another approach.'

'For an assurance,' reminded Cowley. Rhetorically he said: 'What does Gusovsky want an assurance about?'

'That we're no further forward,' said Danilov, answering it anyway. 'Which until five minutes ago we weren't.'

'But now we are,' said Cowley. 'Here's how I read it. The Chechen are sending two men, Zimin and Zavorin, to Sicily: all arranged, Gusovsky said. But they're not going until he's sure.'

Danilov nodded, agreeing with the assessment. 'We can manipulate it, if Kosov comes to me again!'

'*When* he comes to you again,' said Cowley, without any doubt.

More subdued, Danilov took the analysis on. 'A Russian Mafia group is linking with the established Mafia, in Sicily . . .' Repeating the phrase the American had already echoed, Danilov added: 'Maybe it already has: *all arranged*, like Gusovsky said. So what the hell *has* been arranged? It's as frightening as you thought it could be.'

'Worse,' warned Cowley. 'We know the Italian and American Mafia are partners: always have been. Now we've got the global connection: Worldwide Mafia Incorporated. You any idea what that means?'

'No,' replied Danilov honestly. 'At the moment I don't think I have.'

'We can do a lot of damage,' insisted Cowley, a promise as much to himself as a suggestion to the Russian. 'We *can* manipulate it, if we're reading it correctly. If we can catch these two guys in Sicily we can not only sweat them about the murders: we can bust their deal. Maybe break a Sicilian ring, too.'

Danilov felt a sharp and surprising inadequacy, at the enormity of what they were discussing. 'I can't get to Sicily without authority . . . which means admitting the listening devices . . .'

For several moments they sat unspeaking, each trying to assess the loss. The car bug – and Kosov – was their *only* lead, Cowley acknowledged. There was no way to prevent his destruction. So why didn't he take all the responsibility?

Cowley said: 'The eavesdropping equipment is American: nobody here knows anything about it. And they can't ever. I've travelled in Kosov's car. I could have planted it. Be working independently of you, after all the fuck-ups.'

Danilov looked back at the American, head curiously to one side. 'So I don't know you're doing it . . . ?' he groped.

'All you know is what you're told, *by* an American. Which could have come *from* America.'

'And the bugs stay in the car!' acknowledged Danilov.

284

'Unbeknown to anyone except those who need to know,' said Cowley. 'How's that sound?'

'Just fine,' accepted the Russian.

The call came from Kosov two days later, to Petrovka, not to the apartment; an invitation for lunch the following day – 'just the two of us, like old times.' Danilov couldn't remember any such old times, but said he'd look forward to it. He fixed an appointment with Smolin afterwards: Cowley spent most of that afternoon sending messages to Washington and replying to the flurry of questions they prompted from the FBI Director.

Kosov was already seated when Danilov arrived at the *Dom na Tverskoi*, and for once did not attempt the arm-waving flamboyance of champagne and permanently attentive waiters: he actually shook his head against the interruption of one man who began to approach, pouring the red wine himself. They touched glasses and toasted each other's health, and Kosov said at once: 'So it's getting nowhere?'

'We've had to release Antipov,' disclosed Danilov, alert to the reaction.

Kosov nodded. 'I know,' he boasted. 'What now?'

The knowledge could still have been either Mafia or government, decided Danilov. 'Bill's under a lot of pressure from Washington. They're talking of withdrawing him. After all the problems they think he's wasting his time. He seems to think so, too.'

'Which would leave it to you?'

'I suppose so.'

'And there's no way forward?'

'Not that I can see. Maybe I'll get lucky.'

Kosov added to their glasses. 'You thought any more of what else we spoke about?'

'Like what?' Danilov was glad he was not in the car, where he would have known everything was being overheard: self-consciousness might have been obvious.

'Like missing the old days.'

'I don't think I said I missed them.'

'Just some of the benefits.'

285

'Olga certainly misses them.' He didn't like bringing Olga into the conversation, but it fitted.

'Women like nice things. Larissa wouldn't know how to live any other way.'

For a few brief seconds Danilov wondered if there were some hidden meaning in the remark, before deciding there couldn't be. Larissa was going to have to learn. 'It's too late for me now.'

'It doesn't have to be.'

'I've lost contact.'

'You introduced me, once. I could re-introduce you.'

'People will have changed, surely?'

'I've made other friends: important friends. It's much better than it was in your day: better organised.'

'The work I do now is a lot different from a uniformed division. It wouldn't be as easy to co-operate, like it was before.'

'Things can always be worked out. Don't forget I want a transfer. I could be there, ensuring things run smoothly.'

One team replaced by another, recognised Danilov. A lot of careful thought had gone into this approach. 'I need to think about it.'

'You *do* need to think about it. I'm your friend, so I think I can talk honestly: you've been stupid, for far too long.'

Not as stupid as you're going to be proven to be, thought Danilov. 'Perhaps you're right.'

'You *know* I'm right! I can introduce you to the proper people,' persisted Kosov. 'Fix everything.'

Danilov nodded, wondering how far he might be able to utilise that boast. 'Let's keep in touch.'

'*Close* touch,' insisted Kosov. 'Friends should help friends.'

'You're right,' said Danilov. 'They should.' He still had time to meet Larissa, before the Federal Prosecutor. He didn't feel at all hypocritical.

The Tatarovo apartment had two full-sized bedrooms, as well as a separate living room with a dining annexe, and kitchen fittings better even than Larissa's existing flat. It was on the eighth floor, and from the balcony there was a view of the river.

'It's fabulous!' declared Larissa. 'I want it!'

'How much is it?' asked Danilov.

'Four hundred and fifty roubles a month if you're paying in Russian; three hundred if you give the concierge twenty dollars a week for himself. And the bribe to jump the list is two hundred and fifty dollars.'

'I don't have two hundred and fifty dollars.'

Larissa looked at him uncertainly. 'We need it, to get the flat,' she said simply.

Larissa wouldn't know how to live any other way, he remembered. 'I'll have to try to get it.'

'Yes darling, you will,' Larissa agreed. 'Why don't you ask Bill?'

CHAPTER FORTY-FOUR

Danilov went to Pushkinskaya unsure if it would be as easy to convince a trained lawyer as it had been to deceive Kosov. He still believed he was correctly pursuing the investigation by holding things back from Nikolai Smolin, so strongly did he believe the man would make any ultimate decision about the case thinking of government sensitivity first and the law second. But until now it had been nothing more than delaying the information, until he was sure. What he was attempting that afternoon was going further: it *was* deception, even if the eventual outcome might be justified. And if it didn't turn out to be justified, he'd be open to the sort of tribunal that had condemned Anatoli Metkin.

'What's the development?' prompted Smolin. He had a notepad open, ready, in front of him.

'Not here,' warned Danilov, edging out on to creaking ice. 'The Americans have decided it's sufficiently sound for Cowley to examine. I think we should consider my going, too.'

'Going where?'

'Sicily,' announced Danilov. 'The information came from America: specifically Brighton Beach,' he elaborated. 'The rumour, confirmed from several different sources, was of a forthcoming meeting between Russian and Italian Mafia. The American authorities are already liaising with the Italians.'

'What has it got to do with the investigation here?'

'The people named in the Serov documents are thought to be involved,' said Danilov, lying openly.

'It's vague,' complained the Federal Prosecutor.

'I can only pass on what I have been told.' It *wasn't* as easy confronting a legal mind.

'Why didn't Cowley come with you this afternoon?' frowned Smolin.

288

A mistake: it would have been more convincing for an American to have talked about a development supposed to have come from America. 'He's been ordered to leave, as soon as he gets the final go-ahead from Washington,' improvised Danilov. The earlier rehearsal with Cowley provided the escape. 'And there are implications about it I felt best only discussed between the two of us.'

'What implications?'

'I suspect the Americans have had this information for several days,' said Danilov. 'If the decision had not been made to involve Cowley, I don't think we would have been told at all. The Americans and Italians could have handled it quite independently.'

'Meaning?'

'They don't trust us.' Danilov paused, wanting to get the argument absolutely right, although Smolin had earlier not rejected the sort of thing he was going to say. 'They've got every reason not to. If whatever might happen in Sicily *is* linked with our enquiry, and it becomes generally known in advance at Petrovka and in the ministries most closely involved, it will almost inevitably leak.'

'Or *be* leaked?' The Federal Prosecutor was subdued, but showed no surprise at the suggestion.

'It's a danger we've got to accept,' insisted Danilov. Too soon to judge how it was going, but he was encouraged.

'You got names of people you don't trust, at Petrovka or the ministries?'

'If I had I would have given them to you officially,' said Danilov. And still would, if he ever understood the significance of Ilya Nishin and Ivan Churmak and Gennardi Fedorov. What, he wondered, would officially happen after he did?

'Not even an indication of rank?'

'I would have considered that sufficient for an official report, as well.'

Smolin nodded, slowly. 'I suppose the American attitude *is* unavoidable.'

It was moving in the right direction. Danilov said: 'But they *have* told us.'

Smolin took the point. 'So if nothing happens in Sicily – if it *is* a rumour, without foundation – we're damned, suspected of leaking it from here without any chance of defending ourselves?'

'Unless we absolutely restrict the number of people to be told. At the moment there are only four, here in Moscow: Cowley, myself, Major Pavin and yourself. There is nothing in any of the case files at Petrovka.'

'Are you suggesting we do *not* tell Vorobie or Oskin?'

'I think they should have it made clear to them what I believe the American attitude to be, and ensure nothing about Sicily is passed to *anyone* in their departments.'

'That still wouldn't cover us if it *is* an unsubstantiated rumour.'

'The Americans don't believe it is.' Could he escape censure, if it went wrong or nothing *did* happen? Hardly.

'You should go, of course,' decided Smolin.

There was relief but little satisfaction. 'And by a very special route.'

Smolin had given his agreement distantly, as if he was preoccupied with something else. Now he came fully back to the investigator, frowning. 'What special route?'

'We won't be able to avoid people at Petrovka knowing I am away. We need a deception.' It was the moment he and Cowley had accepted to be the most difficult to steer past the other man. It was essential, further to convince Kosov of the collapsing murder case, but it was flawed if examined too closely. Determinedly Danilov pressed on. 'A way has already been suggested: it might, too, reassure the Americans of our genuine co-operation.'

'How?'

'There has still been no public announcement about our having to release Antipov,' reminded Danilov. 'If the announcement about the release *was* made, it would be entirely understandable for me to return to America to review the progress of the case of far, wouldn't it?'

'Review the *failure* of the case so far,' qualified Smolin. 'That's how it would be interpreted.'

'That's how I want it to be interpreted,' seized Danilov. 'It *has* failed: *is* failing. I very much want the people we're trying to find to believe that.'

'By publicly humiliating ourselves!'

'There's no choice about that: it's got to happen, sooner or later. And there wouldn't be any humiliation in the end, if we made it clear we allowed the impression, to create a trap.'

Smolin's head moved, in further acceptance. 'Vorobie and Oskin will have to know the truth, if there is going to be a public declaration.'

'But no-one necessarily beyond them. A return to Washington can be the explanation throughout the lower levels of the ministries.'

'It's a convoluted scheme,' protested the prosecutor, although not forcefully.

'Which could work,' asserted Danilov.

'If it doesn't, we could be made to look even more foolish.'

Me most of all, thought Danilov.

'What in the name of Christ is going on over there!' exclaimed the Secretary of State.

'Not enough. Or maybe too much,' said Leonard Ross. 'I've spent most of the day back and forth with Cowley, trying to make sense of it.' The FBI Director decided late-afternoon meetings at the State Department were preferable to breakfast sessions: Happy Hour bourbon was an improvement on coffee and eggs.

'We're to co-ordinate our statement with that from Russia, regretting the release of a suspect and agreeing the need for consultations?' clarified Henry Hartz. 'The two of them are seen publicly to fly in, to make it look kosher, then take off from another airport to Italy. All because every goddamned policeman and official in Moscow is crooked! Sure these two guys aren't just building up their air miles?'

'Cowley's sure of the intercept: he's bringing a lot of stuff back for the experts at Quantico. But he thinks what they've got already is good enough to move on, and I'm backing him. He's an experienced agent and wouldn't go off half cocked. I've already alerted my guys in Rome to get organised with the anti-Mafia people in Italy.'

'It's the worst of what we didn't want to hear, Mafia worldwide,' recalled Hartz soberly.

'Precisely the reason to go with it,' said Ross. 'If we've got a chance in a million to bust something before it becomes established, I want to take it.'

'I'll cable the Moscow ambassador to release our matching statement as close to the Russians' as possible,' agreed Hartz. 'We can duplicate from here as soon as we hear.'

'You *can* buy things I want!' said Olga, happily, offering the re-written list.

'I'll try,' said Danilov. Would he be able to pad his expenses sufficiently to amass the $250 bribe for the Tatarovo apartment? Where was his much-vaunted integrity now? He waited until Olga went to the kitchen to make supper, before calling Kosov.

'There's going to be an official statement. It's a disaster.'

CHAPTER FORTY-FIVE

They landed in Washington in the literal glare of orchestrated publicity following the announcement of Mikhail Antipov's release, and the inevitable speculation that the investigation was soured from inter-nation rivalry and Russian inefficiency. Cowley and Danilov forced their way stone-faced through the press mêlée at Dulles airport to the waiting FBI limousine, ignoring the shouted questions. The expression wasn't difficult for Cowley: as the car swept off the Beltway on to Memorial Parkway he thought how different his homecoming would be next time. There wouldn't be a blaze of cameras then, and certainly not the convenience of a waiting limousine.

There was a straggle of photographers and one television unit at the vehicle entrance to the FBI headquarters, but the tightly restricted inner courtyard guaranteed an unrecorded arrival. That facility was why Henry Hartz, also unnoticed, travelled in from the more open State Department where the subterfuge could not have been maintained.

Cowley had brought all the tapes, but selected only the one referring to Sicily to play to the Director and the Secretary of State. Hartz did not attempt to hide his scepticism when it finished. 'We're way out on a limb with this.'

'Which we're doing without public awareness,' pointed out Ross. 'Any recriminations will be just between us and the Italians.' He indicated the other tapes and said to Cowley: 'Why didn't we get these earlier?'

'They're evidence of a crooked cop: didn't become part of our case until this . . .' He in turn gestured to the tape they had just played. '. . . I want Quantico to go through all the earlier stuff, for voiceprint comparison and sound and quality enhancement. I also want them to try to get a number, from the dialling, for us to work backwards to locate an address. Snow's going to ship tapes back daily, from now on.'

Ross remained looking at his agent, as if he were going to continue the criticism. Instead, to Danilov, he said: 'This crooked cop a friend of yours?'

'He succeeded me, on promotion,' said Danilov guardedly. He'd expected some sort of conference, but not to be in the presence of the FBI Director and Secretary of State: he wasn't overawed, but frighteningly aware of being out of his depth. If it was ever discovered in Moscow what he was doing, nothing could save him: he hardly deserved to be saved.

'Why target him? You know he was dirty?'

'He made an obvious approach to me.'

Hartz waved generally around the office and the city beyond. 'You think he'll go for all this?'

'There was another meeting, not on tape. He hasn't named a Family but it's obvious who he's talking about. He wants to introduce me. Just before I left Moscow we spoke on the telephone. I said I might like to take up his offer when I get back. He said his friends would be very pleased, and that they would help me any way I wanted.'

'You record that, with a prior explanation to protect yourself?' demanded the former judge.

'No,' admitted Danilov.

'Let's hope he didn't: if he did, you're dead.'

After today – this encounter – he could be anyway, Danilov thought.

Cowley and Danilov left the FBI building by freight elevator and flew to Italy from the totally secure Andrews Air Force base on a loaned CIA plane equipped like no other Danilov had ever seen or imagined possible. The entire fuselage was divided between a lounge, actually fitted with satellite-transmitted in-flight television as well as the predictable movies, and a minuscule but functional bar which adjoined a dining area with full-sized chairs set at a full-sized, white clothed table at which they were served steak and California chardonnay from a closed-off galley. Beyond that were three divided sleeping sections, each with a full length bed, bordering closets and bathroom annexes. They both got six hours' sleep.

Their arrival at the closed-off military section of Rome's Fiumicino airport was frenzied, swarming with uniformed and plainclothes police. It was not until they were halfway towards the city, wedged in the middle of a horn-blaring cavalcade, that they became properly aware with whom they were travelling. The FBI station chief re-introduced himself as Barclay Smith: it was Smith, who was a thin, immaculately dressed man given to languid hand and arm movements, who introduced the plainclothed Italian in the front seat as Guiseppe Melega, the investigating colonel of the Interior Ministry's anti-Mafia division. As he did so Smith said: 'Don't imagine all these outriders are for you: Colonel Melega is currently number one on the Mafia hit list.'

'Maybe we should have taken the airport train,' said Cowley. Why the fuck were they bothering with all the non-leak security in Moscow and Washington to become part of a circus like this, in the very place where they needed the most discreet security of all!

'Much safer,' agreed the DEA agent. 'But no-one's life is complete until they've had a ride in an Italian police car at a hundred miles an hour in traffic.' David Patton was a plump man cutting himself in half with a belt fastened too tightly around a lightweight suit that had long ago been defeated by pasta and Italian heat. That heat was troubling the man now, making him glow pink.

Everyone was at the early-curiosity stage Danilov had come to expect, looking at him as if they expected him to have one eye in the middle of his forehead or six fingers on each hand. He wished he could have satisfied them with some physical oddity.

Melega twisted to smile confidently from the front seat. 'Everything is in place: it will be a perfect trap.' He talked directly to Danilov, enunciating good English with elaborate slowness, as if talking to someone of limited intelligence.

Cowley's concern at the security of the operation only partially lifted when the Italian planning was outlined in detail in Melega's screened, bomb-proofed and electronically guarded headquarters. The man insisted only five people in total in both his controlling ministry and his anti-Mafia division knew a meeting of the Moscow Mafia and the Sicilian Cosa Nostra was anticipated. The two names from Kosov's car telephone – Zimin and Zavorin – were on watch lists at all Italian air and sea ports. The reason had been disguised from Customs authorities by the order being issued through a ministry totally unconnected with Melega's division. Five helicopters, each capable of carrying a fifteen-strong Carabinieri assault force, were on two-hour standby: so, too, were three naval patrol boats, which could transport a total of seventy-five men. To prevent any suspicion of a specific operation on a Mafia-dominated island, no additional officers had been drafted to Sicily itself, but there were fifty mainland Carabinieri who could be mobilised and helicoptered there in under four hours. None had yet been warned of their selection. Detectives and undercover operatives already on the island were listening to informers and sources, but not asking any questions to hint prior knowledge. Obviously there was no watch list for Zimin or Zavorin at either of Sicily's Palermo or Catania airports: all incoming arrivals, apart from holiday charters, had to be routed through Rome.

Danilov pointed out that everything hinged on the two Chechen Family men travelling under their identified names in the first place, and flying direct to Rome in the second. From Moscow, even if they *did* keep their own names, they could arrive at any airport in Europe, travel on to Italy by train, bus or car and cross to Sicily by sea with practically no risk of detection. Although it meant dangerously spreading still more widely the two names, it was agreed Drug Enforcement Administration officers at American embassies in the relevant capitals create a watch list at the most likely transfer airports.

And they waited.

There were daily conferences, away from Melega's possibly monitored office, in restaurants and hotels and 'safe' houses. At each, Cowley passed on what they received through the American embassy on the via Veneto, close to where he and Danilov were living, at the Bernini Bristol.

Kosov's car-phone interception continued to provide incontrovertible evidence of the man's corruption, but nothing more about a visit to Sicily of two Moscow gangsters. Quantico established the voice on the first day of the interception was the same as that on the only tape discussing Sicily. The Sicilian tape had been enhanced to the point of destruction: none of the additional words, six in all, had added any useful material. The American technicians had been unable to decipher a trace-back number from the dialling tone without an identical Russian telephone: Snow had sent from Moscow a duplicate of every car telephone openly available in the city, which included two French and one German, but it was going to take time. If Kosov's equipment was adapted from a European import of which they did not have a copy, a comparison was virtually impossible. Swiss police had not come up with any further information about the Russian named Ilya Nishin; neither had the FBI.

Each evening Patton and Smith tried to entertain them, which was an experience for Danilov and a comparison for Cowley, from his earlier tour of duty as the FBI resident in Rome. The first week Cowley said nothing seemed to have changed in six years, to which Patton replied laconically that nothing had changed in Rome for two thousand years, which was why it was called the Eternal City. Most nights they finished at bars along the via Veneto, which was hardly typically Italian but a place where they all felt comfortable, despite the prices. Never once did Cowley get drunk: several nights he did not drink at all. In the middle of the second week Barclay Smith, who did get drunk most nights, insisted he'd waited a long time to say it but it looked to him like either a bum steer or the bastards had been and gone without them knowing about it. Patton mumbled that he thought so too. Neither Cowley nor Danilov felt like arguing. At the end of that week there was the first suggestion of impatience from Washington, in a personal message from Leonard Ross to Cowley asking how much longer he felt the stake-out justified. There was no indication in the cable of political pressure, but Cowley guessed there was some when Melega raised virtually the same query at that day's conference. The question created the first worthwhile discussion between them for more than a week, opinion ending almost equally divided between the called-off theory and the been-and-gone suggestion.

'It was always on the cards it would be a blow-out,' said the world-weary Barclay Smith. 'How many of these things ever come up with a result? One in ten? One in twenty? Like Caesar said, we came, we tried, we fucked up, so let's call it a day.'

Cowley refused to, immediately. Danilov argued against it as well, both accepting they were clutching at straws because there was nothing else to clutch at, anywhere. Danilov finally got his hair cut and bought three new shirts. He considered another jacket but decided to save the money: he'd already converted his lire advance into $200, and thought he could accumulate the complete bribe for the Tatarovo apartment from incidental expenses. He saw a watch he would have liked to buy to replace the one which rarely worked, but ignored that purchase for the same reason.

It was the next Wednesday that an excited Colonel Melega announced rumours from two independent sources in Palermo – like the Moscow tape, insufficient when separate but intriguing when put together – of a forthcoming meeting of Mafia leaders. A third source, from Catania, confusingly suggested it would be between Sicilian and American dons, with no mention of Russians. Two of the informants put the timing within the next seven days.

On the Thursday, the priority cable to the Rome embassy from the Paris DEA office reported a Maksim Zimin and an Ivan Zavorin transferring from an incoming Moscow flight to an Alitalia service. The alert was so prompt there was still an hour before the Alitalia plane landed at Fiumicino. By the time it did, Colonel Melega had established the Russians were booked for their second transfer connection, still confidently under their own names and with only a ninety-minute stopover, on the local flight from Rome to Palermo. When it took off, six of the new passengers were members of Melega's anti-Mafia squad, the two Russians already secretly photographed and identified from the immigration documents they had surrendered in Rome and upon which both were described as company directors.

Melega, Cowley and Danilov and the other two Americans were already in Palermo airport even before the Rome departure, flown in by one of the helicopters. Thirty additional Carabinieri had also been airlifted in: the rest of the hurriedly mobilised squad were crossing to the island by naval patrol boats, bringing a variety of unmarked cars all fitted with Sicilian, not Roman, registrations.

'Here we go!' sighed Cowley, watching the passengers file off the internal flight. In a brief moment of professional satisfaction he forgot his personal destruction was moving inexorably closer. He soon remembered.

CHAPTER FORTY-SIX

It was not until the two Russians eventually collected their much transferred luggage that the watching policemen realised there was a third, clearly an underling from the way the cases were casually handed to him to carry. In the delay of disembarkation Melega had already collected the passenger list: the obvious third name was Boris Amasov. The Italian was embarrassed the identification had not been made earlier, from the Alitalia arrival in Rome: everyone else in the group felt it should have already been realised, too, but there was no spoken comment.

It was difficult for Danilov to defer to the authority of Colonel Melega, although he knew the Italian had to command an Italian operation, with the rest of them allowed as little more than observers: he suspected the Americans were nervous, too, of their complete dependency. Melega flurried about in constant movement and conversation, juggling – sometimes literally – between landlines and mobile telephones and various subordinate commanders ensuring the surveillance remained absolute, but the rest of the group fell virtually silent, speaking only to make necessary contributions: neither Smith nor Patton attempted the wise-cracking cynicism Danilov had come to regard as endemic among American law enforcement officers.

They didn't form part of the motorised observation: Melega maintained contact from their radio car. When the Italian announced the Russians had booked into the President Hotel, on the via Francesco Crispi, Cowley snorted a laugh and said: 'I don't believe it!'

'What?' demanded Danilov.

'The American *capo di tutti capi*, Lucky Luciano, always stayed at that hotel when he came to Sicily, after being deported to Italy from America after the war. He re-formed from there the Mafia that Mussolini had crushed!'

'They're treating it like a pilgrimage!' declared Danilov, more interested in practicality than history.

'And re-forming the Mafia into something even bigger,' said Cowley.

'Much bigger,' announced Melega, two hours later. By then they had booked into the Politeama Palace on the Piazza Ruggero Settimo, further back from the seafront than the Mafia hotel, in which Melega had installed four officers purporting to be tourists. Melega made the declaration the moment he returned from a contact meeting with them.

'What?' demanded Patton.

Melega, enjoying centre stage, read unnecessarily from a slip of paper. 'John Vincent Palma. Born April, 1943. Given address Waterbury, Connecticut.'

'Go on,' encouraged Cowley.

'He booked into the President Hotel three days ago,' said Melega. 'Reservation is for four more nights. Tonight he had dinner with Maksim Zimin, Ivan Zavorin and Boris Amasov: pasta, with veal to follow. With four flasks of Chianti. At this moment they're toasting each other in grappa.'

His voice distant, Patton mused: 'The rumour from Catania was that it was to be an American-Sicilian meeting.'

'Now Russia completes the chain . . .' said Danilov.

'. . . to create the world-spanning connection we all hoped and pretended wasn't going to happen,' concluded Cowley. To Barclay Smith he said: 'I don't want any leaks now, with open-line telephone calls between here and Rome. Take one of the helicopters back to Rome. Now. I want the name of John Vincent Palma run through every record ever kept in America since the Puritans waded ashore and got met by the Indians. Photographs wired, if they're available. Let's cross-check the name against the Russian ones we have, as well. By tomorrow morning I want to know more about John Vincent Palma than he knows about himself.'

Which was virtually what they got, and at breakfast time, from the unshaven, red-eyed but uncomplaining FBI agent. John Vincent Palma was listed in the FBI criminal computer as a known capo in the New York Genovese Family. There was a failure to convict on a manslaughter charge in 1972; in 1975 an extortion conviction drew a three-year penitentiary sentence. There was another unproven charge of transporting a girl across a State line for the purposes of prostitution. He was married, with two children, lived in Waterbury, as listed on the hotel registration form, and was a respected benefactor of the local Catholic church. None of the Russian names had ever been linked with him. The three wired photographs showed a heavy – although not plump – smooth-faced man, jaw tight in two of them to support the cigar jutting from the corner of his mouth.

'We've got a time frame in which to work,' reminded Cowley. 'Palma's booked for a further three nights, from now. Makes him due out Saturday. Sure, he can extend, but they must be working to some sort of schedule.'

Which they clearly were.

That morning, Palma left the hotel alone and strolled without apparent direction or hurry around the curve of the inner harbour, towards the main thoroughfare of the city. At the Corso Vittorio Emmanuele he took two espressos at the pavement table of a cafe before disappearing inside to use the wall-mounted telephone: the surveillance squad were certain of two separate calls, but there might have been a third. The man took another coffee further along the Corso, after which he set off towards the centre of the town before turning on to narrower streets. At the via Candelai he went into a restaurant to which the three Russians had already been followed, by an independent team of watchers: both teams were at once replaced. Two men from the second group went inside to eat and arrived in time to witness Palma shake hands with Zimin and all four men touch glasses in what was clearly another celebration toast. They managed three more obvious toasts working their way through three bottles of Verdicchio dei Castelli di Jesi: the pedestrian-minded Amasov ate veal again, but the others divided between lamb and liver.

They separated after lunch. Zimin and Zavorin practically retraced the route of the American that morning, lingering on the waterfront and appearing to read the harbour notices.

Amasov went with Palma to a car-hire facility off the via Roma, where they rented the largest Fiat model available. Palma put down an American Express card for security but paid in advance for four days' hire in cash. Five of the undercover police cars brought in on the overnight ferry had matching engine capacity, but all were supercharged.

That night the four ate at a seafood restaurant on the harbour edge. Amasov left most of his fish stew.

At the conference to review the day's developments, Cowley pointed out the duration of the car hire supported his time-frame suggestion. Patton added the fact that they had hired a car at all meant they intended travelling out of town, and guessed Amasov to be the intended driver. There was general agreement the meandering walks around the city were more to kill time than evade any possible surveillance, although Palma's call from a public, untraceable telephone was an obvious precaution.

'Force of habit more than suspicion,' judged Patton. 'These guys think they're as free as the wind.'

The number of the hire car was circulated to all motorised units in the special squad, but withheld from general distribution to island forces.

'We know who they are: what they look like,' declared Melega. 'They're trapped: there's no way they can possibly escape.'

That night Cowley drank more than he had for a long time, although he still did not get badly drunk. At an early stage he said to Danilov: 'Nervous?'

'Yes.'

'Melega's right. We've got them.'

'Not yet.'

'It's been good, working with you again.'

Danilov, who had not drunk as much, was curious at the maudlin tone. 'It's a long way from being over yet.'

'But then it will be,' said Cowley, even more enigmatically. He was still drinking, with the willing Patton, when Danilov went to bed.

They were later to decide the following day's surveillance – and with it the whole operation – might well have been

303

wrecked but for the helicopters. It began smoothly enough. The Mafia group left the President Hotel just before ten and set off eastwards along the coast road, with Amasov at the wheel of the Fiat. Within fifteen minutes of their departure, there were four cars alternating the pursuit, with Melega, Danilov and the three Americans staying well behind and out of sight in the fifth, one of the vehicles brought over from the mainland specifically to act as the command car through its complete range of radio and telephone equipment. From it Melega ordered six more cars on to the road, but with instructions to remain behind them until summoned to replace the closer police vehicles before they became suspiciously noticeable. Just outside Termini one of the immediate surveillance cars radioed back that the group had stopped for coffee. Melega immediately halted their vehicle and made his first change, switching one of the rear cars with one in front.

'Sightseeing?' queried Smith.

'These guys don't waste time on scenery and ancient monuments,' said Patton.

The cavalcade resumed after thirty minutes, continuing eastwards. At once Melega began a rapid conversation in Italian, swivelling and then ducking in his front seat to make it easier to look upwards. Within minutes, without explanation, he pointed and said: 'There!'

The helicopter was painted an orange yellow. The side doors were open and it was flying so low, parallel to the coastline, they could clearly see the crew. Patton and Smith looked, horrified, at one another: Patton shrugged, to Cowley. Melega saw the gesture and smiled, unoffended. There was a babble of incoming Italian on the radio, then abruptly a more blurred reception overlaid with the engine noise of the helicopter. The machine was briefly lost from sight, far ahead, and then soared into view again, climbing high before banking out to sea and completing its turn westwards to go back towards Palermo.

'Wasn't that . . . ?' began Cowley dubiously, but Melega raised his hand, stopping the American to listen to another incoming report.

304

The Italian gave a satisfied head movement. Turning to the rear, he said: 'They've gone off the coastal highway, inland. The mountain road is good, but we couldn't sustain a pursuit all the way across to Catania without being picked up. And certainly not if they went off the main road, to any of the villages.'

'So how we going to do it?' demanded Patton.

'Call off all the vehicles, until we might need them,' said Melega simply. 'The new pursuit car radioed the number of the Fiat to the helicopter they were *meant* to see: it's an air-sea rescue machine, by the way. The colour was essential for the real observer machine, as a marker. The climb you saw was directly level with the Fiat, identifying it for the helicopter you can't see – and which is flying overhead too high for them to see or hear, either.' He gave another satisfied smile. 'Not far in from the coast there's a little town called Sciara. The restaurant is very good there.'

They did not go there in the antennae-festooned command car, transferring instead at Imerese into two ordinary-looking vehicles to arrive separately at Sciara, where they attempted to eat, but with little appetite, eel and mullet and grouper: no-one drank anything but mineral water. Patton's hand kept straying beneath the concealment of the table to the Smith and Wesson on his hip: the man had manoeuvred the seating with his back to a wall, which Danilov thought ridiculous. None of them – apart from Melega – relaxed, each feeling cut off and inadequate without access to the radio telephone and their constant monitor. Melega promised there were other helicopters to airlift them as well as carabinieri anywhere in the mountains a meeting with the Sicilian Mafia might be seen from existing, spy-in-the-sky surveillance, but no-one was reassured. Patton's stomach began to echo, audibly: he apologised for an ulcerous condition.

Melega had a disjointed conversation on a handset driving back towards the coast, but did not get a full account until he talked from the command car. 'Villalba,' he announced. 'It's about seventy kilometres inland: maybe a little more.' He looked up from a map. 'We risked one car: a policeman and policewoman, supposedly lost tourists needing re-direction. Palma and the Russians drank in the only bar but didn't eat. They didn't meet anyone, while my two were in the bar. The helicopter saw Palma and the Russians walk to a farmhouse on the outskirts of the village. From the condition of the ground and the outhouses, it looks deserted. The four of them walked around but didn't go inside. They're on their way back this way.'

'A reconnaissance,' Smith decided.

'Which it always had to be,' said Melega.

'A small village?' prompted Cowley, anticipating the problem from his earlier posting in Rome.

'Everybody will know everybody else,' confirmed Melega. 'We can't do anthing in advance. The two who *did* go in say the place stinks Mafia. If we go anywhere near it again, in advance, nothing will happen.'

'Like the wise man said,' reminded Patton. 'Life ain't easy.'

He'd never thought it was, reflected Danilov.

CHAPTER FORTY-SEVEN

The evening conference unanimously concluded the operation depended heavily upon helicopters: three more twin-rotored Chinooks with a carrying capacity of twenty men each were allocated overnight, making eight in all. Melega additionally increased their manpower by having a fifty-strong army unit seconded to them, completely to seal every route – even mountain tracks – leading to and from Villalba. The Italian agreed with Cowley that such a build-up on the island stretched the security risk beyond breaking point, so the unit and their helicopters were held at Reggio di Calabria, on the mainland just across the narrow Straits of Messina.

That night there was not a lot of drinking and no-one slept well: Danilov was up before seven, and when he got to the breakfast room he found Cowley already there. Smith and Patton arrived within minutes. No-one ordered anything but coffee.

'It might not be today,' said Smith.

'But then again it might,' said Patton.

'I hope it is today,' said the FBI man. 'I want to get it over.'

'I want to get it right,' qualified Cowley. 'It's a bastard not being able to set up anything in advance: I want a wire in that farmhouse, listening to every goddamned word.'

'Which we're not going to get,' deflated Danilov, realistically. He was still worried about exactly *what* they were going to get, even if they made the arrests. Would the Federal Prosecutor formulate a charge under the Russian criminal code to get the three extradited back to Moscow, or would he leave them to Italian jurisdiction and prosecution?

When Melega came in it was from the street, not from his upstairs room. 'They're already up,' he announced. 'According to my people, they're not as relaxed as they were yesterday.'

'Neither are we,' said Patton.

'What about the army unit?' asked Cowley.

'Not yet,' said Melega. 'They're back up. We've got the power of arrest.'

'Let's go and exercise it,' said Cowley decisively.

Their helicopter was a UH-ID Cobra, like the ones Danilov remembered from much criticised newsreels on Russian television of American gunships in the Vietnam war. He realised as the flight sergeant was checking their seat belts – which only crossed the lap and seemed totally inadequate – they were to fly with the side doors open, just like they had in Vietnam, too. He was instantly terrified, believing there was no way, despite the belt, he could avoid falling out if the machine tipped on its side to turn. Even when it did, immediately on take-off, and the centrifugal force kept him firmly on his seat, Danilov still felt uneasy: he saw Patton was gripping the underside of the bench, like he was.

The helicopter rose high enough for Danilov to pick out the coast road along which they had travelled the previous day. From the air it looked much straighter than it had from the back seat of a car. The sun was flaring off the sea, whitening it near the shoreline. There were far more boats dotted on the deeper, bluer water: much further out, probably beyond sight of land, three ponderous tankers wallowed in a follow-my-leader line. On the coast road the tight-together congestion of vehicles made it look as if they were all joined together, like some motorised snake.

Babbled Italian rose and fell in Danilov's helmet, and from the frequent sound fade he guessed they were patched through to the surveillance cars on the ground. It was easy, airborne, to see the sharp inland turn of the road that cut across the island to Catania, and when Melega made hand signals, jerking his finger in a downward pointing gesture, Danilov guessed they were being shown the car they wanted taking the inland route.

The traffic thinned, making it easier to concentrate on the one vehicle to which he believed Melega to be pointing. Just as he began to do so the helicopter banked as well and dropped into a mountain valley, so that they lost sight of the inland road. They were still high enough for Danilov to isolate four more helicopters, all looking the same as the one in which they were flying, and he supposed they were all part of the carabinieri assault force. Then the other helicopters were lost among the mountains and Danilov realised they were going to land.

They did so in a swirl of dust and thrown-about undergrowth on a plateau cut into the side of a mountain. The dust-storm died with the whine of the engine. Danilov climbed gratefully out, stretching, aware of the cramp in his hands where he'd held the underside of his seat for so long.

Melega carried a bundled-up map. He laid it out on the ground, bringing them all down in a crouch. 'We are here!' he announced, pointing to an ochre-shaded area.

A thread of river – the Gangi – was marked on the map, and a village or town described as Alimena, but Danilov couldn't see any evidence of either from where they'd landed: in every direction the mountains were scorched brown and lifeless by the sun, with little green even in the deeper valley below. The only sound, now the helicopter was quiet, was the dry, scratching clatter of cicadas.

'One of our other helicopters made a high pass over Villalba just after we got airborne from Palermo,' resumed Melega. 'There were two cars already outside the farmhouse: I'm guessing the people Palma and the others have come to meet are already there, waiting. I'm not risking another overflight. I've called the army in, from Reggio. They're not going to fly in formation, to avoid attracting attention.'

'Who's going to notice eight platoon-carrying Chinooks anyway?' tried the wisecracking Patton: Danilov decided it was nervousness.

Melega ignored the remark, going back to his map. 'Once the Fiat has taken the Villalba turning, there will be road blocks here . . . here . . . and here. The Villalba road will be completely cut and on either side of it the Catania route will be blocked. We'll use the cleared section of the Catania highway to land at least one of the army machines. Another army group, with some carabinieri, will close the road on the other side of Villalba, towards Mussomeli. I'm going to enclose Villalba itself completely. The army will come in right behind us.'

'So where do we get the signal they're in the farmhouse together?' said Smith.

'It took precisely twenty-five minutes for them to get to Villalba yesterday, from the moment of turning off,' reminded Melega. 'I'm assuming they won't stop at the cafe today. We're going in thirty-five minutes after they've left the main road.'

'In a *fleet* of helicopters making more noise than cats screwing on a tin roof!' openly protested Patton.

'I've talked about it, with the pilot. If we co-ordinate it correctly, we'll be on the ground two minutes from the moment our approach first becomes audible.'

'What happens if it's co-ordinated *in*correctly?' persisted the DEA agent.

'It won't be,' insisted the Italian.

'We should have talked more about this last night,' said Cowley, in quiet despair.

The sun was beating down on Danilov's back. He could feel the sweat forming irritating pathways and he shrugged against them, slipping out of his jacket. He looked up, to meet Cowley's direct stare. Neither had to give any facial reaction to show their uncertainty.

Danilov's action in taking off his jacket attracted Melega's attention. Looking at the Russian, although not directly into his face, Melega said: 'You are not armed?'

'No.' Danilov rarely carried the pistol he was authorised to hold in Moscow, and it had never once occurred to him to bring it on this roundabout journey through airport check-points. Danilov regularly underwent shooting practice – usually attaining a higher than average score – but he had never once fired a weapon in the course of duty. He'd drawn it a few times, making an arrest, but only for effect, which had fortunately always worked.

'Neither am I,' admitted Cowley, who wished he had drawn something from the embassy in Rome.

Melega collected two pistols from the helicopter, offering one to each man. Cowley accepted his more comfortably than Danilov, who hefted the unaccustomed weapon in his hand, examining it intently. A Beretta, he saw: lighter than the Russian standard-issue Makarov or Stetchkin. The safety catch slipped smoothly in and out of lock, a simple thumb action. He made sure the gun ws secured before easing it into the waistband of his trousers, in the middle, bum-crease part of his back, where he'd seen Cowley casually put his. The first of many things, he thought: the first helicopter journey and the first time he would enter a situation in which shooting would be inevitable. Remember to take the safety catch off, he told himself. His stomach churned, rumbling like Patton's had earlier. Did he have an ulcerous condition? Or was he just frightened? Frightened, he accepted honestly.

The Italian returned to the helicopter for its communication facilities. The rest of them wandered about the tiny clearing. There was nothing to say to each other. Danilov went to the lip of the plateau, overlooking the valley. He still couldn't see a river, or a village called Alimena. The cicadas gossiped on. The sun was growing hotter, making him sweat more. He'd need a shower when he got back to Palermo. He took the Beretta from his waistband, looking at it again. It seemed remarkably small, fragile even, to be able to kill somebody. How many bullets had been fired from this very gun: killed people? Click went the safety catch: click again when he reset it.

'You ever worked partner assault?'

Danilov turned at Cowley's question, not understanding it. 'What?'

'Worked with a partner, as a team? Staying close, watching each other's back?'

'No.'

Cowley sighed. 'We'll keep together when we get there. You hear me say "go down" you go down, fast as you can. That's all we've got time to work out. OK?'

Danilov nodded. 'Listen out for me, too.'

Cowley smiled, wanly. 'We should have practised.'

'They turned off the main road!' shouted Melega, from the helicopter. In his excitement he began in Italian, having to stop and start again, in English.

Everyone moved back towards the machine. Danilov stowed his unwanted jacket in the rear, where the tail narrowed, but carefully, folding one lapel across the other so neither would crease, and straightening the sleeves side by side.

'You're right to be careful,' tried Patton. 'Lot of thieves around here.'

None of the others laughed. Danilov forced a smile.

'Let's get ready,' urged Melega.

They took the same seats, like people do in an interrupted journey: there was a lot of noise getting seatbelt buckles engaged. They put on their helmets, plunging their heads into a cacophony of Italian. The pilot depressed switches and buttons: the engine whined and coughed, the whine growing in pitch, and the helicopter lifted off precisely at the moment Melega, hunched over his watch, patted the pilot's back.

They didn't soar, bird-like, into the air as Danilov had expected. Rather the helicopter came cautiously up over the low peak of the mountain and momentarily hovered there, like a player in a grown-up game of hide-and-seek, which Danilov supposed was exactly the game they were playing. Continuing the impression, other helicopters peeped up all around, from neighbouring valleys, like awakening flying things seeking prey. Danilov counted five, then six. A seventh straggled into view. They all abruptly started to move at the same time, in an arrow-head formation. Theirs led at the very tip but they did not go up, like people are supposed to fly, but down to hide again, skimming the valley floors so close Danilov could see the bushes and the scrub and the trees but at the same time *not* see them, not clearly, everything blurred and rushing in front of him. He clamped his mouth against the stomach retch and closed his eyes, which didn't help because with his eyes shut he was more aware of the lifts and drops. One climb seemed higher than the rest and when he looked he saw they were going over the island-crossing highway: cars already blocked it, uniformed policemen motioning protesting traffic back the way it had come. One Chinook was already on the closed-off part of the road, disgorging troops in camouflaged fatigues, and another was flying in, following the road line, the soldiers sitting with their legs dangling over the side, ready to jump before it properly landed. Beside him Danilov saw Patton's mouth forming words no-one could hear: the man's head was moving slowly from side to side, a shake of resignation.

Danilov was never able, later, to separate the crossing of the sealed-off road and disgorging soldiers with what happened at Villalba. Helicopters seemed to fill the sky, a swarming insect cloud. There were snatched glimpses of panicked people running from houses and buildings, to look, and then being driven back to cover by the swirling, deafening whirlwind of descending rotors.

Danilov was aware of running but not knowing where, blinded by the billowing dirt, someone's hand on his shoulder for contact, not for guidance. There were a lot of popping sounds, like a faulty scooter exhaust, which Danilov did not at once realise were shooting: it didn't then — or at any time — occur to him to crouch or take cover. The hand wasn't on his shoulder any longer. Then the dust cleared, and with it his confusion.

The farmhouse was directly in front of him, two helicopters — one a Chinook — beyond. The village was behind and to his left, his view limited to one or two houses and what appeared to be a shop of some sort. People's faces were at its window. He could not see Melega, Cowley or Smith, but Patton was directly ahead and running straight towards the farmhouse. Danilov ran after the American, without thinking of what he was doing. A squad of soldiers in flak jackets, maybe five or six, ran suddenly around from the rear of the building. There was a loud blast, of a shotgun, and Danilov clearly saw a soldier's head blown entirely from the top of his body: another explosion and the flak jacket of another soldier puckered and he went down.

And then there was another shotgun blast, right in front of him. Danilov was never able to remember if he actually heard the shot, ahead of everything else. His first conscious awareness was being hit by something very hard, which stopped him in his tracks: of stinging all over his chest and body, and a lot of blood, and then he was falling. But not by himself; with someone on top of him.

It was Patton, he realised: Patton who had been hurled back into him by the force of the shotgun blast that had completely severed the man's right arm above the elbow: Patton whose blood was gouting all over him and who was initially too shocked to feel any pain and seemed surprised to find Danilov so close – holding him – and who began: 'What the fuck . . .' before they landed one on top of the other in full, unobstructed view and range of the farmhouse, the American virtually cradled in Danilov's lap. Stupefied, they both looked at the shattered, gushing stump. Angrily Patton said: 'My arm! They've taken my fucking arm! Where's my fucking arm?' And then he shrieked as the agony gripped him, arcing up from Danilov as if they were partners in some odd choreographed dance.

The scream broke Danilov's inertia. He heard someone shouting to get down and, recollecting what Cowley had said, tried to pull Patton back to the ground. Patton did slump, and as he did so Danilov looked beyond, to the farmhouse – and saw the double-barrelled snout of a shotgun emerge, aiming directly at them.

Danilov felt no fear: rather, there was an almost serene, disembodied calm in which he knew precisely what to do and how to do it: that he *could* do it. He was unaware of drawing the Beretta or of releasing the safety catch: it was just suddenly in his hand, ready, and he was aiming, unhurriedly, without panic. There was a lot of other firing all around but he was aloof, separate from it, not distracted or worried by the noise. He reviewed his first shot with studied control, sure it was the one that splattered plaster off the window edge, annoyed it was not more accurate. It was still good enough for the barrel of the rifle to be jerked back out of sight, unfired. His next shot entered the window without any deflection, and the one after that, and the one after that: he was shooting without haste, allowing the pause between each trigger pull, cautious against the weapon jamming. Patton was unconscious but still cradled in his lap, his body shuddering in spasm at the blood loss from his massive wound.

Danilov pumped carefully placed round after carefully placed round into the window space, his mind functioning sufficiently for him to wonder if he was hitting people and making them bleed to death like the man he was holding was bleeding to death. When the Beretta clicked empty he groped for Patton's gun, but the waist holster was empty too. I suppose I'll die now, he thought. He hoped it wouldn't hurt too much when the bullets or the cartridges tore into him.

Danilov never saw how the stun and teargas grenades got into the farmhouse: probably through a window on one of the other sides he could not see. There was just the vibrating whump of the stun bomb, which actually made his ears ring, and then the billowing smoke of the gas making it look as if the house was on fire.

The shooting stopped abruptly, one minute aching noise, the next echoing silence. Danilov was conscious of a lot of men in various uniforms, their faces masked, pouring into the house, and of other uniforms crowding around him. Patton was eased away from him but only enough for medics immediately to tourniquet the shattered arm and plunge hypodermics and saline drips into the man's remaining arm. Other soldiers were manhandling Danilov, pushing him to the ground to tear at his saturated shirt. Danilov realised what they were doing – and why – and shouted: 'I'm all right! It's his blood.' And when he became fully aware that it was and how much of it covered him, he vomited, not even able to avert his head when he did so, adding to the foul mess.

Danilov wasn't entirely uninjured. When they cut his clothes away the Army medics found his left shoulder and arm pitted with six separate pellet wounds, but none of them deep nor serious. They injected local anaesthetic to remove the lead shot and cleaned the wounds, and from somewhere a camouflage jacket and trousers were found for him to wear: they were too big, and the trouser bottoms had to be rolled up before he could walk.

Melega broke into the group around him before all the pellets were taken out, urging him towards the medevac helicopter into which the stretchered body of the deeply unconscious and drip-fed Patton was being lifted, with Cowley and Smith attentively on either side. With his unrestrained right arm Danilov waved the Italian away, insisting he was unhurt and didn't need further treatment: Melega didn't argue. When the helicopter lifted off, they were buffeted by the updraught.

Danilov's arm was being strapped to his side, leaving the left sleeve of his camouflage vest hanging limp, when the matchingly grave-faced Cowley and Smith reached him.

Cowley said: 'You all right?'

'Pellet wounds, that's all.'

Cowley offered his hand and instinctively Danilov responded, unsure until they were shaking hands why they were doing it. Cowley said: 'That was the bravest thing I've ever seen in my entire fucking life!'

'Mine too,' came in Smith, covering their hands with his.

Danilov flushed hot with embarrassment. Withdrawing his hand from the cluster, he nodded towards the farmhouse. 'How many are alive?'

'All three Russians,' reassured Cowley. 'Palma, too. There were five Sicilians. One's dead. Another's shot in the head: probably going to die. The Sicilians are from a known Family, the Liccio. They're all being flown direct to the mainland, to the maximum security jail in Rome.'

'I saw a soldier's head blown away?' said Danilov. The anaesthetic began to wear off from his shoulder and arm: it was not a gentle ache but sharp, jabbing pains.

'Two soldiers were killed, and one of the carabinieri. Four wounded,' said Cowley. 'It'll be murder charges, against all of them.'

Danilov nodded towards the medevac helicopter, already a distant speck in the sky. 'What about Patton?'

'Bad,' said Cowley. 'Very bad.'

Seemingly reminded, Smith turned furiously to Melega, who had at that moment returned from the lift-off area. Tight-lipped but yelling, the FBI resident said: 'Why the fuck didn't we have flak jackets?'

'I didn't think of them,' admitted the Italian. '*You* didn't think of them . . .' He paused, to let the rejection settle. 'And it was his arm: a flak jacket wouldn't have saved his arm.'

'Jesus Christ!' exclaimed Cowley, coughing against a choke of revulsion.

There was a moment of confusion, no-one immediately able to understand. Gradually they followed the direction in which the face-screwed American was looking. Very close to where Danilov and Patton had been treated – the ground stained brown from Patton's blood – the man's hand lay perfectly intact, severed from the wrist. It still clutched the revolver for which Danilov had groped, when the magazine of his Beretta had run out.

'Let's get the hell out of here,' said Jones.

'If you want an apology, you've got it!' offered Hartz. 'It was a brilliant operation, justifying to the last cent whatever it cost, and I'm sorry I ever doubted it.'

Leonard Ross, a pragmatist never interested in look-back debates, said: 'There's the possibility we'll have a dead DEA agent. I want the bastards to die for that.'

'What about the Russian?' demanded the Secretary of State.

'You're the protocol experts,' shrugged Ross. 'He deserves an award: according to Cowley, it was like something out of a Rambo movie. If Danilov hadn't sat there, firing every time the bastards raised their heads, Patton would have been shot to pieces.'

'An award might restore goodwill, after all the squabbles.'

'I hope the Italian publicity hasn't screwed things in Moscow.'

Now Hartz shrugged. 'An international Mafia organisation was smashed. Are you surprised the Italians wanted to shout about it?'

'It hasn't gotten us one inch closer to understanding the connection between two murders here in Washington and one in Moscow.'

On the far side of town, in their temporarily allocated FBI office, Rafferty tossed the *Washington Post* across to his

317

partner and said: 'So that's where they've been, not in deep shit as we were told. All that bullshit about mistakes and collapses of relationships were just that: bullshit!'

'Just like the shoot-out at the OK Corral,' reflected Johannsen, reading that morning's account. Lifting from his desk the piece of paper that had arrived at the same time as the newspaper, he said: 'And now there's this!'

'This' was a cable from the Swiss police, hopeful of finding a photograph of Ilya Nishin.

CHAPTER FORTY-EIGHT

There was concerted and government-encouraged publicity, from the moment the manacled mobsters were photographed being led from helicopters at an army base near the capital: there were more photographs as they were led, still manacled, into the high-security Rebibbia jail. In the media release the Italians called the seizures the most severe blow ever to international organised crime: the exaggerated account of Danilov saving the life of David Patton made it seem as if he had protected some of the Italian assault group, as well. It was heightened by the officially expressed gratitude from Washington, describing what he had done as an act of heroic bravery.

Danilov was unaware of any of this until his helicopter followed the Mafia arrival at the same army base: still wearing the borrowed army fatigues, he climbed out to be greeted by a burst of camera lights and jostled demands for him to take part in a hastily arranged press conference with a government minister and Colonel Melega. Danilov refused, careless of any annoyance, more anxious to assess the damage his identification might cause in Moscow: he'd hoped their part in the operation would remain unknown, so they could still manipulate Kosov to guide them beyond the three they now had in custody, to even more important men in the Chechen Family.

Danilov wanted to begin the interrogations at once, but Melega said there had to be official government conferences first. He did, however, agree the three Russians be held in separate cells and refused any contact with each other. Cowley said the bastards weren't going anywhere and his prior concern was David Patton, undergoing emergency surgery.

Danilov finally presented himself at the Russian embassy, to a hostile reception from diplomats who obviously felt he should have registered with them earlier. He refused to be intimidated, demanding communication facilities to send a full account of the successful arrests to Moscow. He gave his part in the shoot-out in flat, factual detail: had he not known Moscow would demand it because of what was being officially released by the Italians and the Americans, he probably would not have included it at all.

That night, the Italian resentment at his refusal of the press conference had gone: Melega had clearly received high-level congratulations. And Cowley and Smith returned from the hospital with the assurance that although his condition was still serious, Patton was going to survive, although it had been necessary to amputate even more of his arm during the operation. The Liccio clan member wounded during the battle had died.

There was easy agreement to divide the following day's interrogation practically between nationalities, Melega to head the Italian team questioning the three surviving Sicilians, Smith to confront Palma, and Danilov and Cowley to examine the Russians.

Maksim Zimin was a fat, bespectacled man who tried the sort of swaggering unconcern Antipov had carried off more successfully in Moscow. He shrugged aside the guards' prodding towards the interview table, lounging back in his chair. It was hot, but not sufficiently so to cause the perspiration shining the man's face, which was dirty from the siege. Cowley, who'd had one psychology assessment confirmed by Quantico, although it had failed in practice, thought he recognised the profile and was pleased. A bully, Cowley guessed: maybe an instigator of violence, but if he were it would always be others who imposed the pain, because men like Zimin were secretly frightened of suffering themselves.

Cowley spoke hurriedly, ahead of Danilov, wanting to dominate the questioning to test his assessment. 'You're going to be in jail for the rest of your life.'

Zimin gave a dismissive wave. 'I didn't shoot at anyone. Didn't have a gun.' He didn't show any surprise at being addressed in Russian by an American.

'What were you doing, in that village?' asked Cowley.

'Minding my own business.'

'With the Sicilian and American Mafia?' said Danilov.

'I don't know what you're talking about.'

'Why did you come to Italy?' said Cowley.

'Holiday,' said Zimin. He smirked, looking directly at Cowley. 'I was going to take lots of holiday photographs. You going to have any souvenir photographs from Moscow?'

Danilov didn't understand the remark. The American's face was rigidly impassive. Forcing himself on, waveringly close to being knocked off psychological balance himself by the obvious inference, Cowley said: 'You were forming links between the Chechen in Moscow, the Genovese in New York and the Liccio here in Sicily.'

Zimin studiously examined his fingernails, not bothering to answer. Danilov was reminded of the encounter with Antipov, not realising how much more fragile Zimin's attitude was. 'Tell us why Ivan Ignatsevich Ignatov was murdered? Shot in the mouth.'

'I don't know anyone named Ivan Ignatsevich Ignatov.'

Cowley wished Danilov had not intruded. 'Tell me about the Chechen.' He anticipated the rejection, expecting nothing that day. But the interview wasn't wasted. He was studying the man, deciding the pressures.

'I don't know who or what the Chechen is.'

Through the frustration, Danilov thought that at least this bastard wouldn't escape justice, like Antipov.

'You frightened, Maksim?' said Cowley. 'I'd be, if I were you. Frightened as hell.'

The Russian didn't reply.

'I'm right, you know. About going to jail. You any idea what it'll be like, in a cage for the rest of your life?'

Zimin stayed silent.

So, too, did Danilov. He guessed the American was using a trained approach, and determined against interfering until he realised what it was.

'You won't do well in jail,' persisted Cowley. 'Look at you! Soft! Flabby! They'll make you into a girl in jail. Fuck you, when they like, how they like. Think about that, Maksim! Think what it's going to be like being held down while everyone takes their turn. No-one to protect you any more.'

There was a nearly imperceptible twitch to the man's face, and a hot smell came across the table from him. 'Stop bothering.'

'I'm not the one who's going to be bothered,' Cowley went on. 'You're not looking forward to being a jail whore, are you? You'll become infected, of course. Venereal disease if you don't get AIDs. Cancer develops from anal venereal disease. Did you know that?' According to the Quantico lectures there had to be the fear of physical violence or assault. Maybe the thought of homosexual rape would not be enough, if the man were gay. How did he know about the photographs? He would have to be fairly high ranking within the Chechen. Which followed, Cowley reasoned: nobody *un*important would have come to set up this operation. Could Zimin be *the* don that Italian rumours had suggested?

Danilov thought he guessed the approach. 'If you talked to us – told us all we want to know – we'd try to help.' Could they cut a deal? The idea of making any arrangement with someone like Zimin offended him, but it would be justified if it solved everything else. Edging towards another compromise, he thought.

Zimin came forward in his chair, hands fisted hard before him, his face wet. 'I'm not going to jail! I didn't take part in any killing.'

'Of course you're going to jail,' insisted Danilov. 'I'm personally going to see that you do. You talk to us sensibly and I'll intercede for you. But go on being stupid and you're going to be locked away forever.'

Zimin strove for bravado. 'You seem very interested in my ass. So I'll do you a favour. I'll let you kiss it. How about that? You like to kiss my ass? It's yours.'

Danilov grinned at the man. 'No, I don't want to kiss your ass. But you're going to be kissing mine, before we're through: before we're through you're going to be grovelling on the ground, begging me to help you. You and Zavorin and Amasov.'

None of them did, not that day.

After Zimin, they tried to question Ivan Zavorin, a thin, neat, clerk-like man with fidgeting eyes and a stutter, neither of which emerged as nervousness they could break. The attitude was different from Boris Amasov, but the refusal was the same. Instead of offering supercilious rejection or ignorance of what had been going on, the fat-bellied, huge-shouldered man with a knife scar down the right side of his face was mulishly stubborn, remaining mute, not responding to anything he was asked.

They had arranged nightly conferences. Everyone assembled depressed in Melega's room. Melega had had the only minor success: the oldest of the three Sicilians had been identified as Antonio Liccio, the son of the man who had given his name to the Mafia clan and who was on the 'most wanted' list of twelve Mafia dons. The other two were brothers, Victor and Umberto Chiara. There were outstanding indictments against all three, the majority for organised crime offences: it meant they could be held for as long as the Italians chose, without any of the current charges having to be proffered until their eventual questioning by the examining magistrate was completed. Liccio had openly challenged Melega to produce a judge brave enough to hear a case against them.

Barclay Smith's only contribution was that Palma spoke Italian as well as he did English, but wouldn't volunteer anything in either language: he had replied to each attempted question by demanding access to a lawyer. His only remark apart from that had been to insist he had been unarmed and taken no part in the shooting. Reminded, Danilov asked Melega about the weapons in the farmhouse. All that had been recovered were the traditional Mafia wolf-hunting shotguns: all bore the fingerprints of the Sicilians, none of the others.

'So Palma and the Russians *do* have a defence that they didn't take part in the shoot-out!'

'Under our law they are equally guilty,' insisted Melega.

'But a plea for a reduced sentence could be entered in mitigation?' pressed Cowley.

'It's possible,' conceded the Italian.

Danilov had an abrupt but vivid recollection of a shuddering man leaking blood all over him, and became hot with anger at the thought of any of them escaping with legal tricks. It was worse for not knowing how he could prevent it.

'I can break Zimin,' declared Cowley quietly. 'I'm sure I can break him.'

There were doubtful looks from everyone else in the room.

Initially the doubt seemed justified.

Day followed day and separate interrogation followed separate interrogation without anyone in the Mafia groups collapsing. Cowley discussed his approach with Danilov, who always let the American lead the encounters with Zimin with the ridicule and threats of jail violence. Several times they both thought the man was going to break, but always he seemed to pull himself back from the very edge. At their nightly review, at the end of the fifth day, Melega said that although there was no concern about the Sicilians, because of the already existing charges, the Italian prosecutors were becoming unsettled at the delay in formal accusations being put against Palma and the Russians: it could be a defence that they had been unfairly subjected to duress, with legal representation withheld.

'I want to do something,' declared Cowley. He'd endured each day's questioning with foreboding of further jibes about souvenir photographs, which hadn't come. It had, he supposed, been naive to expect them. The first remark had been a warning, of a bargaining demand yet to come. It could be soon, if the Italian agreed to what he wanted.

When he explained, Melega said: 'It's a trick.'

'It'll work,' insisted Cowley. I hope, he thought.

It was far worse than any jail pit into which they had ever descended, which surprised Danilov because he'd thought nothing could be as bad as Russian penitentiaries.

The noise was first, hardly recognisable as human sounds: a muttering, growling hum like a beehive where the insects crawl one over the other. And then there was the smell. It was a stomach-souring, retching stink of every conceivable body odour and stench.

They had made Zimin shower and given him cologne, which he had applied, with no way of knowing. The noise came close to a roar – the automatic reaction to authority entering the Rebibbia dungeons – but then Zimin was picked out between them, manacled to identify him from Cowley and Danilov and the guards, and the cacophony began, the shouts and the calls, distorted faces at cell bars and metal- screened windows. There were a lot of arms reaching out, with grasping fingers. They made Zimin walk the entire length of the cell block, slowly, controlling his pace by the tethering chain. The Russian began to shake before he reached the end, trying to pull himself among them, for protection or to hide.

'This is where you'll be,' said Cowley.

'No! Please no!'

A cell had been cleared, at the very end, although it hadn't been cleaned. When he realised he was being led towards it Zimin tried to fight and finally fell, crying, to the ground. He'd won, Cowley knew. The bastard was too terrified even to remember the photographs. He would, though.

The girl, who was freshly bathed and who had already begun her careful, unobtrusive make-up, reacted at once to the telephone because it was the time the telephone started to ring, the start of her working day. She said of course she was free: she could fit in with whatever arrangement. She'd be waiting for him, she promised.

'A full night?' It was always important to establish things at the very beginning. He'd been very demanding last time.

'All evening, all night. That a problem?'

'Not at all. I just didn't want to commit myself elsewhere.'

'Don't do that. Dollars, like last time?'

She hesitated, wondering whether to bargain, but decided against it. 'That'll be fine.'

'Two hours?'

'I'll be there.'

The girl's name was Lena Zurov. She was twenty-eight years old, and a professional and extremely successful prostitute operating in a very select Moscow circle.

Five thousand miles away, Michael Rafferty grinned up from the latest package to arrive from Geneva and said to his partner: 'They may be getting all the glory and all the shit in Rome, but you know who's going to put this baby to bed? The good old Swiss police! And us, because we've made the connection.' He flicked the photograph across the desk to Johannsen. 'Look at that!'

The forbidden cigar-smoking had increased in the past weeks, so that Gusovsky was sometimes racked by paroxysms of coughing; it happened now, stopping the conversation. No-one – not even Yerin – risked reminding the man of the medical ban. The smoke had further fogged the rear room of the Pecatnikov club, already thick with that of his henchmen's Marlboros. Antipov waited with the rest for the spasm to be over.

'It went well?' gasped the Mafia head.

'Wonderfully,' smiled the hitman, a remark as much for his own amusement as an answer to the question. She always had been one of the best.

'You didn't make any mistakes?' demanded Yerin, remembering Washington.

'None,' insisted Antipov.

'Kosov has some explaining to do,' said Gusovsky, quite recovered. 'He said everything was safe and it wasn't. Get him here, to talk to me. Don't hurt him. Just get him here.'

CHAPTER FORTY-NINE

The terror was still juddering through Maksim Zimin when he was led into the interview room. He smelled foul and Cowley guessed he'd wet himself, perhaps worse. He looked with undisguised hatred at both of them, his gaze remaining on the American.

'You quite sure now?' said Cowley.

'Bastard!' It was a hoarse whimper, without any force, the man had screamed so much. 'You know what I'm going to do! And enjoy doing it.'

'Wait!' warned Cowley, not to put off the inevitable but to get as much as they could before it came: he still delayed switching on the tape recorder. 'You don't have them: I guess your people have, but you don't. We're not dealing with that, not now. What we're going to decide today is whether what you tell us is good enough to stop us putting you back in the hole, like last night. And we will. If you fuck us about maybe we'll even give you a shared cell. And go on doing it until we're satisfied we've got it all. You clear on that?'

Danilov sat on the sidelines, bewildered. There'd been no rehearsal, as there hadn't when the American had recognised the man as a bully who could be broken, and Danilov didn't have any idea what this latest exchange was about. Once again he decided to wait, until he got a guide from his colleague.

'Bastard!' said Zimin again, louder this time.

'You're wasting time: risking going back down below. Don't be stupid.' Cowley had realised the previous night there was no way the man would have been carrying copies of the photographs – the photographs Cowley, in fact, did have, locked in the briefcase at his hotel.

'You'll deal!' It was meant as a threat but it came out more as a question. 'My people will make you deal.'

Not just a bully but a fool, thought Cowley. The man had just confirmed who the blackmailers were. It hardly mattered. He couldn't use the information to any benefit.

Did Zimin imagine the American had more influence in Italy than he did, as a Russian? thought Danilov. It had been Cowley who'd manipulated the man's collapse, so he might think so.

Beside him Cowley depressed the start button on the recording machine and said: 'You're Chechen, right?'

Momentarily Zimin hesitated, and Cowley thought he was going to go on with the threats. Then he said: 'Yes.'

'What level?'

'*Komitet.*'

'Inner council?'

'Yes.'

'How many?'

'Three.'

High, seized Danilov triumphantly: high enough to explain everything, surely!

'What was the meeting for, in Sicily?' Another Quantico lesson was that the more they talked, the easier the flow became.

'Big. The biggest ever . . .'

'For them? Or you?'

'Biggest ever for the Chechen.'

'How big?'

'Ten million.'

'Which currency?' The man was exaggerating, trying to make himself sound more important.

'Dollars.'

'You don't have access to ten million dollars!' challenged Danilov, deciding the intrusion was necessary, thinking the same as Cowley. They wanted the truth, not lies from a man trying to avoid being thrown back into the horror they'd shown him. The profit from crime in Moscow had to be enormous, but there couldn't be this much.

'There's more. Ten million was all I was authorised to negotiate this time.'

'For what?' Cowley decided to let the man believe he was

successfully bullshitting them until he tripped over his own lies. Then he'd threaten the hole again.

'Drugs,' declared Zimin. 'Heroin, from the Liccio people here. Cocaine through the Genovese, from Latin America . . .' Zimin went between the two investigators. 'There's a huge market, everywhere in the world. The idea was to make it two way. We were going to set up an organisation in Georgia: move heroin and marijuana from Uzbekistan and Kazakstan . . . ship it out through the Black Sea to the Mediterranean to here . . .'

Zimin was being clever, thought Cowley: mixing what could have been fact with fiction. Before he could make the intended threat, Danilov said: 'You're lying! You don't have ten million dollars!'

'So you're going back to the hole!' supported Cowley, reaching out to turn off the recording machine.

'No!' wailed Zimin. 'There is the money!'

'From where?' demanded Cowley. 'The truth!'

'Government money!'

The announcement momentarily stopped both investigators, each coming towards the same conclusion from different directions. Cowley guessed it was going to throw the entire American government into the biggest loop of this or any other administration. Danilov decided what they were hearing would be officially blocked and diverted and derailed and that all along he'd been a puppet, dancing on a string to convince the Americans of co-operation never intended. *It's like a club, everyone looking after each other.* Leonid Lapinsk's cynicism echoed in his mind, more like a jeer than a warning.

Danilov spoke first. 'Are you telling us – wanting us to believe – your presence here is known about by the Russian government . . . that it's somehow *official*?' The man could still be lying. But Petr Serov had been a Russian diplomat. And Oleg Yasev, a senior and as yet unchallenged Foreign Ministry man, had withheld a name-identifying document. And Gennardi Fedorov, who'd gone to Serov's funeral, was attached to the Finance Ministry.

'Not the government,' groped Zimin, who'd started to sweat badly. 'Not *the* government in control now!'

329

'You're not making sense!' protested Cowley.

'*Listen* to me!' pleaded Zimin. 'It was the coup!'

The American remained lost. For Danilov the fog was still thick, but there were shapes vaguely forming. Serov's concealed diary-entry dates connected perfectly with the August 1991 attempt by the desperate Communist hardliners to overthrow Mikhail Gorbachov and reverse the reforms he had initiated. Danilov's awareness grew. Billions *had* been stolen: stolen and never recovered. A government commission had been established to investigate. If he was correctly interpreting what Zimin was saying, the exposure – if it ever *were* exposed – would be sensational.

'How much, in total?'

'We don't know!' insisted Zimin. 'Twenty million at least.'

'We're talking about the Communist Party funds that were looted? And have never been found?'

'Of course we are!' said Zimin, almost impatiently.

Conscious of the need to get it audibly on the slowly revolving tape, Danilov said: 'The Chechen, a Moscow Mafia organisation, have access to twenty million dollars of looted Communist Party funds?'

'That's right.'

Both Danilov and Cowley were curious at the sly smile that accompanied the admission.

'In Moscow?' pressed Danilov.

'No.'

'No, it wasn't, was it!' understood the American. 'It's in Switzerland! Michel Paulac was looking after it: the local man administering it!'

'Only government officials – *Communist* government officials – would have been able to move a sum of money that large out of Russia?' suggested Danilov.

'I suppose so,' agreed Zimin.

That was slightly off centre, as if the man knew a lot but not all, even though he claimed to be on the governing committee of the crime family. Where was the key? Was it in the past, in August 1991? Or maybe earlier: as early as May of that year, the very first time a name still unexplained appeared in the Serov documents? Abruptly, Danilov said: 'Who is Ilya Iosifivich Nishin?'

Danilov was unsure if the frown was of genuine ignorance or surprise that he had the name. 'I don't know.'

'You must!' pressed Cowley. He was sure he would be tainted with the man's stink.

'I don't!'

Nishin *was* important, Danilov determined. And he thought at last he knew the direction in which to look, to fit another piece into the puzzle. It *would* have needed a government official to move at least $20,000,000 out of Russia. But the coup had collapsed so quickly it would have had to be moved *prior* to the attempt, because there was no time afterwards! May, 1991 – when Ilya Nishin had visited Geneva and then Washington – was very significant. His mind on Switzerland, Danilov said: 'Why was Michel Paulac killed?'

'He was stupid. Wouldn't listen.'

'To what?' came in Cowley.

'That control was going to change.'

'Control of the money in Switzerland?'

'Yes.'

'To the Chechen?'

'Yes.'

'From whom?'

'The Ostankino.'

Finally it was settling into place! Danilov asked: 'Why was Serov killed?'

'A warning.'

'Who to?'

'Those who had to realise it.'

'Why was Ignatov murdered?' demanded Cowley.

'A warning again.'

'Who to?'

'The Ostankino.' He paused. 'I'm getting tired.'

'There's a cell downstairs, in the basement, where you can rest if you want,' said Cowley relentlessly. ' "Control was changing." Changing from the Ostankino to the Chechen?'

'Yes.'

'So the Ostankino had the money first?'

'Thought they did.'

'How did the Chechen learn about it?'

Zimin shifted uncomfortably in his seat, and Cowley decided the man *had* fouled himself. The Russian said: 'A recruit.'

One of the August 1991 ringleaders had been KGB chairman Vladimir Kryuchkov: whose all-embracing, all-knowing, all-pervasive intelligence organisation had probably been the most hard-hit casualty. 'There were a lot of unemployed, weren't there? He must have been high ranking, before. Or been in some administrative position, to learn things?' It was a supposition, but Danilov was sure it was a correct one.

'What was the rank?' chanced Cowley, joining in the guess.

'Colonel,' conceded Zimin.

'We need to get names,' said Danilov. 'Why don't we start with his?'

'Visco,' said the man. 'Georgi Petrovich.'

'Go on,' prompted Cowley.

Zimin nervously allowed himself a faint sneer. He said: 'The KGB had a file on us. On all the Families. Visco knew a lot, about everyone.' He smiled openly at Danilov. 'There were files on co-operative people in the Militia, too. The most comprehensive details of all were about the transfer to Switzerland of the Party funds. He'd heard about it from another KGB officer, Anatoli Zuyev, who had links with the Ostankino and who had somehow – he didn't *know* how – been involved.'

Quantico's teaching had been right, Cowley thought: once the floodgates opened, the disclosures poured through. 'Let's go on with names! All the Chechen! And the Ostankino: as many as you know!'

Zimin's list came to twenty-two, eighteen from his own organisation. The ultimate leadership, the other two on the *komitet*, were Arkadi Pavlovich Gusovsky and Alexandr Dorovich Yerin.

'More!' demanded Danilov, following an idea. 'What is Ivan Zavorin, the man with you?'

'Money man. Accountant.'

'Boris Amasov, the other one?'

'A bull.'

'Like Mikhail Antipov!' seized Danilov.

For the second time, Zimin risked something approaching a sneer. 'Pity you had to release him. An embarrassment.' At the word the man focused on Cowley, seeming about to speak, but at the last minute he changed his mind.

'Those amenable people you learned about from your KGB recruit?' said Danilov. 'Anatoli Metkin one of them? Vladimir Kabalin another?' He intentionally stopped short of mentioning Kosov.

'Please let me stop,' pleaded Zimin. 'I've done a lot: told you a lot.'

They were all tired, Danilov accepted. If they went on they risked becoming overwhelmed, losing sight of what they *were* getting.

'Not enough,' refused Cowley.

'Tomorrow,' said the man, still pleading. 'But don't send me back: please don't send me back!'

Cowley looked enquiringly at Danilov, who nodded. The American snapped the machine off. With the recording off, Zimin said: 'You will help me? I'll tell you everything, but you must help me.'

He wouldn't, Cowley knew. But they'd already got far more than he'd expected. 'You won't be sent back tonight. What happens tomorrow depends on what you *tell* us tomorrow. Before then you can clean yourself up.'

The meeting with Melega and Barclay Smith was the first in which they had anything worthwhile to exchange. Melega said, pessimistically, they might have prevented the link-up this time, but another would succeed soon. The local FBI agent just said: 'Jesus!' Neither was hopeful what they knew now would pressure the people they were questioning into any confirmation or new disclosure. Danilov argued there were still unresolved enquiries in Russia and America which could be hampered by any publicity about the confession, which would be better kept until the eventual trial. Melega reluctantly agreed.

333

After the conference, Cowley and Danilov separated to their different embassies to send their cables. For each of them, incoming messages were waiting.

Cowley was told of the possible Geneva photographic identification of Ilya Nishin and that scientists at Quantico, working through the sample instruments provided from Moscow, believed they had isolated the number dialled on Yevgennie Kosov's car telephone, from which they could trace an address.

After a day solving a lot of mysteries the information at the embassy for Dimitri Danilov created another one, but he put it aside, more anxious to understand the bewildering exchange between the American and Zimin, at the beginning of that morning's interrogation.

Cowley was already in the cocktail lounge at the Bernini Bristol when Danilov got back to the hotel. The Russian accepted a drink at the bar but carried it away to a table, making Cowley follow him.

Quoting, Danilov said: ' "Bastard! You know what I'm going to do! And enjoy doing it." ' He waited several moments. 'What is it Zimin doesn't have but "his people" do?'

'You told us it was safe! Specifically! That's what you had to do! *All* you had to do: find out!' Gusovsky's voice was frighteningly quiet.

'That's what he told me!' protested Kosov. 'He was going back to Washington! The investigation was virtually over.'

'Why would he trick you?' demanded Gusovsky.

'I don't know!'

'You've got to find out,' said Yerin, looking blank-eyed at the Militia colonel. 'And you've also got to find out what's happening in Italy: if anyone's talking.'

'I'll try.'

'No,' said Yerin. 'You won't try. You'll find out. And if you don't, we'll kill you.'

CHAPTER FIFTY

Danilov laid the photographs aside after glancing at only four or five, uninterested in the rest. He thought the girl was very pretty. Her body reminded him of Larissa: a lot of the activity, too. 'I didn't need to see them.'

'A lot of people are going to, very soon now.' They were in Cowley's hotel room. He collected the prints from the table and put them back in his briefcase, as if wanting to hide them away again as quickly as possible. The man was physically bowed, pressed down by a burden he couldn't finally support.

Danilov wasn't sure whether the remark was cynicism or self-pity: perhaps a mixture of both. He had a sickening feeling a very recent puzzle was to become very clear very quickly: he wanted to hear everything Cowley had to say, before telling the American.

'There are newspapers and magazines in Moscow now who would publish them: not the most explicit, but some.'

'In America they'd even use the explicit ones,' accepted Cowley. He hadn't detected any criticism or disgust from the Russian. It was important to make the other man understand it wouldn't jeopardise the investigation.

The query came suddenly to Danilov. 'She was in the bar for about a week before you went with her?'

'About that.'

'Be more specific,' insisted Danilov, almost peremptorily.

'What's it matter?' frowned Cowley.

'How soon, after the night out with Yevgennie Kosov?'

Cowley nodded slowly, in gradual understanding. 'The motherfucker! It fits! The night after: two at the most.'

Danilov nodded back. 'He insisted we all travel in the BMW: I thought he was boasting about the car. But they had to find out where you were staying.' Would the Chechen hit him with the same determination they had hit Cowley, if

Kosov had told them of his black-market dealings in the past? Of course they would. So he'd be destroyed as completely and as effectively as the American. And if the Chechen didn't do it, Kosov still might, when he and Larissa made their announcement. Danilov guessed Larissa would take it much better than Olga. He felt a brief but very positive surge of pity for his wife. 'They *will* try to deal. Blackmail!'

'No deal!' refused the American, loudly. 'I did it! I was drunk, which isn't an excuse, and I was stupid. They set me up and I fell for it, like a jerk. So they won. That time. What we now know is too big – far too big and far too important – for any deal. Which I wouldn't consider, even if it weren't. So in the end, I'm going to win. *We're* going to win. We're getting it now. And we're going to get more. I'll hang in, for as long as I can: as long, I guess, as they'll let me. Which is a pretty shitty thing for an FBI man to have to admit about a bunch of punks! But when I go down, they go down!'

Danilov's admiration for Cowley soared. He wasn't shocked or offended by the pictures – none showed anything he and Larissa didn't do most times they were together – and he was tempted to argue they were not as professionally compromising as Cowley was making out. But deep down he recognised that they were, so to say that would be patronising. Danilov's mind ran on, to a thought that had come to him during that morning's questioning. 'I want to use Zimin: he might even see it as a deal.'

Cowley frowned again. 'How?'

'He knows about the Ignatov killing: that Antipov did it,' insisted Danilov. 'I'm sure he does! About Metkin and Kabalin, too. All of it. He's got to be sentenced here to satisfy Italian justice, but if it could be arranged he serves his sentence in Russia, he could give evidence against all of them.'

'That might not delay the exposure. It won't be Zimin's decision, whether or not to publish them.'

'They don't know what we're getting. Melega's agreed no publicity.'

Cowley smiled faintly. '*Would* Zimin give evidence against them?'

'Depends how frightened we keep him.'

'What about special treatment?'

'Maybe a reduction of sentence,' suggested Danilov. 'It would be worth it to get the other convictions.'

It wouldn't do anything to close the Washington files on Michel Paulac or Petr Serov, but it might just delay his humiliation. Should he feel any different – slightly relieved, perhaps – now he'd shared the personal disaster with someone else, someone who'd accepted it without any critical judgment, professional or moral? If there was going to be any such relief, it hadn't come yet. His only feeling was surprise at how little there had been to discuss about the entrapment. It was practically an anti-climax. Objectively he knew the hostile enquiries and detailed reports – and the scouring criticism – would come later.

Believing there was nothing more to talk about, Cowley said: 'There were things waiting for me at the embassy. We've got the number Kosov was talking to, so we can get an address. And we know who Ilya Nishin is. He's the same guy in the photograph you took from Serov's apartment in Washington . . . !'

'Whom Raisa Serova identified as her father!'

'For the moment we can forget pornographic pictures and blackmail. Get this investigation completely buttoned down!'

'I'm not sure we can forget it, not entirely,' cautioned Danilov. 'The whore in the photographs? Did she have a name?'

Apprehension began to stir through Cowley. 'Lena. That's all. Just Lena.'

'I had a message waiting for me at the embassy, too. There's been another killing in Moscow, with a mouth shot: a high-class prostitute named Lena Zurov.'

'She was killed because of me. It's as if I killed her.' Cowley's voice was distant, cracked.

'It wasn't a Makarov,' completed Danilov. 'The bullet was from a Smith and Wesson. An American gun.'

Yevgennie Kosov waited for Olga to ask, which she did when she realised they were driving through the outskirts of

Moscow. 'Ilyinskoye village. The Izba. You'll love it.' He was having to make it a social occasion, a casual Saturday outing, but it was difficult because he was terrified. She *had* to know something.

'Larissa on duty again today?'

'I don't know why she insists on working. It's not as if she needs the money: she can have as much as she likes.' He shouldn't rush it but it was difficult not to.

'I asked her the same thing,' offered Olga. 'She said she would get bored in the apartment by herself all day.'

'Maybe she's having an affair,' said Kosov. 'Working in an hotel would be convenient, wouldn't it?'

Olga looked sharply across the car. 'Who with?'

They cleared the city and Kosov stamped on the accelerator, taking out his impatience in physical speed. 'I just said maybe.'

'Would it worry you, if she was?'

'We've got a pretty loose marriage,' admitted Kosov. He didn't want to talk about Larissa or marriage! He wanted to talk about her bastard husband, cheating him in Italy.

Was the approach she'd worried about on their first outing going to come now? Why had she *been* worried? She wasn't now. She wasn't sure what she would do, if he made a pass, but she wasn't frightened. Remind him they were friends, probably: say something about not wanting to spoil it. What would it be like, to have an affair? A tiny tremor of excitement flickered through her at the thought. A lot of women had affairs: some women she worked with. It was hardly as if she would be seriously deceiving Dimitri. He didn't have any physical interest in her any more. They only made love when she practically demanded it, which was rare because she didn't have a great deal of physical interest in him any more. The marriage had gone beyond that. She wasn't sure where the marriage had gone *to*. Perhaps nowhere. Perhaps it had just gone. 'What would you do, if you found out she was involved with another man?'

'She'd be very silly, if she was. I've got a lot of friends who could help me.' Who at the moment were probably planning

338

to kill him, if he didn't find out what they wanted to know! He needed to break the inane conversation. He reached across the car, covering her hand. Olga opened her fingers to receive his, returning the pressure. 'Why do you work?'

'Same reason as Larissa, I suppose. And I like having my own money.'

The right direction, he thought. 'Dimitri Ivanovich doesn't keep you short, surely!'

Olga hesitated. 'We have to live on his salary.'

'That can't be easy.'

'It isn't.'

'We had a talk, just before he went away.'

'You're going to help him meet people!'

'I've offered.'

Olga squeezed his hand. 'That would be wonderful. You're a good friend.'

'From what the newspapers and television say, he seems to have been fantastically brave in Sicily.'

'Yes.'

'What's he said about it to you?'

'He hasn't called.'

It couldn't be! thought Kosov, anguished. 'Not at all?'

'I suppose he's been busy. I actually thought he was in Washington.'

He was wasting his time with this fat, stupid, ugly woman! 'So did we all. So you don't know how the investigation is going?'

'Only what I read in the papers. It must be going well if they've made all those arrests.'

At the Risskaya Izba they had smoked fish, with mutton to follow, which was too heavy so she left a lot; when she went to the rest-room to comb her hair and repair her make-up she saw, dismayed, there was a grease spot on the lapel of her cream jacket. Trying to wash it off made it worse.

Kosov, made persistent by fear, suggested walking by the river after lunch. Again he took her hand. 'You do trust me, don't you?'

Olga felt the tremor again. She had to prepare her answer. 'Of course. Why did you ask that?'

The gesture of dismissal came close to being overdone, but Olga didn't see it as that. 'It occurred to me that Dimitri Ivanovich and I talk work a lot: police work. I didn't want to bore you, asking about it today.' He still wasn't sure the bitch wasn't holding back: it didn't seem possible there hadn't been *one* call from Italy, after all the Superman heroics.

'You don't bore me, Yevgennie Grigorevich.' Olga felt warm, heavy-eyed and lethargic from the wine. She was sure he was going to make a pass.

'I don't think Dimitri Ivanovich treats you well enough.'

Olga wished he wouldn't keep reminding her of her husband. 'People get too used to each other.'

'He should have called you from Italy. Any wife would have been worried, after all those stories!'

'He *should*, shouldn't he!' she agreed, in half-drunken belligerence.

'But he didn't?' pressed Kosov, hopefully.

'What?' she asked, confused.

'He didn't call?'

'I told you he didn't: not since the day he left.'

Shit! thought Kosov. 'I'd really like to hear, if he does. I am a policeman, don't forget . . .' He allowed the necessary lapse. 'Did he tell you we'll be working together, soon? That I'll be going to the Organised Crime Bureau?'

Olga wished he would stop talking about boring police business. 'No.'

'We will. Let me know if he calls, won't you? I'd like to hear what's happening. Now that we're going to be partners.'

'If you like,' she said, uninterested.

What could he tell Gusovsky and Yerin, to convince them he was useful, stop them doing anything? 'There should be a celebration when he comes back. You'll tell me, won't you?'

Olga brightened. 'The moment I hear from him.' She was vaguely disappointed when he led her back to the car. Not that she wanted to make love to the man: not as quickly as this. She wouldn't have objected if he'd tried to kiss her, though.

CHAPTER FIFTY-ONE

It was far more difficult to resume the following day. Cowley, remorseful for letting himself be trapped in the first place, was now swamped by the conviction, which Danilov could not argue him out of, that he was responsible for Lena Zurov's murder. And when Maksim Zimin was brought before them the Mafia man was, initially, less frightened.

The second problem was easier for Danilov to handle than the first. He let the resumed interview run for less than five minutes before snapping off the recording machine, calling the other Russian a fool and ordering him to be returned to the life-sentence wing. Zimin obviously did not think he was serious until the guards began to manacle him again. He began to scream, as he must have screamed most of the one night he'd spent there, and fell baby-like on to the floor. Danilov let it go on for quite a long time before calling the guards off.

'Don't fuck with us!' he warned, taking over Cowley's command of the previous day. 'I've seen the photographs. You don't have any pressure, not from here, where you are. We can do with you exactly what we like. I *am* prepared to talk a deal, although not for the pictures you don't anyway control. You do what we want, you won't ever be put in the pit downstairs. Try to be stupid – just once – and I'll guarantee that's precisely where you'll go, after your trial here . . .'

'. . . What do you want?' broke in Zimin.

Danilov told him, without any authority to make the promise, the tape still turned off to prevent a record of the bargaining: it wasn't *possible* for a detective to be completely honest, ever, Danilov thought, in faint justification.

'I want to be back in Russia, before I agree,' said Zimin, in weak desperation. 'Want it discussed, with my own lawyer present. Get the guarantees.'

Danilov was about to press further but Cowley forced himself into the interview, straining his professionalism to the utmost. 'You've got more to tell us here, though: prove your co-operation here and you get the rest. *Our* guarantee.' All the arrangements were going Danilov's way: he still had two murders in Washington he now understood but was no closer to solving. He wanted something, too.

Another unrehearsed intrusion, thought Danilov, irritated. He'd have to let it go. He was later to be eternally glad that he did.

'What?' demanded Zimin again.

'Details of the Swiss account. How it worked. What Paulac did and who he did it with, in America.'

'I don't know any of that.'

'How could you negotiate a ten million dollar deal with Sicilian and American Mafia *without* knowing the details?' challenged Danilov.

'The Swiss part was handled by Gusovsky and Yerin.'

'What about Zavorin?' demanded Cowley. 'You called him the money man.'

'He was to discuss and agree the financial arrangements, if we got to that here: the contracts. But we didn't get to it.'

They could sweat Zimin again in the pit, but Danilov was impatient now. 'Zavorin knows you're on the *komitet*?'

'Yes.'

'Then you're going to tell him – *order* him – to tell us everything he knows. Now! Otherwise it's back downstairs.'

Ivan Zavorin did not need the theatre of dungeon cells to persuade him to talk: they'd broken Zimin, and so it had been the correct, American-led strategy to concentrate upon him, but Danilov thought they would have got something, in time, from this man, too. Zavorin's stutter was more pronounced, after the time he had spent in custody, and he seemed almost pathetically grateful when he was brought into the interview room and told by Zimin to disclose all he knew about the Swiss arrangement.

It wasn't as much as either investigator had hoped, but what he did disclose was enough for Cowley later to admit they should have pressed the accountant harder and sooner. Zavorin's understanding was that the embezzled Communist Party funds were not in a secretly numbered account, as they had wrongly assumed, but held by an *anstalt*, an even more secret trust corporation that could be untraceably manipulated by its founders. He didn't have the directors' names, nor that of the corporation. His role, Zavorin insisted, had been limited to financing the drug-purchasing with accountants to whom the Liccio clan and John Palma had been supposed to introduce him, after the initial meeting at which they had been seized. He did not, personally, have access to the *anstalt*; when they'd left Moscow, that was being negotiated by his lawyer-accountant partner, Sergei Mikolaivich Stupar.

'You don't *have* access yet?' demanded Cowley, confused.

'There was a transfer going through. I don't know any more than that.'

Only Cowley realised at once there was now a paper trail to follow, because only Cowley knew there was a legal treaty between Washington and Bern under which the traditional bank secrecy laws of Switzerland could be abrogated if there was evidence money involved was intended *for*, or the proceeds *of*, drug trafficking. Which Zimin's confession provided. The only thing of which they couldn't be sure was that Ilya Nishin – Raisa's father – and Serov himself would be directors whose names could guide them to the corporation itself.

Both family names *were* there. In less than thirty-six hours, there came confirmation from the Swiss capital that a corporation named *Svahbodniy* existed, with a Geneva registration address: because of the proof of its drug intention, any trading activities of the corporation had been frozen. Neither Cowley nor Danilov commented that *svahbodniy* was Russian for 'free'.

During those thirty-six hours there were two more sessions with Zimin. The man provided a lot more Mafia identities and two addresses – a restaurant on Glovin Bol'soj, and Gusovsky's house on Kutbysevskij Prospekt – which were virtually Chechen headquarters. When Danilov challenged the other Russian that he knew more, Zimin nervously admitted that he might, but that he wanted to be back in Russia before disclosing it. Anxious to get to Switzerland, they decided it wasn't worth pressing him further.

On the eve of their departure, a prominent anti-Mafia judge and three of his bodyguards died in Palermo when their car was blown up. Melega insisted it was a retribution attack for the Villalba arrests. He also said the three Sicilians continued to refuse to talk about Villalba, even though they had been taken point by point through Zimin's admission: so did John Palma. The only reaction to the Russian confession had been Umberto Chiara's soft-spoken insistence that Zimin would be killed in whatever jail he was sentenced to, anywhere in Italy. Danilov thought it would probably be difficult keeping the man alive in any penitentiary in Russia, as well.

That night Melega hosted a farewell dinner in a restaurant near the Spanish Steps, which had an eerie unreality because it had to be cleared of all other diners and surrounded by armed carabinieri. There were toasts to future anti-Mafia successes and assurances of lasting friendships and reunion plans for their return to give evidence at the eventual Italian trial. Throughout, Cowley sat rigid-faced and unresponsive. The only toast for which he showed any enthusiasm – or even properly drank – was to David Patton, who had recovered sufficiently to be flown back to America.

The Geneva meetings were little more than formalities, which Danilov thought they could have completed without an overnight stay, but the reservations had been made. Escorted and chauffeured by the embassy-attached FBI agent, an eager, fast-blinking man named Paul Jackson, they went first to meet Henri Charas, the police inspector handling all the Washington enquiries. It only took an hour to go through the file: there was no doubt the Swiss photograph of Ilya Nishin showed the same man as the print Danilov had taken from the Massachusetts Avenue apartment and which Raisa Serova had been so anxious to recover.

Charas drove with them to the irregularities department of

the Finance Ministry, in Bern. Heinrich Bloch, the director, was a pedantic, stick-dry accountant who had their encounter recorded verbatim by a corseted secretary, and insisted upon giving details of the access treaty, which they didn't want, before getting to the *Svahbodniy* corporation, which they did. The incorporation documents had already been translated into English and Russian, from the original French, for their benefit.

An *anstalt* was a corporation which did not issue shares for the benefit either of the founder or of others. Instead the founder – or holder of the Founder's Certificate, which was a bearer instrument showing all the ownership rights – had power to amend the articles of incorporation, appoint or remove directors and name beneficiaries.

It need not necessarily be profit-making, nor operate as a business: it could be a holding company, which seemed to be the case with *Svahbodniy*. It had been founded with an initial deposit of $30,000,000, in June, 1991: Ilya Iosifovich Nishin was recorded as the founder, and the other directors were Yuri Yermolovich Ryzhikev, Vladimir Aleksai Piotrovsky, Vladimir Alekseivich Kaplan and Michel Paulac – who was protectively identified both by his adopted Swiss name of Paulac and also as Mikhail Panzhevsky.

The change in the board and control of the *anstalt* had come, under the beneficiary clause, in April, 1992, upon the death of Ilya Nishin. None of the $30,000,000 appeared to have been used for any transaction: commission payments, which had been drawn in cash in the name of Michel Paulac, had been met by interest earned upon the original deposits.

In the records of the corporation there was an enquiry by a lawyer acting for Yuri Ryzhikev, concerning the status of the corporation after Nishin's death. Another, separate approach had been made since the freezing of the account under the Bern/Washington agreement.

'We've been lied to,' said Danilov.

'But very well,' agreed Cowley.

'How widely is this drug treaty known about?'

'If it was public knowledge, we wouldn't be able to trace the bad guys, would we?' said Cowley.

'The Swiss are extremely good at keeping secrets,' said Bloch.

'Good,' smiled Danilov.

CHAPTER FIFTY-TWO

Danilov was glad of the silence on the flight from Geneva, preferring to think rather than talk. He tried to work things out in the sequence in which they had to unfold, but as he fitted all the pieces together – guessing at the few still missing – his concentration increasingly focused upon the American. Cowley *had* saved him, in the beginning: unknowingly, a lot of the time, but by his mere presence Cowley had prevented his destruction. Would it be possible for him, in return, to block what was inevitable for Cowley? Danilov wanted to. He didn't, at that stage, know how he could.

He was sure he knew what the official reaction would be to the evidence he already had and which would, he was also sure, be sufficient for a prosecution. And even more than sufficient for an unthinkable diplomatic disaster. Danilov determined, in the next few hours and the next few days, always to keep in mind how he might achieve the favour-for-favour balance, Russian style, to help Cowley. He did not consider discussing it with the American: there was virtually nothing to discuss.

With the importance of sequence – and protocol – in mind, Nikolai Smolin was the first person Danilov contacted upon arrival at Petrovka. He telephoned from the now unoccupied director's suite, which he commandeered without authority. He didn't suspect Galina Kanayev as much as he had her predecessor, but the move freed them from any eaves-dropping and he wasn't sure what he, Pavin and Cowley might have to discuss.

'There's enough for a case?' demanded Smolin.

'Probably several.'

'Involving people presently in government?'

'I think so.'

'Do the Americans know?'

Always the same concern, Danilov recognised. 'Yes.'

'It has to be a full discussion?'

'Definitely.'

Danilov briefed Pavin on what he wanted before the official encounter, not intending to consider anything that had been assembled in their absence until Pavin pointed out the intercept of Olga and Kosov's outing the previous Saturday. There was a transcript, but Danilov insisted on hearing the actual tape.

Cowley shifted, awkwardly, at the disembodied conversation, but Danilov did not feel embarrassed nor angered at anything Olga said. His sole emotion was for Olga herself. She sounded so sadly hopeful, so pleased, at being spoiled and flattered: at being picked out for any sort of attention. His awareness of *why* she had been picked out, which Olga didn't know, worsened the feeling, gouging deeper. He couldn't remember ever having spoiled or flattered her, not even in the early days, when he'd thought he loved her and that she loved him. He'd never bought her a nonsense present, for no other reason except to *do* it: never thought of doing something totally unexpected – which he could have afforded, when he had accepted tributes. What had happened to their marriage had been his fault, Danilov decided, listening to the stilted, almost artificial exchange. Olga had stopped bothering because he had stopped bothering. Olga – poor, gauche, never-getting-it-quite-right Olga – sounded so desperately vulnerable; how lost – how vulnerable – would she be when he divorced her, leaving her quite alone? He wouldn't leave her quite alone, Danilov determined, at that moment. He'd have to support her, and not just financially, but by being there for her, to help her and look after her: see she didn't get into any real difficulty. Larissa would agree – he'd talk it through with her first, of course. Like he had to talk through so much else with her. Larissa had to know how difficult things might be for them, in the very near future.

He was vaguely aware of the discomfited Cowley addressing him.

'It was naive of him to imagine you'd tell her anything on the telephone,' said the American. 'Tell her anything at all, for that matter.'

He hadn't even called her from Italy, Danilov realised: even now, to tell her he was back in Moscow. His only concern had been to amass $250 for the Tatarovo apartment he and Larissa were going to take. 'Perhaps more desperate than naive.'

They were both surprised by the quickness of Pavin's return.

'It was very easy,' said Pavin. 'Ilya Iosifovich Nishin was Deputy Chief Accountant at the Finance Ministry. He died in April, 1992.'

'Kaplan?' questioned Cowley.

'Vladimir Aleksaivich Kaplan is the head of the American directorate at the Foreign Ministry,' said Pavin. 'He has been, for the past five years.'

To Cowley, Danilov said: 'The Serovs would travel on diplomatic passports. Yasev, too. That would make it easier for your people to trace, wouldn't it?'

'I guess so,' accepted Cowley. 'Sure you're not getting *too* conspiracy happy?'

'I want it all!' said Danilov determinedly.

Pavin's files on the murder of Lena Zurov were predictably meticulous. She'd been found dead in her own apartment, on Hasek Street, near the zoological gardens. There was a range of sexual paraphernalia in the apartment: dildos of various sizes, some whips and handcuffs and some vibrators as well as a selection of pornographic photographs, in some of which she appeared. Danilov was aware of Cowley tensing, but Pavin continued without any pointed hesitation. Her birth certificate put her age at twenty-eight; there was no record of her ever having been married; there *was* evidence of sexual intercourse shortly before death. The forensic department at Petrovka was not equipped for DNA tracing, but vaginal swabs had been taken for the semen to be passed on to America. A total of $2,000 had been found in a locked drawer and a further $300 had been scattered over a bedside table, as if in hurried payment.

Among that would be money he'd paid her, Cowley knew: traceably numbered bills he'd drawn from the embassy treasury. In an American investigation, a check on

349

banknote numbers would have been automatic: Cowley did not suggest it here.

It took a supreme effort of will for Cowley to look at the murder photographs. Lena Zurov was sprawled open-legged and naked, half forced off the blood-soaked bed by the impact of the bullets. As in every one of the symbolic murders, there were two body hits, both fatal. The mouth shot, inflicted after death, had taken away half the girl's face.

'The only difference from the others is the gun,' concluded Pavin. 'It wasn't in the apartment. The bullets were cushioned by being fired into the mattress: forensic have some very definite barrel markings. If we recover the weapon, we could make a positive match.'

Where would they find it, wondered Danilov. Or far more likely, where would it be planted? He was sure the danger would occur to Cowley – now if not later – but he made a mental note to warn the man. It was becoming difficult to keep in mind everything they had to guard against and the order in which they had to move. But the conference with the government ministers was very definitely the first priority. He called Yevgennie Kosov before going to it. Reserve matched reserve, but Danilov was held by an ice-hard anger.

The three men remained unmoving while Danilov talked. Several times he offered the documentary evidence he had brought with him, but every time Nikolai Smolin shook his head, almost with impatience. Danilov got the impression there had been another conference, preceding this.

'The American knows: will have told Washington?' repeated Smolin, uttering what appeared to be his only preoccupation.

'Yes,' confirmed Danilov. The lack of response worried him. He didn't think he could openly ask, if he didn't get the guidance he wanted.

'The money is still in this corporation?' queried Sergei Vorobie.

'Yes.'

'Would it be possible to get it back?' asked Vasili Oskin.

The information was in the documents they'd refused: at worse, he could only later be criticised for an oversight. He wasn't going to have to ask, to get his question answered.

'I am not sure about that. Or that a legal conviction is possible, upon the evidence of Maksim Zimin alone,' said Smolin. The opinion wasn't addressed to Danilov.

'America will expect something,' pointed out the Deputy Interior Minister.

There *had* been a prior conference, Danilov decided: they were virtually continuing it now, talking as if he weren't in the room. He wouldn't tell them how he intended going on with the enquiries: it would be easier to have the sort of interview he wanted with Raisa Serova without the intrusion of Oleg Yasev.

The other three men looked among themselves, as if seeking a spokesman. Vorobie said: 'There has been very detailed discussion, after what happened in Italy. And there will have to be more, as a result of what you've added today. But every effort is to be made to avoid this becoming the diplomatic scandal about which we spoke at the very beginning. You are to make no approach to any of the named government officials. Are you clear about that?'

'Completely,' said Danilov. And more, he thought. There was *definitely* going to be a cover-up.

Danilov was an hour later than he'd promised, getting back to Kirovskaya, but Olga was not annoyed. She kissed him, seeming not to notice his half-hearted response as she flustered around the apartment constantly talking, never waiting for him to reply, which after a while he stopped bothering to do. She said the silk scarf he'd bought – again on the plane – from Geneva was beautiful, and showed him all the Moscow newspaper cuttings of his part in the Sicilian gun battle and said how proud she was of him.

It was, in fact, the first time he had seen the complete Russian coverage: there'd only been three clippings from the embassy in Rome. He was surprised how much space he had been given. He thought he looked ridiculous coming out of the helicopter in army fatigues.

Olga made him tell her about it in minute detail, constantly interrupting with small questions when he tried to hurry, and he indulged her, not irritated as he sometimes was. She kept repeating how proud she was. That night she initiated the love-making and he found it easier to respond than he'd thought he would, but afterwards he remained awake long after she had drifted off into a snuffling sleep.

He was soon going to have to find the words to tell her it was all over. What *were* the words? He didn't know yet, but he had to have them exactly right when the moment came, to cause as little hurt as possible. Definitely reassure her that he intended to look after her. Would Larissa have worked out what she was going to say to Kosov? They'd have to talk it through first: get it right between them.

He'd have to call Larissa tomorrow: she'd probably heard from Kosov he was back. Danilov couldn't work out precisely what it had been when he'd spoken to the man, to arrange their meeting. There had been more than simply fury. Fear, Danilov hoped. Would he be able to achieve what he wanted, the following day? He thought so: the Italians appeared to be keeping their word, not releasing anything of the interrogation success. So Kosov's friends would be frantic to know what had been discovered. It pleased Danilov, imagining them frantic. He hoped Kosov was the most worried of all. Not just frightened. Truly terrified. The bastard deserved to be.

CHAPTER FIFTY-THREE

Kosov had decreed the Metropole bar, which Danilov thought entirely predictable, but the man intercepted him as he entered the foyer, announcing that it was too crowded and they would talk in the car instead. Danilov allowed himself to be shepherded back outside, curious at the abrupt change. Distrust, at something he might have set up in the hotel after his misguidance about the investigation? Or was Kosov merely being theatrical, which was also predictable? It didn't matter. Kosov was now compromising himself by insisting on the eavesdropped BMW.

Kosov made no attempt to start the car once they were seated. Instead he gripped the wheel, staring directly ahead for several moments before saying: 'You've made things very difficult for me, Dimitri Ivanovich. Could even have put me in danger. I don't like that.'

It was a poor attempt to sound threatening. 'How did I do that?' Danilov had no difficulty over the conversation being simultaneously overheard by Cowley at the American embassy. But he had to forget the tape, not perform to it.

'By giving me the impression you did!' complained Kosov, loud voiced, turning to Danilov at last. 'I thought we had an understanding. You told me you were getting nowhere. I told other people!'

The suit was blue, a shiny material like silk that Danilov had not seen the other man wear before. The cologne was overpowering in the confined space. 'I'm not running this investigation alone! You knew that!'

'You told me it was getting nowhere!' insisted Kosov.

'Which it wasn't, when we talked!' said Danilov, the explanation fully prepared. 'It wasn't until we got to Washington we heard what was going to happen in Sicily.'

Kosov's attitude softened, very slightly. 'That's where it came from! From an American source!'

'Where else?'

'My friends will be relieved.'

'Why?' asked Danilov, wanting the reply recorded.

'They wanted reassurance about security, here in Moscow.' Kosov started the car as he spoke and Danilov hoped the firing of the engine hadn't blurred the words.

'You talked about an introduction,' encouraged Danilov.

'We've got a lot to talk about first,' said Kosov. He turned away from the Kremlin, driving out of the city. 'You were quite the hero!'

'It was automatic: I didn't realise I was doing it,' Danilov answered, honestly.

'They were interrogated, of course.'

'Of course.'

'What's been said? Admitted?'

'Bits and pieces,' said Danilov, intentionally vague.

Kosov sighed. 'Sufficient for a case?'

'Enough for a murder prosecution in Italy.'

'I mean here, in Moscow!' said Kosov impatiently.

Danilov realised they were driving on the edge of Tatarovo, close to the intended apartment. He had the bribe money ready in his pocket. Larissa would be waiting for him when her shift finished.

He made an uncertain rocking movement with his free hand. 'Maybe. Maybe not. There's got to be a lot of discussion.'

The sigh this time was even more profound. 'So let's start talking properly! Why are we going around in circles!'

'I want to meet your friends. Face to face,' declared Danilov. Kosov didn't have any real choice in how the encounter went, but Danilov did not want to alienate the man too much. It would all come soon enough.

The head shake was patronising. 'Just tell me everything that happened in Italy. And what you want. I'll arrange it all.'

Pompous, arrogant bastard, thought Danilov. He shook his head in return. 'Tell them I want to meet personally.'

'You think you're in a position to make demands?'

'I'm the one who knows about Italy.'

'It's got to be through me!'

'That's not the way it's going to be,' refused Danilov.

'Dimitri Ivanovich! Why are we fighting?'

'We're not fighting. We're avoiding the sort of misunderstandings that occurred before.'

'Just tell me!' implored Kosov. 'I'll pass it all on. And fix whatever you ask for.'

Kosov wanted desperately to restore his credibility with his paymasters, guessed Danilov: maybe he even felt physically threatened. Repeating Kosov's earlier complaint, Danilov said: 'If I deal direct, there can't be any misunderstandings. You won't be endangered.'

'I'm your friend! You can trust me. I'm willing to take the risk! I *want* to help you!'

'Face to face,' said Danilov, adamantly. Was it possible Kosov hadn't passed on the information about his compromising past? It was hardly a reassurance, one way or the other: Kosov would tell the world and his brother when he learned about him and Larissa.

'Somebody did say *something* in Sicily, didn't they?' pressed Kosov, trying to bring the conversation back on the course he wanted.

'There are leads to follow,' allowed Danilov.

'*Are* you going to follow them?'

'I could.'

Kosov seized the intentional ambiguity. 'But you needn't?'

They reached the outer ring road and joined the circle. 'There's a lot to be gone through.' Lying easily, he said: 'It depends what I present to the Federal Prosecutor.' Whose decision, upon whatever I present, I already know, thought Danilov.

'What about Cowley?' said the other man. 'He surely heard all you did: would know if something was . . .' He smiled, conspiratorially. '. . . overlooked?'

'Cowley's interested in resolving the murders in America. What happened here in Moscow is secondary: peripheral, providing he can close the cases at home.' Danilov chose the words carefully, wanting them relayed accurately to defer any use of the compromising photographs. He'd watched Kosov closely, mentioning the American, and didn't think

Kosov knew of the pictures. If he had, he would have surely referred to the whore's murder by now: he'd actually held back, waiting for Kosov to talk about it.

'Let me handle this,' said Kosov, renewing his plea.

'No,' persisted Danilov.

'Without any indication of what happened in Italy they might think it's a trap.'

'*I'm* going to *them*. What sort of trap can I set?'

'They'll want guarantees.'

'*You* give guarantees: you're their man, aren't you?'

Kosov gave a self-satisfied smile, and Danilov felt the revulsion move through him. Kosov said: 'They're going to ask me what you want.'

'To talk about things of interest to both of us,' said Danilov, almost embarrassed by the gangster-movie talk.

'What if they refuse?'

'Tell them they can't refuse: that they'll regret it, if they do.'

'They don't like threats.'

'I'm not making threats. Just being direct.'

'We're going to make a great partnership, Dimitri Ivanovich!' said Kosov.

He had briefly forgotten Kosov's absurd belief they would ever work together. 'A great partnership,' he agreed.

Danilov was conscious of immediate attention the moment he entered the Druzhba hotel: some hotel staff came from the reception area to look at him and smile familiarly, and Danilov was glad he and Larissa weren't going to use one of the unoccupied rooms. She came quickly around the hidden part of the curved counter, where she normally waited. He guessed she was enjoying the recognition.

'Aren't you going to kiss me?'

'I feel I'm on display!'

'You are. You're famous.'

Danilov hurried her from the hotel, wondering why he felt uncomfortable at the recognition, but not at coming directly from his meeting with Kosov to finalise his living arrangements with the man's wife. He waited until she was seated beside him in the Volga before kissing her. 'I've got the dollars for the apartment.'

'Good,' she said briskly, as if there had never been any doubt he would be able to obtain them.

'Before we commit ourselves, you should consider very seriously that Yevgennie could expose me, because of the past.'

'We talked about it already.'

'Don't we need to talk about it again? Life with me is going to be very different from what it is with Yevgennie Grigorevich.' She had the comparison of riding in the shuddering Volga against the smoothness of the BMW as a very real example.

Larissa reached across for his hand. 'My darling! I *want* it to be as different as it possibly can be. I *love* you!'

'There's something else. I won't just abandon Olga. I want to be able to help her – not just with money: if she has any problems. She . . . she isn't very good with things.'

Larissa squeezed the hand she was holding. 'Wasn't I the one to say it would be nice if we stayed friends?'

'I love you,' Danilov returned finally.

At the Tatarovo apartment, he handed over the money and signed the leasing agreement, and the landlord took them around for another tour of inspection, for Larissa to itemise the things they would need. She did so in a notebook, making reminders to herself where she intended to put individual pieces of furniture.

'I hope you're happy here,' the landlord said.

'We will be,' said Larissa, positively.

The Secretary of State had agreed at once to one of their breakfast meetings, but cleared his diary for the entire morning.

It took Henry Hartz a full hour to go completely through what Cowley had sent from Moscow. Finally he looked up to the FBI Director and said: 'So there's a definite government connection!'

'I think we should date it from the coup that didn't work,' warned Ross.

'Serov was a currently serving, accredited diplomat at the Russian embassy,' argued Hartz. 'There are three other names here who are members of the current government!'

'Haven't we ever found a rotten apple in a diplomatic barrel?' asked Ross gently.

'Not a whole goddamned orchardful setting up ten-million-dollar drug deals with Mafia organisations right around the goddamned world!' erupted Hartz.

'Serov wasn't,' pointed out the FBI Director. 'By then he was dead. I'd like to go along with what Cowley suggests: wait a little to see what comes out of the enquiries that are left.'

'I'm definitely waiting for Moscow to come to us,' agreed the Secretary of State. 'They're the ones who've got to do the explaining.'

Two miles away, at the FBI headquarters in downtown Washington, Rafferty looked up from one of the overnight cables from Cowley directed specifically to them, together with all the other additional evidence and specimens. 'Son of a bitch!' he said. 'All the time, we were looking for the wrong face in the pictures, with Michel Paulac.'

'We've got the photographs,' said Johannsen philosophically. He picked up the print that had accompanied Cowley's request from Moscow. 'All we've got to do now is make the match.'

Which they did surprisingly quickly.

'Son of a bitch!' exclaimed Rafferty again. 'We're really getting good at this!'

They got even better. Computerised immigration records threw up a number of exit and entry visas not just for Oleg Yasev, but for Raisa Serova, too.

CHAPTER FIFTY-FOUR

They got to Leninskaya early, before eight o'clock, wanting to guarantee Raisa Serova would be there. The widow opened the door to them in a trousered lounging suit: she wasn't made-up – Danilov decided she hardly needed to be – but her hair was perfectly in place, although hanging loose. It was more of an instinctive than positive gesture, to try to close the door in their faces, and she didn't push against it when Danilov reached out, stopping her.

'Don't be silly,' he said.

'I shall complain . . .'

'. . . Stop it!' interrupted Cowley. 'It's over, Raisa. We know.'

For several moments she remained at the door, gazing at them, then stood back, unspeaking, for them to enter. She went to her usual couch, in front of the widow, and huddled into it, her legs tucked beneath her as if she was trying to make herself inconspicuous. They sat where they had before. Pavin got out his notebook, ready.

'It was Italy, I suppose,' she said dully.

'And America: it was in America, after Italy, that everything was pulled together,' said Cowley. They intended, in the beginning, to be intentionally obscure, to lure her into saying more than she otherwise might.

'Would you believe me, if I told you I am relieved?' said Raisa.

It would have been easy to feel pity for her, but Danilov didn't. Instead of replying, he reached sideways for the damning evidence Pavin had waiting. One by one, on the table between them, he set the photographs from both Geneva and Washington, jabbing his finger on each print as he enumerated them.

'This is a copy of the photograph I took from your apartment in Massachussets Avenue . . . a photograph you were extremely anxious to have returned. It shows your late husband with your father, Ilya Iosifovich Nishin, also now dead . . . Here is your father with Igor Rimyans, a known Ukrainian gangster living in the United States of America. It was removed from his house in the Queens district of New York . . .' Danilov hesitated at the photographs that had only become significant in the last forty-eight hours, since Rafferty and Johannsen had carried out the comparison Cowley had requested on his return to Moscow, then his finger jabbed again, three times, in separate identification.

'In each of these Michel Paulac, a naturalised Swiss financier whose family came from the Ukraine, where their name was Panzhevsky, is shown at official Washington receptions . . .' The finger pointed very definitely. 'And here . . . here . . . and here . . . you are shown at those same functions, although the invitations were in your husband's name and you never signed or gave your correct name in the registration records that are kept at these events . . .'

'. . . I don't think this should continue!'

For several moments it would have been difficult for either Cowley or Danilov to continue. Oleg Yasev stood at the entrance to the bedroom corridor. He was unshaven, hair still disordered from sleep. He wore trousers and his shirt was undone at the neck, without a tie.

Determined against his previous arrogance, Danilov said: '*We* will decide what should or should not continue, like we will decide whether to believe your explanation of why you tried to withhold the name of Ilya Nishin from the documents you returned from the Foreign Ministry. Come in and sit down!'

Yasev did, with unexpected humility, on the edge of Raisa Serova's encompassing couch. Automatically she put her hand out to rest on his thigh. Just as automatically, he took it in his.

Cowley came into the questioning, as they'd arranged. Offering duplicates of the *anstalt* agreement, he said: 'These are legal Swiss documents, translated into Russian for our benefit although I am sure you have a similar copy some-where, of a secret financial corporation established by your late father with thirty million dollars of stolen Communist Party money, just prior to the coup against Mikhail Gorbachev in August, 1991: an escape fund, if the coup failed. Which it did. But for which none of the main ringleaders – apart from your father and a few others – ever managed to evade responsibility. And which they were never properly able to utilise anyway . . .'

'. . . Please, no more . . . !'

'. . . And this,' persisted Danilov relentlessly, '. . . is another legal Swiss document, the passing over of the Founder's Certificate – the absolute control – of the secret Swiss holding. It legally passes that control to you, Raisa Ilyavich Serova.'

The room was icily silent.

Raisa stirred from her curled-up position. 'If my father hadn't already been so ill, it might have been different! It could have all been reversed . . .' She reached up, for Yasev's hand. 'At least we tried . . .'

Neither Danilov nor Cowley understood her response. Danilov pressed on: 'Petr Aleksandrovich was never properly part of it, was he? He was the clerk, because he was brilliant at detail: but you were the person who always negotiated with Paulac . . . tried to retain control of the money . . .'

The woman interrupted, which was fortunate because Danilov was close to going ahead of himself. 'Petr Aleksandrovich was happy to do what he was told: happy to stay forever in America, which was what he wanted.'

'What did *you* want?' asked Cowley, looking between the woman and the man perched at her side.

She took the full meaning. 'To get out of the mess I was in.'

It was becoming splintered, difficult to follow. 'Your father was operating for the plotters, right?'

She nodded. 'Some of them: the KGB chairman, certainly. I think there were others like my father, but I don't know any names. He didn't. He believed in the old system, you see. Quite sincerely. He couldn't imagine – couldn't believe – it was all coming to an end. He wasn't well, even then. Knew he couldn't be active, in the attempted overthrow . . .'

Cowley intruded, in an effort to get more coherence into the account. 'Why the Ostankino? Why *any* Mafia group? Your father was in the government: the deputy chief in the Finance Ministry! It doesn't make sense.'

'KGB,' said the woman shortly, barely helpful.

Something that slotted into the Rome interrogation, isolated Danilov. 'Who?'

'Vasili Dolya. Director of the First Chief Directorate. He was a university classmate of my father's. They remained friends, afterwards. At least, my father thought they were friends. Dolya was part of the coup, with the chairman, although he was never found out. And he knew how things operated outside the country: that was the expertise of his division, after all. He said there should be contingency arrangements, if it went wrong. It was Dolya who introduced my father to Paulac, in Switzerland. And the two of them who suggested the Ostankino cells in the United States be brought in: he said they would know how to make the money *work* in America.'

'The Ostankino weren't necessary, were they?' took up Cowley, ahead of the Russian but equally aware of the value of what they were learning. 'So Paulac was the first to cheat?'

Raisa nodded. 'We didn't know. Not at first. Not for a long time.'

'Was it Paulac's suggestion that Yuri Ryzhikev and Vladimir Piotrovsky should be *Svahbodniy* directors?' pressed the American.

There was another agreeing nod. 'He told my father it was the proper, necessary business arrangement: Ryzhikev, from here, would direct his American partner.'

'Igor Rimyans?' suggested Danilov.

The nod came again.

'How long before the Ostankino started the pressure?' guessed Cowley, more experienced in Mafia take-overs.

'It was Paulac, to begin with. He tried to persuade my father to move most of the money from Switzerland into America: said there was no point in holding it in Switzerland, just earning interest. That it had to be used to generate more money. But the coup had failed by then. Everyone who'd supported it but escaped arrest was waiting, terrified of the knock on the door. My father most of all, because he'd set up the escape fund that nobody – none of the plotters, that is – was going to be able to use. That's why Paulac began coming to Washington so often, to meet me: that was the route, you see? My father kept Petr Aleksandrovich in Washington so there was a channel of communication from Paulac to me to my father, back here in Moscow. Everything we wrote to each other went back and forth untouched and unread by anyone else, through the diplomatic mail . . .'

Danilov did not want to interrupt the flow, but it was imperative to establish the extent of official government involvement. 'So Petr Aleksandrovich was almost incidental: a cipher kept in Washington for the diplomatic convenience through which you could handle things with your father?'

Raisa smiled, a sad expression. 'That's one of the most ironic parts. I told him not to do it, but he said it was a way to protect us. We didn't want to be involved, you see. We were both ciphers, for my father. Isn't that funny! Without the names you would never have found out, would you?'

Another reaction they hadn't anticipated, recognised Danilov. Before he could pursue the most intriguing remark, Cowley said: 'Paulac was the man who began the pressure?'

'Then it got frightening, from here,' took up the woman. 'My father was ill by then: his fear at being implicated in the coup had a lot to do with it, I think. These men, gang people, began openly threatening him: said if he didn't transfer the money like they wanted, they'd make public what he'd done, have him arrested and put on trial, like the rest of the plotters . . .'

Knowing the original deposit in Switzerland was untouched, Danilov said: 'But he didn't give in to the threats?'

She shrugged. 'I pleaded with him to return it. End the whole stupid business.'

'Why didn't he?' said Cowley.

'He was very ill. He asked Dolya to do something. Frighten them off. Dolya told him the KGB was being broken up, into internal and external services: in chaos. It didn't control everything, like it once had: Dolya said the Ostankino were prepared to expose him, as well as my father. There was nothing he *could* do.'

'Whose idea was it to go to another Family?'

'Dolya's. Some of his former officers were involved with the Chechen, apparently: a lot of them are in crime now. The Chechen promised to protect us: said we had nothing to fear any more. But they wanted access to the Swiss holdings . . .'

'. . . Which your father gave them?' said Danilov – a trick question, because he knew the documentation in Switzerland was still in the name of the Ostankino leaders.

'No!' she said. 'He went to hospital soon after: wasn't fit to do anything legal. That's another irony, isn't it? Having to do something legal with men who only break the law . . .'

He hadn't tricked her, Danilov accepted. 'And then you inherited control, upon his death.'

Raisa looked down when she nodded, a moment of sadness. She came up again, breathing deeply, determined to explain. 'It didn't take us long to realise we'd simply exchanged one pressure for another – one worse, in fact – by going to another gang. I'd always intended to return the money somehow, when I realised that one day I'd be in charge of it. I didn't *want* the damned money . . . It was stolen!'

'You told them you were going to give it back?' asked Cowley.

She made an uncertain shoulder movement. 'I told Paulac, the last time we met. Paulac got very frightened: he hadn't told the Ostankino about the Chechen being brought in for protection: that they were pressuring me to change the directorship. He said to change the names would get us killed. Like giving the money back would get us killed. I didn't believe him. I thought he was just trying to scare me . . .'

'You came back to Moscow to return the money? The sickness of your mother was the excuse?' queried Danilov.

'This time and a lot of times before. All I wanted to do was protect my father's name and get rid of the damned money. I told Paulac I wasn't scared. I said I'd tell the Ostankino man,

Ryzhikev: made Paulac give me a telephone number, to reach him . . .' She halted, shuddering. 'Then the murders happened, Paulac and Petr Aleksandrovich . . . and the first one here . . .'

'So you didn't contact Ryzhikev?'

'I was terrified: we both were . . .' She smiled up at Yasev again. 'I knew Paulac hadn't been exaggerating . . .'

'The day after Petr Aleksandrovich's funeral a man came to my flat,' said Yasev, surprising them with the intrusion. 'He said he'd been with the KGB before the coup and knew what had been set up. He said Raisa had to sign over the Founder's Certificate to people he would take us to: that the Chechen were assuming full control. I knew by then they weren't exaggerating, either.'

'You told her she had to?' Danilov asked him.

It was the woman who answered. 'We didn't know what to do! It was another way of getting rid of the money and the pressure, wasn't it! Just give them what they wanted . . . !'

Why had the money still been intact in Switzerland, wondered Danilov. 'When did you do it?'

'Three or four days after all the stories in the papers about what happened in Italy.'

'The same man who came to my flat arranged it,' volunteered Yasev. 'We went to a big house in Kutbysevskij Prospekt . . .'

The address they'd got in Rome, recognised Danilov. 'Who did you meet?'

'There were a lot of men: we weren't told who they all were.'

'You must have had a name to pass over the Founder's Certificate!'

'Arkadi Pavlovich Gusovsky.'

Another Italian confirmation! He was aware of Cowley nodding beside him, in matching awareness. 'Anyone else?'

'Someone called Yerin . . .' she shivered. 'He made me very nervous. He's blind, milky-eyed, but he looks at you as if he can see you.'

'You signed,' encouraged Cowley. 'What happened then?'

'I had to sign as well, as a witness,' said Yasev.

'How was the transfer to the Chechen to work?'

'When the investigation died down and it became safe to access the *anstalt* I was to instruct a Swiss lawyer to substitute what I'd signed over for what already existed there. They'd sent someone to Geneva to find out how to do it.'

'Giving the Chechen the whole thirty million?'

'And us relief, at last,' said Yasev.

The man appeared content to remain subservient, Danilov thought. Had Raisa Serova dominated her husband as completely as she clearly dominated her lover? It was a passing reflection, leading to another. Dominant or not, he was going to have to adjust his attitude towards the woman, if what she'd said was true. And he had no way of proving she hadn't intended to return the money, before being terrorised into parting with it.

The questioning continued for a further two hours, coming down largely to filling in dates and details. Raisa Serova produced the telephone number of the Ostankino leader, Yuri Ryzhikev, and Yasev gave the exact day when the *Svahbodniy* documents had been signed over, which was only one day before the Swiss authorities froze the account, supporting Danilov's guess there had been insufficient time to plunder it. Yasev volunteered the relationship between himself and Raisa dated from their overlapping posting to the Russian embassy in Paris: Raisa volunteered that if they had been able to return the money, she had intended divorcing her husband to marry Oleg.

'Putting something else right, as it should have been a long time ago,' said Yasev.

'What's going to happen to us now?' demanded Raisa. 'The blind man, Yerin, said we would be killed if we ever told anyone.'

'I think, for the moment, you should come into protective custody.'

'I think so, too,' agreed Yasev anxiously.

'You'll arrest them, both gangs, won't you?' said the woman, just as anxiously. 'We won't be safe, Oleg and I, until they're locked up.'

'We'll arrest them,' assured Danilov. Against how many charges would be possible?

Yasev and the woman went together into the bedroom, to collect clothes to take with them.

'That didn't turn out at all like I expected it to,' admitted Cowley.

'Nothing in this case turns out like we expect it to,' reminded Danilov.

It took most of the remainder of the day to go through the protective custody formalities and prepare a full report, accompanied by a transcript of the statements of Raisa Serova and Oleg Yasev, for the Federal Prosecutor. Because the Deputy Interior Minister had taken over the ultimate authority for the Organised Crime Bureau, Danilov duplicated to him, as well.

'I wish you wouldn't go ahead with this other thing,' said Cowley. 'It has no purpose.'

'We don't know that, yet.'

'Any more than we know your people are going to cover up as much as you suspect they will.'

'Trust me,' said Danilov glibly.

'I do. And I think you're taking too much of a chance. In any court that even admitted in evidence the tape of you and Kosov in the car, a clever lawyer could make you sound the crookedest cop in the history of corruption.'

Danilov conceded that at the moment the American was right. 'I want to *see* them: know what they're *like*. I need to be ready, in advance of whatever the official decisions are.'

'If it's an official decision, it's an official decision!' argued the exasperated American. 'You've solved a case. They decide how to take it from here.'

'We've solved an embezzlement case, which we didn't know we had. We haven't solved four murders. Which we knew we *did* have. The Italian convictions will be theirs, not ours.'

'Where else is there to go?' exclaimed Cowley, in despairing cynicism.

'Maybe where I'm going.'

'If they'll see you,' cautioned Cowley.

'They'll see me. They can't ignore me.'

'You'll be as exposed as hell!'

'I'll cover myself.'

'Nobody knows where the hell you're going,' objected the American. 'You're totally at their mercy.'

'The car's bugged,' reminded Danilov. 'You can listen.'

'Maybe to the sound of the gun going off,' completed Cowley.

'We'll hear what he's got, before we show him how we can hurt him,' said Yerin.

'He'll deal,' predicted Gusovsky.

'We've got to have Zimin killed,' said Yerin conversationally. 'It doesn't matter whether he's talked or not; he's got to be killed.' He paused. 'We should have done it a long time ago.'

CHAPTER FIFTY-FIVE

It was the Metropole again, but the man wasn't waiting to intercept him in the foyer, nor in the bar itself, when Danilov arrived, a few minutes ahead of the arranged time. The waiter peremptorily tried to move him from the booth, until Danilov said he was waiting for guests and didn't intend occupying it alone: he deliberately ordered beer, the cheapest drink on the list.

Danilov welcomed a few minutes by himself. He was about to try the biggest bluff of his life. Cowley, still not entirely knowing what he was attempting, had continued to argue against it. So had Pavin, who had come from their original office, where he still had his files, to announce the number deciphered from Kosov's car phone had been traced to the Kutbysevskij address. Pavin had wanted to order foot and motor patrols around Kutbysevskij and the restaurant on Glovin Bol'soj until Danilov pointed out both were in Kosov's Militia district, and that it was inevitable the man would learn about them. He refused, too, to have any squad personally imposed for protective surveillance. His most positive rejection was to Cowley's suggestion he wear a body microphone and transmitter.

Danilov did not seriously believe he was in any physical danger – not this first time at least – but it was not until after he'd made the final arrangements with Kosov that he realised how few precautions there were to take. He wrote a detailed statement, listing as much as he suspected about the man's links with the Chechen, to supplement the stack of incriminating tape transcripts. In particular, he itemised that day's date and included timings for a provable and continuing narrative implicating the man in the imminent Mafia encounter. He intended to supplement it even further with whatever identifying conversation would be recorded from the BMW.

Kosov was fifteen minutes late. The reluctant waiter became smilingly attentive when he bustled towards the booth, looked disgustedly at the beer, and ordered Chivas Regal, widening his thumb and forefinger to make it double. Danilov was aware of three men entering the bar at almost precisely spaced intervals after Kosov. They wore Western-style suits and upon one there was a glint of gold, from a bracelet and a ring on the same hand, but the features were Slavic. The one with the gold reminded him of Mikhail Antipov: Danilov was glad he had not agreed to a similar escort, which would have been not so well dressed but just as obvious.

'So there's no hurry?' said Danilov, as Kosov began to drink.

'There's time to talk. These men – the people you're going to meet – like respect. They're big . . . very big.'

'Do I play the peasant or the kulak?'

'Just trying to help,' said Kosov. He was subdued, close to being openly frightened.

It would be wrong to offend the man. 'Who will I be meeting?'

'They'll tell you their names, if they want to.'

'Where are we going?'

'It's quite close.'

Both Kutbysevskij and Glovin Bol'soj were quite close. For a few moments he sat regarding Kosov, not speaking. Kosov would definitely be as vindictive as possible. He'd try to ride out the exposure, Danilov decided: certainly not resign, unless it was demanded. And resist that demand, as strongly as possible. 'What else should I know about them?'

'They're very generous, to people they consider friends.'

'I would have to prove the friendship, of course?'

'Of course.'

There was nothing to be gained by pressing further. 'They very worried about Italy?'

Kosov's face clouded. 'They're still furious at being misled.'

'Not by me. And you know how that happened.'

'It would help if you explained again to them, in person.'

'I'll make a point of it.' Danilov was suddenly caught by the irrational wish to play the car intercepts back to the man: particularly the one involving the sadly flattered Olga. He dismissed the fantasy, irritably, looking up in time to see two of the men who'd entered closely behind Kosov both looking at him: one turned away too quickly.

Kosov smiled at the assurance. 'It's going to be very good, when you're connected like I am: when we're really a team, officially and otherwise.'

Danilov thought 'connected' had some American Mafia connotation, but wasn't sure. He looked pointedly at his watch, which was a waste of time because it had stopped again. 'Shouldn't we go?'

The BMW was parked prominently outside the hotel. Danilov didn't bother to check the three followers he was sure would be leaving directly after them, more concerned with feeding the incriminating tape. 'How far do we have to go?'

'I told you, it's quite close.'

'Where do they meet, the Chechen? Are there special houses . . . restaurants . . . public places . . . what?'

Kosov, who was heading back in the direction of Red Square, looked sharply across the car. 'Who said anything about the Chechen?'

Shit! thought Danilov, caught out. Quickly recovering, he said: 'That's who the Americans think is involved.'

'They move around,' offered Kosov, after a pause.

He had to give as much as possible of the route. Seeing the illuminations ahead, Danilov said: 'I would have expected the Kremlin stars to be taken down, wouldn't you? It's a Communist symbol, after all.'

'I haven't thought about it,' dismissed Kosov, impatiently. 'You're not armed, are you?'

'No.' Should he explore the demand? It hardly required an explanation, and he didn't want a too-persistent question-and-answer exchange.

Kosov turned on to Sverdlova. As they passed the US embassy – aware that briefly the American, at the listening apparatus, was only yards away – Danilov said: 'Cowley says conditions inside the embassy there are terrible. The KGB bugs in the new building should have all been located by now, wouldn't you think?'

'I haven't thought about that, either,' said Kosov shortly.

Kosov had not attempted to play either his radio or taped music: so he was too distracted – concentrating upon other things – to show off. Or worried. Perhaps the Metropole drink hadn't provided sufficient buoyancy. They were passing the monolithic Peking restaurant and Danilov was about to introduce it as another marker when Kosov pulled sharply into the underpass for the inner peripherique in the opposite direction. 'What the hell are you doing? We're going back the way we came!' He'd keep to their optimistically devised monitoring but Danilov already knew he was in free orbit, virtually untraceable. The hope of maintaining a street-by-street identification had always been impractical.

'Making a detour,' replied Kosov flatly.

Recognising another name-identifying chance, Danilov said: 'Surely you – and the Chechen – don't think I'd surround myself with bodyguards! So we're being checked out by minders?'

'I don't know.'

'Of course you know! This is ridiculous, Yevgennie Grigorevich!'

'It's not my idea!'

'How much longer do we drive around and around like this?'

'I said it wasn't my idea!'

'They were too obvious.'

'Who? You're not making sense!' protested Kosov.

'Your three Chechen protectors, back at the hotel.'

'I don't know anything about three men at the hotel.'

Enough, decided Danilov again: he had the Chechen linked by name with Kosov. 'The Kammeny Bridge! This really is the conducted tour!'

Kosov did not reply.

If Moscow were divided by the Mafia into a cake they were a long way now from what was acknowledged to be the Chechen slice: certainly a long way from Kutbysevskij

Prospekt or Glovin Bol'soj. Danilov was curious if they would continue, to complete the inner ring road. But once again Kosov made an abrupt and unannounced underpass turn to reverse yet again the direction in which they were driving. Preposterous though it was, Danilov conceded it would have been impossible for any surveillance car to have remained with him this far without being identified. They re-crossed the Kammeny Bridge and went by the embassy and the Chinese restaurant a second time but almost at once turned off Sverdlova, on to minor roads. On what Danilov thought he recognised to be Kisel'nyj Street Kosov unexpectedly slowed, to be passed by two cars flashing their lights.

'I'm glad they're satisfied,' said Danilov.

'Shouldn't you be glad they're so careful?'

'I don't know yet what I have to be careful about.'

They only drove for another few minutes and Danilov managed to get the place name when Kosov visibly began to slow once more. For the benefit of the tape, Danilov said: 'Finally we get to Pecatnikov, which we could have done in five minutes if we'd come direct!'

'I told you it was close,' said Kosov.

Close indeed, to the favoured restaurant, Danilov recognised: Glovin Bol'soj was only two or three streets away. He half expected Kosov to go through the connecting alleys to reach it, but the man didn't. Instead he pulled up within yards, in front of a huge, pre-revolutionary building which at first appeared a blank-walled, unlit block. Only when they went through a passage into an inner courtyard was there any sign of life or even habitation, which even then was still dimly lit.

Danilov guessed they were going into one of the apartments, but they didn't. Kosov led towards a far basement corner, where there was a brighter light for the stairs leading down, but no nameplate to mark what it was. He absorbed everything as he followed Kosov, appreciating the absolute security. It was not, he acknowledged, protection against any sudden raid by a law enforcement agency. This was security against rival gang incursions, and was perfect. He hadn't seen the surveillance, but the passage from the road would somehow be constantly monitored: any suspected entry would be identified halfway along and the occupants of whatever it was in this far corner warned before the intruder reached the courtyard. Danilov guessed there were enough exits from the rabbit warren he was entering for it to be cleared before an interloper began to cross the square.

Directly inside the basement entrance was a small, curtained-off vestibule with a reception counter to the left. An extremely attractive, heavily busted girl in a blouse too tight and too low smiled at him. The gold-adorned man from the Metropole blocked a further curtained entrance to whatever lay beyond: Danilov could hear the muttered noise of people. The man smiled, too, and advanced towards Danilov, hands familiarly outstretched for a pat-down search.

Danilov extended his own, halting hand. He'd have to concede, but it would be a mistake not to protest, now and later. This was the only chance he'd get: if he failed tonight, here, he failed in everything.

'He's OK. I asked,' tried Kosov.

'Orders,' said the man, simply.

Would it only be a weapon search? Or would the man be feeling for a wire, too? Whatever, Danilov was glad he hadn't gone along with Cowley's suggestion. 'This once,' he accepted, tensing against the man's hands going over his body. He would have welcomed the Militia – certainly the Militia at Petrovka – being this cautious.

'OK,' approved the man, stepping back.

'Who was on guard when you were at the hotel?' asked Danilov.

The man smiled again but didn't answer.

A club, decided Danilov, as he pushed through the curtain. Hardly a public one, if every customer had to endure a body search. Another records check for Pavin tomorrow, to discover in whose name the property was registered. The room was very small, circular until the far end, where it flattened out into a roughcast, whitewashed wall, in which were set three doors, all closed. There was a small dance floor, surrounded by tables and chairs, and a tiny stage to the left. That, too, was curtained-off: to one side, from a glassed cubicle, another extremely attractive girl with displayed cleavage rivalling the receptionist's was at a turntable. The music was quiet, American jazz. No-one was dancing. Danilov guessed there were about thirty people in the room, far more men than women. They were smoking well-packed Western cigarettes; the emptying bottles on the tables bore the labels of Western gins and whiskies. Three or four girls were alone at tables: he wondered if Lena Zurov had come here often.

No-one paid them any noticeable attention as they skirted the dance floor towards the far wall. Danilov expected them to go through one of the doors, but Kosov stopped at a table almost hidden by the unused stage, where a dark-haired, sallow-faced man sat alone.

He smiled up at Danilov, indicated a chair and said: 'It's good to meet you.' He extended his hand but didn't stand.

Danilov didn't sit or accept the offered hand. 'I will speak with Arkadi Pavlovich Gusovsky.'

The man lowered his hand but remained smiling. 'You're speaking to him.'

Danilov breathed out, heavily. He hadn't expected, after all the caution so far, immediately to meet the Mafia leader, but they should at least have surrounded whoever this substitute was with others, to make it look right. It was unthinkable Gusovsky would have greeted him without escorts. Unthinkable, too, that the real ganglord would have smiled at the handshake refusal. 'I've been through enough theatrical shit tonight. I'm not going through any more. Go and tell Gusovsky I want to meet *him*. I don't care how many others he wants around him, but I'll only deal with him direct. He's got five minutes to make up his mind. If I'm not with him in that time – and satisfied that it *is* him I'm meeting – I'll leave, having wasted my time. Tell him in those words. You got all that?'

The smile faded, into blankness. 'I'm not used to being spoken to like that,' tried the man.

'I'm sure you are,' said Danilov. 'And you're wasting

time. Tell Gusovsky I want to talk about murders. And drug deals in Italy. And about fund-holding corporations in Switzerland. And about all the mistakes you've made and are going to go on making – make worse, in fact – unless we speak.' He looked at the watch that wasn't working. 'You've already lost one of your five minutes.'

For a moment or two longer the Mafioso remained where he was. Then he pushed the chair back, noisily, and disappeared through the left-hand door.

'What are you doing!' hissed Kosov, beside him.

Briefly Danilov had forgotten the other policeman. Kosov's face was twisted in frightened bewilderment.

'Establishing ground rules,' said Danilov. It seemed a long time since he and Cowley had done the same.

'I told you . . .'

'. . . I'm here now, Yevgennie Grigorevich! From here on I'll decide how to behave: what to say and how to say it. You don't have to be involved, associated with it.'

'This is madness . . . ! Terrible . . . !'

'You know what Gusovsky looks like? I want a sign that it's him.'

'No . . . no . . .' muttered Kosov, looking nervously around the room. 'This isn't right . . . not how it should have been . . .'

Danilov wasn't sure whether that was a denial or a refusal: either way it didn't matter. Kosov was clenching and unclenching his hands, eyes rolling in a fruitless search for nothing in particular: probably, Danilov thought, it was escape. An ancient record on the turntable – Louis Armstrong singing 'Mac the Knife' – had reached the phrase about oozing blood, which Danilov hoped didn't turn out to be appropriate. He guessed it was an in-joke against them, for the benefit of the others in the room. They were being stared at now, standing obviously by the stage. 'I'll make my arrangements my way. If they don't like it, it's my . . .' He paused at the cliché shared between East and West. '. . . It's my funeral.'

Kosov was too disoriented to make any coherent response: he positively moved back, as if retreating, when the man

376

who had greeted them emerged from the nearby door, trying to compensate for his own rebuff by simply jerking his head, for Danilov to enter. Kosov shifted, from one foot to the other, but was spared a problem he didn't want by a further head movement, forbidding him to follow into the inner sanctum.

Beyond the door was a small, private dining room. There were only three tables. At one sat two men, the older with unnatural milky eyes. His companion was totally non-descript apart from the physical thinness of a man suffering a prolonged illness. His face had a chalk-white pallor and his skin, particularly on the hands he now held in front of him, resting his chin to examine Danilov, looked paper thin, as if it might tear. The appearance was worsened by a crumpled grey suit that was too large, sagged off the shoulders, the jacket sleeves partially covering the hands, despite the way he was sitting with his arms up. There was a finger-wide gap between his shirt collar and his neck.

Only one of the other tables was occupied. One man, wearing a turtlenecked sweater under a chamois bomber jacket, was a stranger; the other two had completed the watching group at the Metropole, with the gold lover outside. Definitely street people, Danilov decided. And he knew who the blind man was: so the chances were it *was* Gusovsky he was meeting. There were bottles and glasses on each table, but no food.

Danilov went to the table with the two men and sat, uninvited. To the thin man he said: 'I still don't know who you really are : . .' He half turned, to address directly the man unable to see him. '. . . But I know you, Aleksandr Yerin . . .'

The most obvious stir at his awareness of a name came from the escort table: there was one very noisy grating of a chair. Yerin leaned forward, so adjusted to his disability that if the eyes had not been opaque it would have seemed he could see. Danilov's impression was that he was sniffing, like an animal sniffs the scent of another, to gauge danger. Only the thin man remained totally expressionless. Still with his chin on his hands, he said: 'I am Gusovsky.' The voice was surprisingly deep, a rasping timbre.

'I hope you are,' said Danilov.

'My man outside said you were insolent,' said Gusovky, as if he were confirming something. He pointedly poured red wine into his own and Yerin's glasses. There was a third glass on the table: the man put the bottle down without offering it to Danilov.

Danilov thought it was an artificial gesture, like so much else. 'I'm guessing it was Georgi Visco. He should have carried off the deception better than he did, with his KGB training. And you should have put people around him, like you have here. That was bad attention to detail. And the three you sent to watch my meeting with Kosov, to make sure I was alone, were a bad choice, too. They couldn't have been more obvious with signs around their necks.' Danilov was surprised how easy he found it to force the arrogance.

There was a fresh shuffle of movement from the adjoining table, at the introduction of the KGB colonel's name and the personal sneer at two of the men sitting there. Gusovsky's mouth tightened just very slightly, at the unprecedented lack of respect. 'So they did talk, in Rome?'

'You can't be sure of that, can you?' He had to be extremely careful not to connect source to fact: everything had to confuse them, worry them as much as they had to be worried, to allow him this close, this quickly. He breathed in, readying himself. A lot had been known before – and then afterwards – by the KGB who were now spread among all the Families in the city, hadn't it? he said. Neither replied, listening like statues. They shouldn't forget, he suggested, that it was virtually instinctive for the KGB, even disbanded, to infiltrate organisations to gain control. Had they thought about that, being overthrown not by rival gangs but by recruits they thought loyal? And then there was America. A lot had come out there. And Switzerland.

Opposite him Gusovsky and Yerin remained impassive, not drinking, not interrupting, not doing anything.

One by one, Danilov enumerated the Chechen names he *had* obtained in Rome, but which could have come from many other leaks. He threw in, quite superfluously, a lot of Genovese and Italian Mafia identities, to thicken the smoke-screen. How much did Gusovsky think the Genovese consiglierie and the Liccio clan had to pass on? How certain would Gusovksy be there wasn't an informant here in Moscow, deep in their own organisation? Sure he'd created sufficient obscurity, Danilov concluded: 'You couldn't plug all the leaks even if you knew where they were.' He didn't want, this early, to introduce the Geneva *anstalt* and the attempted Chechen take-over.

'So we know what you've got,' accepted Yerin. The man spoke softly but with precise pronunciation, for every word to be heard.

'I don't think you do,' further lured Danilov.

'What do you want?' demanded Gusovsky. It was a contemptuous question from a man accustomed to dispensing favours to the frightened or the bribable.

Danilov allowed some silence. 'I'm not the supplicant. You are.'

'Don't treat us like fools.'

Danilov thought the blind man had difficulty controlling his voice that time: they really weren't accustomed to anything but abject respect. 'Let's not treat each other like fools.'

Gusovsky's mouth tightened further, and his pallor accentuated an angry redness. 'We were told you wanted to discuss things of mutual interest.'

'More your interest than mine.' Very soon now, he'd find out if Kosov really had kept the past to himself. Or whether he had offered it to ingratiate himself with these men, to arm them with the sort of pressure they always sought.

'Why don't you tell us what you think our interests are?' demanded Gusovsky. He indicated the bottle at last. 'Take some wine.' It was an order, not an invitation.

Danilov was tempted to accept but wait for the other man to pour, but he didn't. He had no intention of obeying the expected rules by acting cowed or subservient, even on their own territory, but there was no benefit in unnecessary antagonism. He filled the available glass and drank, but without any meaningless toast. 'I think one major interest is in forming an association with other Mafia groups, in Italy and in America and in Latin America. I think you believe you have funds available, to finance that association. I think you're concerned how endangered that intention is, by the arrests in Italy: you'd be stupid if you weren't. There's the confrontation with the Ostankino . . .' He let the recital trail, waiting intently. Would they pick up on the half-intentional clue about imagined funds? He hoped not, this soon. He did not want to play every card without an indication of what they were holding, in their attempt to outplay him.

Neither responded at once. The sightless Yerin bent slightly sideways to the other man, deferring to him the right to speak first, which Gusovsky eventually did. 'Quite a catalogue!'

'Your shopping list, not mine.' They were going to trap him, if he didn't soon get what he expected thrown back at him. Make me bargain, thought Danilov desperately.

'The Italian arrests didn't come from here? It was American information?' said Yerin.

Kosov the faithful conduit! thought Danilov. 'That's how it happened. From America.'

'You work closely with the American?' asked Gusovsky.

'Yes,' embarked Danilov, cautiously. This was the way he'd wanted it to go: the opening hand, card for card.

'He confides in you?' asked Yerin.

They were close to overplaying, thought Danilov: or in too much of a hurry. 'There's a full exchange.'

'There are probably some things he doesn't share with you,' suggested Gusovsky. He smiled for the first time, pleased with himself: the dentures were too large for his mouth, as if they had been made when he was much fuller featured, or he had borrowed them from someone else.

Danilov began to revise his opinion of the man as non-descript. He was unsure whether to pre-empt them about the photographs or let them over-extend with their announcement. Give it a little longer, he decided. 'I doubt it.'

There must have been some sort of shelf or container beneath the table and a signal between them Danilov didn't see. Yerin knew immediately where to reach. He passed the package to the expectant Gusovsky who in turn offered it across the table. 'Isn't it strange, how some men get so much pleasure from screwing whores?'

Danilov refused to accept them, stranding the Mafia chief with them unlooked-at in his hand. 'Those!' said Danilov. 'I thought Lena looked very pretty. Fantastic body. I've never considered the male motivation, until you mentioned it, but I've always been curious why girls as attractive as she was become prostitutes. I would have thought it would be easy for them to get grateful husbands. Perhaps it isn't so simple, in Moscow. Or perhaps it's just sex: that they like variety. You didn't have to kill her, though. That was panic, after the Italian arrests. Stupid.'

Danilov's nonchalant dismissal of the blackmailing pictures – the only part of the encounter for which he was half prepared – and the obvious fact he'd already known about something he didn't regard as a threat, caused the greatest shock of anything he'd said or done since entering. Gusovsky remained with them in his outstretched hand for several moments before putting them on the table. For the first time Yerin was disoriented, moving his head jerkily as if he'd lost the direction from which the voices were coming. There were audible sounds of astonishment from the other table.

Danilov was savouring the moment, believing he had achieved precisely what he wanted, when Gusovksy's remark exploded in his mind. He connected it with Pavin's detailed account of Lena Zurov's murder and for the briefest moment he had the physical sensation of tightness, all over his body, a ballooning of excitement. It was only a guess, he warned himself: a wild, snatch-in-the-air guess. But one he could follow and possibly prove, because as always Pavin had been meticulous. And this time it would be done right.

'You don't think it would be embarrassing if these photographs showing a woman later murdered with an American pistol reached newspapers here and in America?' challenged Gusovsky.

'Cowley will have to resign, certainly,' agreed Danilov. 'But he's already decided to do that. And it will be an

American embarrassment. It won't affect what happened in Italy, or influence any prosecutions I originate here . . .'

'You sure about that?' interrupted Yerin.

They *did* know about his compromising past! At least he had the confirmation: could calculate from now on from *knowing*, not from guessing. 'Yes, I'm sure about that,' he lied, grateful there was no uncertainty in his voice.

Yerin dipped sideways again, once more for Gusovsky to offer a photograph, which he did by sliding it across the table. And this time, the shock was Danilov's.

It was fortunate he was looking down, concealing any facial surprise, although he didn't think he showed much. The glare of the camera flash had shown up the fade in Olga's black dress. She was caught looking vaguely surprised, the smile slack, as if she were slightly drunk, which she probably had been. From his later visit there, Danilov was able to recognise the balcony of the nightclub on Tverskaya.

'You might not recognise her with her clothes on,' said Gusovsky. 'The girl beside your wife is Lena Zurov.'

'I know,' said Danilov, looking up, sure he'd regained his control. 'It was the night Yevgennie Kosov took her to Nightflight. I was in Washington at the time.' Once more his casual acceptance discomposed them. Inwardly he boiled: some day, somehow, he was going to make Kosov hurt in every way possible, and he didn't give a damn about any retribution the man might attempt against him.

'Kosov told you!' blurted Yerin.

'No. My wife did. Was there any reason why she shouldn't have done?'

'Doesn't that compound the embarrassment though?' persisted Gusovsky. 'A cocksucking whore who serviced your American partner, also at a nightclub with your wife?'

'It will make headlines,' agreed Danilov. He put a sneer into his voice. 'But think about it far more sensibly than you obviously have, so far. If I brought against you, personally, the charges I can – and then a lot more against people in your organisation, which I also can – wouldn't that show *exactly* what those photographs are; a cheap and clumsy blackmail which didn't work anway? Cowley's already decided to quit.

And Olga would be shown to have been what? A guest at a nightclub, taken there by a policeman friend, innocently having her photograph taken with a woman she didn't know was a whore . . .' It was sounding far better than he'd hoped. '. . . Balance it,' he said, making it sound like an order. 'Murder, extortion, massive theft and a huge drug-smuggling operation on the one hand. On the other a drunken man tricked by a whore and a naive woman, inveigled by a crooked policeman . . .' He smiled. 'I think I've won, don't you?'

'Now let's get . . . !' began Gusovsky, outraged, but the calmer Yerin talked over the other man in his soft but clear voice.

'From what you've just said it would seem so. But there's a lot more we need to know, because so far you've talked in riddles. I think you'd better start discussing things properly. So we'll all understand what we're saying to each other.'

Danilov did not, at this stage, want to go one step further. But he needed to end everything on his terms and with them even more unsure. He hoped his luck would hold. He looked briefly to the second table, aware of the bewilderment of the three men who had never before witnessed Gusovsky or Yerin treated with such contempt. He said: 'These others aren't necessary. From now on the discussion will just be between the three of us. I want them out of the room.'

'*You* want them out of the room?' boomed Gusovsky, incredulous.

'That's what I said.'

'I don't know what the hell you think you're doing, what you're saying!' erupted Gusovsky, his anger finally taking over, which was what Danilov had hoped. 'Have you any idea who you are talking to? What we can do to you? You're a little person, you hear . . . ?' He held out his thumb and forefinger, but in a narrowing gesture, not like Kosov's in the hotel bar, earlier. 'That little. That's all. You can't make demands, about anything. That's what *we* do. So now you start showing respect! You sit there like the little person you are and you say what you think you've got that's so important and you say please and you say thank you . . .'

The man stopped, breathlessly. He gulped, heavily. 'You've annoyed me, little man. It's not good for anyone, when I lose my temper.'

Perfect, judged Danilov. It could still fail – he wouldn't know he'd succeeded until he was outside in the street, and not be sure even then – but he thought he'd got away with it. Why did they always defeat themselves by arrogance! 'So you're not going to tell them to leave?'

In front of him Gusovsky visibly trembled, the patchy redness against his normal complexion making him look ridiculous, like a painted clown. It was Yerin, again, who better suppressed his rage. 'You've been told what to do.'

Here comes the test, thought Danilov. He pushed his chair back, standing. He was conscious of the three bodyguards instantly coming up, too, but he did not look at them, remaining staring down at the two Mafia chieftains. '*I* control the *Svahbodniy* holding in Switzerland, not Raisa Serova! Let Kosov know when you want to talk again.'

All three guardians were barring the exit when he turned, and Danilov felt a stir of uncertainty. Without looking behind him, he said: 'Tell them to get out of the way.'

It seemed a very long time before they moved, although later Danilov guessed it could only have been a minute or two: not even that, just seconds. It must have been a gesture, because no-one spoke behind.

Kosov was at the table by the dance floor. He rose the moment Danilov emerged, scurrying alongside as he continued towards the outer door.

'What happened?' demanded Kosov, anxiously.

'I annoyed them,' admitted Danilov.

It pleased Danilov to terrorise Kosov further by refusing to discuss the encounter, beyond saying he expected the Chechen to want another meeting. Just to drive Kosov to the edge – an edge over which he was now absolutely determined to push the bastard, for all he had done – Danilov warned Kosov they might want to talk to him, as well.

'You told them I hadn't misled them: that it wasn't my fault?'

'Of course I did,' assured Danilov, who had forgotten.

Kosov returned him to Kirovskaya, where he remained only long enough to phone Cowley and say he was on his way to the hotel. Olga asked why he'd bothered to come home if he intended going out again so soon: Danilov said something unexpected had arisen and left her blinking uncertainly when he kissed her, as he left. He wasn't sure why he'd done it, either.

Cowley had been drinking but wasn't drunk when Danilov got to the Savoy. For the first time, Danilov explained in precise detail what he was trying to achieve, concluding with the wild possibility that had occurred to him during the actual encounter with the Chechen hierarchy.

'You'll never get it all together,' protested the American, awkward in his gratitude. 'I can't believe you're trying to do this, for me! Why should you?'

'You were very necessary to me, in the the beginning,' reminded Danilov. 'And now it isn't just for you. There's Olga.'

'I don't know what . . .'

'Then don't say it,' stopped Danilov. 'It hasn't worked yet.'

'And won't,' insisted the impossibly depressed Cowley.

Danilov's first instruction the following morning was for the re-arrest of Mikhail Antipov. He put Pavin in personal charge of the seizure, with specific instructions that everything necessary in a proper investigation had to be brought in this time.

He didn't have to ask for a meeting with those in ultimate charge of the investigation. There was already a Foreign Ministry summons waiting for him.

It was not until the middle of that day that the hurriedly despatched Sergei Stupar telephoned Gusovsky at Kutbysevskij Prospekt. 'Our lawyer made an approach, claiming it was an investment enquiry. The *anstalt* is frozen.'

Gusovsky replaced the telephone, looking across to the blind man. 'The bastard was telling the truth! He *does* control it.'

CHAPTER FIFTY-SIX

The Justice Minister, Roman Barazin, was an addition to the group awaiting Danilov at the Foreign Ministry. Danilov guessed there had been a prior discussion, but his presence was not practically ignored, as it had been upon his return from Italy. He was, instead, the object of instant attack.

The Deputy Interior Minister, who had announced his supervision of the Organised Crime Bureau but done little to implement it, began it. 'You've flagrantly ignored specific instructions, by arresting the widow of Petr Serov! And Yasev, an executive government official! They are to be released.'

'I don't think they should be,' said Danilov calmly. 'And they're *not* arrested. They're being held in protective custody. To which they agreed. It was all made clear in my overnight report.'

Vasili Oskin was at once deflated. Smolin tried to help, a lawyer wanting more facts before committing himself. 'Why do they need protective custody?'

'I also want to know that: I've not seen the overnight report,' said Barazin. He was a fleshy, permanently red-faced man with a moustache as full as Vorobie's: because of the man's bulk, it suited Barazin better than the Deputy Foreign Minister.

Keeping to the sequence supplied by Raisa Serova, Danilov felt quite relaxed verbally repeating the woman's confession. He introduced Yasev's function in what, with the possible exception of Barazin, the government officials already knew, and set out the pivotal role of Vasili Dolya, the Director of the KGB's First Chief Directorate, in involving not one but two Mafia Families.

'We should still have been consulted *before* you attempted to interview Mrs Serova,' insisted Oskin, trying to recover.

'At our last conference I was authorised to continue the

criminal investigation,' reminded Danilov. 'It was Raisa Serova who inherited the control of the Swiss corporation from her dead father. I made that quite clear, at that conference. I considered interviewing her, after her lies at our other meetings, an essential part of that criminal investigation. I did not know Oleg Yasev would be with her until I arrived at her apartment on Leninskaya.' It was pedantic, and they might suspect he was stretching the truth to its utmost, but there was no way they could confront him. Caught by a further thought, about questions he still wanted to put to the widow and her lover, Danilov said: '*Has* Raisa Serova asked to be released? Or Oleg Yasev?'

Oskin frowned, irritated at the questioning turning upon him. Seeming reluctant, he said: 'I was officially informed, through the Ministry.'

'By whom?' pressed Danilov.

Oskin's frown deepened, but before he could speak Barazin said: 'What importance can that have?'

'I don't know, not yet,' said Danilov. He'd made a mistake, trying to get too much, but now he was enmeshed in it.

'Well?' demanded Barazin impatiently, but to Oskin.

The Interior Ministry official spoke looking with fixed dislike at the investigator. 'It was a senior permanent secretary, Konstantin Utkin. Why is that important?'

I don't know, but I'm sure it *is*, thought Danilov, the satisfaction stirring through him: Konstantin Vladimirovich Utkin was another of the three unexplained names in the letter Leonid Lapinsk had sent him just before committing suicide.

'Well?' repeated Barazin sharply, speaking this time to Danilov.

'No,' said Danilov, because he couldn't explain it, 'I don't think it has any significance.'

'You have untangled a very complicated situation, involving past and present members of the government,' said Sergei Vorobie, coming into the discussion. 'But not *everyone* is involved in a world-ranging conspiracy.'

'I don't look upon what we have so far learned *as* a success,' said Danilov. 'We still have three unsolved murders we are sure are connected, and one curious case of a prostitute killed in the same way.' They couldn't catch him out on that lie, either. But they would, later, unless he prevented the Chechen publishing the compromising photographs of Cowley with Lena Zurev.

'Nothing in Mrs Serova's confession changes the decision already made,' insisted Vorobie. 'The government officials who appear to have been involved will be questioned and required to resign. There will be no prosecution.'

Needing the guidance for an uncertain future, Danilov said: 'There has been an enormous amount of publicity, most of it regrettable. Two murders were in America: two others here attracting a lot of attention. How can they *publicly* be explained away, without any reference to how they're linked?' He should tell them what he'd done: was *doing*. A later explanation that it was an unresolved part of the enquiry wouldn't save him if he were wrong. Nothing would save him if he were wrong. So why tell them anything?

'That's for us to decide,' said Oskin briskly.

'No!' denied Danilov. 'Of course I know there is going to be the biggest cover-up possible: I've guessed that from the start . . . ' Which was why, he thought – enjoying the American phrase – he had already, for a variety of reasons, gone so far out on a limb. 'But how can we persuade the American administration privately, to go along with it?'

'Far easier than perhaps it will be to satisfy public opinion,' said Barazin, close to being dismissive. 'In the case investigated by yourself and Cowley a little over a year ago, there was intense pressure from Washington to allow the mistaken arrest to remain the accepted solution . . .'

It was brilliant, accepted Danilov, knowing in advance what the diplomatic blackmail would be: absolutely brilliant.

'. . . Our most recent psychiatric information, about the man detained here, shows indications of recovery. If that recovery were to continue I, as Justice Minister, would have to consider releasing him. A public explanation would have to be given, of course . . .'

There would even be such a preliminary psychiatric

388

report, Danilov knew, prepared by a puppet psychiatrist, of which the security authorities of Russia still contained an abundance, from the previous era. 'Which still isn't a public explanation for the murders now! This time we don't conveniently have a mentally deranged man!'

'Which is why I am taking part in today's discussion,' disclosed Barazin. 'I've read everything so far, apart from the woman's confession. I want your personal assessment of what we've got, to compare against our opinions.'

Danilov desperately wished he'd had time to think through his answer, to avoid leaving himself exposed. Cautiously, he said: 'In Italy I indicated to Zimin we'd reach an agreement, in return for his giving evidence here. The man knows Mikhail Antipov *is* guilty of the Ignatov killing. He hinted he knows about the lost gun, which could implicate Metkin and Kabalin, too. He claims to be a member of the Chechen *komitet*, and we know the Chechen tried to take over the Swiss fund, although we've only got the woman's word for it, no documentary evidence. If Zimin is that high in the Mafia organisation, it's conceivable he'll know what happened in America as well. If we make the deal, his telling us about America could be part of it . . .'

'It's linked with the embezzlement of the Party funds and the government, which you've been told must not come out!' broke in Smolin.

'Everything I have so far suggested would be restricted to a Russian enquiry which could finally culminate in a Russian court,' pointed out Danilov. Looking between the Justice Minister and the Federal Prosecutor and measuring every word, he said: 'We – you two, most of all – control the evidence and the prosecution presented before a Russian court . . .'

Barazin smiled, bleakly. 'A point well made. What else?'

He *was* covering himself, Danilov decided. He moved towards further protection. 'I have this morning ordered the re-arrest of Antipov, for further questioning. I'm convinced he knew the murder weapon would disappear. This time he won't have any idea what I've got: what I might have learned in Italy. So this time the interview is going to be very different . . .' If he told them what else he'd ordered – or intended – regarding Antipov he ran the risk of being caught out, because everything else still remained a guess. '. . . If you decide to offer Maksim Zimin the deal, there will need to be discussions between yourselves and the Italians. Possibly the return to Italy of Cowley and myself, to get as much as we can in advance of any trial of what the man can tell us, to satisfy Washington . . .'

Barazin gave another smile, more like a facial stretching exercise. 'This is good.'

Their acceptance was such that Danilov decided to press on. 'And I think it is important I continue the investigation, beyond what we already have and know,' he lured.

'Why?' asked Oskin.

'According to the woman, she has signed over control of the Geneva *anstalt* to the Chechen leadership. But we know, from the Swiss, they haven't tried to access it. I think it's important we find out why: for me to return there, for that purpose. Vasili Dolya was closely involved with creating the Swiss arrangement. I want your permission to arrest and interrogate him, *before* he knows there is not going to be a prosecution . . . And I want to talk to Raisa Ilyavich Serova again. As well as Yasev. I think there is more for them to tell. So I would resist their being released, until I can question them again. As I said, it is *protective* custody.'

'You're straying back into government problems again!' warned Smolin.

'Until we know *completely* what those problems might be, we won't properly be able to prevent that happening,' insisted Danilov, with unarguable logic. 'The investigation *isn't* properly concluded, not yet. It needs to be, before you can be entirely confident of avoiding any government embarrassment.' If he got it all, he even had a slender excuse for making personal contact with the Chechen leadership.

Danilov was kept only briefly outside Vorobie's ornate office, for the government officials to have another un-recorded discussion. When he was recalled, Barazin said: 'You are to continue with the investigation. And with providing daily reports, through Federal Prosecutor Smolin.

Which will include *everything*. We will open discussions with Washington on other matters.'

'Thank you,' said Danilov. They would never know how complete his gratitude was. He hoped they never knew, either, how he'd twisted his requests.

A lot awaited Danilov when he returned to Petrovka. Mikhail Pavlovich Antipov had been re-arrested, on this occasion after a minor struggle, and was in a holding cell. At the Ultiza Fadajeva apartment he had once again been in bed with the mother-and-daughter whores. Danilov hoped that was encouraging.

'And the rest?'

'Cowley's already collected everything. He's waiting for you,' said Pavin.

'What about the hair?'

'That's what caused the struggle. He's got this' – Pavin hesitated, realising Danilov wore his hair in a crew cut too, 'short hair,' he resumed. 'But we got enough.'

The telephone number Raisa Serova had provided for the Ostankino Family had been traced to a large house on Wernadski Prospekt. Danilov ordered round-the-clock surveillance, supplemented at all times by photographs from which they could attempt positive identification to go with the names they now had. Yevgennie Kosov had tried to make contact on three occasions, always leaving the message he would call again. When he did, from the BMW, Danilov said he wouldn't be able to talk for at least three or four days. There were other developments which had to be handled before then: everything had become very tricky. When Kosov demanded to know what he should tell 'his friends', Danilov said just that. Danilov's final instruction to Pavin was to arrest Vasili Dolya, for which there was signed authority from the Interior Ministry. Dolya was to be held in solitary confinement, like Antipov.

Danilov and Cowley considered amusing themselves by going to the Metropole bar because they felt it was appropriate but didn't, meeting in the Savoy instead.

'You could just be right!' greeted the American, trying to

climb from his despondency. 'I've put an action-this-day priority on everything.'

'I'm certainly right about something else,' said the Russian. It only took minutes to disclose the pressure Moscow intended imposing upon Washington.

Cowley's initial, desperate thought was for Pauline, if the Russians disclosed who the real Moscow serial killer had been. It would destroy her: drive her from Washington, maybe even into a new identity. 'Doesn't anybody think of anything other than blackmail, for Christ's sake!'

'I don't see how your people can resist it,' said Danilov.

'Nor do I,' said Cowley. Please God don't let them try, he thought.

It took Danilov longer to recount the rest of the meeting with the politicians.

'Our luck can't hold,' insisted Cowley. Pauline could be faced with a double exposure, he thought: him *and* a mass-murderer husband.

'We're committed now,' said Danilov, equalling the insistence.

'I'll cable Bern we're coming back,' undertook Cowley. His message crossed one directed to him from Switzerland, from the case-monitoring police inspector Henri Charas, that a Swiss lawyer had made an investment enquiry about the *Svahbodniy* corporation.

'Why the hell has Antipov been re-arrested?' asked Yerin.

'I don't know!' pleaded Kosov. 'All Danilov said was there had been developments . . . that I was to tell you that.'

'Get him here!' order Gusovsky.

'He said three or four days.'

It had to be at the investigator's whim, Gusovksy accepted. For the moment: but only for a very limited moment. Softly, at his most menacing, the thin man said: 'This is very serious. We want to know what's happening. And why it's happening. And if you don't help us do that, the person for whom it's going to be the most unfortunate is you.'

'I'll do everything I can. I really mean everything!'

'Kosov is useless,' insisted Yerin, after the man had left the cafe at Glovin Bol'soj.

'We need him for the moment,' said Gusovsky. 'He's our link.'

CHAPTER FIFTY-SEVEN

The second finance conference was for the Russians' benefit, with Cowley little more than an observer, like the Swiss police inspector who travelled with them from Geneva to Bern: their practical involvement would come later. On this occasion Danilov needed guidance on the specific legal details of the *anstalt*, and the precise-minded Heinrich Bloch took an expert's pleasure in expanding his earlier explanation.

At its end Danilov said: 'So according to Swiss law, Raisa Ilyavich Serova still controls the corporation once it is unfrozen?'

'Absolutely.'

'And how is it unfrozen?'

'A formal declaration from America, with whom our treaty exists, that they are satisfied the assets were not intended for or the proceeds of drug trafficking,' recited Bloch, as if he were reading from the statute. 'In the circumstances, there should perhaps be supportive affidavits from the Russian authorities.'

'What if, covered by notarised authority from Raisa Serova, a new Founder's Certificate were presented, transferring control to someone else?'

'It wouldn't be effective with the *anstalt* suspended,' said Bloch at once. He appeared disappointed at what he believed to be Danilov's lack of understanding.

'What if it were no longer suspended?'

Bloch frowned. 'The transfer would need to be additionally confirmed by her authority sworn before a Swiss notary.'

Danilov felt a jump of satisfaction. 'So the transfer certificate by itself is insufficient?'

'My government protects itself with the second document. A Swiss notary has to be satisfied the person

394

surrendering the Founder's Certificate understands they are abandoning all rights.'

'This is always explained, at the formation of a company?'

'It is the law that it should be done,' said Bloch.

'But the transfer papers, by themselves would still constitute legal documents, in court?'

'If there were need for them to be produced,' confirmed Bloch stiffly.

'We've travelled from Moscow to hear that,' said Danilov. And got far more into the bargain, he thought.

Bloch gave a frigid smile. 'What has the investment enquiry got to do with this?'

'A great deal, I hope,' said Danilov.

'Do you want the lawyer examined?' offered Charas.

'No!' said Danilov urgently. 'He'll only be acting as a nominee anyway: I don't want anything to alarm him. Or the people he's acting for. What I do want are the transfer documents when they are presented.'

'You are sure there is going to be an attempted transfer?' queried the official.

'Positive.'

'I hope you fully understand what the regulations require.'

'Absolutely,' assured the Russian.

'And they will be accompanied by the necessary legal release from Washington?' persisted Bloch, a man for whom everything had to have a written authority. He directed the question at Cowley.

'Yes,' promised the American.

'And with supporting Russian representation,' said Danilov.

'You any idea what could happen if anything – just one thing – gets mistimed!' demanded Cowley, over dinner that night at their hotel. He was allowing himself wine.

'The money isn't at risk,' reminded Danilov. The legal requirements precluded that particular débâcle, but he wasn't so sure about other potential disasters.

'You think they'll collapse and confess?' demanded the American.

'We'll be lucky if they do,' admitted Danilov.

395

'It's still supposition.'

'I'm right,' insisted Danilov. He was going to test another guess when they got back to Moscow the following day: one he was intentionally not sharing with Cowley. The deception worried Danilov. If he were wrong, it was something the American need never know. If he were right, Cowley would learn about it, at some time. Danilov thought he could still explain it away to convince the American he hadn't risked their personal understanding. Or could he? What sort of man would Vasili Dolya be? He'd know soon enough. Unless Dolya tried some futile defence, it shouldn't take long. Danilov was surprised, now they were reaching what he believed to be the conclusion of everything, how little time it was taking to slot the final pieces of the jigsaw into place. Not one jigsaw, Danilov reminded himself: several. 'You'll advise Washington, ahead of whatever my Foreign Ministry ask?'

'They're going to be one very pissed off group of people,' predicted Cowley.

'They'll be happy enough in the end,' insisted Danilov.

The guess about Vasili Dolya did prove to be right.

There was almost an hour's delay on the return from Geneva to Moscow, and Danilov feared at one stage he would have to postpone the encounter, but they made up time during the flight, and Pavin was still waiting patiently at Sheremet'yevo. On the way into the city, he said there was a note waiting from the Justice Ministry, saying that Raisa Serova and Oleg Yasev had formally sought release from protective custody. They were being put off – as Danilov had requested – by the insistence there were arrests still to be made. Stephen Snow had relayed a message from Washington that the forensic examination on the Mikhail Antipov material would be completed within forty-eight hours.

The chairman of what had formerly been the KGB division responsible for foreign espionage entered the Petrovka office trying to maintain what would once have been inherent superiority like a piece of familiar clothing, despite the disorientation of solitary confinement. He was a small, pinch-faced man of contrasting mannerisms: his eyes flickered constantly, absorbing every detail, but his voice and movements were measured, every word reflected upon before being uttered, every gesture considered: Danilov didn't think the man would have ever done anything spontaneous or unpremeditated in his life. Then he remembered the reason for the interview. The failed 1991 coup had been a hastily conceived, disorganised shambles from confused beginning to quickly capitulating end.

Dolya wore civilian clothes – a grey suit, white shirt and muted patterned tie – but there was an Order of Lenin ribbon in his lapel. Danilov realised, for the first time, they both held the same rank of lieutenant general. His was an acting promotion, he remembered; he supposed that gave Dolya a slight supremacy, and he was glad he had retained, still without permission, the vacant director's suite. Yuri Pavin sat so unobtrusively in a far corner that Danilov wondered, despite the moving eyes, whether Dolya registered there was an official notetaker.

'Why have I been arrested? I demand an explanation!' said the man at once. The voice was high-pitched – although not yet from obvious nervousness, which Danilov hoped would come soon.

In their halcyon past the KGB had disdained any Militia authority. Probably, thought Danilov cynically, with every justification. He had to stop it becoming a game of verbal gymnastics. 'You have been shown the signed authority for your arrest?'

'Yes.'

'So let's stop wasting our time.' He put Raisa Serova's statement on the expansive desk between them, not needing it as a reminder, and took Dolya through every part that implicated him, from the university friendship with Ilya Nishin to the identities of the former KGB officers who were now part of the Ostankino and Chechen Families. As he talked Danilov realised it would still be possible for the former intelligence chief to deny the accusations, but towards the end Dolya discernibly began to wilt and Danilov

397

suspected, relieved, the confidence was more fragile than it appeared on the surface.

Dolya's instant response made the attitude understandable. 'I was obeying orders, from a superior office,' he declared.

It was confirmation, but not of what Danilov wanted confirmed. More bluff, he acknowledged, before continuing: not as dangerous but perhaps more desperate than the confrontation with the Chechen leadership. 'Whose orders, about the gun that killed Michel Paulac and Petr Serov?'

The eye shudder now *was* fear. The man's head moved, too, looking rapidly around the office, and Danilov reckoned it was the first time the man saw they were not alone and that the conversation was being recorded.

'I don't know what you're asking me.'

'Of course you do,' said Danilov, bullying. 'You know, because there's been enough publicity about it, that I've been to Washington. Carried out a very full investigation at the embassy there . . .' Openly lying but knowing there was no way Dolya could challenge him, Danilov went on: 'It's odd that you should say you were obeying orders. That is what Nikolai Fedorovich Redin told me.'

'The bastard said . . .' blurted Dolya, no longer thinking before he spoke, trying too late to bite the words back.

Danilov let the virtual admission hang in the air between them for several moments. 'He lied. So whose order was it? Gusovsky? Yerin? Zimin?'

The awareness of the names further disoriented the man. 'A message, through Visco,' mumbled Dolya.

'Your former KGB officer?'

Dolya nodded without replying, so Danilov repeated the question, making him say 'Yes' for the record. Having spoken, Dolya hurried on: 'I didn't know what it was for. I was just told to send it to Redin, at the embassy. That it would be collected.'

Danilov was thankful he'd excluded Cowley. Nikolai Redin, the still-serving security officer in Washington, had to be got out before his link in the murders was known by the FBI. Danilov accepted the most important part of the confession was yet to come. 'Who *did* collect it?'

'I don't know.'

'Don't be stupid,' said Danilov loudly. 'You expect us to believe your officer was simply going to hand over a gun to a complete stranger, without any identification?'

'Someone from the Chechen,' said Dolya, still trying to avoid an answer.

'*Who*, from the Chechen? I want a name!'

'Antipov,' said the man, mumbling again. 'Mikhail Pavlovich Antipov.'

'How?' persisted Danilov remorselessly.

'They met, somewhere near the embassy. A park.'

'Lafayette Park?'

'Yes.'

Danilov knew he could take any risk now. 'And Redin had to show Antipov a photograph, didn't he?'

'Yes.'

'Of whom?'

'Petr Aleksandrovich Serov.'

He'd got it! There was a sweep of lightheadedness, at the final success, but Danilov's satisfaction was at once tempered by reality. Cowley would have to know he had been cheated, which could damage their relationship. And although they could bring Redin home from Washington to avoid an immediate diplomatic confrontation, Danilov didn't see how Dolya – or Redin, for that matter – could be kept out of any eventual prosecution against Antipov, which in turn would be necessary legally to resolve a double murder committed on American soil. So the inevitable government embarrassment was merely being postponed, not avoided. Not my concern, Danilov told himself. Then – sneering at his own irony – he thought, I am only obeying orders.

The Federal Prosecutor accepted his call without Danilov having to persuade aides it was a matter of priority.

'We'll bring Redin out tonight,' agreed Smolin instantly, not needing to consult the other ministers. 'You're detaining Dolya?'

'Pending any decision you and the Justice Minister make.'

'What about Switzerland?'

'There's a comparatively easy way to get the money back,'

disclosed Danilov. He gave a brief explanation, promising a fuller written report overnight.

'Raisa Serova will need to be properly detained now.'

'I've already issued the order,' disclosed Danilov. 'Against Yasev, too.'

'Anything?' asked Cowley, when Danilov telephoned.

'Nothing,' said Danilov. All the other lies, to trick people into admissions and confessions, had been easy. This one stuck in his throat, close to being a physical discomfort.

'Sons of bitches!' exclaimed Henry Hartz. He'd summoned the FBI Director directly after the departure of the Russian ambassador, who had requested the meeting to talk of the wrongly-detained Russian mental patient showing signs of recovery.

'He make the threat openly?' queried Leonard Ross. He'd already alerted the Secretary of State to the possibility of the approach, after Cowley's warning. Hartz had said he wouldn't believe it until it was formally made. Now he did believe it.

'He didn't need to, did he!' said the outraged Secretary of State. 'Said his government felt they should bring it to our notice and that they would welcome our views.'

'There's going to be another request, shortly,' said Ross, who had two hours earlier received Cowley's account of the Swiss conference.

'Does that give us anything to bargain with?' wondered Hartz, when Ross explained.

'We could be difficult about it, I suppose: give them a bad time,' said Ross. 'But it ends with the same decision for us: can we have it made public that an insane Bureau agent was a serial killer, with a senator's niece as one of his victims? And that we did a deal to cover it up from everyone, including the senator?'

'Of course we can't!' accepted Hartz, exasperated. 'And they damn well know it. How about the killings here, in the current investigation?'

'Forensic are doing what they can.'

'I'm not going to do anything about getting their thirty

million back until we get an acceptable prosecution!' insisted Hartz.

'At the moment there's no way of knowing we're going to get that,' warned Ross realistically.

'So we'll have to deal, in the end?'

'Yes,' said Ross bluntly. A fair-minded man, he added: 'But they did it the last time. And we'd do exactly the same as the Russians, if we were in their position.'

'I like *making* the demands,' said Hartz, in matching honesty. 'Not having demands imposed upon me.'

The photographic surveillance of Wernadski Prospekt revealed a large house partially hidden behind a protective wall. There always appeared to be a large number of Mercedes parked around it. A total of twelve men were repeatedly pictured, who were assumed to be staff or bodyguards. Women came and went; none were thought to live there permanently. The written reports, linked to the photographs, talked of a very definite attitude of respect towards one particular man, a thickset, hunched figure who always appeared to move head down, sure a path would be cleared ahead of him.

'Yuri Yermolovich Ryzhikev?' queried Danilov.

'There's no comparison picture in our records,' said Pavin.

'There's bugger all in our records!' reminded Danilov.

CHAPTER FIFTY-EIGHT

The protective custody had necessarily meant their separation in male and female facilities, and Raisa Serova's first interest on entering Danilov's self-appointed director's suite was in Yasev, as his was in her. She came through the door a few moments after the man, who at once felt for her hand, smiling. Neither showed any awkwardness about the open affection, but then they hadn't at the moment of discovery, at Leninskaya. Raisa, as always, was immaculate, perfectly made-up, perfectly coiffured, despite having spent the past three days in near-jail conditions. They both appeared relaxed and confident. It wouldn't last, after he announced their formal detention, but Danilov guessed they would eventually be released, because of the government decision already made, and their sanitised version would be the one officially accepted. There should be some satisfaction, he supposed, in telling them they'd failed.

As Yasev helped Raisa into her chair the man noticed Pavin, waiting in his notetaking corner of the room and frowned, although only slightly. The same look encompassed Cowley, close to the window. Danilov looked, too, nervous of what was likely to emerge during the questioning: should he lie to the American, to preserve their relationship? Or retain his integrity and tell the truth?

'You've arrested them?' demanded Raisa at once. 'Is it all over?'

'It's all over,' said Danilov, which was not an answer to her question.

Yasev smiled at her again, more widely this time. 'So it's safe for us to leave?'

'You're no longer in danger, you mean?' came in Cowley, from the window.

Yasev looked uncertain. 'That was the point of our agreeing to come into custody, wasn't it? For protection?'

'We've been reconsidering some aspects of the case since our last meeting,' said Cowley. He was having to make a determined effort to concentrate: Washington's overnight message was that no decision had been reached on whether to agree to the Russian pressure. Which meant Pauline was still at risk.

The woman shook her head, bewildered. 'What aspects? What's going on?'

'The search for the *absolute* truth,' said Danilov, answering literally. 'You see, we don't think you've been totally honest with us. Everything's there, perhaps. It's just the order in which you've told it that's wrong.'

She made another head movement. 'You *have* the truth! We came voluntarily into your protection. We no longer need it. We will go now.' She started to rise, followed by Yasev.

'I agreed that it was all over,' said Danilov, stopping both of them. 'Not that the Chechen leadership is in custody. So far, the only one arrested is the man in Italy.'

'Tell us,' urged Cowley, 'did you still think there was a way to get the money?'

The woman and her lover slowly regained their seats. Raisa said: 'I was trying to find a way to return the money and get rid of the pressure. And protect my father's name. *That's* the truth.'

'No,' refuted Danilov. 'We've had the Swiss company incorporation rules explained to us. Where did you learn about the transfer of an *anstalt* Founder's Certificate? From your father? Or from Paulac? Maybe both: we know you would have had to go through the process when your father signed over the beneficiary agreement.'

'I don't know of the transfer regulations,' insisted Raisa.

With both possible sources dead, that denial was beyond challenge. Danilov said: 'Just one thing didn't fit, from the beginning. Just imagine, if it *had* worked! A perfect double murder and a thirty-million-dollar fortune . . . !'

'. . . On which to live happily ever after,' Cowley finished. He no longer had any doubt about this supposition of Danilov's, although there could never be sufficient evidence to bring a prosecution. He wondered why Danilov wanted to go through the charade.

Yasev reached out for Raisa's hand again: Danilov got the impression it was a warning more than a gesture of affection. At the same time, the ministry official looked directly at Pavin, industriously recording every word.

'That was the idea, wasn't it?' persisted Danilov. 'Getting the money and disposing of Petr Aleksandrovich?'

'This is ridiculous!' persisted Yasev.

'The one thing that always worried me – that I couldn't reconcile, however much I tried – was how the Chechen hitman who killed your husband and Michel Paulac knew the precise date and place where they would be meeting in Washington,' said Danilov. 'It couldn't have come from Paulac, could it? His loyalty was to a rival gang. And Petr Aleksandrovich was a clerk, standing in for you . . .' He looked between the man and the woman, hoping one of them might speak. Neither did. '. . . There was only one other person from whom the information could *possibly* have come. You, Raisa Ilyavich! You who always made the ongoing plans with the financier, at the conclusion of every conference. Finding you two together at Leninskaya helped us towards understanding: realising you were having an affair and weren't after all the grieving widow. And that affair has been going on for a long time, hasn't it? Ever since Paris. We've become very good at tracing immigration records: entries and exits from countries. We know just how many times you two shuttled back and forth, between Moscow and Washington . . . and we know, Oleg Yaklovich, that you hold an exit visa valid over the next month . . .'

'This is fantasy,' broke in Yasev. 'Total and utter fantasy . . .'

'But so *logical*,' took up Cowley. 'Paulac knew how violent these Moscow gangs are: you *told* us how he warned you. Called them killers. But you weren't frightened of the Chechen takeover. It was perfect for you. You could get rid of an unwanted husband and the financier close enough to have interfered. And you knew the money was safe because it remained yours until you'd legally sworn the necessary Swiss authority, quite irrespective of any transfer document you might sign here, supposedly giving everything to the Chechen. But they wouldn't know that: probably still don't . . .'

'. . . Who was there to stop you?' resumed Danilov. 'No-one connected with the 1991 coup could complain if the money disappeared. They would have incriminated themselves. And by the time the Chechen learned how you'd cheated them, you would have cleaned out the *anstalt* and been living as far away from Russia as you could. A thirty-million-dollar fortune was worth the risk of their trying to find you, wasn't it? And with that amount of money you could have easily got new identities, couldn't you?'

'If the Chechen hadn't tried to expand internationally as quickly as they did – and had a treaty not existed between Switzerland and America under which the account could be sealed – it would have all worked,' said Cowley. He pinched his thumb and forefinger together. 'That close!'

Directly addressing the woman, Danilov said: 'You didn't want the Chechen to get it wrong, did you? You even provided a picture of Petr Aleksandrovich, so the killer would know what he looked like.' Danilov detected a stir of movement from the window behind him, from Cowley.

'You're talking nonsense!'

'Dolya's confessed.' He was opening the way to lie later, to Cowley, he realised.

'I did not identify my husband to anyone!'

Yasev's warning hand reached sideways again. 'Fantasy,' he repeated. 'It's all utterly without foundation. Any of it.'

'Why have you a visa to travel out of the country?' demanded Danilov, of Yasev.

'We told you at Leninskaya, I was trying to find an acceptable way to return the money. If I could devise something, I was going to travel to Switzerland with Raisa Ilyavich, to help arrange for the transfer back here, to Russia.' The man told the blatant lie staring unblinkingly across the desk at the two investigators.

'But you hadn't found an acceptable way?' said Cowley, close to mockery.

'I no longer had to, after our last meeting. The *anstalt* was officially known about, along with Ilya Nishin's part in it: he couldn't be protected any more. It became a simple matter of repatriating assets I didn't have to concern myself with.'

It was Yasev and Raisa Serova who were really mocking them, Danilov decided: Yasev had certainly recognised the inconsistencies weren't sufficient for any prosecution. So what had they achieved, arranging this confrontation? The satisfaction of letting the couple know it hadn't, after all, been a foolproof scheme, he thought again. It seemed a doubtful victory now, no more than a sop to his own pride.

'No,' he agreed, stressing the sarcasm. 'It isn't something you've got to concern yourself with any more . . .' Turning to the woman, he said: 'And you are going to get your wish to give the money back. Every cent of it. That will please you, won't it?'

'Yes,' she said tightly.

Still not much of a victory, decided Danilov. 'Upon the authority of the Federal Prosecutor, you are both now being formally arrested, pending further enquiries.'

Yasev tried to bluster, demanding access to the Foreign Ministry and then a lawyer. Raisa's face closed like a mask and she said nothing. Yasev's parting words, as he was led away, came in a shout. 'You have no proof!'

'He's right,' said the American, from the window.

'And he knows it,' agreed Danilov. 'At least where they're going to be held now won't be as comfortable as the last two or three days.'

Cowley put himself directly opposite, on the other side of the desk. 'Dolya confessed?' he echoed.

'It was . . .' started Danilov, then stopped. He wouldn't do it! He could claim the confession was made to someone else – to an official in the Interior or Security Ministries – but he wouldn't do it. 'There had to be some way a Russian pistol got to America. Airport security is too tight for it simply to be carried on and off planes.'

'Redin, the Washington security man?' Cowley's voice

was dull, not outraged. He should have thought of it himself: might have done, if he hadn't been awash with alcohol and remorse.

Recognising the cliché before he uttered it, Danilov said: 'He was obeying orders. Dolya was, too. From the Chechen, not from the government. He told me about the gun and he told me about the identification.'

'Redin's back, out of American jurisdiction?' said Cowley, in further dull acceptance.

'Overnight,' confirmed Danilov. 'He would probably have been beyond your jurisdiction, under diplomatic immunity, anyway.'

'What made you realise?'

'Italy,' admitted Danilov. 'Just before we went into Villalba, and Melega realised neither you nor I were armed. I started thinking how we couldn't have been, unless we'd got special dispensation from the airlines. Our embassies were the only other way.'

'Another guess that turned out right,' said Cowley.

'We agreed at the beginning there might have to be a limit on the co-operation, for obvious reasons,' reminded the Russian. 'This was one of them.'

'I know.'

Danilov had expected more disappointment from the other man. 'And there's no way Washington need ever find out how it really happened: the recall could have been unknown to either of us.'

'I know that, too.' He'd have done it himself, Cowley acknowledged: had done things very similar during the serial-killing investigation the Russians were now using for diplomatic blackmail.

'No hard feelings?' pressed Danilov hopefully.

'No hard feelings,' assured Cowley. Objectively, he said: 'We're too close to the end for it to become a problem again.'

They realised just how close when Stephen Snow telephoned Cowley from the embassy: there was a positive DNA comparison, and forensic had also made a provable match with clothing fibre from the grey Ford. The evidence was on its way, in the following morning's diplomatic pouch.

'Which takes care of your two murders,' Danilov said. More pointedly, he added: 'And that of Lena Zurov.'

'How the hell can it ever be separated, for any effective cover-up?' asked Cowley.

'I don't know,' admitted Danilov honestly. 'But it will be. It's called the art of diplomacy.'

The shotgun scars were completely healed, although there was a vague tenderness when Larissa traced them on his arm and shoulder, as she was doing now. Olga seemed to have forgotten about the injury, after the first night.

'It'll seem strange, not doing this any more,' she said. They were in bed, in one of the conveniently empty rooms at the Druzhba.

'I'll be glad,' said Danilov. He was uncomfortable at the giggled recognition whenever he arrived at the hotel now.

'Thanks!' she said, in feigned offence.

'You know what I mean.'

'So the case is almost over?'

'There are still one or two things to sort out.' Which included a decision about officially prosecuting her husband.

'So *we* can settle things?'

'Yes.'

'I want to do it the way I said. The four of us. At the same time. Sensibly.'

'Yes,' agreed Danilov again. Would it be easier, all together? Or more difficult? Not easy either way. He supposed if they were together he wouldn't have to prepare all the words to ease Olga's feelings. The priority was to let her know she wasn't being abandoned.

'We need some furniture in our flat, first,' said Larissa decisively. 'Do you have any friends?'

'No,' admitted Danilov, knowing what she meant.

He detected a tiny sigh of disappointment. 'It'll be ridiculous trying to get anything from a State shop. We'll need to go on the open market. It would be useful to have dollars.'

'It'll have to be roubles.' Danilov was uncomfortable how quickly the temptation to fall into the old, compromising ways came to mind. His thoughts ran on logically. After tomorrow there would have to be another meeting with the Chechen. It was the one risk of the mistiming of which Cowley was frightened. Danilov was, too.

'You're not doing what you've been told,' said Gusovsky. 'Do you really think we'll wait on his convenience! This is all down to you, Yevgennie Grigorevich. You told us he wanted to talk about friendship and all he did was sneer. We're not going to be treated like this. And you're very stupid not to have realised it.'

'We're making you personally responsible,' said Yerin. 'You know what I mean, don't you?'

'Yes,' accepted Kosov, thin voiced. It shouldn't have been like this! It should have been simple, everyone making comfortable arrangements. Why the hell was Danilov behaving like this?

'So get him here!' said Gusovsky. 'Now!'

CHAPTER FIFTY-NINE

Holding Mikhail Pavlovich Antipov completely incommunicado for so long – and in far different circumstances from before – gave them the psychological edge of which the FBI's Behavioral Science experts would have approved as a disorienting device, but ethically disapproved of as a Fascist torture and outlawed by every legislation – up to and including the Supreme Court – throughout the United States. But Danilov and Cowley were not in the United States. Cowley had given it a passing, unremembered thought; Danilov not at all.

Antipov came into the interview room shuffling and stinking and arguably verminous. Because he – and his wardrobe – had been stripped of every article of clothing, he wore prison canvas made stiffer by the filth of earlier wearers. A ginger-speckled beard was once more furring his face. There was an indentation in the crew-cut, where the sample had been forcibly taken: Danilov saw that even hacked away the man still possessed more hair than he did. The gold Rolex on the list of confiscated articles was probably still working, too: after a brave remission, Danilov's fake Cartier had permanently expired.

But Antipov was animal-strong, not as eroded as Vasili Dolya or Maksim Zimin. But not, either, contemptuous and bombastic, like he had been at the first confrontation. Instead the attitude was wary, a predator knowing other predators, circling to define boundaries, the direction from which the sudden pounce might come. He looked intently at the clothes that had been seized. Most of them had been tossed into a pile – another psychological pinprick for someone as clothes-conscious as Antipov, and again guessed at by Danilov – near to Pavin and the recording apparatus. Some had been isolated. There was a fawn jacket, hung carefully from a specially brought-in metal rack. Next to it were trousers, also on a hanger over which they were just as carefully folded, and a shirt. All were sealed in plastic bags far thicker than normal cleaners' wrap. Next to the clothes, in a smaller plastic container, were a pair of heavy, dark brown brogue shoes.

'We've got you, in the end,' announced Danilov. The plan was for him to open, generally: Cowley had to take over when it became more technical.

The refusal to respond wasn't theatrical arrogance now but protective caution, waiting for the proper attack.

Danilov's attitude was different from the previous occasion, too, knowing he had every reason for superciliousness. 'For three of the murders, this time . . .' He gave a palms-upwards, so-what gesture. 'Which leaves us without a legal conviction for the Ignatov murder but we know you did it, so everything's wrapped up. We score four out of four. No-one could have done better than that, could they, Mikhail Pavlovich?'

'You're talking shit.'

'Oh, no!' corrected Danilov. 'This isn't going to be like last time. No evidence is going to disappear. And you know what? We don't even need your confession: not a word! How about that?'

'Fuck off!'

'Not before you know just how bad it is for you. Not before I've told you of the talk I had with Vasili Dolya, about how you got the gun: about the meeting with Nikolai Redin in Lafayette Park, to get the identification of Serov, so you didn't make a mistake. Doesn't that worry you, Mikhail Pavlovich: knowing the evidence they're going to give? And then there's Maksim Zimin, whom we're bringing back from Rome to testify against you, under the deal we've done with him and the Italian prosecutor . . .'

Antipov went back in his chair, as if trying to pull away from the litany. There was no outward indication yet, but Danilov knew the man was frightened: he had to be. And this was only the beginning. Danilov thought he was going to enjoy terrorising someone whose life had been spent terrorising others.

'. . . And all because of sex!' Danilov jeered. 'You know that? If you'd kept your dick in your trousers just for once – and not liked whores so much – I would never have thought of you . . .' He hesitated, knowing he had to be careful here because everything he said was being taped: so he couldn't refer openly to the Pecatnikov club and Gusovsky's sneer about men liking whores when the Chechen leader had produced the photographs of Cowley. It was almost time for the American to come in. '. . . Someone said something about men screwing hookers and I thought about how you were first arrested, in bed with the mother and daughter pair we found you with again this time . . . and then I remembered that there was forensic evidence of Lena Zurov having had sexual intercourse just before her death. Just couldn't stop yourself, could you? Told to kill her but you had to fuck her as well, didn't you? It excite you in a special way, fucking whores? Something to do with their having to do whatever you want, maybe?'

'This going to go on very long?' tried Antipov.

'You've got a lot to hear yet,' said Danilov, looking towards the American to prompt his scientific entry. 'We want you to know just how much we're going to produce against you to put you in front of a firing squad . . .'

'You ever heard of DNA?' demanded Cowley, taking his cue. Speaking more to the recording apparatus than to Antipov, for the benefit of tape from which the later prosecution would be formulated, he went on: 'It's the abbreviation for deoxyribonucleic acid: it's found in the nucleus of human body cells. DNA is the blueprint for the physical difference between each and every individual ever born, anywhere in the world. And so no two people's DNA is the same – apart from identical twins, and we're not discussing identical twins: we're discussing you. Scientists can extract an individual DNA tracing from any cellular material. And the best source of all is semen. A lot was recovered from Lena Zurov. All we needed was a comparison . . .'

Cowley put his hand up to his own head, covering the spot where the sample had been hacked from Antipov's skull: an

American defence lawyer would probably have argued physical assault and had the DNA evidence declared inadmissible. '. . . A minimum of twelve separate hairs are necessary for a match. And we got a lot more than that from you, so the FBI technicians at a place in Virginia named Quantico got three separate but quite positive sets . . .'

A nerve abruptly started to tug at the left of Antipov's mouth, jumping discernibly under his skin. It was discernible to the man himself. Antipov put his hand up, scratching as if it were an irritation, using the cover to swallow heavily, several times. The growing apprehension wasn't hidden, and both investigators saw it.

'That first arrest was always a joke, wasn't it?' picked up Cowley. 'Because there was the gun, briefly, there didn't seem the need for all the rest that should have been done. And which *was* done this time, seizing all your belongings for scientific examination . . .' Cowley reached out, picking up the plastic bag containing the shoes. 'You did a lot of shopping in America, didn't you, Mikhail Pavlovich? These are a very popular make of shoe. Florsham. The colour, ironically, is oxblood. But it wasn't oxblood the Bureau scientists found; it was human blood . . .'

He paused, opening a file on the table between them, where the enlarged photographs better identified the spot. 'See that!' he invited, pushing it closer towards the other man. 'Deep into the welt there, where the sole is stitched on to the upper part of the shoes? It's very strong twine, but it absorbs. That's where it was found. Blood isn't as good as other cellular material, for DNA discovery: red cells don't have a nucleus, so there's no DNA. It's got to come from the white cells, which means you need a lot of it. But there was a lot when you killed Petr Serov. So much I had the highway authority hose the scene down, when we'd finished with it. You didn't have any on your clothes – because we've checked them – and you may have wiped your shoes clean, but you did step in it and enough went into the welt to soak into the twine to give us a trace . . . a trace that's again been positively matched with the DNA of Petr Serov . . .'

The nerve near Antipov's mouth was vibrating now, and

he wasn't trying to cover it any more: 'Bastards!' he said, in weak defiance.

'There was other material on your shoes, which we can use,' continued Cowley. 'In the welt again, where it isn't easily brushed away. Minute particles of cement dust, but sufficient to make a batch comparison. There's more, in the cuffs of those trousers there – the trousers you wore the night you killed them. The Bureau have a special scene-of-crime vacuum device. Sucks up everything. They ran it over the entire area where Serov's body was and picked up a lot more. There was some in the Ford Paulac hired from Hertz, and on his shoes and trousers, too. Did you make him watch, when you killed Serov?'

Antipov's eyes were bulging, and he looked hurriedly around him, a rat looking for its escape hole.

Cowley turned the pages of the file. 'Here we are! All the dust was traced to batch numbers 4421 and 4422, manufactured by the Hardseal Cement Corporation based in Johnstown, Pennsylvania, and shipped two weeks prior to the murders to the Dart and Bell Construction Company of Silver Spring, Virginia. The Dart and Bell company are carrying out warehouse repairs to a block fronting the Potomac, at the bottom of Wisconsin Avenue: they started work four days before the killings. They're still doing it . . .'

'Awesome, isn't it?' goaded Danilov, to give Cowley a minimal break. 'See how closely you're tied in with everything?'

Antipov shook his head, swallowing heavily again.

'And then there's this!' announced Cowley, offering a glassine envelope containing four threads, one thicker than the other three. 'All clothing manufacturers keep batch records, too: all part of their quality control, which is a Federal requirement. Ever noticed how new clothes always have the odd pieces of cotton or fibre attached? That thicker grey strand there is polyester which accords absolutely in dye colouring to those pants of yours that held the cement dust. So does the cotton. Both, through the dye, were traced by the Bureau to the Fashion First company in Trenton, New Jersey. Their records showed the pants had been shipped, with the jackets, to five stores in New York and two in Washington, a week prior to the murders . . .' He had to pause, dry-throated. 'The polyester fibre and the three cotton threads were recovered from the Ford car, in which Paulac's body was found . . .' The American smiled. 'You know what I thought, when this case began? I actually thought it wasn't going to be helped much by the Bureau's scientific expertise. Just shows how wrong you can be sometimes, doesn't it?'

'We've told you what we know,' said Danilov. 'You want to tell us all *you* know?'

Antipov did. It took him four hours. When he came to the murder of Lena Zurov he said he had been ordered to kill her, without a reason being given, which was fortunate. The reference to the whore came before either expected it, and there would not have been time to switch the tape off if the man had named Cowley as the intended blackmail victim.

Danilov finally took the call he had been refusing, pleased at the fear in Kosov's voice. He guessed it was being made from the car, although the reception was very clear: Kosov must be parked somewhere.

'What the hell's going on! You any idea the situation you've put me in?'

'Everything's got to be timed just right. It's taking a lot of planning.'

'They say they won't wait!'

Danilov wasn't ready: wouldn't be until he learned the final decision upon the entire case file – with the exception of the intercepts from Kosov's car – that he had presented. All there had been so far was a formal acknowledgement from the Federal Prosecutor that it was being considered.

'Tell them they must . . .' Danilov hesitated, unsure if he could make the commitment. Deciding he had to, he said: 'Just two more days. Make arrangements for a meeting the day after tomorrow. Tell them I'll have the deal in place by then.'

'It's not going to work!' said Cowley, making his usual protest when Danilov finished talking.

'Yes it is,' insisted the Russian.

That evening Cowley received a copy of the official response from Washington agreeing to every demand made by Moscow. Danilov decided it was reason enough to approach the Federal Prosecutor rather than wait for Smolin to contact him.

Cowley decided it was reason enough for several whiskies in the Savoy bar, because it meant Pauline was safe from public humiliation.

CHAPTER SIXTY

Danilov went worriedly to Pushkinskaya. The conclusion had to have been reached at Ministry level – at presidential level, even – and should have been given to them from one of the baroque, chandeliered chambers, not the Federal Prosecutor's office. So perhaps the final decision had *not* been made. Perhaps they weren't going to be told in detail: there was no official requirement. Danilov hadn't thought of that until now. It was even more reason to worry. Yet Smolin had agreed to Cowley's attendance, which surely gave the encounter some semblance of officialdom. Would there be enough at least for him to go on with the move into which he was inextricably locked?

Maybe it wouldn't be what they'd already told him and upon which his entire plan was founded. Maybe they would after all go for a major show trial, naming and charging everybody, even the identified Mafia leaders. No, he told himself, bringing the see-saw down in the other direction. They'd diplomatically pressured Washington, using the serial killings, and Washington had agreed to go along with a limited prosecution. But did that limitation exclude any charges against the Chechen? It was the most obvious surmise, because there had not been any orders to make arrests and he would surely have been the officer-in-charge of any such operation.

Danilov sighed, beside Cowley in the back of the Volga: for every argument there was a counter-argument, for every reassurance a deflating doubt. He believed Kosov, about the Chechen impatience: so he'd have to keep his arranged appointment, whatever he learned – or didn't learn – today.

He was surprised by the reception awaiting them, guessing Cowley was too. It actually *was* a reception, although very low key: there was vodka and small dishes of *zakuski*, but only the three of them to celebrate. Nikolai Smolin played host, pouring the vodka, and made a self-conscious toast praising the success of the investigation.

Danilov felt matchingly self-conscious. He hadn't expected the open praise – and didn't think Cowley had either – but if the gratitude was to be as muted as this he thought it would have been better not to have bothered at all. Muted or not, it *was* a celebration of sorts, so the extent and degree of the prosecution *had* been determined. Tentatively he said: 'So all the decisions have been made?'

'We think so.'

'We,' isolated Danilov. Why was Smolin being left to make the announcement, if indeed he did intend telling them everything? Where were the others who'd felt it so necessary to involve themselves until now?

'I've heard from Washington there has been agreement on how the case should be prosecuted,' encouraged Cowley. He wanted the vodka, but had only taken token sips to respond to the Federal Prosecutor's toast. He knew the sequence Danilov wanted and was even more anxious than the Russian about whether it would be possible. He genuinely didn't see how it *could* work but it was the only chance of survival he had and he was clutching it, a drowning man hanging on to the thinnest straw.

'There have been a lot of exchanges with other governments, apart from America,' disclosed Smolin. 'With Italy and with Switzerland. We think it has been resolved very satisfactorily.'

'How?' demanded Danilov directly.

The prosecutor looked between the two investigators and for a brief, stomach-dropping moment both Danilov and Cowley thought the man was going to refuse to answer. Instead Smolin said: 'The priority has always been establishing – or perhaps confirming – confidence between governments . . .' He smiled bleakly at Cowley. 'Particularly in America, where the crimes began – or at least were thought to have begun. Washington have accepted completely there was no official Russian connivance in any organised illegality, through our embassy. That what connection there was came from the past, and from people and crime *of* the past, not the present . . .'

Danilov thought that statement stretched the known facts but he didn't consider interrupting with a question, wanting Smolin to talk himself out.

'There is no doubt the murders of Michel Paulac and Petr Serov have been solved, and the American government know it,' insisted Smolin. 'We have a complete admission, together with supporting and corroborating confessions and more scientific evidence than any other murder case I have ever known. Mikhail Antipov will be properly tried and properly sentenced, under Russian law. Every legal requirement will be satisfied. Legal representatives from the Swiss and American embassies will attend, as observers.'

'Then the rest must come out, publicly,' said Cowley, risking the intrusion from which Danilov was holding back.

Smolin shook his head. 'The trial of Mikhail Pavlovich Antipov will be in a closed court. Statements will be issued, at the end of each day's hearing.'

'How can that be justified, legally?' persisted Cowley.

'It would unquestionably have been a matter of state security if a Mafia cell *had* been operated out of an accredited Russian embassy, wouldn't it?' demanded the prosecutor. 'There is *every* justification for hearing and fully examining such evidence in camera, to prevent the sort of unsubstantiated sensationalism that followed the revelation of the Mafia names in Serov's possession.'

'And after the full examination of the evidence, it will be declared an unsubstantiated allegation?' anticipated Danilov.

'Which is the truth,' said Smolin easily.

'So how did Paulac and Serov get shot in the mouth?' demanded Cowley. They *couldn't* parcel it up like this! It would have to leak out!

'We're denying ongoing, entrenched Mafia presence,' said Smolin patiently. 'Not that there was *any* criminality. Petr Serov *was* involved in organised crime. But by himself, without the knowledge or assistance of anyone else in the embassy or the government. And Michel Paulac was also involved in crime. We will issue a detailed apology that a Russian diplomat was so engaged, at the end of the Antipov trial, when his sentence is announced. Which will be the truth, because we do regret it. Switzerland will do the same, which is again the truth, because *they* regret it. And Washington will publicly respond by welcoming our assurance that there isn't a Mafia cell in the embassy. Which again will be the truth, because there isn't.'

The prosecutor stopped, for them to assimilate the explanation.

It *was* possible, Cowley conceded, although still unsure there was not an oversight somewhere. As Smolin was setting it out, there were no lies, no dishonesty: just events and evidence sanitised to satisfy everyone and everything.

They *were* the facts, conceded Danilov: it was the truth viewed through a reversed telescope, the proper images minimised instead of being magnified. But it worked: simply, logically, acceptably, it worked.

It was the sceptical Cowley who tried to point out a flaw. 'What about the Italian trial? That won't be controlled, with the public excluded. The Italians have already publicised it as much as they can.'

'Publicised what?' returned Smolin, appearing to enjoy the debate with the two people most closely involved with the entire investigation. 'It will be a murder trial! A murder trial which will detail the smashing of a Mafia chain that was going to span the world! That's what all the publicity will be about. That it was a link-up to smuggle drugs will be a factor, but how it was to be financed will be a very incidental part of the prosecutor's case: certainly there will be no mention of funds in Switzerland looted from Communist Party sources, or of people in Moscow who until very recently still had political influence being involved.'

There *had* been a lot of exchanges with other governments, acknowledged Danilov. 'What if Zimin talks about it in open court, as part of his defence?'

'It doesn't provide any defence,' argued Smolin. Heavily he added: 'It might affect our thinking about returning him here to serve his sentence, though.'

'Which he will be told, before any public trial?' anticipated Danilov. It was easy to understand why policemen became totally cynical if they didn't become totally corrupt.

'There will be the need for you to go to Italy again, ahead of even the preliminary hearing,' said Smolin, answering the question without provably suggesting Danilov exert the pressure. 'You will need to re-interview him, about the evidence he can offer here, against Antipov.'

Danilov's first thought was that the trip would give him the opportunity to juggle lire into dollars conveniently to help him set up home with Larissa. At once he despised himself for it. Still wanting the information he needed to bring the case to what he would personally regard as its absolute end, Danilov said: 'We could charge a lot more people in the two Mafia Families here: badly disrupt a lot of organised crime.'

Smolin regarded him almost irritably. 'We have already badly disrupted organised crime. The people to whom you're referring, in both the Chechen and the Ostankino, were involved with the stolen money. Which they did not succeed in getting. So a crime was not perpetrated: the man who did steal the money is dead, beyond punishment. We know a lot of Mafia identities, which we didn't before. How they operate, even. That could be useful, in the future.'

Was it solely to control government embarrassment? wondered Danilov, giving his cynicism full rein. Or were there still unknown people in places sufficiently powerful to influence these judgments and decisions? He thought the question possibly provided an answer to an earlier un-certainty. Having made their arrangements and compro-mises, the other members of the government with whom they'd dealt before had now retreated into the background, never to be accused of political or legal manoeuvring. It made feasible his intended manoeuvring, too, so there was no benefit in his arguing in favour of prosecuting the Chechen. Instead he said: 'What about Metkin and Kabalin?'

The Federal Prosecutor gave another negative head shake. 'You took Antipov's confession. He never identified them by name. Just that he was told to laugh at your interrogation about Ignatov: that no prosecution would be made.'

'So there is to be no trial?' asked Cowley.

'They will be dismissed from the Militia, with the loss of all pensions and privileges, by a disciplinary hearing.'

'Raisa Serova?' queried Danilov. He didn't expect there would be another opportunity, so they had to learn everything now.

'America has agreed to withdraw any restriction on the *anstalt*. We are providing the supporting documents, as was suggested to you . . .' The prosecutor looked directly at Danilov. 'You will personally take her to Bern, to supervise her signing over the money to Russia.'

If he were present, the one uncertainty – the danger of the timing slipping out of sequence – was removed! And he had his answer, about any further Chechen prosecutions! So he could do it! He glanced quickly at the American, to see if the man had realised, but Cowley didn't answer the look.

Instead Cowley said: 'But not accused of any criminal act?'

'No,' confirmed Smolin.

'Yasev?'

'Dismissed, with the loss of all pensions and privileges. So is every other serving member of permanent government who's been implicated.'

The punishment of the old – but perhaps returning – days of Communism, thought Danilov: those not facing a court were being reduced to the status of non-persons. 'What's the post-trial statement, about Ignatov and the woman?'

Smolin shrugged, the wording both undecided and unnecessary. 'Rival gang fights: there's enough of that practically every day on the streets of Moscow. Whores get killed all the time. It hardly needs explaining.'

Cowley shifted uncomfortably. 'Washington is still your weakness,' he insisted. '*Why* was Serov involved?'

'What's wrong with the truth again?' asked Smolin. 'He was the American-based liaison between the Russian gangsters living there and whose names were in his possession – and the Swiss financier whose family came from a republic of the former Soviet Union. That's sufficient inference, for their connection. If the tie-up between Russian, Italian and American Mafias had been formed, there would have needed to be a liaison, wouldn't there? We can even speculate they intended using the security of the diplomatic mail as a conduit between Moscow and

Washington. Which is true again.' He straightened, briskly, looking between the two investigators. 'Anything left out?'

'No,' said Cowley.

'No,' said Danilov.

'There'll be something,' predicted Cowley, back at Petrovka.

'He was using us, like he – and the others – have been using us all along,' contradicted Danilov. 'We're the closest to it all, so we had to be the first: the filter. It'll be refined and polished and rehearsed, long before it gets to any court. By the time it does, it'll be perfect.'

'I forgot how good you guys were at fixing courts!' There wasn't any real criticism in the remark.

'Which you guys were happy enough with the last time and are going along with now,' retorted Danilov, unoffended.

'And the only poor bastard wrongly accused will be Petr Aleksandrovich Serov, the messenger boy who's going to be made out to be a diplomatic Al Capone.'

'You realise I can control the timing now, don't you?' demanded the Russian. 'That the one danger is out of the way.'

'It's the *Mafia*, Dimitri Ivanovich,' lectured the American. 'Danger isn't *ever* going to be out of the way.'

'After what we've been railroaded into doing!' protested the Secretary of State. 'You've got to be joking! Tell me you're joking!'

'We agreed he should get some recognition! He saved the life of an American agent, for God's sake!' argued Leonard Ross.

'They can go piss into the wind,' rejected Hartz.

'Danilov didn't put the pressure on us! He did his job. Bravely. We should do something,' insisted the more reasonable FBI Director. 'I thought it could be something unusual.'

'Like what?' said the Secretary, unimpressed.

'If an FBI agent had done what Danilov did, in the line of duty, he would have got our Medal of Valour.'

'We making honorary FBI agents now?'

'Why not?' asked Ross. 'That's all it would be: honorary. It's in my authority to give the award, doesn't require any special discussion or decision, and would have just the right touch, publicly.'

'God protect me from a liberal, legal mind!' said Hartz. 'I bet you never sentenced anyone to death in your whole goddamned career.'

'I did,' corrected the Director. 'Five, in fact. But I never condemned anyone wrongly. That's the important thing.'

At the end of five days the surveillance of the Ostankino had confirmed three more meeting places. Danilov had become convinced the thickset man was Yuri Ryzhikev and was frustrated he couldn't confirm it, although realistically accepting it was a professional disappointment. The information was just for background files, after all. He told Pavin to suspend the observation after a further week.

CHAPTER SIXTY-ONE

The detour around the Moscow streets was even more convoluted than before so Danilov guessed they were not going to Pecatnikov, the address he already knew and which would have made the precaution pointless. It was, he supposed, a sensible precaution for them to take: by now they would be frantic, not knowing if Mikhail Antipov had talked. Danilov hoped so. From Kosov's demeanour – and stumbled demands to know about Antipov's arrest – he certainly was. The man had insisted on three drinks before setting off, hands jerking so nervously he came close to spilling them, sweat leaking from him. He'd never properly finished anything he began saying, which wasn't necessary because it had almost all been complaints at the way Danilov had behaved, personally, towards him.

Danilov had enjoyed every whining protest. His determination to destroy Kosov was as strong as ever, but he was unsure when or how to submit to the Justice or Interior Ministries the dozens of tapes they now possessed from the BMW in which they were at that moment zig-zagging around the city. It couldn't be before Cowley left: they had decided to stick to the story of the bugging as an entirely independent American operation, with the tapes being surrendered as a departing gesture. Danilov was sure he could sustain the deception of not having known.

What he was even surer about, after the latest discussion with the Federal Prosecutor, was that Kosov would not be disgraced in a public trial, which was what Danilov had always envisaged: there would be an unpublicised disciplinary tribunal and an unpublicised dismissal, and that would be the discreet end of it all. No, he corrected at once. If they dealt with Kosov the way they had dealt with everyone else, the man would be stripped of all government privileges, so he would lose his worth to the Chechen and whoever else from whom he took bribes and favours. And he was going to lose Larissa. So Kosov *would* be destroyed: not publicly, perhaps, but in every other way. Danilov didn't admire himself for the vindictive satisfaction.

And if everything was to be resolved discreetly, maybe his own past – compensated for by what he had achieved at Petrovka – might be treated with less than an outright dismissal. His survival, at some level within the service, would be a minimal guarantee for his and Larissa's future. Olga's too. Recognising it as hypocritical, he decided nevertheless that he really had to remember to buy Olga some of the things she wanted when he made the trip to Switzerland. And try to convert some money into dollars, for the Tatarovo apartment. Double hypocrite, he thought.

'You any idea of the pressure you put me under?' demanded Kosov.

'You told me several times.' The man was becoming more coherent, although repetitive.

'What's Antipov said?'

'There've been a lot of interviews.'

'That isn't an answer! I can't work with you like this! I need to *know*!'

'He's talked about a lot of things. It comes down to what is presented to the authorities and what isn't.' Danilov liked the sound of it, believing it would be as good when he repeated it later. From the surroundings, he recognised they were coming into the district regarded as the Chechen slice of Moscow. He hoped the journey would soon end.

'So he's named names?'

They'd undoubtedly question Kosov independently. So there was benefit at this stage in the man believing he knew just how serious it could be for his paymasters. 'He's named everyone he knows.'

The only initial sound was a wheezing intake of breath. 'This is terrible!'

'Didn't I tell you everything was taking a lot of planning?'

'Did he name me? Had he heard of my connection?'

'No,' said Danilov, which was the truth.

This time there was a relieved sigh. 'What are we going to do?'

'Not panic,' insisted Danilov. 'There's a way.'

'What way?'

'I need to talk it through, with the others.'

'Tell *me*! Aren't we working on this as partners?'

No, thought Danilov: nor would they work as partners on anything, ever. 'I've got to judge their attitude before deciding what is possible and what isn't.'

The hitherto unseen monitoring cars swept by, light flashing, and Danilov recognised they had arrived. He recognised where, too. The cafe was hidden in an unexpected loop off Glovin Bol'soj, little more than an indentation in the line of houses, and was not as secure as the club to which he had been first taken. The only similarity was that it was in a basement, with a receptionist behind a small desk, this one not revealing as much cleavage.

The same gold-bedecked man was at a table just inside the actual restaurant. He began to rise when he saw Danilov, who shook his head in warning refusal: the bull finished getting to his feet, but didn't approach for a body search. A sign of concern, judged Danilov: they were letting him play his independence game. He was still glad he'd again refused the urging of Pavin and Cowley to wear a body microphone, which apart from risking everything would have picked up any reference to incriminating photographs.

The guard slotted in directly behind as Danilov passed, following him through the restaurant. It was a long, corridor-style room: Danilov guessed the doors to the kitchens, creating a break halfway along, formed the division between genuine customers intentionally positioned in the front and Chechen people in the booths at the rear. A group of intruders could not, unopposed, make the sort of still unsolved firebomb attack mounted in the last week or so on the suspected Ostankino restaurant in Ulitza Moskina: innocent people, unwittingly forming a human barrier, would be hurt or maimed, but the Chechen could escape through either the kitchens or the rear, with minimal casualties.

In the booth closest to the doors to the private dining facilities, Danilov recognised two of the men who had sat guard at the separate table at Pecatnikov. He smiled at them. They ignored him. Before he reached them, one disappeared through a central door, re-emerging almost at once and holding it open for Danilov to enter. Danilov didn't turn to check, but he had no impression of Kosov entering behind him.

Apart from Gusovsky and Yerin the room, set with four other tables, was empty. Again there was no evidence of any food before either man, although there was a wine bottle and two already filled glasses. As Danilov sat, Gusovsky poured wine into the third.

'We've been trying to make contact,' announced Gusovsky. The overlarge dentures were displayed in a supposed smile.

'I've been busy,' said Danilov. There really wasn't a lot to say, but they had to be too frightened at the end even to begin thinking clearly. He knew they would be.

'We know,' said Yerin. 'Why was Mikhail Antipov arrested?'

'Because you used a careless man,' said Danilov. 'Which I warned you about. Antipov made mistakes: dropped clues that couldn't be missed. He *had* to be arrested.'

'We didn't begin well last time,' said Gusovsky. 'We want to establish our relationship properly tonight. That's what we're meeting for, isn't it?'

'I hope so,' said Danilov. The humility must have taken a supreme effort of will from the emaciated man.

'We're concerned about the mistakes Antipov has made,' conceded Yerin, in his carefully enunciated tones. 'Not just before but *after* his arrest.'

'You should be.'

'Please don't be so aggressive,' said the blind man.

'I want you to understand how serious it is, for you . . .' Danilov hesitated. '. . . Personally serious.'

Gusovsky topped up Danilov's glass. 'That's precisely what we want to understand.'

'He's named you: both of you. Zimin too, obviously.

Told me everything he knows, in fact. Hierarchy, structure, at least twenty other names. All your locations of which he's aware. Rackets. What the operations are. Identified hits you've ordered. With his evidence – and what could come out in Italy – the Chechen won't exist any more. You two – and a lot of others – could go to jail for life. You'd be finished.' Danilov supposed he was in the Federal Prosecutor's position, the previous day: looking at the truth through the turned-around telescope. And it *was* the truth: in his panic to mitigate what might happen to him, Antipov had talked of every one of those things, in as much detail as he knew. Knowing he had to swamp them with a lot of that detail to satisfy them he *did* know, Danilov gave examples, selecting three murders – of other Mafia members – at random and itemising airport heists and hotels where they ran the prostitutes, taking particular care to include Lena Zurov to let them know their photographic blackmail had been further reduced.

They *were* swamped. So completely that, when Danilov finished, Gusovsky turned speechless for response to the blind Yerin, seeming to have forgotten the sightless man could not see the gesture.

It was Yerin who did speak, recovering first. 'You've come here.'

'Yes.'

' "Told *me*," ' echoed Yerin, verbatim, having identified another qualification in what Danilov had said.

'Yes,' agreed Danilov. The blind man was very definitely the cleverer of the two Mafia chiefs.

' "*Could* go to jail for life," ' continued to isolate the other man.

'Yes,' said Danilov, for the third time.

'So it could all be avoided?' said Yerin.

'I think so,' declared Danilov simply.

Tension eased from both men, as if the too-taut wires supporting them had been slightly relaxed. 'You'd better tell us how,' said Gusovsky. The resonant voice was still hoarse, from the shock of all he had been told.

'It wasn't possible for Antipov to tell us all he did, at one

429

session,' said Danilov, embarking on the unchallengeable lies. 'It took a long time: one of the many reasons I couldn't come any sooner. I was careful, how the interviews were conducted. It would be extremely easy to prepare Antipov's final confession in a selective way.'

Gusovsky smiled in understanding. 'How selective?'

'He *has* to go before a court. There has to be public satisfaction in America that the murders there have been solved and the killer convicted. But neither of you need personally be mentioned. We could cut out a lot of the other names, too. And most of the detail. It was the Ostankino who were involved with Serov and Paulac, not you. That Family could be substituted, a lot of the time . . .'

There were expressions of satisfaction from both men. Yerin said: 'You're talking of satisfying American opinion. Does Cowley know about your meeting us? About this conversation?'

Definitely the cleverer, thought Danilov. This was probably going to be the most difficult part. 'You have some photographs of him, with the dead woman. And of my wife with her, as well.'

The smiles went, replaced by expressions of wariness. Gusovsky said: 'So that's the exchange? The photographs – and the negatives, of course – for selectively presenting Antipov's evidence?'

'No,' said Danilov, causing the confusion he wanted.

'What then?' frowned Gusovsky.

'We haven't talked yet of Switzerland,' reminded Danilov.

'We were going to,' promised Yerin.

'Let's do it now,' suggested Danilov. Already knowing the answer but having to ask the question, he said: 'Did you try to access the account?'

'It's blocked,' said Gusovsky.

'With thirty million dollars in it,' enticed Danilov.

'At your last meeting you said you controlled it,' said Yerin.

'It becomes unfrozen the moment I officially inform the Swiss government the investigation is complete. Which it is,' said Danilov.

'Go on,' urged Gusovsky, beginning to smile again.

'The government are going to recover it. The bureaucracy will take time. I'm involved at every stage, but not directly *responsible*, if that bureaucracy goes wrong. Which bureaucracy often does . . . So I can orchestrate everything. I'll trigger the release the day after tomorrow. You've got the replacement Founder's Certificate: present it at the opening of financial trading that day. It will take a further day to be formally registered . . .' He paused, wanting the announcement to be dramatic. '. . . Four days from now, at the opening of trading in Switzerland, you'll have unrestricted control of thirty million dollars, maybe for as long as a week. It won't take you more than a week to move it all somewhere else, will it?'

Again – although more briefly this time – the Mafia leaders didn't speak. But again it was Yerin who did break the silence. 'I think we could probably do it in under a day.'

'So what's the deal you want?' persisted Gusovsky.

'I can't suppress or edit the evidence alone. Or by myself create the untraceable delay in recovering the money. There'll have to be substantial payments to others,' declared Danilov. 'I want a *very* substantial payment, for myself and for the others involved, a week from now . . .' He allowed the brief silence, although it was obvious he had not finished speaking. '. . . And I want, *before* I do anything about the money in Switzerland or about adjusting the statements that incriminate you, all the photographs and all the negatives . . .' He allowed himself to smile at last. 'It'll be payment in two parts: photographs first, then money. How does that seem?'

'I think that's very fair,' said Gusovsky, without bothering to consult the other man.

'We haven't decided what substantial means,' said Danilov.

'What's your figure?' asked Yerin.

'What's yours?' bargained Danilov.

'Our relationship is to be ongoing?' said Yerin.

'That's what we both want, isn't it?' said Danilov.

'How about a clear million dollars from the Swiss money?'

sugested Yerin. 'We'll fix a permanent weekly retainer: no need to hurry about that, we'll decide the figure when all this is settled. But it'll be good; very good. You name the Western car you want and you get it. Anything, in fact – clothes for your wife, whatever you want for your home. You're never going to have to worry about anything for the rest of your life . . .'

Was this the sort of arrangement Kosov, cringing outside, enjoyed? He had the car, and there was always the wad of dollars. 'A *clear* million?' qualified Danilov. It would be wrong to appear overwhelmed, although he was. 'Deposited in Switzerland, I think.'

Gusovsky nodded. 'How much, for the others?'

'Two-hundred-and-fifty thousand.'

'Is Cowley one of those others?'

'Additional.'

'So he knows?' said Yerin.

'How could he *not* know?'

'What does he say?' asked Gusovsky.

'All that is necessary for America is a conviction for the two Washington murders. He has no interest in anything else: anything in Russia. Unless, of course, it's forced upon him.'

Yerin gave a hunch of his shoulders at the threat, as if he were laughing, although he didn't. 'What does he want?'

Danilov smiled. 'To hear the outcome of my meeting with you today.'

'Suggest half a million,' said Gusovsky. He stretched across the table, offering his hand. 'This is going to be a very good arrangement.'

Danilov completed the handshake. Yerin extended his hand, sensing his partner's gesture, and Danilov shook that as well, then said: 'There is one problem, of course. Antipov will know his statement has been tampered with, when he gets to court. He's made it as full as he has, to get a prosecuting deal.'

'*His* problem,' said Gusovsky at once. 'You've got access to him: remind him we forgive him, so far. But just this far. He's to take things the way they're presented, to the

432

prosecutor and then in court. He'll have to serve some time, after the sentencing, until he's forgotten in the system. Then we'll get him out and he'll be looked after very well. He knows it's possible, because he's helped us do it before . . .' The thin man stopped and Yerin took over, almost as if they had prepared themselves, which Danilov accepted wouldn't have been possible.

Yerin said: 'If he doesn't – if he argues or thinks he can get a better deal from the authorities – you tell him we will have him killed. Not at once. For as long as it pleases us there won't be a moment when he'll be safe from attack: not even if he goes into solitary confinement. And he will be attacked. Badly. He'll be crippled and he'll be blinded and then he'll be killed. You tell him all those things, just like I've told you. He'll believe it because he knows we can do it.'

Danilov certainly believed it. Antipov would be tortured and killed: so would Maksim Zimin, when they learned the man was being brought back from Italy after his trial there. Danilov didn't think any precaution or protection he tried to evolve would prevent it happening. 'I'll make sure he understands.'

'A very good arrangement,' repeated Gusovsky.

'I want it even better,' said Danilov. 'I don't see any reason to go on arranging our meetings through Yevgennie Kosov. You'll have my direct line. I want always to be able to contact you quickly . . .' Danilov finished the demand by offering the card with his Petrovka number.

Gusovsky at once responded with the number Danilov already had, of the house at Kutbysevskij Prospekt.

'And I'd like the photographs and negatives. Tomorrow. They're no further use to you, now we've reached this understanding.'

'None at all,' agreed Yerin. 'Best got out of the way. Forgotten.'

'Be our guests for lunch here,' suggested Gusovsky.

'I'd like that,' accepted Danilov.

'Will the American join us?' invited Gusovsky.

'I'm sure he'll be delighted.'

★

'It could be a *really* good arrangement,' said Gusovsky.

'The best,' agreed Yerin. 'By releasing the photographs, we get the money. From it we can easily pay out less than two million dollars to get not just one but *two* investigators on the payroll. Once we create an account for Danilov in Switzerland, he's *ours*. We can bargain the details of wherever we pay Cowley his money to the Genovese in New York, which gives *them* a senior executive in the FBI. It's perfect! And it doesn't cost us a single kopek!'

'Antipov will have to be killed *before* any trial,' said Gusovsky conversationally. 'We obviously can't take the chance of his staying alive. Danilov will have to organise that, the moment he's taken the money and committed himself: he'll have to arrange for the bastard to be held where we can most easily get to him.'

'Let's hope the Liccio people can get to Zimin, like they say.'

'That would make it complete, wouldn't it?'

'More than complete,' agreed Yerin. 'We'll have won absolutely.'

'There's no-one in the world who can't be bought,' said Gusovsky, wistfully.

'Let's hope there never is,' said Yerin.

'You think they want to gloat, having me personally accept photographs of my dick in a whore's mouth?'

'Probably,' accepted Danilov.

'I've never met Mafia dons. Punks, yes. But never dons.'

'You want to know something?' said Danilov rhetorically. 'They frighten the shit out of me.'

'So what's it going to be like, later?'

'I don't know,' admitted Danilov, still honest. 'There's not much they can do.'

'You don't know that.'

'There's only one way I can go now.'

'Kosov going to be with us tomorrow?'

Danilov shook his head. 'He almost wet himself with relief, on the way back. But it was a great recovery. Before we got here, he was making plans for what it was going to be like when he's transferred and we're a team.'

'You any idea until today he was on the sort of deal they talked about with you?'

'There was the car,' said Danilov. 'But no, not really.'

'It occur to you we could handle this another way?' asked Cowley, solemn-faced. 'That we could accept the money?'

'From the moment it was offered,' replied Danilov, just as seriously.

'The Medal of Valour!' exclaimed Rafferty, reading the FBI internal bulletin. 'A Russian's going to get the Medal of Valour. What about us guys who stayed at home and did all the mix-and-match stuff!'

Johannsen grimaced at the apparent resentment. 'Stayed at home, safe and warm,' he pointed out. 'Not sat on our asses in the Sicilian dirt and got shot at with wolf guns.'

Rafferty pulled down the corners of his mouth, apologetically. 'Just talking, that's all. Just talking.'

CHAPTER SIXTY-TWO

The notification of the award was duplicated to Cowley, who reached Danilov at Petrovka slightly ahead of the official advice from the Foreign Ministry, to which it had been formally communicated by Washington. Cowley made the congratulations light, saying if Danilov kept thinking the way they'd both been doing before they'd parted the previous night, he could be the richest honorary FBI agent in history. The Foreign Ministry message was signed personally by Sergei Vorobie, who along with his congratulations called it an honour of which they were all proud: the information was being released to the press. Danilov telephoned Larissa before Olga with the news. Larissa said it was wonderful and could she tell everyone: Olga asked if it was just a medal or whether a cash award went with it.

During the morning, while he was arranging the following day's trip to Switzerland with Raisa Serova, congratulatory notes arrived from the Deputy Minister and the Federal Prosecutor. Nikolai Smolin repeated the praise when they spoke, for Danilov to learn that a Foreign Ministry lawyer would accompany him, carrying the Russian documentation in support of the official American release of the *Svahbodniy* corporation. When Danilov telephoned, Heinrich Bloch said that as well as Cowley, the American side was going to be represented by a legal team from the US embassy in Bern: the small luncheon party he had arranged, prior to the formalities, could now be extended into a small celebration for the American recognition of bravery, of which he'd just heard. He added his congratulations, too.

Despite the interruptions, Danilov still reached the Savoy in time for a drink with the American before they had to go to Glovin Bol'soj. They talked generally about the forthcoming encounter but agreed there was no purpose in the advance

436

preparation that had gone into their interrogations in Rome and Moscow: the last thing they could appear to be doing that day was interrogating anyone. As a worried after-thought, Danilov asked Cowley if he'd fitted himself with any recording apparatus. Cowley said he hadn't.

On their way to the Mafia restaurant Cowley disclosed Washington were pressing for a return date; he'd vaguely indicated another fortnight, but guessed it could probably be sooner. Danilov had grown so accustomed to spending most of the day and many evenings with the American it was difficult to imagine their not being together much longer. The thought seemed to be with the American, too. He said he looked forward to their meeting in Rome for the eventual trial there, although he guessed the restrictive security under which they would have to live would become a pain in the ass after a while. It reminded him to pass on that David Patton was on day release from hospital: the story was he'd a DEA headquarter's job when he was fully recovered. Patton had also sent a message of congratulation about the medal, through the embassy. Of them all, it was the one Danilov appreciated most.

Their reception at Glovin Bol'soj was extreme, the courtesy and smiles stopping just inches short of patronage. Cowley decided they did want to gloat, and that all the men who nodded and grinned broadly at him, as he walked through the restaurant to the private rear room, probably had seen the photographs of him with his dick in a whore's mouth. Lena Zurov had died because of him, Cowley thought, in familiar recrimination. She hadn't been a whore, despite her profession: she'd been a chosen victim, like he'd been a chosen victim. He was sure he was going to enjoy – savour – what was going to come.

They were ushered into the private salon without the attempted body search of which Danilov had warned the American. A small bar had been installed – which Danilov decided was to provide at least one minder, acting as bartender – and there were elaborate flower arrangements which both investigators thought funereal. There were generous introductions and effusive handshakes. Yerin,

437

sufficiently at home to move around without hint of blindness, offered champagne but announced for Cowley's benefit there was every American liquor: all Cowley had to do was name it. The American asked for Chivas Regal, not to be awkward but from preference. There were numerous toasts to health and lasting association.

There was sufficient food for a banquet for a starving African nation: a starving Russian nation, for that matter. Beluga caviare formed the centrepiece of the *zakuski*. There was smoked sturgeon, separate selections of dumplings and mushrooms in sour cream, *basturma* cured meats, meat-stuffed Siberian *pelmini* – the Russian ravioli – and chicken and pork *shashlik*. Again to impress Cowley – and themselves – there was a selection of Californian wines to go with other choices from France and Georgia. Cowley had limited himself to one whisky and took only one glass of wine: toadying to their posturing, he chose Napa Valley chardonnay.

That posturing stopped very positively halfway through the meal: so, too, did most of the eating, both sides impatient with the pretence. Gusovsky called themselves businessmen, and thought there were going to be a lot of business opportunities in the future. From now on each would be mutually dependent upon the other: Cowley was not to imagine his involvement limited to this one occasion. Despite the setback of Italy, links *would* be formed with American organisations, so what was being established today would be a continuing situation when Cowley returned to America.

Again the conversation was split between the two Chechen leaders. Directly to the American, Yerin repeated, with chilling casualness, the threats against anyone who talked openly in any court, and insisted Cowley made it clear during any pre-trial interviews in the future, with anyone involved. With businesslike practicality, he demanded how and where Cowley wanted his money paid. It was one part of the encounter Cowley and Danilov had rehearsed: Cowley said he thought he'd keep it in Switzerland, as Danilov intended to, and would let them know the bank details when they were fixed. He responded well aware the posturing was beginning again: they were going to make him and Danilov plead for the photographs.

'Part of our arrangement is to begin today?' he said. He didn't resent appearing to beg: he was going to get more enjoyment out of the game than they were, although they didn't know it yet.

'For both of us,' came in Danilov, accepting like the American they were expected to demean themselves, despite the business-together shit. He was as unoffended as Cowley, sure now the final victory was theirs.

From the guessed-at recess beneath the table where they always sat Gusovsky took two sealed manila folders, one thicker than the other: he pushed the thicker towards Cowley, saying: 'You'll want to ensure every negative corresponds with a print?'

'No,' said Danilov. 'We trust each other, don't we?'

Picking up on their own double act, Cowley said: 'We're partners now.'

Gusovsky said: 'This is forgotten by us: we regret it. We hope it is forgotten by you.'

'Entirely,' said Danilov. No, he thought.

'Completely,' said Cowley. No, he thought.

'The sort of misunderstanding that arises sometimes in business,' said Yerin, the false apologies all part of the affectation.

Cowley thought there was a lot adopted from Hollywood: except that in Hollywood the players were acting. These two – one who appeared to be dying from some wasting disease, the other a white-eyed blind man – weren't acting but were, literally, deadly serious: they could still have stepped from the screen of any Mafia movie he'd ever seen. Or any parody of one.

Hands came out and were shaken. Gusovsky's grasp was cold, like lifeless people were cold: Yerin's hold was warm, cloying.

'I'm worried about the money,' said Danilov.

'You've no need to be,' said Yerin.

'I meant getting control, from Switzerland. It's got to be exactly right.'

439

'It's already being done.'

'Don't let us down,' said Danilov.

'Don't let *you* down!' said Gusovsky.

'Don't let either of us let anybody down,' said Cowley. 'We're just anxious to make everything work out as it should.'

'The replacement Founder's Certificate will be presented at the opening of trading tomorrow,' assured Gusovsky.

'That's perfect,' said Danilov, for the satisfaction of Cowley and himself.

'A week from now you'll be rich!' said Yerin.

'A week from now we'll all be rich,' said Cowley. 'And getting richer in the future.'

Danilov took a meandering route when they left, at first with no direction at all, in the first few moments actually checking to see if they would be followed from Glovin Bol'soj. He didn't detect any shadowing cars.

'Well?' Danilov demanded of the slumped American beside him. 'You've met your first dons.'

'Yes.'

Danilov frowned sideways. 'Well?' he insisted again.

'They're *real*!' said Cowley, as if the discovery surprised him.

'Of course they are,' accepted Danilov.

'They'll kill you,' said Cowley. 'There's no *way* they won't kill you. They'll have to.'

'They won't be able to,' said Danilov. 'You won't be with me next time. But you were today. So you can identify them. Know what it's all about. And you'll hold all the proof.'

'That won't be enough, you crazy bastard!'

'Yes it will.'

Danilov became aware of where they were when he drove past the Botanickeskiy Sad metro and at once took the side road to the Botanical Gardens. Each had travelled with their sealed envelope in their lap. Danilov opened his, looking down with renewed sadness at the woman he was about to abandon. The photograph Gusovsky had produced as a threat was the best, but there were two other shots taken

440

from slightly different angles: she appeared bemused but very happy in each. There were two sets, as well as the negatives.

Cowley, beside him, hadn't opened his package.

'Shouldn't you look?' prompted Danilov.

'I've seen them.'

'Not the negatives.'

Almost uninterestedly, Cowley eased the flap open. He didn't extract what was inside, merely parting the contents with his fingers. 'They're here.'

'There's rubbish bins in the park,' said Danilov.

The American followed Danilov inside the gardens and watched while he made a bonfire in an empty metal basket of the photographs of Olga in the Nightflight club. Just before the fire died, Cowley extracted the contents of his own envelope and fed them one by one to the flames. The negatives were last, causing the biggest flare. Towards the end several people stopped on the pathways to look curiously at them.

'How many copies do you think they will have kept?' said Cowley, as they walked back to the Volga.

'A set or two,' accepted Danilov. 'They might have kept a negative back, from the prints they supplied to you in the first place.'

'They *will* kill you,' insisted Cowley.

'You're my guarantee,' repeated Danilov, just as insistently.

'What if they release the photographs out of sheer revenge?'

'Then we both die,' said Danilov, with courage he didn't feel. 'Just in different ways.'

The government lawyer, Vladimir Olenev, was a small, bespectacled man thrust into unusual circumstances and made nervous by them. He was waiting in the foyer of the Foreign Ministry with a briefcase held before him in both arms, and after he got into the Volga with Danilov and Raisa Serova he remained with it clutched in his lap. The lawyer looked intently at Raisa, knowing what she had almost succeeded in doing: she stared back at him until Olenev became embarrassed and looked away.

The woman had still not been formally released from custody, but as always looked as if she was about to step out on to a model's catwalk. Danilov wondered how she had managed to get her change of clothes and kept it uncreased. Her immediate demand, when he had collected her from the women's detention centre on Ulitza Bucher, had been about Yasev. Danilov, who hadn't seen the man since their last interview, said Yasev was all right, as far as he knew. Politely, no longer arrogant, she asked if she could be allowed to see him. Danilov, who supposed her detention would end after she had completed the surrender of the *anstalt* that day, said he thought it would be possible.

There was even less room in the car when they picked up Cowley from the embassy. Olenev's uncertainty worsened in the presence of the American. There was nothing for any of them to talk about and they travelled out to Sheremet'yevo in virtual silence. Danilov supposed he was officially Raisa's escort, so he sat beside her on the flight. She refused anything to eat or drink and spoke only once, asking when a decision was going to be made about herself and Yasev. Danilov said very soon, once the Swiss-held money was returned.

The smiling Paul Jackson was waiting for them at Geneva airport, fortunately in a larger embassy car than the Volga. The local FBI man at once congratulated Danilov on the valour award and made a remark about his being one of them now: Raisa frowned questioningly, but didn't ask.

The lunch was a courteous attempt at diplomatic hospitality by Heinrich Bloch, but it didn't really work. Raisa was even more the object of curiosity from the American party, which she treated with the same defiance as she had faced down the Russian lawyer. She seemed surprised when two of the Americans expressed sympathy at the death of her husband. Danilov wondered how fully they had been briefed, from all that Cowley had sent back to Washington. Olenev's English was limited and Danilov frequently had to translate. Once or twice, to amuse herself, Raisa actually contributed. Despite the stilted difficulties, both Danilov and Cowley allowed themselves to relax, Danilov gesturing a silent toast to the Americans: Bloch's first remark, when they met, was to confirm the presentation of a replacement Founder's Certificate, naming Arkadi Pavlovich Gusovsky the new controller of the *Svahbodniy* corporation.

The hand-over formalities were more time consuming than Danilov expected. Bloch didactically insisted upon the procedures being explained in Russian, English and Schweitzer-Deutsch, with each set of lawyers signing documents of understanding. Raisa looked bored when her part in the proceedings came, and bemused when she was handed copies of every document recording her surrender of the *anstalt*. Olenev obviously approved the preciseness of the ceremony and queried whether he was not the proper recipient of the inoperative replacement certificate; Danilov guessed he might have persisted had not Cowley joined in his own insistence that it was rightfully theirs, as criminal evidence, and nothing to do with the return of the $30,000,000 to the current Russian government.

It was too late by the time they left Bloch's office for Danilov to buy the intended gifts for Olga, but shops were still open at the airport. He left Raisa Serova in the charge of Cowley and the lawyer and bought a beige skirt and matching shoes, using the measurements he had copied from clothes in her closet before leaving Moscow. He didn't have sufficient money left for the blouse to complete the outfit.

It was past nine before they got back to Moscow and Danilov was able to try the Kutbysevskij number, but Gusovsky was there.

'We need to talk,' announced Danilov.

When he got home to Kirovskaya, Olga said she would have preferred the skirt in a darker colour and she wished he had bought a blouse to finish it all off.

CHAPTER SIXTY-THREE

Gusovsky's house on Kutbysevskij Prospekt was very large, close to being a mansion; there were similarities between it and the surveillance photographs of the Ostankino leader's home. Both were cordoned behind high stone walls, with huge metal gates closing off the protective grounds, and outside each were fleets of cars: the Chechen appeared to prefer BMWs, which explained Kosov's choice. Danilov thought the Volga looked insignificant and shabby, parked at the end of the convoy, but for once, he guessed, his wipers and wing mirrors would be safe.

He had to announce himself at a control panel set into one of the gate pillars, and a man who had watched his Metropole meeting with Kosov came to the gate to confirm his identity before it clicked open on an electronic release. As it snapped shut behind him, Danilov felt the dip of genuine fear. At that moment he thought Cowley had been right, all along: that they'd had sufficient to counter the Chechen threats and the evidence they'd retrieved from Switzerland was unnecessary. Cowley's most forceful argument – ending in a shouting tirade – had been against this personal confrontation: they'd parted at Petrovka an hour earlier with the American yelling red-faced it was ridiculous, absurd, a macho affectation to impress no-one but himself and that he'd come to believe his own heroic publicity. Danilov certainly didn't feel heroic now. He felt frightened, weak-legged and sweating, and if the gate hadn't been barred behind him and at least eight guards watching in front he would have turned back: maybe even run.

The man who'd checked him at the gate said something Danilov didn't hear. Danilov just nodded back, following across a wide gravelled forecourt which divided the two halves of the garden. In the middle of the forecourt was a cherubed fountain from which no water spouted. There were three more BMWs to the left, with men around each: two were vaguely polishing the vehicles but others either sat inside or lounged against the bonnets and boots. They all watched him: someone must have made a remark, because abruptly the two on the closest car laughed. Danilov was surprised no-one attempted to search his briefcase. I'm a trusted, bought policeman, he thought.

The house was pre-revolutionary, and the baroque and rococo of the period had been intricately restored in the carved woodwork and the ornate plaster cupolas of the high ceilings. The hallway was marble-floored and escorting the full climb of a huge, encircling staircase was a flight of cherubs from the same flock as those on the fountain outside, sculpted here from the solid stone walls. Heavy brocade tapestries which couldn't have been genuine but which appeared old hung from other sections of the walls.

Arkadi Gusovsky and Aleksandr Yerin were waiting for him in a wood-panelled study on the far side of the hallway. Like everything else about the house, the room was enormous, two walls dominated by bookshelves, another hung with more tapestry. There was a wide, leather-inlaid desk in front of leaded windows, but Gusovsky was in a deep leather armchair to one side of a stone fireplace big enough for a man to have stood upright beneath the mantel. Most of the other chairs and couches were also leather, but Yerin sat on a more upright, brocaded chair. For the first time the man's disability was covered by shaded glasses.

Gusovsky rose at Danilov's entry, going towards a regiment of bottles on a side table, asking what Danilov wanted as he walked. He looked fully at the investigator for the first time when Danilov said he didn't want anything, the cadaverous smile uncertain. It was Yerin, a man who used his ears for the eyes he did not have, who cocked his head to one side and said: 'You're by yourself. Where's the American?'

'This only needed me,' said Danilov. He hoped the perspiration wasn't obvious on his face. He could feel it wet on his back.

Gusovsky came away from the liquor table without pouring anything. 'There is a problem?'

445

'Not now,' said Danilov. He went further into the room, towards the two men. All the convenient seats and couches were low: having listened to everything Cowley had ever said about psychology, Danilov decided it would be better if he remained standing.

'What is it?' demanded Yerin.

'I *am* going to reach an agreement with you, but nothing like you imagined,' announced Danilov. 'I'm not taking any payment from you, now or in the future. Nor coming on your payroll. Ever. Neither is Cowley.'

Gusovsky didn't sit either, but came up to stand behind his partner's chair: there was the slightest turn when Yerin realised the presence behind him. Yerin, the quicker thinker, said: 'What has happened to the money in Switzerland?'

'It has all been returned to its rightful owner, the Russian government. You haven't got it. I never intended you should.'

Gusovsky felt forward, lightly touching Yerin's shoulder. Silence filled the room. Coldness, too, although sweat still glued Danilov's shirt to his back.

Gusovsky said: 'Oh, you silly man. You very silly little man.'

'Maybe,' agreed Danilov, finding the calmness difficult. 'It was an enormous temptation: we even talked about it.'

'Do you know what's going to happen to you?' said Gusovsky. He sounded very calm, too, his normally resonant voice soft, as if he were savouring something.

'I could guess a lot you'd *like* to do,' said Danilov. 'Particularly here, which is practically as secure as the Kremlin and with all your people around you. But you're not going to do anything. Now, or later. You can't afford to.'

Yerin reached up, touching the other man's hand warningly. 'You tell us why you're so sure about that?'

'That's what I've come to do,' said Danilov. He considered moving closer to the fireplace but weighed the psychology again and didn't: he would have looked small in comparison to the huge surround. 'I didn't tell you all the evidence I could bring against you. I didn't tell you about the KGB deputy's confession, about the gun that killed Petr Serov. And why

446

we had to bring the security man out of the embassy in Washington. Or even a quarter of what Antipov has told us, about what he did for you. Which I could put to Zimin in Italy and get even more, if I wanted to. So I'll tell you now . . .' Which he did, not needing any prompting from the copied material he carried in his briefcase and which he was still unsure whether to show them, in the evidence form in which it was assembled.

The two Mafia chieftains remained motionless, but Danilov detected the now familiar redness coming to Gusovsky's face: he abruptly realised he was clutching the briefcase to him, like the nervous lawyer during the brief trip to Switzerland, and hurriedly put it beside him.

'Complete, wouldn't you think? But I *don't* think it is, you see. It would certainly seem so, on the surface: they're all properly recorded confessions and you're personally named, over and over again. But where's the *proof*! It's their word overwhelmingly against yours, but it could be argued against. And I *do* know how powerful you are. I believe you've got other people in ministries whose names I don't know: people you could force or bribe to help in some way. The judiciary, too, so you might be able to influence the judges: even get those who've got to do what you tell them ruling on the admissibility of evidence. And I know you *could* get people killed, even in jail. I'd certainly have a hard job introducing the confessions of dead witnesses, wouldn't I . . . ?' Danilov's confidence was growing. Not by much, but the hollowness was lessening: he actually managed to smile. 'I know you'd do all those things. In your position, you'd be mad not to. So you're not in so much danger, after all . . .'

'Which makes me think you are,' intruded Gusovsky. He was very red, as always resenting being treated as the inferior.

Danilov held up a halting hand, intentionally overbearing. 'I'm going to open the briefcase,' he warned, more for his protection than theirs. 'You know what it is I am going to show you, but I want you to understand the position it puts you in . . .' Very slowly, he unclipped the case and extracted

447

the photocopy of the replacement Founder's Certificate for the *anstalt*, announcing what it was for Yerin's benefit as he handed it beyond the blind man, to the standing Gusovsky. '*This* is proof! You know we have the original. It carries both your names and both your signatures . . . I guess you were guided to the place where you had to sign, Aleksandr Dorovich, but the signature is still provably yours. I now hold irrefutable documentary proof of your attempt to gain control of a government fortune. But not held *here*, in Moscow. Evidence can disappear in Moscow, can't it? The original is already back in Washington, sealed, in Cowley's name. You can't get it or interfere with it . . .'

Once more it was the rational Yerin who spoke. 'You said, at the beginning, you were going to deal.'

'I know and Cowley knows you kept copies of the photographs,' said Danilov. 'It was always inconceivable you'd part with something as useful: you must have thought us very naive, unable to think beyond the amount of money you were talking about. But the deal I offered then still stands, *exactly* as I set it out. I will ensure no prosecution against you. And you will never use those photographs. If you do, Cowley will in turn produce the original Swiss document, and no influence you think you've got could keep you out of jail . . .' He paused, not wanting to show the fear but knowing how he had to finish, for his own safety. 'And that is why I am going to walk out of here today, without any interference. Why I'm not in any personal danger. You'd agree about that, wouldn't you? Understand now why Cowley isn't here . . . ?'

Gusovsky's face blazed, and he had to grip the back of the other man's chair to keep his control. Yerin said: 'A stand-off, this time. What about next time?'

'I shall investigate as hard and as properly as I can. And bring whatever prosecution I can. And if you tried to fight me off by using the photographs, then I'd have a second prosecution with the Swiss case, wouldn't I? Cowley would have to resign, but we've already gone through that. Like we've talked of how I'd respond to the pictures of Olga being released.' The future was the weakest part of the whole bluff.

And not just with future investigations into one of the major crime Families in Moscow: there was always the outside possibility the Justice Ministry and the Federal Prosecutor might change their minds, later, about bringing against these men precisely the prosecution they'd decided *not* to pursue. There was, he accepted philosophically, always going to be a nagging uncertainty. It was just another, to go with all the rest: he wasn't sure in which order.

'You *were* silly,' insisted Yerin. 'Of course we kept copies of the pictures. But I don't think we would ever have used them. You would have been far too valuable. Worth the money and everything else we would have given you.'

'I'm more comfortable this way,' said Danilov, recognising the closeness to pomposity. 'You know why it was so easy to trick you? You can't imagine anyone being honest, can you? That's what the director before Metkin said: that everyone in Russia is still too entrenched in the old ways . . .'

'Leonid Andreevich Lapinsk certainly knew how to work the old ways in the old system,' agreed Yerin. 'We lost a good and grateful friend with his retirement. He managed to block your succession, but Metkin was never good enough to be the sort of director we wanted. He was far too stupid and far too greedy.'

Gusovsky's control went completely after Danilov's un-opposed departure, the man's fury fuelled by his impotency to orchestrate a situation of which he'd imagined themselves in charge. Yerin, no less furious but contemptuous of time-wasting performances, said in rare impatience to the other man: 'Stop it! It's not achieving anything.'

'I *want* him!' insisted Gusovsky. 'No-one treats me – no-one treats either of us! – like that!'

'He's got us, so that's exactly what he can do,' accepted Yerin. 'He's got protection, with the American, that we can't touch. You know it and I know it but most importantly, he knows it. He's fucked us. Absolutely.'

'He *can't!*'

'He has,' said Yerin flatly. 'But he has to be reminded how vulnerable he'll always be.'

CHAPTER SIXTY-FOUR

It should have been pleasant – an enjoyable culmination, the farewell party – but it wasn't. He'd achieved everything and more than he'd ever imagined possible. But too much was soured for Danilov to think of enjoyment. Leonid Lapinsk was the biggest disappointment: Lapinsk, whose admired protégé he'd always imagined himself to be, and to whom he'd disclosed the progress of every case upon which he'd ever been engaged for Lapinsk to decide against whom to proceed and whom to protect, depending upon the bribe being offered: to realise – totally and for the first time – the real reason for Lapinsk's head-down attitude that take-over day at Petrovka, when Metkin had been performing not to humiliate Lapinsk but to amuse the old man – to amuse everyone – at his expense. He tried telling himself Lapinsk had committed suicide from remorse and actually sent a letter of apology, but the cynicism was now so bomb-proof Danilov suspected the regret was probably more that he would eventually discover Lapinsk's crookedness than belated penitence. Danilov was surprised Pavin hadn't known, to warn him. Perhaps Pavin *had* known, all along. Perhaps, Danilov decided, he was everyone's fool.

Another distraction was having not Larissa but Olga beside him for the ceremony. Not because he felt embarrassed by Olga and would have been prouder of Larissa, although the sweater Olga wore with the Swiss-bought skirt and shoes showed a moth-hole neither had noticed until too late, beneath the left arm. He wanted Larissa because it was all too cruel to Olga: she was moving around the American embassy dazed, smiling and nodding but not speaking because she was frightened, believing herself in surroundings to which she had still to become accustomed and in which she must learn how to behave in the future. And in just over twenty-four hours, when the confrontation was finally to be staged, Olga was to learn she was being discarded: that she was never again going to be in such a situation, never again have to worry about how to cope.

Danilov accepted he was moving around smiling and nodding and near dazed, like Olga, because he had never expected to receive the FBI's Medal of Valour like this. He'd thought it would simply arrive: in the post even, a wrapped package – although if it had been delivered that way, with an American postmark, it would have been stolen. He certainly hadn't expected a formal presentation ceremony in the American embassy, before a phalanx of Russian and American cameramen (which made him glad he'd taken the precaution of a short haircut) and with Sergei Vorobie and Vasli Oskin and Nikolai Smolin as invited guests, which was to prompt later comment in the media of both countries on the continuing investigative rapprochement between Moscow and Washington such an invitation indicated. There were legal restrictions about what could be said, so the press conference and television interviews were limited. Cowley participated in both but apart from that remained determinedly in the background, letting it be Danilov's day: they had their own farewell plans for later.

The American ambassador made a speech of platitudes, the only highlight another relayed message from David Patton, and Danilov delivered a matching set of clichés. The objects of the toasts became confused, after four, and Danilov kept raising and lowering his glass automatically, although he was drinking very little. There was still the parting meeting with Cowley to come and after that the final arrangements for the following day to be made with Larissa, who was expecting him at the end of a split-shift duty at the Druzhba.

The event over-ran, although it still ended by mid-afternoon. When she realised Danilov was driving her back to Kirovskaya, Olga said: 'I thought we might have gone on somewhere! Had a party.'

It was the last deceit Danilov would have considered, letting her imagine there was anything to celebrate. 'I've still got a lot to tidy up. Cowley's going the day after tomorrow:

there are things to do. I'll be late home tonight.' For the last time, he thought.

Olga was hardly listening, still held by what had happened at the American embassy. 'I was photographed ten times: I counted! Four times by myself.'

And once at a nightclub with a murdered hooker that doesn't count any more, thought Danilov. 'You'll probably be in the papers tomorrow.'

'I want you to buy every one. And I might be on television tonight.'

'Make sure to watch.'

'You going to wear the medal?'

It had been ceremoniously pinned on to his lapel – worrying him it might puncture the cloth of his Italian jacket – but he'd taken it off before leaving the embassy. 'It's not that sort of medal.'

'I thought you looked very handsome today!' she said.

'I thought you looked very attractive,' he said, dutifully.

'Let's get together with Yevgennie and Larissa soon! I want to show your medal off to them!'

'I've arranged something tomorrow night,' said Danilov. Committed! he thought.

'*You* called them?' frowned Olga.

'I telephoned Yevgennie,' Danilov lied. 'He wasn't there but Larissa was. I invited them over.' He was making the decision on how it was to be done without consulting Larissa. Now she'd have to agree.

'You want to eat in?' protested Olga.

'No!' said Danilov. 'Drinks. Then we'll decide what to do.' She'd hate him for this conversation, later.

'Will Bill come, too? He told me today he wants us to go and stay with him in Washington: said I'd like it.'

'We'll see,' avoided Danilov.

'I'm so happy!' said Olga. 'Aren't you?'

'Yes,' said Danilov, thick-voiced.

Danilov thought it was a considerate gesture for Cowley to have invited Yuri Pavin, as well. And there was the additional benefit, as far as Danilov was concerned, that

Pavin's presence prevented the American repeating yet again he didn't know how to thank Danilov for what he'd done about the photographs. The American had said it twice, in the bar while they were waiting for Pavin, and Danilov now thought there'd been enough gratitude.

Because Danilov said he had an appointment later, they ate early in the ornate dining room of the Savoy, at a discreet table quite near the street entrance. Each agreed it was difficult to imagine it finally over, and Pavin pointed out that it wasn't really, because Cowley would undoubtedly have to return for the Antipov trial and there would also be the reunion in Italy, for the Mafia hearing.

Cowley said all the eavesdropped tapes from Kosov's BMW – a total of 56 – had been returned from America and were waiting, together with the transcripts, at the embassy. 'Taking up quite a lot of space,' he added.

Danilov hadn't thought of where to store them, until he made his professional move against Kosov: one step at a time, he thought. He supposed they could be conveniently lost among his now established chaos in the Petrovka office he did not actually occupy any more.

'And there's still the bugs, in the car,' reminded Cowley. 'Our technical people are dismantling the recording and listening apparatus in the next few days, but at the moment it's all still live and hearing everything Kosov says or does. I guess you'll be able to get them out easily enough, on some trip or other?'

He wouldn't, Danilov realised. After tomorrow night he'd hardly be a welcome guest in the ostentatious vehicle. And he wouldn't be in it before then. 'What happens if I can't?'

Cowley shrugged. 'They stop functioning when we disconnect at our end, I suppose. And I guess the magnetism of the fixings will give out, sooner or later. So they'll fall off in the car. When he finds them he'll know what's happened.'

He'd know that anyway, recognised Danilov. He'd just let the microphones stay where they were. To Pavin, Danilov said: 'We'll collect everything tomorrow.'

Cowley said: 'You want what's still coming in? There's

453

been nothing much since you went to Kutbysevskij. Quiet, in fact.'

'We'll take it all,' decided Danilov. If evidence was available he wanted it, even if he didn't know its worth at that stage.

'It was quite a bunfight at the embassy today,' smiled Cowley.

'My one and only medal!'

Cowley appeared briefly uncomfortable. 'But not the final presentation.' He reached into his inside pocket, bringing out two gift-wrapped packages. 'You weren't the only guy shopping at Geneva airport.'

Danilov's gift was a heavily calibrated chronometer, with three time-measuring dials in addition to the second hand. Pavin's was a tortoiseshell-bodied fountain pen.

'You always seemed to have difficulty with the time,' grinned Cowley, to Danilov. '. . . and you sure as hell do a lot of notetaking,' the American completed, to Pavin.

Both Russians were embarrassed, Danilov more so, because it hadn't occurred to him to buy anything for Cowley, and although there would be time before the American finally left Moscow Danilov couldn't think of anything *to* buy, in the meagrely stocked shops. Perhaps Larissa would have an idea. Both Danilov and Pavin stumbled their thanks and Cowley said pointedly he had more to be grateful for to them than they had to him.

The American, who was drinking but not excessively, lifted his glass towards Danilov and said: 'Here's to the final recognition! Your directorship!'

It had once seemed very important to him, remembered Danilov. Lately it hadn't crossed his mind, not even when he'd taken over the controller's suite.

He was only a few minutes late arriving at the Druzhba but Larissa was already waiting, almost impatiently, in the foyer. 'A surprise!' she announced.

Danilov allowed himself to be bustled into the car and obediently drove out to the Tatarovo apartment. She led excitedly from the elevator, opened the door ahead of him and then stood back, inviting his inspection.

There was a table and chairs already arranged in the dining annexe and a couch, with matching chairs, in the living room. There were flowers – deep red blooms the name of which he didn't know – in a vase on a side table, and a television on a stand. In the main bedroom – the only one furnished – was a made-up bed, covered with a deep blue duvet, with a matching dressing table opposite the built-in clothes closet. Both the living room and the bedroom had scatter rugs over the wood block flooring. There were a cooker and refrigerator in the kitchen, with pots and pans and a rack of knives neatly arranged. Everywhere smelled fresh and new.

'You had to use Yevgennie's friends, to get all this!' he said, immediately alarmed.

'No,' Larissa said, pleased with herself. 'One of the girls who shares our old arrangement is the ordering manager for the hotel. We're refurnishing two of the top floors. So we told the suppliers what was necessary for them to get the order . . .' She twirled, encompassing everything. 'And this was what was necessary!' With a final flourish she opened the already stocked refrigerator. 'Champagne, for tomorrow night's celebration!'

'You're wonderful!' he said. Favour-for-favour, he thought.

'I'm going to be, for you.'

'I've decided where we're going to tell them,' he announced. 'Not a neutral place, like we discussed. I want it to be at Kirovskaya. Tell Yevgennie I've a particular reason to want to see him.'

'Why Kirovskaya?' she frowned.

'It's Olga's home. I want her to realise she's being left with something she knows; something she recognises. I think it's important.' More psychology, he thought.

'If you think so,' said Larissa.

'It's not going to be easy, is it?'

'But worth it,' she insisted. She looked towards the prepared bed. 'There's no real reason to wait, until tomorrow night.'

'Yes there is,' refused Danilov. 'Tomorrow night it will be

right.' He didn't want to make love to her before that: it *wouldn't* have been right.

CHAPTER SIXTY-FIVE

It was the beginning of the trial-preparation period, a concluding stage he normally enjoyed for the opportunity to examine the entire enquiry in detail. There was no pleasure this time. Danilov went through a lot of the preliminary routine almost automatically, his mind more occupied by the approaching evening. He repeatedly tried to arrange the words, in advance, on the occasions when neither Pavin nor Galina were in the room actually muttering the attempts, until he realised the foolishness of it. Nothing sounded right anyway. All the words and phrases he could think of were stiff and unnatural, as if he were reading from a printed speech. Tonight wasn't something he could practise, something he could make easier. It was going to be . . . be what? Tearful? Obviously. Any love between them might have gone long ago but Olga would still be shocked, bewildered, by the upheaval. She'd certainly cry.

What would Kosov do? Totally unpredictable. Danilov didn't think the man, who had all the bombast and pretensions of a coward, would be physically violent. He'd shout and rage – maybe even threaten to fight – but it would be in other, already feared ways the man would try to get his retribution.

Danilov wasn't as apprehensive now as he had been. He supposed it was the comparative ease with which the confrontation with the Chechen leaders had gone, being able to match threat for threat. He knew he could do precisely that, if Kosov started talking of the past. Go as far as playing the incriminating tapes, as tangible proof. There'd been the unreasoning fury when he'd learned how Kosov entrapped Olga, but although it was still with him the anger was colder now, not so all-consuming. Kosov would have lost his wife and his prestige with his paymasters and know there was never a possibility of their working together as partners at

Petrovka. So did he need to go any further, to drive the man entirely from the Militia, which had been one of the first of the several unthinking resolutions he'd made?

Danilov did have to concentrate to prepare the evidence edited in the way the Federal Prosecutor decreed for the limited arraignment that had been decided, accepting as he did so the ultimate irony that he was doing precisely what he had promised the Mafia bosses, although not for the reasons they believed. Nikolai Smolin's decision, not his, reflected Danilov, so Smolin could be the final arbiter of what was included. Accordingly Danilov set out to prepare what, in effect, was a précis of a statement or evidence account, attaching markers to events and facts Smolin might want either to add or omit. Because he respected the man's ability, he frequently consulted the meticulous Pavin, so it was a time-consuming operation which he guessed would take him a further week to complete: maybe even longer. Danilov stopped earlier than he would normally have done on an initial preparation day, not wanting his personal distraction to affect his professional judgement.

He talked with Pavin about what they could buy Cowley. Pavin couldn't think of anything in Moscow to compare in either quality or price with what Cowley had given them, but didn't think that was necessary anyway: taking their lead from Danilov's medal, why didn't they go to the Arbat souvenir precinct and buy the American one of the dozens of genuine military decorations discarded by the greatly diminished army, and stage a valour presentation of their own? Danilov thought it was an idea that would appeal to Cowley.

Olga had tried very hard. She'd prepared hors d'oeuvres and set out bottles. In the forefront the FBI medal was on show, the presentation box open and propped up, for it to be displayed.

'I don't think that's a very good idea,' he protested gently. 'It looks far too boastful.'

'They'll want to see it!' she said, disappointed.

Danilov closed the box and took it from the table. As he walked towards the bedroom, he said: 'If they ask we'll show

458

them. But not until they ask.' He tossed it casually into his bedside drawer.

'Yevgennie would show it off, if he had one,' she said petulantly, when he returned to the living room.

'Yevgennie and I do things differently,' he said. There was already a mark on Olga's new skirt.

'Where are we going tonight, after the drinks?'

'Why don't we talk about it when they get here?' He'd have to be the person to say something, first. *Larissa and I have something to tell you*, he thought. That wasn't right. It transferred the announcement to Larissa. *I have something to say. About Larissa and me. We're in love – have been for a long time – and we're going to get married.* That was it, wasn't it? He'd spent all day – and a lot of days before that – trying to wrap the declaration up in soft words and phrases, but there weren't any soft words or phrases to make easier what they had to say. So he'd come out with it like that, bluntly, brutally. Olga or Kosov would say something then – Kosov, most probably – and then would come the tears and the arguments about divorce. And the last thing that would interest any of them would be an American medal. He had to remember to take it, he realised, suddenly. He hadn't thought of packing anything yet – wouldn't have been able to pack anything yet, without Olga asking what he was doing – but his clothes were all conveniently arranged, the shirts still folded suitcase size, from the trips abroad. He'd try to do it tonight, if Olga wasn't too distressed or angry: make the break abrupt and clean. If he couldn't he'd still take the medal, at least.

'What time did you say?'

Danilov looked unnecessarily at his new watch. 'Six.' It was five-thirty. If they were going to be on time they'd be leaving now, to make allowances for the rush hour.

'Do I look all right?'

'Fine. But there's a mark on your skirt.'

Olga look down, surprised, hurrying into the bathroom. Danilov heard the taps running. He poured vodka to the rim of the glass. Stage-effect, he thought. The dampness, where she'd tried to sponge it, made the spot look much worse

459

when Olga emerged. He hoped it would dry before the others arrived, for Olga's sake.

'It's going to be a good evening!' predicted Olga brightly. 'I know it is!'

Danilov jumped at the sound of the telephone, close to spilling his drink. He hurried to it, knowing it would be Larissa.

But it wasn't.

'I think something's happened,' announced Cowley.

'What!'

'The tape has just recorded the biggest goddamned noise I've ever heard. Now it's dead.'

So were a great many people, one in particular. And within thirty minutes of the telephone call, briefly, inside, a blindly deranged man who loved her and wouldn't let her go, even though Larissa wasn't there any more – wasn't anywhere any more – to be held and loved and protected, like he was going to protect her forever.

It was to take a week to establish that eight people had been killed and twenty more injured, two seriously. There were insufficient remains to identify Yevgennie Kosov or his wife Larissa, who had been sitting literally on top of at least four pounds of Semtex that exploded the moment the BMW ignition was fired. By a quirk – as obscene as the quirk that threw David Patton's gun, still in David Patton's hand, aside in the Sicilian shoot-out – Kosov's ornately-jewelled watch was thrown clear by the blast: it was still working when it was found, close to the apartment wall. It was not attached to a wrist. Its discovery was officially logged in Militia records; it had disappeared when an identity-check search was made, three days after the atrocity.

Every window of the block was shattered, and the ground and first floors so badly imploded the entire section was declared dangerously unsafe and fifteen familes evacuated. The crater in Nastasiskij Prospekt was three metres deep and extended the entire width of the street.

The fire brigade were still dowsing the blazing wreckage of the car when Danilov got there. The heat of the explosion

460

was so fierce the metal had burned, like paper: only the chassis suggested it might have been a car, and that was uncertain. What had survived was red, like blood, a cruel effect of water upon white-hot metal. It hissed and smoked, whitely, like awakening ghosts.

Danilov took it all in yet saw nothing. He trembled, like someone naked in the snow, but he was so hot his skin felt tight. He waved his police identity like a flag to get through the barriers to the very edge to the crater, staring down, knowing it was going to be all right because it had to be all right, and that she would be down there: injured, obviously, but still alive, able to recognise him when he got to her and went with her in the ambulance wedged between two fire trucks. He'd tell her it wasn't important about Tatarovo and the wine tonight. They'd do it when she was better.

He stared wildly around, not understanding why he couldn't see her, but there were a lot of people and a lot of swirling steam, so he had to be in the wrong place. He dodged in and out of firemen and uniformed Militia and when he still couldn't see her he hurried to the ambulance and demanded to be told where she was, waving his police authority again, not realising – not caring – there were others injured and killed, and that the bewildered medic didn't know what he was talking about. When he did see the man's confusion Danilov said Larissa's name, over and over again, and tried to describe her: her blonde hair and chiselled nose and the way she held her head sometimes, oddly twisted, as if she was withdrawing from whoever she was talking to. When the medic shrugged and began to walk away Danilov snatched at the man to stop him, but rescuers were pulling angrily at him now. He shook them off, yelling his rank, trying to get down into the hole where men still wore safety suits and reinforced masks, to protect them from the heat.

The hands became stronger, refusing to be shrugged away, and then voices penetrated, voices he knew, Cowley's and Pavin's, and he turned gratefully to people he recognised. 'Help me! She's down there! She's probably hurt. Can you see her? I can't see her.'

461

'Come out,' said Cowley. 'They're getting her. You're in the way. So come out.'

'You're sure? They've got her?'

'Come out.'

Danilov scrambled up, needing their help, because he was still shaking badly and his legs were very unsteady. The other two were on either side, arms cross-linked to cocoon him, getting him away.

'Where is she! She'll need me to go to the hospital.'

They kept walking, not speaking. It became abruptly dark, out of the search floodlights: briefly Danilov's vision fogged completely, a wipeout of consciousness. When he became aware again, he was on the edge of the rear seat of the Volga, his feet and legs still outside the open door.

'She dead, Dimitri,' said Cowley, refusing Danilov his fantasy of shock. 'She wouldn't have known anything. But she's dead.'

Danilov began to cry then, knowing it was true but not wanting to know it was true, racked by great, convulsive sobs and needing the arms that still held him. They stayed that way for a long time, the three of them in a tight group, Cowley repeating Larissa was dead until finally Danilov mumbled that he knew, but softly, so that if it wasn't true it wouldn't matter. He became aware of where he was and of the two men supporting him: became properly aware for the first time of the full horror of the atrocity itself.

'OK?' asked Cowley finally.

Danilov nodded.

'We need to talk. For you to hear things.'

Danilov nodded again.

Cowley held him tightly, very briefly. 'I'm sorry.'

Danilov was fully conscious of what had happened and what he was doing and where he was, but he still moved and reacted dully, needing to be prompted and guided as they entered the darkened, night-staffed embassy and were led by Cowley to the FBI office: Pavin remained at the rear of the procession, a cautious hand hovering at Danilov's shoulder.

'I'm all right,' insisted Danilov when they got there.

'Thank you, but I'm all right.' He looked questioningly between Pavin and the American. 'How?'

Pavin said: 'I've known for at least three years. It was your weakness: how you could have been attacked. I've never understood why you weren't. I always tried to cover your back.'

'Yuri telephoned, after you called him to find out from the uniformed division what had happened,' expanded Cowley. 'I figured you might need help.'

'We were going to tell them tonight,' said Danilov, not really addressing either man. 'Olga and Yevgennie. Talk about divorce and then get married . . .' He gave a shrill laugh, momentarily close to the edge. 'We've got a flat. We were going to celebrate with champagne tonight.'

Just as introspectively, Cowley said: 'Holy shit!'

'We came here for a reason,' reminded the pragmatic, less emotional Pavin.

Cowley straightened, reaching for the tape which had been carefully marked, so he could cut it off before the sound of the explosion.

'*We told you to come!*' echoed Gusovsky's voice. '*When we say come, you come!*'

'*I couldn't. Not immediately.*' Kosov was snivelling, a trapped animal.

'*You set us up!*'

'*I didn't! He cheated me, too.*'

'*You're no good to us any more, Yevgennie Grigorevich. We can't trust you.*'

'*No! I'll speak to him!*'

'*There's nothing to speak about.*'

'*Let me try!*'

'*No good to us any more,*' repeated Gusovsky, monotonously. '*He laughed at us, as fools. Did you both laugh: think we were fools?*'

'*No!*' wailed Kosov.

'*You're the fool, Yevgennie Grigorevich.*'

Cowley snapped off the replay button, at the warning marker. 'They did it.'

'I know,' said Danilov simply.

'It was the last conversation we recorded.'

'I want to hear the explosion!' demanded Danilov.

'No you don't,' said Pavin, gently. 'There's no point.'

'They probably brought someone in from another republic to do it,' said Danilov, close again to personal musing. 'They'll never be charged, not Gusovsky or Yerin.'

'No,' agreed Cowley. 'That's the way it's done.'

'It's not the way it should be,' said Danilov.

CHAPTER SIXTY-SIX

The investigation was not given to the Organised Crime Bureau but to a general criminal unit, which spared Danilov from inevitable participation. When it was learned it had been the car of a Militia district commander, the newspapers speculated it was a revenge killing by someone whom Kosov had arrested: police records of all his cases were being examined, for a likely motive through which to trace the killer. Television as well as newspapers carried photographs of Kosov and Larissa. It was a good picture of her – posing in her head-tilted way – and he cut it from two different newspapers because he didn't have a picture of her. Olga cried a lot but Danilov didn't, not after the breakdown that first night, by the crater. He took to arriving at Petrovka by eight in the morning and not leaving until six or seven, but never later, because it was unfair to leave Olga alone.

The man from whom Pavin bought the medal on the Arbat insisted it was for bravery under fire: they were doubtful, but that was what they told Cowley on the day he left Moscow, and he was as delighted as Danilov had guessed he would be. They talked over the reunion plans that didn't need any more discussions: there had been no reference, from either Cowley or Pavin, to Larissa's death during the four days since they had got him away from the scene. Only at the moment of parting, at Sheremet'yevo, the last thing Cowley said was: 'I really am sorry.' Danilov thanked him.

Danilov hadn't discussed with the American what he intended doing, because there was no reason for Cowley to know. He didn't tell Pavin, either, although he guessed the man would realise later because it was Pavin he told to organise the swoop on Wernadski Prospekt, to bring in the Ostankino leader.

Yuri Yermolovich Ryzhikev was much heavier than he'd appeared in the prints, bull-chested and thick-necked, with very full black hair and the dark complexion of someone from one of the southern republics: Danilov thought occasionally there was the trace of a Georgian accent. There was a lot of gold adornment, which seemed to be the requirement of every mafioso in the city: the man came into the Petrovka suite with a camel-coloured topcoat slung cape-like around his shoulders, over a brown silk suit. The shoes were crocodile. There wasn't the arrogance of the Chechen chieftains, but there was no apprehension over the arrest, either.

He sat where Danilov told him but asked at once if Danilov knew what the fuck he thought he was doing. Danilov quietened the attitude at once by offering across the table the copies of the original *Svahbodniy* Founder's Certificate and the second certificate transferring control to Raisa Serova upon her father's death, both of which held Ryzhikev's name. The government had recovered the money, Danilov said. Ryzhikev had been stupid like the Chechen had been stupid, but in Ryzhikev's case it hadn't happened once but twice, first losing it to the Chechen and then to the Russian authorities. So he did know what the fuck he was doing. He was giving Ryzhikev a warning.

No action was being taken over the embezzlement, and they knew all the murders had been committed by the Chechen. But no Mafia clan was going to be above the law any more. They had a file on the Ostankino, like they had on every other Family: they knew Wernadski Prospekt was the main house, but they had all the other clubs and restaurants as well. To prove it, Danilov listed those they had discovered, during the surveillance, adding the one that had been fire-bombed by the Chechen. They didn't just know the locations, they had identities, too, he continued, and to prove that recited all the names listed in Zimin's confession, as well as the few Pavin had managed to assemble from the sparse Petrovka files. They didn't rate the Ostankino as seriously as the other Families, because they knew it would be swept up by the Chechen, who were already taking over whatever they wanted. When he said that, Danilov offered the certificate that had never become operable, replacing the Ostankino directors with Gusovsky and Yerin.

'The Chechen are going to take you over: look how easy it is for them to kill your people, whenever they like. So by eradicating them we get rid of not one but two mobs, don't we?'

They already had a massive file on the Chechen. They had over thirty names and they knew the meeting places, at Gusovsky's home on Kutbysevskij Prospekt and the restaurant on Glovin Bol'soj and the well-protected club on Pecatnikov.

Danilov made it a condescending lecture, once waving the man down when Ryzhikev appeared about to speak, and when he finished the man's face was puce and he was hunched forward in his chair, looking more bull-like than before, as if he were about to charge.

'You can go now,' dismissed Danilov. 'Until you're absorbed, just remember what I've said. We know who you are and where you are. We can swat you like a bug, whenever we want.'

'You're out of your fucking mind,' managed Ryzhikev at last. 'You got it wrong. All wrong.'

I hope I haven't, thought Danilov, at the end of that day. He was in the basement, where the incinerator was housed, feeding the car tapes and the transcripts into the flames, carefully and individually, wanting it all completely consumed, like Larissa had been completely consumed. Technically it was evidence, he acknowledged. But as Cowley had agreed, at the embassy the night it happened, Gusovsky and Yerin would never be punished for ordering the assassination. What he had tried to achieve today was much better: justice without trial. The ultimate personal compromise, for a policeman.

The double funeral was at Novodevichy cemetery, like Serov's. Olga cried. Danilov felt nothing, emptied. Having been at the scene he wondered what, if anything, was in the coffins. There were representatives from the Justice and Interior Ministries, as well as a sizeable contingent of uniformed Militia, eight of whom formed an honour guard. A uniformed Militia colonel whom Danilov did not recognise gave a graveside eulogy in which Yevgennie

Kosov was described as an outstanding policeman of integrity and leadership and Larissa as a loyal and loving companion. No matter how long it took, the perpetrators would be brought to justice for one of the vilest crimes in Moscow's criminal history.

'It was true, wasn't it? What a fine man Yevgennie was?' said Olga, on their way back to Kirovskaya.

'Yes.'

'I just can't imagine what it will be like, not having them any more.'

'No.'

'At least Larissa went too. She wasn't left by herself. I couldn't bear to be left by myself.'

Danilov said nothing.

Danilov gave up the Tatarovo apartment the following day. The concierge's immediate concern was that he would want his dollar deposit back; he didn't relax until Danilov made it clear he wasn't asking for a refund. He wasn't asking for the advance rent back, either.

'What are you going to do with the furniture?' asked the man, surveying the living room.

'Why don't you sell it for me? Either on the open market or to the next people who want the flat.' It was unthinkable to transfer it to Kirovskaya, with some easy excuse for Olga, although everything here was better than theirs.

The concierge beamed at the prospect of even greater profit. 'We'd better take an inventory. You put the prices against the items and I'll do my best to get them . . .' Hurriedly he added: 'Not sure I'll be able to get what you want, though. Might have to come down a bit.'

'Why don't you just get what you can?'

'We'll still make a list.' At the refrigerator he said: 'There are things in here. And a bottle of champagne.'

'You have them,' said Danilov. 'The champagne, too.'

The man began to stack the food on the worktop, the champagne last. He said: 'I'm sorry things didn't work out for you. Sometimes they don't.'

'No,' said Danilov. 'Sometimes they don't.'

CHAPTER SIXTY-SEVEN

The war broke out two days after the funeral. The Chechen restaurant on Glovin Bol'soj was raided by Ryzhikev's gang. Three Chechen bulls were maimed – one blinded, two others crippled – and three innocent customers in the front section were badly injured: one was a twenty-one-year-old girl who lost an arm. The restaurant was torched with engineering expertise, fires set so it was not only gutted but the structure so weakened the roof and walls collapsed.

The attempted Chechen retaliation, ambushing a convoy of Ostankino lorries supposedly entering from Poland, was in reality an ambush in reverse. Nothing had come from Poland. Each truck held waiting squads of men more interested in humiliation than death and injury: one Chechen man was killed and two others injured – just as four Ostankino were injured – in the initial confrontation, but the remaining twelve, once overpowered, were stripped naked and left handcuffed and manacled in chains that had to be cut off with oxy-acetylene burners, and with signs around their necks identifying the Family they represented. Photographs appeared in four Moscow newspapers.

The Chechen did succeed better with a counter-attack at an Ostankino cafe, killing two, but five of the attackers were badly hurt and they didn't manage to set it alight, which they had intended. The Ostankino retribution was again public mockery, but more effective on a second level because by hitting Kutbysevskij they showed they could get to the very heart of the Chechen empire, the residence of Arkadi Gusovsky himself. They blew up three BMWs parked in the road outside and set light to another two, intending them to burn more slowly. When Gusovsky's guards tried to get out of the gates, they discovered they had been chained closed by three separate ropes of thick metal, so the alerted newspaper photographers this time had shots of the imprisoned guards pulling from the inside of the gates in frustration. The day after, two separate publications carried satirical cartoons of black-masked, striped-jerseyed gangsters running in opposite directions around a circle of money, piling up in head-on collision while a police group watched.

Danilov thought it was a good portrayal of his intentions, but it still wasn't complete. It became so at the end of the third week. It was never discovered how the Ostankino got into Pecatnikov without being detected, although the rumour arose of a disillusioned defector. The frontal group managed to burst through the door of the club before any alarm was raised, and sprayed the interior with Russian RPK and Yugoslav Mitrajez M72 machine guns. The Chechen were utterly surprised and the battle was over very quickly, with eight dead. The delay was still sufficient for Gusovsky and Yerin to escape from the rear dining room through the labyrinth of corridors honeycombing the complex: both would have survived if they'd hidden in Yerin's upstairs apartment, but their only thought was to get completely away.

The second assassination squad must have followed Gusovsky from his home to isolate and mark his car. As the thin man bustled from a rear entrance of what he'd thought an impregnable fortress, hurrying the blind man towards the BMW, waiting gunmen opened up with more machine guns – RPKs and M72s again – catching both in triangular fire. Three bodyguards and the waiting driver died as well.

The killing of Gusovsky and Yerin ended the inter-Mafia conflict: the fighting that followed was between second-level Chechen battling for succession to the leadership.

'It was how it should have been settled,' said Pavin, when they learned of the death of the Chechen leaders.

'There isn't any satisfaction,' said Danilov.

'There shouldn't be, not in vengeance,' said the other man.

It was the day the summons to the Interior Ministry arrived, from Vasili Oskin.

There was tea and further congratulations, this time for the way the prosecution evidence had been assembled and presented. There was also the news that the Rome trial was expected to begin in November. It was predicted to last three months, and the Italian authorities had been assured Danilov would be available throughout the entire hearing.

'So you will be away from Moscow for a considerable time,' said the soft-voiced deputy minister. 'It could even extend beyond that period.'

Was he here for nothing more than a hypothetical discussion about a trial he'd always known he'd have to attend? 'I'll make a diary note of the date, to avoid any overlap with cases here.'

'However long it takes, it will mean your being away from Petrovka,' said the man. 'And there is still the unresolved matter of the directorship. I clearly can't continue as the titular head.'

It wasn't a hypothetical conversation, Danilov accepted. 'Clearly not,' he agreed cautiously.

'There's been widespread discussion, about your being appointed,' disclosed Oskin. 'There is a strong feeling among many people the position is rightly yours, after the success of this most recent case . . .' He hesitated. '. . . and another strong body of opinion that precisely *because* of that success, you are far too valuable an investigator to be elevated into an administrative role . . .'

They weren't even bothering to change the excuse. Danilov waited to feel disappointed – robbed again – but nothing came.

'. . . And then there is this further long absence, in Italy. The Bureau could not be left without a commander for an indeterminate period . . .'

'No,' agreed Danilov. If there was a feeling, it was boredom.

'So the appointment is to be made from within this Ministry, not from the Militia,' said Oskin. 'A trained lawyer. Vadim Losev. A very able man. He will have the title but in effect it will in future be a joint command. And you're being promoted, to full General.'

'I am sure we will work well together,' said Danilov.

That evening, as he had done on several nights since her

death, Danilov detoured to Novodevichy cemetery on his way home to Kirovskaya to stand by the marked grave, knowing he had to stop doing it but unwilling to, so soon.

'They did win, darling,' he said. 'I fought like you said I should, but they still defeated me.' He wondered if he would ever learn who they were. And what he could do about it, if he ever did. He wouldn't bother to tell Olga, not yet. She'd only become upset, even with the confirmed but meaningless promotion. He'd tell her about Italy, instead. She could start making another shopping list.